Advance praise for *Things We Keep Hidden*

"A compelling story of friendship, hope and the ties that tear us apart... and hold us together. Jill Lynn writes with wit and emotional depth in this page-turning women's fiction novel that will leave you longing to hold all your loved ones a little tighter."
—Brenda Novak, *New York Times* bestselling author

"*Things We Keep Hidden* is an absorbing novel about friendships and the secrets that surface during a 'friendcation' weekend involving three couples and the teenaged daughter of one. I could relate to their stories and struggles and thoroughly enjoyed this novel, as will many other readers, no doubt. From its intriguing opening to its satisfying conclusion, it kept me turning pages."
—Eileen Goudge, *New York Times* bestselling author

"In *Things We Keep Hidden*, Jill Lynn highlights lives that may seem idyllic on the surface, but are riddled with dysfunction. The bonds of friendship are tested as secrets from the past rise to the surface, threatening the present. Suspenseful and moving, this novel will tug at your heart strings while keeping your pulse racing. A riveting read!"
—Belle Calhoune, *New York Times* bestselling author

"*Things We Keep Hidden* is a poignant story that highlights the joys and hardships in relationships, and the beauty that can be found in sharing our vulnerabilities. Jill Lynn is masterful with her depiction of friendships, marriage, and parenting, portraying them all with a realism that draws the reader deeply into the story. Filled with heart-tugging moments and hints of suspense, this is one read you won't put down until the final page has turned."
—Susan L. Tuttle, bestselling author of the Treasures of Halstead Manor series

Also by Jill Lynn

Love Inspired Trade
The Summer of Keeping Secrets

Love Inspired
Falling for Texas
Her Texas Family
Her Texas Cowboy
The Veteran's Vow

Colorado Grooms
The Rancher's Surprise Daughter
The Rancher's Unexpected Baby
The Bull Rider's Secret
Her Hidden Hope
Raising Honor
Choosing His Family

For additional books by Jill Lynn, visit her website, www.jill-lynn.com.

Things We Keep Hidden

JILL LYNN

If you purchased this book without a cover you should be aware that this book is stolen property. It was reported as "unsold and destroyed" to the publisher, and neither the author nor the publisher has received any payment for this "stripped book."

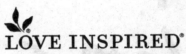

Stories to uplift and inspire

Recycling programs for this product may not exist in your area.

ISBN-13: 978-1-335-04500-3

Things We Keep Hidden

Copyright © 2025 by Jill Buteyn

All rights reserved. No part of this book may be used or reproduced in any manner whatsoever without written permission.

Without limiting the author's and publisher's exclusive rights, any unauthorized use of this publication to train generative artificial intelligence (AI) technologies is expressly prohibited.

This is a work of fiction. Names, characters, places and incidents are either the product of the author's imagination or are used fictitiously. Any resemblance to actual persons, living or dead, businesses, companies, events or locales is entirely coincidental.

For questions and comments about the quality of this book, please contact us at CustomerService@Harlequin.com.

® is a trademark of Harlequin Enterprises ULC.

Love Inspired
22 Adelaide St. West, 41st Floor
Toronto, Ontario M5H 4E3, Canada
www.LoveInspired.com

HarperCollins Publishers
Macken House, 39/40 Mayor Street Upper
Dublin 1, D01 C9W8, Ireland
www.HarperCollins.com

Printed in U.S.A.

To Jen, Holly and Kelli. Happy twenty-five years to us.

Chapter One

Isley Stanton *would* make this weekend a success. Somehow. Because she *and* the charity started in honor of their high school friend needed a win.

There had to be a light at the end of this stressful, depressing tunnel she'd been cowering in.

At least, that's what she kept telling herself as she wiped down the outdoor furniture of her Breckenridge, Colorado, vacation home in preparation for the arrival of her childhood girlfriends and their husbands.

Minus one. Always minus one.

Isley, her husband, Trevor, and their son, Aiden, had skied and snowboarded in Breckenridge during Aiden's growing-up years, and she and Trevor had long dreamed of having their own place, finally purchasing this house six months ago.

Right before Aiden's world—and subsequently theirs—had come to a screeching halt.

Speaking of their son...it would be nice if their recently

turned nineteen-year-old would simply answer Isley's email to confirm he was (a) alive and (b) didn't hate them.

But it had been a week since she'd had a response from him.

Isley had been aware of the rehabilitation center rules from the start. Patients were their priority...communicating with family members, significant others, and friends was not.

At the time they'd been hurriedly hunting for the right rehab, Isley had thought the rules sounded good. Progressive even. Team Aiden. She'd believed the sole focus on assisting his rehabilitation seemed like just what her son needed. But she'd also been desperate to redirect Aiden's trajectory from serving time to treatment and recovery.

Now, she just wanted her son to answer an email.

It was reminiscent of his high school years when he'd only respond to her texts if it suited his needs.

Isley gave the striped all-weather pillow an interior decorator chop and stationed it in the corner of the outdoor L sofa.

"Anyone home?" a female voice called, and Isley spun from her spot on the deck, peering through the wall of glass doors that she'd slid open to embrace the gorgeous seventy-degree afternoon.

She let out a squeal and jogged into the house, meeting Payton Collins and her husband, Liam, by the kitchen island. She'd left the front door unlocked, knowing they'd be arriving soon.

Despite the fleeting moment of tension that had erupted between the women during their last friendcation weekend, Isley's spirit sagged with relief at the sight and presence of her friend. They'd trudged through the depths of grief and despair together, and with the events that had been going on in Isley's life over the past months, she could use someone as steady, as permanent a fixture in her world as Payton.

The embrace lasted long enough to combat a small slice of the two years since they'd last seen each other. Their biennial friendcations had started after college as a way to not lose contact when time and space separated them. The vacation weekends had also been inspired by their friendship with Cecelia Finch. Cece had been their fourth throughout their high school years, and in so many ways, even with her late addition to their friend group, their ringleader. After her death, they'd been bonded in ways that no one outside of the three of them understood.

And they'd vowed after that loss not to grow apart.

Isley stepped back from the embrace and greeted Payton's husband, Liam, with a hug.

"Thanks for having us," Liam said warmly.

"Of course. Clara and Hank should be here any minute too." Clara and her husband ran Hank's family farm in Veil, Colorado, where the women had grown up. Veil was a flat farming community in eastern Colorado. Not to be confused with Vail, Colorado, which was a high-end ski resort town.

A clarification they had to make whenever they were asked where they were from.

Even though Isley and Clara only lived a couple hours apart, due to their busy schedules, the planned long weekend every other year was typically the only time they saw each other in person.

Isley's friends didn't know about Aiden's stint in rehab yet. But when she'd considered relaying that information over text or a phone call, her brain had just...refused. Almost as if saying the words out loud would make the situation more painful.

She would find a way to tell them this weekend, somehow.

Isley covertly attempted to wipe moisture from under her lower lashes.

Payton noticed, her expression sympathetic. "You okay?"

Isley nodded. "It's just..." *Been a rough half a year.* "There's something about us."

Payton's smile arched, yet it held edges of sadness or pain or something close to those that had Isley's alarm bells ringing. "There absolutely is. We're the best."

"It's definitely not humbleness," Liam delivered wryly. His accompanying grin declared he knew exactly what he'd walked into this weekend and he was #blessed to be included. *Smart man.*

A couple years into their friendcations, the women had voted to allow The Husbands to join them on future trips. And they always made sure the men knew how special it was to be graced with their presence.

"The house is gorgeous. You're never going to be able to get me to leave." Payton scanned the modern rustic kitchen that connected to the living room, her gaze tracking to the expansive deck and the pine trees that lined it.

Due to the open glass doors, a scent particular to the mountains filled the house—a mix of evergreens and earth that had been soaked in snowmelt.

"Thanks." Isley's heart gave a swift beat of appreciation. The previous kind elderly owners of the house had dubbed it The Haven, and Isley and Trevor had continued using the fitting moniker. "We love it."

"Is Trevor here?"

The *we* would imply that, wouldn't it? "Not yet." He'd promised to arrive before their guests, but when Isley had last checked their tracking app, Trevor had still been at his office in Denver.

"Give him a break." Liam's cheeks creased. "He did work hard enough to purchase this house for all of us."

Isley laughed. "True." She was thankful for how hard Trevor worked and that he'd experienced so much success as a hedge fund manager throughout the years. But despite what his brother thought of her, Isley hadn't fallen for Trevor when they'd met in college because he'd come from a family with a higher socioeconomic status than hers. Though that wasn't exactly hard to do. She'd fallen for the way he'd made her feel—safe.

Before driving up from Cherry Creek yesterday, Isley had popped into numerous places near their house for provisions for this weekend. And once she'd arrived in Breckenridge, she'd been all over town procuring more supplies.

Trevor had declined to join her in Breckenridge early, claiming he needed to work. Since he would miss a chunk of today—Thursday—and all of Friday at the office before returning to work Monday, she believed him. And yet, the distance between them felt palpable to her.

But then, she was the one who, unbeknownst to Trevor, had caused that separation.

Payton's brow furrowed. "Is." Though her name was pronounced Eyes-lee, those closest to her shortened it with a soft *I* sound. "There's something I have to tell you."

Isley's throat constricted. "What is it?" She'd already experienced more than enough upheaval in her world over the past months. She wasn't sure how much more her system could handle.

"How about I just show you instead. And then you can forgive me. I hope." Payton grabbed Isley's hand, leading her outside, where Isley caught a glimpse of movement in the back seat of Payton and Liam's vehicle.

She paused on the front step to analyze. "Is that Reagan?"

Payton nodded. "She's been going through some stuff, and I didn't want to leave her at home. I would explain, but it feels like it's hers to share, not mine. And I'm sorry for not saying anything earlier and that I'm just springing this on everyone."

"Pay, you don't have to explain *anything*. I'm glad she's here and that she's okay."

Especially after what the women had gone through with losing Cece.

Payton's logical research scientist approach to problem-solving meant that she would never cart Reagan along on the trip unless something serious drove her to make that decision.

"Thanks, Isley." Liam's quiet appreciation came from behind her.

She swiveled to respond. "Of course. Happy to have her." Making room for another guest at the house wouldn't be a problem. But figuring out how to add someone to this weekend's scheduled activities might take more finagling.

Tonight's sailing excursion had a six-person limit.

So, Isley would either need to sweet talk the captain into an additional guest or sit this one out. Which would be fine. She could experience Summit County anytime.

"She doesn't need to join us for the activities," Payton supplied, as if reading Isley's mind. "I mean, it's great if there's room, but if not, she can hang out at the house. Or something. I haven't thought it all through." Payton sounded frazzled. As worn as Isley felt. Their situations mirrored each other in a way. Because it appeared neither of them knew how to navigate the current issues happening with their child. Although, Isley would guess Reagan's problems were nowhere near as serious as narrowly avoiding serving time, like Aiden.

"It won't be a problem. We'll figure it out."

This summer's friendcation had dual purposes.

To see each other. And to assist Finch's Hope—the suicide prevention charity that Cece's mother, Belinda, had started shortly after her death—out of the financial troubles they'd recently found themselves in.

Isley had procured donations from various Breckenridge businesses for activities and products. The items would be part of a vacation package in the upcoming online fundraising auction for Finch's Hope, including a four-night stay at a resort that their family had frequented before purchasing The Haven. Isley had shared about Cece and the charity started in her honor with the resort's general manager, and he'd readily agreed to donate.

Turns out the GM had lost his stepdaughter to suicide when she was fourteen.

Stories like that were so painful they stole Isley's breath. If only Finch's Hope could save everyone contemplating such a decision. If only they could orchestrate a ghost of Christmas future and show people the stark, unbearable pain that their void would create in the lives of their loved ones.

According to Belinda, Finch's Hope had secured everything from jewelry to household items to gift cards as part of the online auction. To create extra buzz for the fundraiser, their group planned to participate in the Breckenridge activities that would be included in the auction package over the course of this weekend and then photograph and share about them on the Finch's Hope blog.

Let it be enough.

Payton and Isley approached the small SUV, and Payton opened the back door. "Are you going to get out at some point, Rea?"

"Are you sure you want me to?" Reagan heaved her waif-like body out of the back seat as if she had two industrial bags of flour strapped to her back. "It would be easier to control my actions if you locked me in here for the weekend."

Payton's weary sigh spoke volumes. Isley nearly laughed at the well-crafted teenage snark spouting from Reagan. She'd *been* that teenager once upon a time.

"It's really good to see you, Reagan." It was. And it made Isley miss Aiden *so* much. She squeezed Reagan's arms in lieu of a hug, unsure if the teen would welcome physical affection. Aiden had certainly gone through years of refusal in that regard.

Based on Reagan's shuttered body language, it was vividly apparent that she had not agreed to this trip without a fight... or more likely hadn't agreed to it at all.

"Um...you too." Reagan's attempt at a polite reply garnered amusement from Isley once again.

Children! Why couldn't it be easier to parent and easier to be a kid? Sometimes it all felt so overwhelming.

"She can share a bed with me," Payton said. "Liam can sleep on the floor or a couch. We don't want to be an imposition."

"Righto." The skin flanking Liam's eyes pinched almost imperceptibly. "No problem by me."

Isley waved her hand dismissively. "The basement couch is a sleeper." She addressed Reagan. "We'll get you set up in no time at all with a space that's yours."

Reagan's teeth pressed into her lip. "'Kay, thanks."

"That's...perfect. Thank you, Is." But Payton followed her gratitude with a frown.

What was that about?

A horn sounded, and they turned in unison to see Hank and Clara's minivan pull into the driveway. Clara waved from the driver's seat and nearly exited the vehicle before it was fully stopped.

The women gathered in a group hug. When Clara stepped back from it, her lips pinched, telltale emotion shimmering in her milk-chocolate eyes that matched her shoulder-length hair. "Are we okay? I know last time—"

"Over and done." Isley quickly halted her line of questioning. That subject was the last place she wanted to go again.

Belinda Finch was a surrogate mother to each of them. They would do anything for her. Anything to ease her pain and not increase it. Which Isley reminded herself of whenever she questioned the choices they'd made over the years.

Trevor pulled into the driveway as Payton tugged Clara aside, likely giving her the same sparse explanation regarding Reagan's unexpected presence.

Clara's response to whatever Payton quietly told her was a swift, tight hug.

Trevor kissed Isley's cheek. "Hi." The warm ivory skin surrounding his gray-blue eyes crinkled with remorse. "Sorry I'm late," he whispered in her ear before turning to greet everyone. To his credit, Trevor didn't miss a beat and began chatting with Reagan as if her joining them had been the plan all along.

"Isley and Trevor, this is so generous of you to share your home with us and Finch's Hope," Clara gushed. Even back in high school, Clara had been the most compassionate and gracious of the four girls. Their peacekeeper. Their little bit of sunshine, sporting golden retriever vibes.

"We're so glad it worked out. When Belinda first called me about the charity's issues, I was at a loss." Cece's mother had shared the news about the charity likely having to close its doors due to lack of funds just two days after Aiden had been dropped off at rehab six weeks ago.

Two days that Isley had spent riding an emotional roller coaster…and making plans she should have never followed through on.

"But then you created an amazing weekend for us *and* the charity." Payton's smile still held hints of sadness that Isley desperately wanted to unpack.

"And organized an online auction for Finch's Hope," Clara added. The charity's logo had a finch sitting on a blooming tree branch. A fitting representation of life and hopefulness.

"I didn't *organize* the online auction. I just suggested it." Isley had referred Belinda to the online auction company they'd used before for Aiden's school PTO, because she'd known she didn't have the bandwidth to head up the fundraiser herself while Aiden was in rehab. Somehow, even though he was technically safe, she felt so raw and worn. She'd definitely been functioning at half-mast.

"*Just* that. Most days I feel like I can barely put on matching shoes. Not that it would matter anyway. It's not like the crops or pigs are checking out my fancy Walmart T-shirts and jeans." Clara's eyes brightened with humor and then dimmed swiftly. When they'd first discussed using their friendcation weekend to focus on the charity, Clara had seemed quite relieved that they would be staying at Isley and Trevor's vacation home.

She'd mentioned money was tight and that they were helping their daughter Ava with the cost of college as much as they could, so Isley was glad the house and food for the weekend wouldn't cause them additional strain.

"Let's head inside. Grab your things and I'll show you to your rooms."

Hank hefted his camouflage hunting backpack and Clara's quilted duffel bag from the back of the van. Trevor carried Reagan's bag, and Payton and Liam each retrieved carry-on suitcases.

Reagan stopped to use the half bath upstairs, and Isley led the rest of the group downstairs to the family room and additional game area, which housed a pool table.

"Payton and Liam, I have you in the Peak Eight room." Which she'd decorated with antique store finds—a map of Breckenridge's original ski runs, wooden skis, and framed vintage resort advertisements. "And Clara and Hank, you're in the Dillon Reservoir room." In that space, she'd brought in soothing nautical blues and local artist pieces of the reservoir.

Both bedrooms had en suite bathrooms that also connected to the communal living room space.

"We have a little something for you as a thank-you. It doesn't exactly go with your gorgeous decorating, but I thought…" Clara's shoulders lifted. "It's a small piece of home." She unzipped her bag and pulled out a package wrapped with brown paper and tied with a simple string. "You can open it now. It's nothing big."

Isley accepted the gift. "You didn't need to do this." She pulled back the wrapping to find a rectangular photograph of a sunlit field filled with round bales of hay. The shadows and shapes and whatever Clara had done while developing the print gave it an artistic, creative feel. "This is gorgeous. It should be in a gallery."

"Thank you," Hank emphasized. "That's what I tell her all the time."

"Don't be silly. That's over the top."

"It's not," Isley protested. "Good thing we have you on retainer for the weekend. See? We're all helping with the charity. Not just me." Clara enjoyed digital photography and even developed film in the darkroom Hank had built her as an anniversary gift a few years ago, so they'd roped her into being their photographer for the activities this weekend.

"My only contribution comes in the form of Liam," Payton said as she examined the photograph.

"I don't mind." Liam was an English professor and had agreed to write about the Breckenridge weekend for the blog. "I might not have known Cece, but I feel like I did through you all."

Clara sniffled. "This is why we let The Husbands tag along. They have redeeming moments." A collective amused groan came from the men.

"Clara, this is beautiful. I want one. I'll pay."

"I'll send you one," she answered Payton, "but I'm not accepting money for it."

Isley ran her fingers along the weathered frame. "I love this frame. Where did you get it?"

"I made it with some old barn wood we had on the farm."

"You made it? Like with a saw?"

Clara grinned. "Yes. Saw, nails, hammer."

"I'm so impressed." Isley strode over to the fireplace and adjusted the candles and other items on the mantel to make room for the photo. "Fits perfectly. Like it was made for this spot. Thank you."

"You're welcome."

Reagan came downstairs, her dread at joining the adults nearly palpable.

Again, Isley's heart went out to her and whatever turmoil had brought her to their doorstep.

"Reagan." Isley strode in her direction, meeting her behind the sofa. "This can be your area down here." She motioned to the couch and wall-mounted television. They had a video game console and a boatload of games, but she doubted Reagan would be interested in those the way Aiden and his friends were. "The adults can stick to the upstairs living room. And I was adamant about getting a quality mattress, so it *should* be comfortable. I'll get the bed made up now."

"We'll do it," Payton protested. "You don't need to—"

"I don't mind at all. Everyone get settled and then meet out on the deck for hors d'oeuvres when you're done."

While Trev retrieved his weekend bag from his car, Isley located bedding for Reagan in the basement linen closet.

She removed the sofa cushions, and Reagan joined her, tugging on the mattress until it unfolded.

Isley had meticulously made each of the beds yesterday—hospital corners, top sheet finished side down and folded back, bed spread evenly distributed, pillows positioned with a final chop. Her desire for an impeccably decorated and organized space had started in high school, and she'd loved her perfectly systematized room, which she'd outfitted with thrift store and garage sale finds...and a locking doorknob she'd installed with a friend's help one afternoon while her mom hadn't been home to harp on her about it.

Isley's hand settled on her lower back. To the spot she'd sought so hard to hide and heal over the decades. But despite barely being visible after the creams and laser therapy, it always seemed to pulse beneath her fingertips.

Reagan caught the other side of the fitted sheet that Isley spread over the mattress.

"You don't need to help, Reagan."

"I don't mind. I'm sorry that I'm here. That I'm causing more work for you. Trust me, I'd rather not be." Her hazel eyes that were a perfect match for Payton's flashed wide with panic. Even their hair was similar—a pretty deep brown, worn long and parted down the middle that complemented their apricot skin. "I didn't mean that like it sounded."

Isley laughed. "No offense taken." She ballooned the top sheet over the fitted.

Reagan half-heartedly stuffed the corner under the mattress. "My grandparents are on a Mediterranean cruise they already had planned, so they couldn't come stay with me."

Liam's parents were usually great about helping out with Reagan for friendcation.

"And Mom refused to leave me with a friend because apparently she's trying to control everything about my life."

Isley correctly tucked the top sheet and barely resisted moving to Reagan's side of the bed to do the same. "I wish I were innocent when it came to that type of overprotection, but I still do the same thing with Aiden and he's nineteen. Speaking of, do you mind if I redo that corner? It will stay tucked so much better and not drive you crazy coming loose in the middle of the night."

A flicker of a smile surfaced from Reagan. "It's all yours." She stepped back, watching Isley with crossed arms and full-blown amusement. "I thought my mom was the only one who obsessed over small stuff."

Isley spread the blanket and bedspread. "Oh, honey. Her issues are nothing compared to mine."

Chapter Two

Payton walked upstairs as Isley carried a tray filled with two pitchers and stacks of glasses onto the deck. She followed, stepping outside to find the gorgeous Colorado blue sky she'd grown up with showing off.

It was prettier than anything Payton had encountered in Texas.

Though if anyone in the Lone Star state heard her utter such a thing, they would chase after her with pitchforks yelling *blasphemy*! Despite the fact she'd desperately wanted to get out of Veil and escape her family when she'd been a teen, this state would always be home to her.

Veil was only a few hours from Breckenridge, but no one else in the group outside of Isley and Trevor had ever visited the quaint mountain town. Payton and Clara had jumped at Isley's offer to combine friendcation with the charity fundraising and use the Stantons' new vacation house as their home base.

"What can I do to help, Is?"

"Not a thing." Isley motioned to the table, which held a massive live edge wood charcuterie board artfully arranged with vegetables, dips, crackers, fruit, meat, and cheeses that could easily feed twenty. "Trevor is my assistant tonight, so you just sit and relax and eat."

Payton was tempted to force the issue, but Isley was a perfectionist when it came to hosting. Probably because she'd done so much of it over the years for Trevor's business partners and clients.

"I'm here." Trevor joined them on the deck. "Give me a job."

"Find out if they want smoked honey lemonade or the sparkling blush drink and then get to pouring."

No one in their group drank alcohol for various reasons, so both would be mocktails.

"Yes, ma'am," Trevor retorted with a teasing grin as Isley buzzed back inside. "She scares me sometimes when she's in hosting mode."

Payton laughed. "You and me both. I'll do the pink drink." She took a seat at the table that showcased the pretty view of the evergreens on the property. "I'm so glad you two finally made this house happen. You've been talking about it for a long time."

"Thanks. Us too. Now I just have to figure out how to not work so much so that we can enjoy it more."

Clara, Hank, and Liam joined them as Trevor handed Payton her drink.

Liam took the seat next to Payton, which made her emotional pendulum swing from happy to sad back to some middle ground of tired, confused acceptance.

Ever since her husband had announced The Plan, Payton had been reeling. Treading water. Wondering what to do with the fact that Liam wanted to stop being married but stay best friends.

How did one navigate that? Not to mention tell their daughter.

"Ooh, what's that?" Clara asked as she and Hank sat across the table from Payton and Liam.

"I believe it's sparkly and pink and made with unicorn dust. Wasn't that what she said?" Trevor asked Payton.

"Something like that." Payton's mouth curved after she sipped from the heavy lowball glass. "It's yummy."

"I want." Clara clasped her hands together in anticipation. Trevor poured her a glass and started on a smoked honey lemonade for Hank after asking his preference.

"Is, this is perfection," Clara said as Isley returned to the deck with a water pitcher and additional glasses. "You even ordered ideal weather."

"This *is* perfection." Hank's delivery held his underlying hint of dry humor as he accepted the drink from Trevor. "We are grateful you two did this." His tone lowered with a serious edge. "I hope it gives the charity what it needs. And Belinda too."

Unlike Trevor and Liam, who'd come into their lives during and after college, Hank had known Cece too. Had grown up with her like the three women had.

They'd had a fun friend group during high school. Hank and Clara had started dating freshman year, but they were low-key about it, so that had been nice. And then there'd been lanky Scout, Cece, Isley, Payton, and Scout's friend Erik had hung out with them a fair amount. And then during junior and senior year, Cece pulled her boyfriend Konnor into their group.

According to Isley, Konnor planned to attend the catered dinner party in honor of Finch's Hope that would close out the vacation weekend on Saturday night. Scout had also been invited, but he lived in Germany for work and declined the invitation. Though Isley had also spilled the tea that Scout had sent a generous donation in lieu of being able to attend.

Which was so very Scout.

Or at least it matched the person Payton had known twenty-plus years ago.

He and Cece had been really close, so his support of the charity made perfect sense.

The dinner party had been yet another Isley brainchild. Clients whose lives had been saved in part by the charity, plus their significant others, would be attending the dinner along with Belinda and some of the charity's staff members. Video footage and photos from the evening and interviews of the survivors' stories would be used for additional blog content that would hopefully funnel more attention and support to the online fundraising auction.

The charity and their friend group were pulling out all the stops, because if they didn't, Finch's Hope might cease to exist.

And they all needed good to come from the ashes of Cece's untimely death. Without that, all they had was the biggest regrets of their young lives.

All three women struggled with guilt over the night Cece died. It was why Clara had broken their unwritten rule and broached the subject to Isley and Payton on their last friendcation.

Payton understood exactly where Clara was coming from. Certainly Isley did too.

But it was too late to change any of it now.

Trevor asked Liam's drink preference, and he also chose the lemonade.

"Where's Reagan?" Isley scanned the living room as if expecting their daughter to follow. "Does she know there's food?"

"I asked her before I came up, but she said she's not hungry." Though it was far more likely that Reagan was protesting being forced on this trip. "I think she's watching something. But I'm sure she'll surface shortly."

Payton couldn't believe she'd pulled a stunt like showing up for friendcation with her teenage daughter in tow. She was grateful that Isley, Clara, and their husbands had handled the situation with grace and understanding.

She should have given them a heads-up, but everything had just unraveled so quickly at the end.

Sometimes life just....*lifed*. Of course that wasn't a word, but Payton couldn't think of a better description.

She and Liam had tabled separating or even telling Reagan about The Plan after Payton had found that box under their daughter's bed.

Payton still hadn't come to terms with what the contents meant even though they'd been dealing with the ramifications for months.

And then, just when Reagan seemed to accept and settle into her counseling sessions, girl drama had started online. Rumors. Rude comments. Lies. Payton and Liam hadn't even known it was happening until the school counselor had called. Ms. Grate had done her best to put an end to the online commentaries and gotten most of the content removed, but the damage had been done.

The biggest saving grace in all of it had been that none of the online fodder had revealed Reagan's private issues.

Thank God.

"What's first on our agenda for the weekend?" Clara walked around the deck, the *click-click-click* of her camera capturing the food, the view, the people.

"We're doing an evening sail on Lake Dillon," Isley answered. "I would have scheduled it for tomorrow so you all had a moment to relax, but this was the only night they had open."

"That's sounds fantastic. I think Reagan will love that." Liam popped a grape into his mouth.

"What will I love?" Reagan stepped onto the deck through the open glass wall.

"Isley booked us an evening sail on Lake Dillon."

Reagan's nose wrinkled at her dad's answer. "I don't have to go to that, do I?" Her expression flashed apologetically in Isley's direction before her eyes narrowed and landed on Payton. "Mom, you said I could just hang out at the house." Her tone was clipped, icy teenage perfection that Payton had patented herself.

"I'm not saying you *have* to go." She kept her response smooth and unruffled. "But you should consider it. Wouldn't it be nice to experience this part of Colorado while you're here? Who knows if you'll ever be back again." Payton checked with Isley. "Providing there's space for her?"

Isley placed a small portion of smoked salmon onto her plate. "We can make that work."

"Rea, why don't you eat something and think about it?" Maybe some fruits and vegetables would help regulate her mood. Liam had taken Reagan to the store for road-trip supplies, and they'd returned home with mostly junk food.

Usually Payton and Liam flew to wherever the group was meeting for their trip. They'd been to numerous cities over the years. Nantucket last time. Coronado before that. But this year they'd opted to drive because it had felt as if Reagan's life were imploding, and Payton had wondered if they would need to cancel attending friendcation at the last minute.

She probably would have if the whole weekend wasn't focused on Cece and Belinda and Finch's Hope.

After the girl drama, Reagan had spent the first two weeks of summer barely leaving the house with little to no friend contact. Except for Killian, a girl in their neighborhood who was a year older, and who Payton still didn't know well enough to discern if she was a good influence or not.

Reagan had begged to stay with her this weekend, but Payton had refused.

The last thing Payton had wanted to do after her daughter's recent troubles was leave her with a family she knew nothing about.

She'd decided escape was the answer. For all of them.

Suddenly, she'd been loaded into their small SUV with a seething Reagan and a disgruntled Liam, plus luggage.

The road trip versus flying created an imposition for Liam because it meant extended travel time and the need to find a sub for the summer class he was teaching. Payton had almost suggested he stay home with Reagan, and she go on the trip, but then she'd have to tell her friends about The Plan. And she was in no way ready to process any of that. Not when she barely understood it herself. And the idea of her husband being the only one missing when photographs of this weekend were going to be blasted all over the Finch's Hope blog? *No, thank you.* She wasn't ready to deal with that at all.

Last night they'd stayed in a roadside hotel in Raton, New Mexico. Reagan had been so angry about where they were and being forced to go along on the trip that Payton had been a little afraid she might murder them in their sleep.

Joking...for the most part.

Reagan dropped into a chair and released an amplified huff. She grabbed a plate and began piling on cheese and meat, meticulously avoiding anything that grew on a tree or in the ground. Another noise—this time more of a grunt of annoyance—slipped out.

Reagan had certainly mastered the art of speaking her mind without uttering a word.

Payton didn't need to glance around the table to confirm that Reagan's antics were causing a scene. Eyes wide, Payton sent Liam a nonverbal SOS. Shockingly, he read her like a favorite manuscript and pulled the attention away from their irritated daughter.

"Hank, how are things with the farm?"

Her heart gave an exhausted thump of relief while Hank hacked as if he'd swallowed down the wrong pipe.

He took a few small sips of his drink until his coughing subsided. "The farm is great."

Clara plucked an olive from the charcuterie board with the serving tong. "It's actually been—"

"We had a major drought year before last," Hank filled in, a divot dividing his ruddy forehead. "But weather's been better since then."

Clara appeared to clamp her lips shut at that. Strange. Payton could count on one hand the number of times she'd witnessed Clara frown.

Even at her mother's funeral in the sixth grade, she'd conjured faint, polite smiles for the attendees that had greeted her after the service.

Payton remembered because Clara's ability to always reach for the positive astounded her, even then.

"Mom." Reagan glanced up from her phone. "Can I *puh-lease* just—"

"Rea, why don't we talk inside." Payton released her own huff. What had she been thinking bringing Reagan on this trip? No wonder Liam had pushed back on that idea. He would have left her with Killian even though they didn't know her. Which of course made Payton the bad guy.

"Fine." Reagan shoved back from the table and stalked into the house.

"I'm *so* sorry, you guys. I just... I wanted to do this weekend for Cece and the charity and Belinda. But I should have canceled. Or at least told you Reagan would be joining us. I've been a mess." There was no other way to explain her strange decision-making skills lately.

"We'll take you any way we can get you, Pay." Clara spoke softly but firmly. "I'm so glad you didn't cancel. Maybe something good will come of this weekend for you and Reagan."

At this point, Payton would be surprised if they lasted the whole weekend let alone garnered good from it.

Liam set down his glass with a clink. "You want reinforcements?"

"Yes, please."

They met Reagan in the kitchen. Hopefully that would be far enough away that they wouldn't disrupt the group outside.

"Mom, I was thinking that part of the reason you probably don't want me to just be at the house is because you don't want me on my phone. I know how much you hate electronics. You talk about it all the time."

Did Payton resemble a punching bag? She should check a mirror. "I don't hate them. I do dislike how they change your brain and cause depression and—"

"*Mommm*, I already know all that. So, what if instead of staying at the house while you're gone, I walk around Breckenridge." Reagan beamed as if she'd solved a physics equation. "It looked tiny when we drove through. Like it can't be more than a handful of streets. I'm sure it's safe."

How had Reagan noticed anything about Breckenridge? Even with Payton's attempts to get her to look out her window on the drive, she'd been glued to said phone.

"You want me to see Colorado. Let me do it on my own terms."

"So basically, you're willing to do anything but join us on the sailboat."

Her exhale answered that question clearly. "I do *not* want to be stuck on a boat with a bunch of old people."

Payton laughed. What else could she do?

"We're not *that* old," Liam said with offense. "Mom and her friends are only forty-two." And Liam was one year older than her while Trevor was two years older than Isley. "If you let yourself hang out with them—with us—you might actually enjoy yourself."

Go Liam!

Reagan's arms crossed. "Yeah, that's not gonna happen."

"I don't think it makes sense for a fifteen-year-old to go exploring alone when we don't know the area."

Reagan snorted. "Exploring? I'm not climbing a mountain. I'll walk through some shops. What could possibly happen?" Not a question to pose to Payton right now. She could fill a whole notebook with outrageous scenarios. "You do realize I handle myself in Dallas just fine, and it's a thousand times the size of this town."

Payton stemmed a smile at the gross exaggeration. But she did know how capable and aware Reagan was. And outside of interactions with her parents, she acted pretty mature.

Payton was running out of excuses.

"Reagan," Liam directed. "Earmuffs for a second."

Reagan rolled her eyes. It was something they'd done when she was little if they didn't want her to overhear.

"What am I, two?" Despite the complaint, she slapped palms over her ears and began humming obnoxiously.

"Maybe you should ask Isley what she thinks?" Liam suggested. "She'll be able to tell you what she would feel safe doing, at least."

True. "Good idea."

Liam motioned for Reagan to remove the earmuffs while

Payton strode outside and waited a few beats for a lull in the conversation.

"Is, not to put you in a weird position, which is exactly what I'm doing, but do you think it's safe for Reagan to walk around town by herself?"

Isley's mouth pinched apologetically. "I would say yes. When we used to come up when Aiden was in middle school, we let him and his friends snowboard together and check in with us throughout the day. The bus is free in town, and she can hop on or off anywhere. Or there are like two Uber drivers if she wants to get back to the house before we return. And we can give her the code to the garage. But if you need me to provide a different answer, I can."

The mark of a good friend. "I appreciate that, but the truth works fine." She returned to her family in the kitchen. "Okay, kid. You win this one. We'll drop you in town when we head out for the sailing tour. Keep your phone volume up at all times and answer my texts when I check in. Deal?"

"Deal." The faintest trace of a smile surfaced, but Reagan quickly stifled it. "Since I don't have any space of my own on this forced trip, I'm going to take a shower in your bathroom. That one in the motel last night was like something out of a crime scene. Do not come downstairs for at least thirty minutes."

She pounded down the stairs, her footsteps reminiscent of a baby elephant or a T. rex. From the moment she'd learned to walk, Reagan had never been one to move quietly or gracefully, and Payton was secretly amused by that idiosyncrasy.

"You're welcome. We love you too," she called after Reagan even though she was out of hearing range.

Liam laughed. "I think, loosely translated, that was teenager speak for 'thank you—you're the best parents in the world.'"

"Uh-huh. *That*'s what you took away from that conversation?" It was nice to be on the same team as Liam again. Despite his claims about nothing changing between them when he'd first made his announcement regarding their marriage, Payton had felt so disconnected from him since then.

She was just going to have to trust that Reagan would be safe. It had to be better than leaving her back in Dallas, didn't it?

"She'll be fine, Pay. Anything she does at home she can do here and vice versa. The choice is hers wherever she is."

And wasn't that the worst part of it? That lack of control was the equivalent to being buried alive.

Payton couldn't go to school with Reagan or sleep on the floor next to her bed at home. Both options she'd unrealistically considered after finding that box. Payton had to come to terms with the fact that she couldn't control Reagan's choices. But that left her with no idea how to protect her daughter.

"Take a minute to regroup. I'll see you outside." Liam paused as he passed her, almost as if he were going to lean in and hug her. Kiss that spot on her temple he'd labeled *the thinker* back when they'd been dating. But like a fuzz in the wind, his brief halt was simply that. He floated onto the deck while Payton crashed back to the reality of the last few months.

With the new distance between herself and Liam, Payton had felt as if she were carrying Reagan's issues on her own. Like she was the only one fighting for Reagan even though that wasn't true. Payton was doing her husband a disservice to imply he didn't love their daughter as much as she did.

But she'd felt so *alone* in all of it.

The past months had been eerily representative of the isolation she'd experienced growing up—before Clara, Isley, and then Cece had walked into her world and saved her.

So maybe being here with the two friends who knew her better than she knew herself wasn't the worst decision she'd made, after all.

Chapter Three

Clara had hoped that much like restarting a glitching electronic, friendcation would be a reset for Hank. A distraction from the farm stress and a chance to remember that their family was far more important than a piece of land—even if it had been in his family for generations.

But considering that her husband was currently in the marina restroom emptying the contents of his stomach, she would say her plan, at the moment, was failing.

Clara sat, knees bent, on the small sandy beach of the Frisco Marina waiting for Hank. The rest of their group remained on the catamaran, moored off the dock where they'd recently deposited the two of them in the hopes that getting Hank's feet back on solid ground would stem the motion sickness that had started immediately after the boat left for their sailing tour.

Since she hadn't seen Hank in almost ten minutes, Clara would say that that plan had also failed.

She felt like an inept emotional support wife—a running theme for her lately.

Though she had earned a grin from Hank when he'd been on his way to the marina bathroom and she'd sarcastically offered to join him to hold his hair back.

In typical Hank fashion, when his hair had started receding in his late thirties, he hadn't fought it.

He'd just shaved his head and grown a beard.

The change had given him an edgier look, and Clara liked to tease him that he'd entered his farmer-slash-rock-star phase.

He was five-nine—which aligned just right to Clara's five-foot-five height—with a stocky frame and strong shoulders that had been supporting her since her mom died.

When the brain aneurysm happened, most kids hadn't known what to say to Clara, so they'd just ignored her mother's death. But a week after the funeral, Hank had walked up to her—despite the awkwardness between boys and girls at that age—and declared he didn't know what to say, but he was real sorry about her mom. At which point he'd marched off and rejoined his friends to the sounds of teasing and laughter.

It was possible Clara had started loving him right at that moment.

"Hey." Her husband slowly eased himself to a seated position next to her.

"Hi, how are you feeling?"

"Excellent."

She laughed and then grunted with upset. "I can't *believe* I forgot about your motion sickness." It never bothered him in a moving vehicle. Only on water. "I think I was just so excited about sailing on a catamaran that I completely spaced about that very thing nearly killing my husband."

Skin retaining a clammy green hue from his recent exploits, Hank chuckled. "I don't think motion sickness has ever killed anyone."

"I'm sure Google—and your body right now—would beg to

disagree." She groaned, annoyed with herself and with the hiccup this was throwing into the group's evening. "Why didn't you remind me? Why didn't we do medicine beforehand?"

"I didn't think about packing medicine for landlocked Colorado."

Of course not. Why would he?

"And when Isley mentioned this activity for tonight, I didn't think I'd react as strongly to a lake as I do the ocean."

"You were incorrect in that assumption."

"I'm aware." He flashed a faint smile. "You were so excited about sailing. I didn't want to ruin it. And this—" he motioned to them sitting on the beach and then to the boat slightly offshore containing their friends "—certainly didn't ruin anything. I mean, who doesn't want to listen to someone they can't get more than a few feet away from retching continually?"

Clara laughed and then quickly sobered. "Now you're probably even more upset with me for saying yes to this trip."

"I wasn't upset." Hank's indigo eyes were weighted with questions. "I just didn't understand why you didn't discuss it with me. It's not like us not to talk things through."

He was correct to say it wasn't like them. But he was generous not to state the whole truth.

Clara had broken their cardinal rule. They made decisions together. They always had.

It was one of their best features, and she'd completely disregarded it.

"I was afraid you'd convince me that we shouldn't go."

His vision transferred to the stunning view before them. Boats bobbed in the water, and a couple in kayaks glided away from shore. The mountains were a kaleidoscope of colors—grays and blues and greens and the occasional shimmer as sunlight kissed their peaks.

"Obviously we needed to be here for Cece and Belinda. But our lack of funds would have held me back."

"Thankfully it's not an expensive trip. Not with all the donations." Clara had been extremely relieved to find out they would be staying at Isley and Trevor's vacation home and the weekend had been filled with donated activities.

Their biggest cost would be the drive.

Clara loved their biennial friendcations and the escape they provided from day-to-day life.

It had always been such a grace to get away from the stress of running the farm, even from the kids. It made Clara a better, more patient parent when she refueled with her friends and their husbands. It was a weekend she could be herself, fully and completely, because no one knew her like Isley and Payton. No one had experienced what they had together.

"I know how hard you've been working to save lately."

Clara had gotten creative with their grocery budget recently by following advice from a few coupon blogs. She'd focused on sale items and using staples from the pantry.

"But…" Hank swallowed, Adam's apple dipping. "How are we paying for this sailboat ride? Did you ask Isley?" His eyes were somehow soft and broken at the same time. As if he'd undergone a beating over the last year and his body refused to heal.

"It's donated. You know that."

"I know that the activity being auctioned off with the vacation weekend is donated. But I doubt this outing is."

"It is. We needed to document everything for the blog. Needed pictures and content that would bring in traffic to the site. The more interest, the more money the vacation weekend and the other auction items will bring in. Isley orchestrated all of it. You know the levels of her charisma and charm. The woman could make a cat tap dance if she waved her hand."

"True." Hank's sad smile sprouted. In the last year, Clara wasn't sure when she'd seen his truly happy one. She missed that carefree version of her husband. There was an ache, a sadness, an unworthiness that Clara continued to sense in him. As if he *was* the farm. As if his value was intricately linked with it.

Clara had almost fallen off the expensive high quality outdoor chair she'd been occupying when they'd been eating on the deck earlier and Hank had referred to the farm as *great*. Why would he do that? Why hide their troubles? These were their people. Why not lean on friends who would support and understand?

She doubted Hank was *hiding* the farm issues as much as he was just incapable of discussing them. It was so painful for him. Clara had attempted to get him to articulate his emotions and not bottle everything inside, but the man was a vault.

She knew much of his turmoil was because it was a family farm, and the thought of possibly losing what had been his grandparents' and parents' was devastating.

Clara understood that deeply.

But she also understood that they had to figure out how to weather this turmoil even if their hearts were broken or their pride demolished. God forbid they fully lost the farm and had to start over from scratch, there was still plenty to live for.

Including four beautiful children.

Ava was nineteen and had just finished her first year of college. Clara still wasn't okay with the fact that she'd stayed near her school for the summer to take part in an internship, but she was trying to be.

Ava had always been Clara's mini-me and her best helper. Golden tan skin, silky walnut hair, milk chocolate eyes compliments of Clara's grandmother who'd been full-blooded Shawnee. They shared the same slightly round cheeks, though Clara's were from weight while Ava's were from being young and flawless.

In contrast, their younger three kids had taken on Hank's fairer skin tone, his eye color, his darkest shade of blond hair that lightened in the summers. Or at least used to before it had faded to oblivion.

Sam was sixteen, Aaron fourteen, and Talia ten going on twenty. Despite the occasional mood swing from any one of them, they were good kids who didn't grumble—for the most part—about their chores and pitching in on the farm. But they were still children. They fought with each other and believed the world revolved around them.

If they lost the farm, Clara knew the kids would rally and adjust. She just needed Hank to believe the same thing about himself.

"Do you think one of those two Ubers Isley mentioned might be able to pick me up here and get me back to the house?"

"Good idea. And we can grab some medicine on the way back."

"Already done." He patted his pocket. "The marina store had some. I got the kind that will make me sleepy, so hopefully it will knock me out and I'll wake up good to go."

She pulled her phone from the pocket of her ankle-length jeans. "I'll just let them know we're heading back to the house so they can get back out on the water."

"Clara Rose, you are not coming with me."

"But—"

"I'm going to sleep this off. And you're going to get back on that vile catamaran. Because I'm certainly not going to be signing us up for another sailboat ride in the future, so this is your chance."

"What if you get sick on the drive? You'll need—"

"I am not ninety. I can get myself to the house. And I don't think there's anything left inside of me, but if there is, I'll figure it out. I'm a big boy. I won't take no for an answer on this one. You're just going to have to concede."

A smile tugged at Clara's lips. "So bossy." And so Hank to insist she continue the sail. "Always the chivalrous one." It was good to see a spark of the old version of Hank shimmering under the surface. Surely Clara would be able to unearth the rest of him during the long weekend ahead.

Outside of nearly killing her husband, tonight was one of the best experiences of Clara's life. They'd flown across the water. Her hair was knotted and probably resembled a doll's in a two-year-old's grip. She'd assisted with trimming the sails like Captain Jay had taught her, so she was practically a seasoned sailor at this point. And she didn't remember the last time she'd felt such a sense of freedom.

Especially once she'd received the text from Hank confirming he'd made it back to the house without enduring another bout of sickness and was in bed.

With a short amount of time left before the sun would slip behind the mountains and Captain Jay would return them to the marina, Isley had asked if they could anchor near the Dillon Amphitheater. Now, faint threads from tonight's bluegrass concert skimmed across the water. They were hemmed in by incredibly gorgeous mountains, and the lake was a stunning inky blue.

"May I pretty please have my cameras back? I only need a few more."

Clara had taken so many photographs of the gorgeous views during the evening that eventually Isley had stolen her cameras and forced her to lounge on the catamaran trampoline with the rest of them.

Isley forked both her digital and film camera over. "You do

realize you're not on the clock, right? This weekend is supposed to be a combination of supporting the charity and vacationing."

"I love taking pictures. It's not a chore." Plus, with these views, how could she resist?

Clara snapped a couple photos of the sun shimmering across the lake's surface with her digital camera and then switched to her Minolta SRT film camera. She'd started playing around with the highly recommended beginner camera for developing years ago and loved it so much she'd never graduated beyond it.

She was already excited to process the film when she got home. Creating in her darkroom was a hobby for her. A stress relief. Though she'd cut back lately because the supplies were costly.

"This is definitely one of the best outings you've planned, Is." Trevor was on the trampoline, his back against the hull, and Isley was leaning against him.

She peered over her shoulder at her husband. "Except for poor Hank."

Isley had packed them a cooler with some snacks and sparkling flavored waters. At her mention of Hank, those currently with a drink in hand raised their can.

"To poor Hank," they all said in unison.

Hank would laugh when Clara relayed that he'd become the subject of their toasts after his departure.

"I feel so terrible that I didn't remember he had motion sickness." Isley released a frustrated growl. "We could have stopped for meds on the way over. Could have asked Captain Jay. Why didn't he say anything?"

"Always have some motion sickness meds at the hut. Should've mentioned it." Captain Jay had pulled his cap down and was positioned at the back of the boat—aka the stern now that Clara was a sailing expert—giving them as much privacy as the small craft allowed. Clara had thought he was snoozing beneath the rim of his hat until he made the remark.

"He didn't say anything because he's Hank." Liam sat across the trampoline from Isley and Trevor while Clara and Payton reclined in the middle of it. "He would never want to draw attention to himself by asking us to stop for him."

"I think if he could go back now, he'd pick that option versus the one that happened." No doubt her husband was embarrassed about becoming ill. But Liam was right that Hank didn't like to be the center of attention. "No one should feel bad but me. He's my husband, and *I* didn't even remember. I was too excited about sailing."

"It was a *great* night for a sail," Trevor emphasized. "Poor Hank."

"Poor Hank," they echoed.

"Everything else has been perfect, Is." Trevor tightened his arms around Isley. "Right down to the blanket your friend is covered in."

"Hey!" Payton laughed. "I came from Dallas heat. Sixties is frigid compared to that."

"Your husband doesn't need a blankie."

Payton plucked a carrot from the snack tray and tossed it at Trevor. He laughed, deflecting it, and it plopped into the water and sank.

Payton checked her phone and then returned it to the pocket of her summery linen pants that she'd paired with a black tank top and sweatshirt. She laid back against the taut trampoline deck beneath them, hands behind her head, vision cast to the cobalt sky streaked with wispy clouds and airplane contrails.

"Are you guys worried about Reagan?" Clara asked.

"Why?" Payton jerked to an upright position. "What do you mean?"

Oops. Clara had just mowed over an underground hornet's

nest. From the moment Payton had drawn her aside earlier and relayed the world's shortest explanation for Reagan's presence on this trip, Clara should have known not to prod in any fashion. Whatever was going on was private to Reagan, just like Payton had said. Clara only hoped she was okay. Certainly, with what they'd gone through with Cece during their senior year of high school, the women in particular were aware that was all that mattered.

"I just meant that she's walking around Breckenridge and it didn't necessarily sound like you wanted her to do that."

"Oh." Payton eased back to the trampoline, her elbows propped behind her. "Yeah, I wasn't sure about it at first. And of course her location sharing isn't working for some reason—maybe because of the mountains? So, that isn't helping. But she's been checking in with me, and she's actually going to a movie now. I guess she found a cute little theater. I'm not sure when she'll be done, but maybe we can pick her up on our way back through town. If not, Liam or I will just run over to get her when she's done."

"That sounds perfect. Glad she found something to occupy herself that didn't involve putting up with us old fuddy-duddies."

"She would appreciate that term for us." Payton grinned at Clara.

When Captain Jay announced it was time to return to the marina, everyone let out a collective whine that earned a lopsided, short-lived smile from the stoic man.

After disembarking the catamaran, Clara climbed into the third row of Isley's SUV since, without Hank, she was effectively a fifth wheel. Though, come to think of it, she wasn't sure she'd witnessed even the slightest of touches tonight between Liam and Payton. Usually Liam was the affectionate one while Payton was more like Hank—not a PDA fan.

Clara had made a game out of embarrassing Hank with affection in public. His ruddy cheeks would turn bright red, and he'd practically squirm out of her reach.

He made it too easy.

By the time they pulled onto Isley and Trevor's street twenty minutes later, Clara's eyelids were heavy.

Finch's Hope being the main focus of the weekend added an extra element of emotion to this trip. Clara prayed the blog content they were planning to provide for the charity would increase interest and participation in the online fundraising auction as a whole.

They owed Cece and Belinda that and more.

She was grateful that Payton and Isley weren't upset about the conversation she'd brought up last time they'd been together.

Logically Clara knew they couldn't go *there*—back to that night. But twenty-plus years later she was still tormented by it.

Trevor stopped the vehicle partway up the driveway for some reason. Maybe to open the garage door.

"Did Reagan come back to the house tonight while we were gone?" Trevor's voice held an edge.

"No," Payton responded. "She shopped and now she's at the little movie theater. Remember, I asked if she wanted us to grab her on our way back and she said the movie wasn't over yet? Oh," Payton's voice dropped. "That's strange."

"What's strange?" Clara shifted to peer around her friends.

The front door of the house stood wide-open, light from inside spilling across the cement steps.

Clara half expected Hank to be standing in the door frame, but he wasn't. No movement came from inside the house, and a creepy, crawly sensation slithered up her spine.

Clara had witnessed the effects of motion sickness meds on Hank before, and they made him nearly comatose. Had he sleepwalked and wandered out of the house?

Trevor put the vehicle in Park. "I'm going to head inside and check on Hank. Make sure everything is okay. Stay here a minute." He popped out of the vehicle, and Liam followed in his wake.

"Maybe the door didn't latch well when Hank got back and the wind blew it open," Isley said from the front seat, but unease blanketed her statement. "It has to be a simple explanation like that. Right?"

"Except you didn't give Hank a key to the house." Apprehension tightened Clara's throat, and the sides of the vehicle felt as if they were squeezing in all around her. She scrounged for the middle-row seat release for the spot that Liam had just occupied so that she could get out of this cramped back seat and check on her husband. "You gave him the garage code."

Chapter Four

Before Isley registered what was happening, Clara was out of the vehicle and darting for the house.

"Guess we're going in." Isley unbuckled as Payton did the same. They hurried after their friend, but by the time they entered the house, she'd already descended to the basement.

At first glance, it didn't appear that anything was missing or out of place upstairs.

Isley and Payton headed down to find Trevor and Liam standing near the pool table. Clara and Hank's muffled voices filtered from the Dillon Reservoir room.

"He's fine," Trevor confirmed. "Was sleeping when I got here." He pressed a few buttons on his phone. "I'm still calling the police because the front door showed signs of forced entry."

It had? Isley had rushed by so fast that she hadn't noticed.

"Maybe an intruder was here and then realized someone was home and took off. Who knows." Trevor walked away from the group as he began answering the emergency operator's questions.

"I checked the rest of the basement when we first came down," Liam confirmed. "There's no one here now."

"I can't believe someone was in the house," Payton whispered. She whipped out her phone and swiped clumsily at the screen. "What if Reagan came back early for some reason? What if she was here and—"

"She wasn't." Liam gave Payton's arm a gentle, grounding shake. "We *just* texted with her on our way back."

"I still need to talk to her. To hear her voice." Payton shoved the phone to her ear.

"Fine. But maybe don't tell her what's going on until we know what's going on."

Payton gave an agitated nod.

A sleepy Hank followed Clara out of the bedroom, rubbing a hand over his shaved head. "Clara says the front door was open? I didn't come through that way. I used the garage."

"We assumed." Isley leaned shakily against the pool table. "Trevor says it looks like someone forced their way in."

"What?" Clara hissed, her expression clouded with worry. "Was anything missing upstairs? I ran down to check on Hank without looking."

Payton's phone buzzed, and she answered immediately. "Reagan, are you okay?"

Based on the snippy tone shooting back through the phone, Reagan was indeed in one piece and her irritation with her mother for needing confirmation of that when they'd communicated thirty minutes earlier on their drive back from the lake didn't appear to be well received.

Payton walked into the Peak Eight bedroom to continue the conversation.

Trevor joined the group near the pool table. "They're going to send someone out. They said we should wait outside in case an intruder's still in the house. But I would think that's not an issue at this point, though I guess I should check upstairs just to confirm." His vision swung to Hank. "Did you notice anything weird when you got back to the house? I assume the front door was closed?"

"I was pretty out of it when I got back here, but nothing appeared out of place. And I would have noticed an open front door."

"But if someone had broken in while you were here, surely you would have heard something," Clara supplied. "You're a light sleeper."

"When I'm not medicated. I don't know that I would have tonight. Especially since I was in a downstairs bedroom."

"We should all check if anything is missing or stolen before the police arrive," Trevor suggested. "I'll verify the main level bathrooms and bedroom are clear."

"I'm going with you. There's no way anyone is still in the house at this point." Isley needed to know if anything had been taken. Her iPad? It linked to her credit cards and their bank account. It would be an absolute mess to cancel everything. But at least they were all okay and no one had been harmed.

Nothing mattered beyond that.

The group dispersed in pairs to check their possessions. Trevor walked in front of Isley as they made their way upstairs in what she knew was an attempt to protect her should they encounter anything unexpected. Nothing seemed out of place in the living or dining room, and they confirmed the half bath was empty before continuing on to the bedroom.

Trevor scanned the closet and bathroom while Isley checked the nightstand for her iPad.

It was right where she'd left it.

"All clear." Trevor paused in the doorway to the closet, brow creased. "Our jewelry is here."

"My iPad is here. Nothing is missing. Trev." Isley's voice

shook. "We haven't been able to get ahold of Aiden in a week. What if he's not at rehab and no one relayed that information to us? What if he left and he's using again and he forced his way into the house only to realize we were staying here?"

"Aiden would never..." She watched the recognition of what she'd said roll across his features like a summer storm.

They'd both thought their son would never do all sorts of things. Like use oxy to get high. Or hand out oxy unknowingly laced with fentanyl at a college party along with one of his lacrosse friends.

One of the girls had almost died. Freya Edwards had been in a coma for the longest three days of Isley's existence.

"Before I drove to Breck today, I sent Aiden an email like you asked me to so we could see if he would answer me for some reason when he wouldn't answer you."

Relief caused a rush of air to escape. "Did he reply?" Isley had no desire to discover that their son wasn't on speaking terms with her, but she also desperately wanted to hear *something* from him. And confirmation that tonight had nothing to do with Aiden would be a godsend.

Trevor shook his head, and her spirit deflated.

"We'll call the rehab facility tomorrow and confirm he's still there. Just because he stopped communicating with us, doesn't mean we should jump to wild conclusions. Aiden knows that he'll be prosecuted and serve time if he doesn't finish rehab. He wouldn't risk his future." Yet that's exactly what he'd done at that party. His and others.

"So, when the police get here..." Isley's stomach revolted, and she swallowed to overcome the nausea. The instinct to protect their son was so strong it swarmed around her midsection and plunged to her feet like the Tower of Doom ride, causing weakness in every muscle along its path. "What do we—"

"Don't bring him up. As far as we know, he's at rehab."

There was a hesitancy to her husband's delivery that sparked dread in Isley. "Let's go see if the others are missing anything."

They walked out of the bedroom as their friends came up the stairs.

"Nothing of ours was messed with or stolen. At least not that we can tell," Liam announced, Payton on his heels.

"Us either." Clara and Hank joined them at the top of the stairs.

Isley scanned the living room again and then walked into the kitchen. There was a glass next to the sink. Likely Hank's from when he got back from the excursion. Isley knew it hadn't been there when they'd left because she'd tidied up before the sailing tour. She had some...issues with cleanliness.

Aiden used to tease her about her need to keep the house organized at all times. Nothing on the countertops. Nothing strewn around the living room. He would laugh and say, *Museum looks good, Mom.* Or some other quip like that. And then he'd hug her, or nudge her, or throw an arm over her shoulders—he'd been taller than her for a good five years—and she'd laugh off the neurosis that had started after one of her mother's particularly terrible boyfriends.

"What's that on the island?" Isley stepped toward the white piece of paper barely noticeable against the backdrop of the white marble countertop as police sirens wailed in the distance. "Hank, did you write a note when you got back?"

"Nope."

Trevor's hand stopped hers before she could slide the note closer. "Don't touch it."

Isley leaned forward, deciphering the scrawled handwriting written in all caps.

Tell the truth or I will. What? What did that mean?

"That's strange and concerning." Trevor studied the note without moving it. "What could that be about?"

Blank, anxious stares answered him. No one spoke. The note didn't make any sense.

Except...

"No one touch it. Maybe the police will be able to pick up a print from it. I'll go out and meet them."

Hank and Liam strode outside with Trevor, the men's voices agitated.

Clara and Payton flanked Isley at the edge of the island.

"What if..." Clara pressed her lips together.

Payton's eyelids shuttered. "Do we *want* them to get a print from it? What if it has to do with *us*?"

"There's no way it's about that." Isley spoke in the same hushed tones as her friends. "No one even knows. If they did, they would have said something a long time ago."

"We *are* here to support Finch's Hope and raise awareness for their fundraiser," Clara supplied. "And everyone back home knows this weekend is happening."

The sirens were so close now that the house and Isley's heart reverberated with the wail. "That's impossible. We were just kids who made a poor decision," Isley protested weakly. "How could someone hold us accountable?" And yet, that's exactly what they'd feared at the time and in the years since. They all carried so much guilt over Cece's death.

"If that's true," Clara's chin inclined, "why didn't we ever tell anyone?"

Chapter Five

Cece

I carry a tray of microwave popcorn, chips, candy, soda, and carrots into the living room and deposit it on the floor between our sleeping bags, pillows, and blankets.

"Cece, your mom is amazing." Payton leans forward, snagging a Coke. "Mine thinks soda is evil."

"She wouldn't buy this stuff just for me." And before eighth grade, she wouldn't buy it at all.

I'm certain my mom wants the girls to feel welcome at our house because she was so desperate for me to have friends.

I don't relay that info because I don't like to think about last year. Eighth grade feels like a bubble. Like a TV sitcom rerun that's fake and outdated.

I still cannot believe my mother moved us to this Podunk town after she and my dad divorced. It has a *grain elevator*.

But, I have friends. Actual friends who don't talk behind my back. At least not that I know of. We have a sleepover nearly every weekend. Most often at my house, because Clara's house is full of boys, Isley's house includes her chain-smoking, ornery mother and her boyfriend-of-the-month, and Payton's is as cold as a museum.

I thought my parental sitch was messed up until I met Pay. Hers are unemotional and uncaring but weirdly still provide for her physical needs. Based on outward appearances, it would seem she has it pretty good. But once you're part of her inner sanctum, you see the strange robotic interactions they have with her.

Payton doesn't like to discuss her family, and I don't blame her. I don't like to talk about my family stuff either.

Isley sticks *My Best Friend's Wedding* into the DVD player. We watch it every time we hang out, and it's become like background noise. We know the whole soundtrack and all the lines.

Isley presses Play and then plops down on the living room floor, clutching a pillow to her stomach.

"Who's up first?" she asks.

"I'll go." Clara crosses her legs and faces us instead of the TV.

"Truth or dare," Payton asks.

"Truth."

Clara's whole life is a truth. There's almost nothing I don't know about her, and I've only lived here and been friends with these girls for eight months. Clara is the literal definition of an open book.

"Is Hank a good kisser?" I ask. It's a silly question because of course she'll say yes. But we only have so much for subject-matter options. Nothing goes on in this town. Which would explain why we're playing truth or dare at one in the morning.

Clara's blush is visible even in the faint light from the television.

Isley laughs outright.

Payton takes a drink of her soda. "What comparison does she have?"

We all laugh because it's true. From what I've been told, Clara and Hank have liked each other since at least sixth grade.

Still, she's the only one of us who's kissed someone besides Isley, who let Mick Knot make out with her in the hallway after the homecoming dance.

She hasn't spoken to him since.

Clara sighs, her skin now resembling a bright red Christmas sweater. "We haven't kissed."

Silence fills the room, and then everyone explodes with questions at once. The main one being *why not?*

We all just assumed that Clara didn't want to dish about it like the rest of us would if we had a boyfriend.

"We've only been together a few months!" she exclaims.

"On a technicality." Isley pops a carrot into her mouth, and it crunches loudly through her closed lips. "You guys have loved each other for like forever."

"That's not true." Clara folds her hands primly. "I didn't even know if he liked me until he asked me to the homecoming dance. And even then, I thought it might be just as friends."

The rest of us groan good-naturedly. Only Clara could be that oblivious.

"I knew Hank liked you the first week of school," I chime in. "It was a well-known fact when I started Veil High. Clara, you are by far the sweetest, most innocent person I've ever encountered." Which is part of what makes her so loveable. The whole world could be falling apart—and from what she's told me, hers pretty much did when her mom died—and she would still be kind and supportive and grace-filled.

I clap my hands. "Okay, now someone give me a dare. And make it a good one this time."

"Climb up on the roof and howl like a wolf." Isley beams.

Our rule is that if we don't follow through on a dare, we have to walk up to someone at school who we think is cute—again, the options are slim—and tell them we had a dream about them.

No one has refused a dare yet.

I'm certainly not going to be the first. I pop up and stride for the front door.

Everyone scrambles off the floor, chasing after me. "Cece, you can't!" Clara exclaims. "Your mom will hear!"

"What if she doesn't let us come over anymore?" Payton tugs on my arm in an attempt to keep me from unlocking the front door. "We *need* the level of junk food she allows. Isley will give you a new dare." Of course, what she's actually saying is that we need a place to hang out where everyone is comfortable, and our house *is* that.

"I will." Isley bobs her head in agreement. "And you won't have to do the punishment. I was just messing around. I forgot you'll do pretty much anything."

I grin at her as I back out the screen door. "You didn't forget. You just wanted to see how far I would go."

Our house is a small rancher with a rock wall lining a portion of the front. I climb onto it. "Someone give me a boost."

The three of them—two amused, one concerned—stand there staring at me.

"If you don't give me a boost I'll have to open the garage to get the ladder out, and then—"

"Fine." Payton marches over. She joins me on the rock wall and threads her fingers together, creating a place to put my foot. "But if we don't get to hang out here anymore after this, you're telling five people at school you had dreams about them."

"Deal." My mom won't care. She's just grateful I'm alive. With Payton's assistance, I wiggle my way onto the roof. Then I stand, throw my arms wide and let out a howl that feels oddly satisfying. Giggles answer me from below. I glance down to see the three of them bent over with laughter.

"Now get down before we get caught and never get to come over again!" Clara calls out in a hushed reprimand that makes us laugh even harder.

I shimmy off the roof on my stomach and drop to the ground, but I don't tell them why my mom would never ever refuse to let them come over.

Some truths are better left untold.

Chapter Six

When the police arrived—two uniformed patrol officers followed by a sergeant—they quickly ticked through a list of questions with the group, ascertaining who'd been home, who'd been out, that the door had been closed upon Hank's return to the house, that no one had touched the note when they'd found it or recognized anything about the paper or the handwriting.

And that no one had an inkling as to what the note was referring to.

Clara had swallowed hard at that question.

She *didn't* know.

But that hadn't stopped her from leaping into a deep dark ocean of overthinking. She'd never been at peace with the events leading up to Cece's death. She'd always wanted to confess all to Belinda Finch. But Clara hadn't been the only one with skin in the game. And back in high school, she'd let Payton and Isley talk her into remaining silent even though that went against *everything* in her.

Then again, she hadn't put up much of a fight. Her friends

had been afraid of any repercussions for the three of them if their involvement the night Cece died was revealed. And Clara had been terrified of the same.

Hank knew she felt guilt over Cece's death. But he thought it was the typical kind that came after a suicide. The *I should have known better—why didn't I see this coming and stop it?* kind.

Clara certainly had that version too.

At Sergeant Miller's suggestion, the group—minus Payton, who'd left to pick up Reagan—gathered around the dining table since the police were focused on the island, the note, and the front door. They were attempting to get prints from those areas but said a match would only come up if someone was already in the system.

From what little Clara understood so far, it appeared the odds of them uncovering where the note came from or who had broken into the house were small.

Unless someone followed through with the threat. But when would that be?

Hard to navigate, considering they didn't know what truth the note was referring to.

Since nothing had been amiss when Hank returned to the house, the consensus was that someone had entered the home and left the note while he was sleeping.

Which absolutely petrified Clara.

If she'd been the one present during a home invasion, she'd never sleep again.

But Hank had taken *that* news in stride. Unlike his downward spiral regarding the farm issues.

Sergeant Miller walked to the edge of the dining room area. He was maybe early thirties and built like he spent an hour in the gym every day, with a buzz cut, russet skin, and piercing green eyes.

"Sir," he addressed Hank. "When you came back to the

house, did you notice anything at all? Lights on or off? Any vehicles parked nearby or at a neighbor's? No detail is too small."

"Hank?" Clara touched her husband's arm, and he startled. The two of them were sitting across from Isley, Trevor, and Liam at the table. "Seargent Miller asked you something."

Sergeant Miller repeated the question.

"No vehicles that I noticed," Hank responded. "And ours were all in the three-car garage here because we moved them inside when we took Isley's SUV to the lake. But the house was well lit. The outside lights were on, as were the kitchen lights when I came in from the garage. I assumed Trevor and Isley wanted to make it appear like someone was home while we were out tonight, so I left everything the way it was. Then I went straight to bed to sleep off the motion sickness. Sorry I'm not more of a help."

Sergeant Miller wrote in his little leather-bound notebook as Clara studied her husband.

She'd always teased Hank that he was a terrible liar. And she had the sense right now that he was hiding something. But what? Why? It wasn't like Hank had broken into their friend's house—which he had access to—and left the note himself.

Clara's radar must just be off because someone had been in the house while her husband was sleeping. Yeah. That was *definitely* messing with her.

"Hello? Anyone here?" The voice came from the front of the house, where the door was slightly ajar but blocking the visitor from sight.

"I'll handle it." Sergeant Miller stopped in the kitchen to talk with Officer Yates and Officer Sanchez before continuing to the door.

Hank rubbed a hand over his stomach.

"How are you feeling?" Clara asked him quietly.

"Okay. Just a little off from the boat still, I guess."

"Do you think it could also be the altitude?" Isley stared vacantly at her hands, which were twisting on the table in front of her. "It causes all sorts of problems. Shortness of breath, nausea, headaches, dizziness. I know you live in eastern Colorado but with the increase in altitude, it's still possible. I would get you a glass of water, but…" She shrugged.

"I'll get you a cup of water, sir." Officer Sanchez strode over to the cupboard and filled a glass at the sink. She delivered it to Hank, her braided raven hair swishing across the back of her uniform.

"Thank you." Hank took a small sip, reminding Clara of when their kids had the stomach flu and she encouraged them to start rehydrating slowly.

"I think we're almost done," Officer Sanchez supplied. "There's not much more we can do. And since the note isn't threatening anyone's well-being, that de-escalates things."

Did it? To Clara, the note felt just as menacing as a physical threat. Especially since someone had obviously wanted to send a message by breaking in to deliver it versus leaving it in a nonintrusive way.

Officer Sanchez studied the front door where Sergeant Miller was in conversation with a man mostly blocked from their view by the sergeant's frame.

"Guy needs to get a swipe card," she murmured.

"Frequent customer of yours?" Clara asked.

Sanchez's mouth flickered. "Something like that."

Officer Yates directed a scowl in her direction, and Sanchez quickly wiped the smile from her face. The older officer had a constant pucker under his white mustache.

Sergeant Miller walked back in their direction, and the man from the front door followed. He was fair-skinned and close to six foot, with short sandy hair and a complexion Clara would give a kidney for. Would it be weird to ask his skin-care routine? It probably involved one-hundred-dollar facial cream. He wore laced leather boots with jeans and an untucked button-down shirt made of quality fabric that screamed *money*. Sometimes—like in the case of Isley's wardrobe—it was just obvious.

But perhaps that was because Clara shopped in the section of the World Wide Web, which contained items that screamed *it's okay if you ruin me*. That way she didn't panic when she inadvertently stained them or, her personal favorite, gained a hole rubbed from the button on her jeans.

"This is your next-door neighbor, Kyle Elrod." If Clara was following correctly, this man's house was the one almost diagonal from Isley and Trevor's. The two homes were located at the end of the street, and both bordered a ravine. "He wanted to check on you all and see if we needed anything over here."

Kyle was put together in a yuppie way—the aforementioned skin elasticity, the casually stylish clothing. But he was also *too*...something. Clara got a weird sense about him. But then, she would probably get a weird sense about anyone right now.

"Mr. Elrod has offered us the footage from his surveillance system. We're not sure what it catches of your house, but it's worth a look."

Certainly surveillance cameras were the norm these days, but the idea that his captured anything from Isley and Trevor's lot felt...invasive.

Clara was being so dramatic. Obviously everything just felt heightened due to the home invasion.

"That's really great of you." Trevor stood and shook Kyle's hand. "Sorry we haven't met before now. We're in and out from Denver."

"Glad to help any way I can. I live here full-time, so I tend to keep an eye out for a lot of the neighbors who are part-timers."

A very slight, very quiet, very cynical puff escaped from Officer Sanchez.

Kyle scanned the inside of the house with blatant curiosity. "Hope you didn't have too much stolen."

"We—" Trevor glanced at Sergeant Miller, who gave a barely visible headshake. "Thank you. Appreciate that."

"Kyle." Sergeant Miller slapped a hand on his shoulder. "Thanks for the help. I'll walk you out." He directed Kyle toward the front of the house, the faint hints of more questions being asked and answers avoided along the way.

Was the neighbor just a snoop? Or was Clara turning into a cynic?

During the turmoil of the past two years, she'd tried so hard to remain optimistic, cheerful, and encouraging. But the burden of lifting up her husband and herself was growing heavier, and she wasn't sure how much longer she could continue without assistance.

And now someone was attempting to force a truth from one of them. It felt eerily reminiscent of the games they'd played in high school.

Except those had been fun and innocent.

And this didn't fit that description at all.

Sergeant Miller returned to the group seated at the table. "If we find something of interest in Kyle's surveillance footage, like a person or a vehicle, we'll need you all to watch it to see if you can identify anything familiar."

Isley sensed her eyes widening, and she did her best to stem the surprise and panic surely scrawled across her features.

The idea of someone breaking into their home was bad enough. But the notion of having to identify that person or their vehicle, especially when Isley and Trevor weren't entirely certain of their son's whereabouts, was debilitating.

Trevor calmly answered the sergeant in the affirmative while Isley continued unraveling into tiny stress-filled particles.

"I need to use the restroom. Is it okay if I do?" This whole situation made Isley feel like she was in trouble even though *their* house had been broken into.

But then...she had made some terrible choices way back when. And more recently. It was hard not to jump straight to those scenarios when one received a cryptic note hand-delivered with a crowbar.

"Of course," Sergeant Miller responded. "We're just finishing up and then the house is all yours again. Unfortunately, there will be a bit of a mess from the fingerprinting."

"No problem. We'll get it cleaned up." Isley strode for the primary bedroom and entered the en suite bathroom. She pressed her palms against the countertop, her body bent over as she struggled to lengthen her clipped breaths.

Her therapist considered deep breathing the first line of defense against anxiety, but Isley often felt it did little to combat hers.

If Aiden had left rehab, wouldn't someone have communicated that with them since they were footing the bill? Except... he *was* nineteen. The rehab center likely wasn't required to tell Isley and Trevor anything.

Stop assuming Aiden's not at rehab just because he hasn't communicated with you.

Yet not answering her or Trevor really wasn't like Aiden.

No doubt it looked to the outside world like they had a son who'd gone off the deep end and was partying nonstop and handing out drugs like candy.

But that wasn't the version of Aiden they knew.

They knew the athlete. The student who received A's and B's and compliments from his teachers. The kid who'd always been able to make them laugh and was quick to assist when she arrived home with a trunk full of groceries.

As Isley had asked herself many times before, how had her

sweet boy gone from waving at her during preschool programs to his current scenario?

It all felt like a nightmare. Like she would wake up and find out Aiden was still *Aiden*.

Isley and Trevor had talked to Aiden about drug use in high school, specifically the dangers of fentanyl. He'd laughed off the idea of him or his friends using, as if it was absurd. He'd teased Isley and Trevor about buying their own helicopter so they didn't have to rent one for every over-parenting mission.

After being thrust into the substance-abuse world unexpectedly after Aiden's arrest, Isley and Trevor had quickly learned that they weren't the only parents shocked by such a development in their typically well-adjusted child's life.

Controlled substances were an epidemic. The answer on so many college campuses to stress or pulling an all-nighter to finish a paper or project. Maybe helping others avoid what their family was currently going through could be her next cause.

Right after she survived this strange break-in and note.

The note was the part that gave Isley hope, because it didn't make sense for Aiden to have written it.

Even if he was (a) out of rehab and (b) knew what she'd done, he likely wouldn't blame her.

He'd wanted to do the same before being shipped off to rehab, but Trevor and his brother, Jeremy, had vehemently fought him.

Jeremy was a personal injury lawyer who'd assisted throughout Aiden's case. He'd referred them to Aiden's defense lawyer. He'd been present for every meeting.

And he'd always had a chip on his shoulder when it came to Isley.

Jeremy fully believed, no matter how long Trevor and Isley were married, that she'd chased Trevor because he came from a wealthy family. That she'd somehow roped him into marrying her.

If anything, Isley had done her best to avoid Trevor's interest in her when he'd been a TA in her Principles of Business class. She'd known they weren't cut from the same high-end cloth. That he deserved better than her or what she'd come from.

Trevor thought Isley was overreacting when it came to his brother's opinion of her, so she tried not to say *anything* about Jeremy. But if he had somehow become aware of what she'd been up to after Aiden's deferred sentencing, Jeremy would definitely be game for outing her.

But why threaten her with a note? Wouldn't he be more than happy to run to Trevor and relay her offence? And the idea of Jeremy breaking into their home was ridiculous.

He *wouldn't do it. He'd hire someone to do it* for *him.*

Wow. That thought had popped into her brain without prodding.

Tell the truth or I will.

Jeremy could be giving her a chance to fess up.

Or her mind could be spinning so severely right now that nothing she was thinking made any sense at all.

Isley splashed water against her cheeks, glancing in the mirror to find hollow eyes and stressed, sagging skin staring back at her.

Cece had also been blonde with blue eyes, though Isley's hair color now came from an expensive salon. In high school, people had often commented that the two of them looked like sisters. Sometimes they would joke they'd been separated at birth, because they'd wished they were.

But if they'd really been that close, Isley should have known what Cece was going through.

Was Isley missing something again?

Could the note have something to do with Cece's death?

It felt impossible. But Clara was right that all of Veil knew what they were up to this weekend. Had someone also known what they were up to the night Cece died?

Chapter Seven

The phone rang in Payton's SUV, startling her.

Liam. She exhaled unsteadily and answered. "Hey."

"How's it going? You two okay? You've been gone a while."

"The movie has a little more time left so I'm just sitting in the car waiting for her."

Payton had known she would be early, but she'd used picking up Reagan as an excuse to leave the house the moment she felt it wouldn't draw attention to her so that she could process all that had happened.

She definitely wasn't looking forward to telling their daughter someone had broken into the house and left a strange note.

Lately Reagan felt like an expensive breakable vase that Payton bobbled and nearly shattered every time she removed it from the shelf for dusting.

"I didn't want to stress out Rea," she continued. "And I felt like demanding she leave the theater early—"

"Would definitely do that," Liam filled in. "Good plan. I just walked onto the deck to get out of the way for a bit.

The police are almost done here. Outside of the note and the tampered-with front door, they don't have much to go on."

Why wasn't the note addressed to someone? Did that omission mean it was intended for Trevor or Isley?

It *was* their home.

It can't have anything to do with us. We live the farthest away.

Though someone breaking into the house to leave the note definitely reeked of unhinged behavior.

There'd been a student at the beginning of last fall's term who'd been obsessed with Liam. One morning, he'd arrived at school to find her sleeping in his office. She'd claimed the door had been unlocked. Twice she'd shown up at events Liam had attended where she wasn't on the guest list.

He'd had to get the university involved. They'd made sure that anything that could reflect badly on Liam—and therefore the institution—was swept under a rug.

Things had settled back to normal after that, and then, six months ago, Liam had sat Payton down and announced that he believed they operated better as friends than spouses. He wanted to divorce and then raise Reagan as friends and partners.

Live in separate houses but do holidays together.

Have their own lives but also be intricately involved in parenting Reagan as a unit.

"Let's be the best friends we already are," he'd declared.

Payton had been so blindsided she hadn't known how to respond. She'd just sort of...shut down.

And Liam had taken her silence as agreement.

Now, everything was in limbo because of the troubles Reagan had been going through. Which left Payton so confused. Not to mention awkwardly on a semi-vacation, semi-fundraising weekend with her semi-separated husband.

"Reagan is walking out now."

Their daughter strode toward the vehicle, head down, long brunette hair partially covering her face.

At least Payton knew the note couldn't have anything to do with Reagan's issues. And yet, they'd experienced so much heartbreak in the past months she was no longer sure of anything.

Including the ancient Cece stuff that had instantly jumped to the women's minds.

Reagan got in and shut the door as a guy her age exited the theater. He glanced around the lot, his vision landing on their vehicle for a millisecond before bouncing away.

"Who's that?" Payton nodded toward the teen as he got into a small car and drove out of the parking lot.

"What do you mean?" Reagan snapped. "How would I know who that is?"

"I just thought—" He'd looked directly at Reagan before averting his gaze. Hadn't he?

"Hey, Rea." Liam spoke.

"*Dad's* on the phone? What's going on?"

"Something strange happened at the house tonight," Liam filled in. "Someone broke in through the front door and left a weird note on the kitchen island."

"What? When did this happen?"

"Most likely after Hank came back early from sailing." Payton didn't want to relay the details of the note to her kid, but Reagan wasn't the type to let something like this go. "The note says, 'Tell the truth or I will.' It wasn't signed or addressed to anyone."

"I don't get it. Why would someone do that? What's it about?"

"That's the problem." Payton spoke calmly despite the tension zipping through her body. "No one knows and no one recognizes the handwriting. It's all very strange."

"The police are here now. They're taking the note with

them, so Clara snapped a photo. They tried to get prints from it and the island and door too."

"Did this person steal anything?" Reagan's voice wobbled.

"We don't think so. We all looked through our possessions and didn't find anything missing."

"A neighbor just stopped by to offer his surveillance footage, so the police will be checking that."

That was an interesting development that Payton had missed while she'd been out.

"And if it captures anything," Liam continued, "they'll have us watch it to see if we recognize a vehicle or—"

"What?" Reagan squeaked. "There's video?"

"Does the surveillance footage bother you, Rea?" Liam could obviously sense her upset, even without the visual of her strangling her seat belt or pressing teeth into her upper lip.

"Of course." She blinked back tears and inhaled shakily. "It's freaky enough that someone was in the house. But the idea of them being caught on video makes the whole thing real."

Too true. "I'm so sorry this happened, Rea. Here I was trying to get you away from drama and stress and we're right back in it."

"We're not staying there tonight, are we?" She shuddered. "We're getting a hotel, right?"

"I...hadn't thought that far," Payton answered. It would be expensive for all of them to stay elsewhere. And the danger was gone at this point, wasn't it? Unless someone came back. But even then, the note wasn't threatening physical harm. Plus, they had the whole weekend planned for Finch's Hope. They couldn't just forgo that. Belinda and the charity needed them.

"Just come back and we'll figure everything out," Liam responded. "Love you. Bye."

Liam disconnected, and Payton sat in stunned silence. He hadn't spoken those words to her since he'd first announced

The Plan. Even though he'd also assured her nothing would change and that they would continue to love each other. As non-romantically involved partners.

All Payton had been able to think at the time was *consciously uncoupling*. Wasn't that what Gwyneth Paltrow had labeled her divorce?

The endearment had likely been directed at Reagan, but it still steamrolled Payton in a completely different way than the break-in and note.

"Mom?" Reagan squeezed her hand in a rare physical display of affection. Even as a baby, she'd had long slim fingers. Payton had tried to get her to play piano when she was younger, but she'd never taken an interest. She'd stumbled upon horseback riding herself. Of course it was the most expensive extracurricular activity. And of course Payton didn't begrudge her one second of the money or the time commitment. Unlike her own parents would have done.

"Sorry. Zoned out for a second."

"Totally. Makes sense with what happened tonight."

If only the break-in was the lone thing confusing Payton's brain cells.

She drove out of the lot, passing the spot where the young kid who'd exited the theater after Reagan had been parked. He'd left immediately after getting into his car. No more glances in their direction. He *had* focused on their vehicle when he'd walked out the doors, hadn't he? Payton was certain she hadn't imagined that.

But then, Reagan was stunning. She was always playing with makeup and accentuating her unique hazel eyes. Her hair was shiny and long.

It certainly wouldn't be outrageous for her to garner attention.

"Nobody was weird with you at the theater, right? You felt safe?"

Payton sensed Reagan's eye roll even though her vision was on the road. "Yes, Mom. Nothing was weird. You know I'm hyperaware about that stuff. Hey, I need to stop at the store on the way back to the house," Reagan announced as they crossed Main Street.

"Why?"

"I...got my period and I need stuff for it."

"Oh. Okay. Can you look up a grocery store or something like that?"

"Already did." She hit directions and handed her phone to Payton.

It wasn't too far. Just a quick jaunt out of the way. Payton ignored the wave of exhaustion that swept over her and adjusted their route.

As she pulled up to the grocery store entrance, a text popped up on Reagan's phone screen.

Zion: LMK what happens.

She handed the phone back to Reagan. "You have your card?"

"Yep." Reagan hopped out, and Payton found a parking spot.

She texted Reagan.

Let me know when you're checking out and I'll swing up to get you.

LMK = Let me know. Payton understood that texting acronym. But who was Zion? She'd never heard Reagan mention that name before.

What was he referring to in that text?

Curiosity slid along Payton's skin, which was reacting to the dry Colorado climate as if she were an amphibian sporting scales.

Between the contents of the box under Reagan's bed and the social media bully blitz she'd endured, Payton was on high alert when it came to her daughter's social sphere.

If Reagan had left her phone in the car—which she would never do—Payton would have scrolled through it just to quiet her concerns.

After almost ten minutes, Payton sent another text.

Ready??

Kk. Gimme a sec.

Did that mean she was checking out or just getting started?

Five minutes later, Reagan walked out of the store, and Payton zoomed out of her spot and up to the front.

"Did they have what you needed? What took so long?"

"They didn't have my brand so I had to figure out what to get."

"But you're good now?"

"Yeah."

"Great." Payton resumed the short drive to the house.

"Did you check with anyone? What's happening with the break-in now?"

"I didn't. We'll find out shortly."

When they arrived, the unmarked police car remained at the curb, but the cruiser was gone. Payton pulled into the driveway behind the third garage stall.

She turned off the engine and unbuckled, but Reagan remained frozen, her forehead pinched with worry as she stared at the house.

"I don't want to go in."

"We don't have to. If you want me to grab your stuff and head to a hotel, we can." Payton wasn't going to force Reagan to stay here if it would cause her fear or stress.

"Will the detective ask me questions if we go inside?"

That's what Reagan was worried about?

"You weren't at the house, so I can't imagine Sergeant Miller would need to do that. He's actually quite young and not imposing."

"This all feels so true crime documentary."

"Try finding out someone had been in the house *and* the GPS tracking still wasn't working on your phone. Logically I knew you were at the movie theater and not here, but I just... lost it. Sorry I made you call me. I just had to hear your voice and confirm you weren't being held hostage or something."

Reagan laughed. "I'm being dramatic because I'm a teenager. It's like my job. What's your excuse?"

Amusement tugged Payton's lips into the first smile she'd worn since they'd arrived at the house tonight to find the door wide open. "I'm a mom. It's like *my* job."

They watched as Sergeant Miller exited the house. He approached their vehicle, and Payton cracked her door since she'd turned off the engine and couldn't roll down her window.

"You two okay?"

"We are, thank you."

He stepped back to allow Payton room to exit the SUV. "Do you think it's safe for us to stay here tonight?" She left her door open so that Reagan could hear his answer. This way, she didn't have to decide. They could listen to the expert.

"The alarm system will be armed—it wasn't earlier. And I'm going to send some patrols through the neighborhood over the weekend. So yes, I think you'll be fine staying at the house." Sergeant Miller tugged a card from his pocket. "I already left my card with Mr. and Mrs. Stanton, but here's another."

"Thank you." Payton tucked it into the back pocket of her wide-leg linen pants as Sergeant Miller continued to his vehicle.

She faced Reagan, who still occupied the passenger seat. "What do you think? Should we blow this Popsicle stand?"

Reagan groaned, laughter following. "*Ugghh*, Mom, you're so *old*."

Payton beamed and gave her brunette hair a flip. "Thank you so much."

"It wasn't a compliment." Reagan unbuckled her seat belt. "If everyone else is okay, then I'm good with staying."

Strong Reagan. Payton loved that about her stubborn daughter. It was probably why she'd come through everything recently as well as she had.

They encountered Trevor, Hank, and Liam at the front door, working on securing it for the night.

Reagan walked straight into Liam's arms, and he hugged her tightly and kissed the top of her head. "You okay, kiddo?"

She nodded and continued into the kitchen, where Isley and Clara were wiping down the island.

"Reagan!" Isley pulled her into a hug. "I'm so glad you're okay." She eased back, hands still on Reagan's arms. "So glad you weren't here when this all happened."

"Me too." A slight sheen reflected in Reagan's eyes.

Interesting. Reagan had become quite adept at burying her emotions lately. This strange break-in was messing with all of them.

"Are you hungry?" Isley asked Reagan, her attention also swinging to Payton and Clara. "I was thinking about putting out some food."

"I ate popcorn at the movie, so I'm good. But thank you."

"I can't believe you're cooking at a time like this, Is." Payton had no desire to eat right now.

"You know I don't cook. I assemble."

"I'm not hungry," Clara piped up. "And I'm always hungry. I doubt anyone needs food."

"Then how am I going to keep myself occupied?" Isley lamented. "What are we supposed to *do*? I know Sergeant Miller said it was fine to stay here, but it definitely feels...tainted."

That was a fitting word.

Isley fanned her face with her hands. "Trev, are we really doing this? Staying here? Continuing the weekend? Don't we need to figure out a plan?"

The husbands stopped their discussion by the door.

"I don't know what else *to* do." Trevor shrugged. "Trying to find a place for all of us to stay would be a mess. And then what? We can't avoid the house indefinitely. I would say we get the door secured and then sleep on it tonight. And then in the morning we can all make a decision about the weekend."

Isley's breathing visibly calmed, and Payton felt her system mimic her friend's.

"That's a good idea. Reagan, you can sleep in the bedroom with me tonight. I'm sure Dad will take the sofa bed so you don't feel vulnerable with the basement windows and doors."

"Happy to." Liam sent Reagan a reassuring glance. "Besides, this all has to be some weird misunderstanding. It's not like that threat makes sense for any of us."

Liam sounded so confident. That should be comforting to Payton. But right now, she only felt weary and confused. Sleep was the right idea. Provided any of them would be able to accomplish it.

Isley emitted a haunted sigh. "This is definitely the strangest, worst thing we've ever had happen on friendcation."

"I have to disagree," Hank intoned. "The time I got food poisoning in Austin was worse, and *I'm* the one who was here sleeping when someone broke in and left the note."

"Oh, Hank." Isley pressed a hand over her mouth. "I forgot you were sick on a previous trip!"

Payton had too.

"Apparently I have the intestinal system of a newborn."

Laughter followed Hank's quip. The air in the room shifted and settled. They'd been through a lot together over the years. Surely they could navigate this too.

"Poor Hank." Clara raised a mug with a tea label hanging from it.

"Poor Hank," the group echoed the cheers that they'd started on the catamaran.

Hank chuckled, head shaking. "I don't even wanna know."

"Y'all are weird." Reagan wrinkled her nose. "Is it okay for me to go downstairs?"

"Of course." Payton grabbed her purse from the island. "I'll go with you."

Surprisingly Reagan didn't balk at that.

Once in the basement, Payton motioned to the narrow table flanking the back of the sofa. "I didn't mention this to anyone else, but I noticed some of your things were behind the couch. I wasn't sure if they were here earlier, before we left."

Reagan picked up a long-sleeved shirt from the table. "I moved this stuff out here."

"Even still, you should check your things and just confirm nothing is missing."

"What would I even have that's valuable?"

"AirPods? Money?"

"Both were with me, not here."

"Okay, that's good. But let's try to keep your belongings in the bedroom versus out here so we're not cluttering the living room."

"I doubt Isley cares." Then Reagan didn't know Isley well. "You're the one making a big deal out of nothing," she continued, a bite to her tone.

"I'm not—"

"So, I left some stuff out." Reagan huffed. "Sorry." She grabbed the small pile of toiletries and clothing and delivered it to the bedroom, dumping the items haphazardly into her open bag on the floor. They cascaded onto the carpet, creating a hazard that could easily take down Payton during a middle of the night bathroom run.

Something she didn't open her mouth to complain about. Payton would have appreciated some points for that.

Reagan returned to the living room. "There. Happy?"

Interestingly enough, no.

Chapter Eight

Clara lay under the incredibly soft, fresh-scented down comforter, eyelids shuttered against the abrasive sunlight reaching tentacles around the closed blinds. She must have slept in this morning.

Not a huge surprise based on how long it had taken her to fall asleep last night after the police left.

At first she'd heard noises—wind and house creaks, most likely. Though they'd felt sinister in the dark. Then Hank started snoring. Then her mind had gone wild with outrageous scenarios.

Eventually she'd slept. And dreamed that she'd received a note from Ava. *Mom, admit that you wanted me to come home this summer. Admit that you're disappointed!*

Clara could acknowledge as much, though she would never deny Ava the opportunity to take part in a career-impacting internship. Even if it required her to live on campus in summer housing.

But maybe, *just maybe,* Clara was mourning this summer without her oldest child more than she'd realized.

Ava's absence was a blow in the midst of the farm strain and the morose mood that tension created in Hank.

Clara felt like her world was crumbling around her. She kept trying to grab the falling pieces and lug them into place, but her efforts were too slow and clumsy.

She glanced over to find Hank's side of the bed empty.

Had he woken at the same unreasonable hour he did at home? When they were first married, Clara had attempted to get up at the same time as him so they could start their day together.

But she'd quickly learned that farmer's hours were not Clara's hours.

She slept a bit later than him at home and then made breakfast for everyone before the kids headed off to school. Which Hank joined them for.

They'd done a good job figuring out what worked for them over the years, and they'd never gone through the turmoil and adjustments that so many couples did when they were first married.

Maybe, *just maybe,* that was also why this new scenario with this unrecognizable version of her husband felt so debilitating.

Clara checked her phone on the nightstand. It was eight thirty. She'd left it on Do Not Disturb with the option for the kids or Hank's parents, who were in charge of the kids, to call in case of an emergency. She clicked off the setting, and the screen flooded with emails and other notifications that caused a surge of anxiety.

Clara swiped them to the side. She was on vacation—if that label still fit after yesterday's events. She would deal with real life later.

Where are you? She texted Hank and then popped up from

the world's most comfortable bed to open the blinds. Sunlight streamed in, and green vegetation and undergrowth stretched underneath the tall pines outside, creating a pretty picture.

The door edged open as Clara climbed back into bed.

Hank stepped inside. "I was about to head down to check on you when I got your text."

He handed her a coffee cup, and Clara inhaled the dark, nutty roast. "She made lattes?"

"Would you expect anything less?" Hank sat on the edge of the bed, and Clara scooted toward the middle to make room for him.

"No. But I thought Isley might sleep in this morning." Then again, she was the perfect hostess. Everything Isley did, everything she provided, was quality. Right down to the sheets Clara didn't want to remove herself from. "Did Is get up early to make breakfast? I hope not."

"No. She's only been up about twenty minutes. Trevor set out pastries, fruit, granola, and yogurt this morning."

"Yum." Her stomach clamored for the food it would have revolted against last night. Clara's mother had a saying—*everything is better in the morning*. Even now, decades after her death, Clara still used that truth with herself and her children. Sleep made things so much clearer and more bearable.

"What time did you get up?"

"About six."

"Oof." Clara winced. "That's painful."

"Compared to five, that's sleeping in."

"No one on the planet has ever considered six sleeping in. I assume you were the first one up?"

"Yep. It was peaceful. I don't know the last time I stopped trying to fix everything at home and just…existed. I read. And drank coffee after Trevor got up and made some. I was afraid to touch the fancy coffee maker."

Clara laughed. She would be too. The coffee maker probably cost as much as a month of their mortgage. But she didn't harbor jealousy over Trevor and Isley's monetary success. They were both incredibly generous.

Plus, Clara had witnessed firsthand how Isley had grown up. She knew the girl who hadn't always had food in the house even though her mother had never run out of cigarettes. The girl who'd driven to another town to find clothes at the thrift store in the hopes of not wearing anything her classmates had donated to Treasure Thrift in Veil.

"I'm glad. Hopefully a break from the farm gives you some rest and perspective." Clara clamped her tongue to the roof of her mouth to stop herself from saying more. Her goal was to support Hank. To carry him through this and out the other side. Not nag and screech at him. Even though there'd been moments over the last year plus when that was exactly what she'd wanted to do.

The most frustrating part of the failing farm was that it wasn't due to Hank's lack of effort. He worked literally nonstop.

After the drought had caused poor wheat conditions and a loss of a major portion of their crops, he'd rallied, leveraging the land to add in three new income streams.

But instead of helping, those had caused additional strain.

Hank couldn't have foreseen that happening. Neither of them could have.

Clara sipped the latte, a moan of appreciation following. "This might be the best coffee I've ever tasted."

"Right? Even the plain stuff Trevor made this morning was pretty life changing."

"Isley probably had it flown in fresh."

Hank released a short laugh. "It did come from a fancy bag."

"How's the motion sickness? Any other problems with that?"

"No, ma'am. All good."

At least one issue from last night had been resolved. Now to deal with the bigger one as a group, like they'd planned. "What's everyone up to?"

"Hanging out. Eating breakfast. Liam's reading of course. Payton just came up a few minutes ago. And Reagan is still out."

"Good for Reagan. I'll get ready and be up in a few so we can discuss the weekend."

Hank left and Clara rushed through her morning routine, then slipped on heather gray shorts with a black T-shirt. After tossing her shoulder-length hair into a ponytail, she ascended the stairs to find Trevor, Isley, and Payton at the table. Hank and Liam were seated in the living room—Liam with a novel in his hands and Hank thumbing through a coffee table book that appeared to be about the history of Summit County.

Clara was greeted with a round of good mornings as she parked herself and her delicious latte next to the platter of pastries that she had absolutely no willpower—or desire—to resist.

Isley looked up from her iPad. "I'm so glad you slept." She sipped from a ceramic coffee mug. "My adrenaline just wouldn't quit last night, so I took something to help me sleep." Her mouth quirked and she rolled her eyes. "So of course now I'm still groggy from it *and* I have annoying dark circles under my eyes."

"Same on taking forever to fall asleep and the dark circles. Last night was..." Clara's head shook.

"Exactly." Payton cut through a piece of pineapple and popped half into her mouth.

"Clara, I'm so sorry Hank was here during the break-in." Isley leaned forward, her expression pained and earnest. "How are you handling that? Are you okay?"

"I mean... I don't love that Hank was here. But I'm just trying to be grateful that he's fine and nothing worse happened."

"I am in the room if anyone wants to talk to me directly." Hank rose and joined them at the table, taking the seat next to Clara. "Besides, Isley, it's not like you're responsible for what happened."

"Considering it's our house, it's hard *not* to feel that way."

"Trevor's not blaming himself."

"He's an anomaly," she retorted.

"I wouldn't say I feel *no* responsibility," Trevor replied. "But certainly, Is has me beat in that regard." He scanned the group. "So, what's everyone thinking this morning?"

Liam closed his book and joined them at the table.

Hank rested a hand against Clara's shoulder. "As far as I'm concerned, it's up to you girls. Staying doesn't bother me. Neither does going."

"I agree." Trevor pinched the bridge of his nose. "I'm upset that someone broke into the house, but hopefully the police can handle that part. There really isn't much we can do about the note at this point. Not without knowing who left it. Like Sergeant Miller said, at least there wasn't a threat of bodily harm or a demand for money. The whole thing is just very strange."

Isley set her latte on the table with a clink. "I needed the distraction of this weekend because—" she glanced at Trevor before continuing, and he encouraged her with a nod "—Aiden's in rehab."

What? Clara's heart sank to her toes. Ava and Aiden were the same age. She couldn't even comprehend the news Isley had just delivered.

"I would have said something earlier, but every time I started to text or call, I just...couldn't follow through." Moisture filled her ocean-blue eyes, and Trevor squeezed her hand in nonverbal support.

"I'm so sorry, you guys. That's a lot to handle." Payton glanced at Liam. "We might not be in the exact same position, but we can empathize."

"How is Aiden? Is he doing okay in rehab?" And to think, Clara had been struggling with Ava not coming home because of an internship!

"We assume so, but we really don't know because we haven't heard from him in the last week. The rehab's focus is on healing the patient. Communicating with families isn't their top priority."

"Hopefully that's a good thing because it means they're helping Aiden." Clara's voice dipped with empathy. "But not knowing has to be awful."

"It is." Isley wrapped her hands around her coffee mug. "We're definitely at their mercy as to when or if we get an update on him. For me, Belinda's cry for help was almost a godsend. Organizing this weekend and the Breckenridge vacation package for the auction gave me something to do besides worry about Aiden. And now that we put all this work into it—"

"*You* put all this work into it," Clara corrected.

"We're all contributing something, and we're all emotionally invested," Isley stated. Which *was* true. "So... I'd like to follow through. For Belinda. And Cece. And all the lives Finch's Hope has already saved and will save in the future."

"I one hundred percent feel the same." They couldn't let a strange note stop them from supporting Finch's Hope. This upcoming auction was make it or break it for the charity, and Clara, Isley, and Payton needed Finch's Hope to keep their doors—aka texting and phone lines open—for so many reasons.

The charity had never experienced money issues in the past, but their bookkeeper had been skimming funds for the last two years.

What kind of person stole from a charity? It was sacrilegious beyond comprehension.

She'd been fired, obviously, but Belinda had refused to press charges because the woman was a young single mother. Clara had heard through the Veil grapevine that the woman was now in counseling and receiving assistance through a local low-income program.

That also had Belinda Finch written all over it.

Liam sat back in his chair. "As long as Reagan feels safe, I'm good with staying."

"Agreed. We do need to confirm with Reagan that she's comfortable continuing the weekend." Payton swirled the remaining coffee in her mug. "But canceling feels like letting whoever broke in win. I don't love that it happened. I'm still not sure why it did." Her vision toggled between Clara and Isley. "But we can handle whatever comes, right?"

Isley nodded, as did Clara.

They knew exactly what their friend was asking—if the note was about their actions the night Cece died and someone was trying to reveal those, would they survive that?

And the answer didn't really matter, because continuing the weekend was the right thing to do.

Clara wasn't sure that Payton and Isley realized how much Belinda had stepped in for her in the wake of her mother's death. And Clara hadn't even met Cece and Belinda until years after her mom passed. Yet, Belinda always knew just when Clara needed encouragement.

So, even if their involvement the night Cece died was somehow uncovered, Clara would handle the repercussions.

Except...the last thing she wanted to do was cause Belinda Finch pain.

Which was the biggest reason she'd kept silent all this time.

Chapter Nine

Reagan huffed loud enough to send the chipmunk on the trail near them scampering in a different direction.

Run, Chippy, run. Save yourself.

Payton had illogically assumed that because Reagan had agreed to stay for the weekend, she would have a good attitude about the weekend's activities. She'd also assumed that once Reagan got out in the fresh pine-scented air and experienced the gorgeous views, she would get over the fact that she didn't want to be on a hike with her parents and their friends.

Payton had assumed incorrectly on both counts.

Since their next scheduled activity that would be included in the vacation package wasn't until this afternoon, the group had decided—at Isley's suggestion—to do a simple hike this morning in the hopes that it would clear last night's break-in from their minds.

Plus, it would create extra blog content for Finch's Hope and could be listed as a free activity option with the vacation package.

The trail meandered along a small creek, was surrounded by evergreens and Aspens that created plenty of shade, and supposedly ended at a small mountain reservoir. It should be a relaxing, calming experience.

Instead, it felt tainted by the waves of annoyance radiating from Reagan.

Payton slowed her pace to align with Reagan's, who was lagging at the back of the group, arriving just in time to glimpse another woodland creature—this time a robin—fleeing for its life.

"Rea, I'm so confused. I thought you were okay being here. If you're not, why didn't you say something when Dad and I talked to you this morning?"

When she and Liam had spoken to Reagan after the breakfast conversation, Payton had fully expected Reagan to declare she was freaked out and wanted out of The Haven and Breckenridge. It was the perfect opportunity for her to do so. Especially after the fuss she'd put up back home when Payton first suggested she join them on the trip.

But Reagan had surprised them by agreeing to stay so they could support the charity—despite the break-in and the lack of her own space.

"I was just thinking about how none of last night made sense," Reagan had relayed from her perch in the middle of the queen bed this morning. "That note was like a second-grade threat. What was the point?"

Liam laughed quietly. "So true." He'd tousled Reagan's hair. "That's my girl."

"Dad! Don't touch my hair. I *seriously* hate that."

Payton had laughed internally, because she'd committed that same offense previously. Unlike Liam, she'd learned her lesson.

Now Reagan tugged an AirPod from her right ear, leaving the left one in. "What?"

Payton repeated herself.

"I'm fine staying. I just don't want to be *here*." Translation: with them. "I get that you didn't want me to be alone at the house while you guys were on this hike. I didn't want to be there either after last night." She tugged the sleeves of her gray, long-sleeved, cropped shirt, which she'd paired with black bike shorts, past her wrists. "But why not just let me hang out in town instead of this? I don't get it. Why can't you just let me do my own thing?"

"Because you're fifteen." Payton soaked in the sun warming her shoulders, attempting to use it to diminish the tension radiating from her trapezius muscle.

"And incredibly mature for my age."

Her current disposition might imply otherwise.

"Can you just..." Reagan made a shooing motion and reinserted her AirPod.

Fine by me. Payton marched forward to join her friends, passing Hank in the process.

After the hike, they planned to check out the town of Breckenridge so that Liam could write up a description and Clara could grab photos. They also needed to pick up a couple gift certificates that were being donated by local stores. Isley had procured those when she'd been running errands in Breckenridge before their arrival.

The woman was a fundraising machine.

Lately, Payton had only been accomplishing the bare minimum—her work as a research scientist, which usually felt rewarding but lately felt demanding, carting Reagan to and from school and riding practice, and preparing meals with Liam's assistance.

They cooked together on the nights that Liam didn't have class and had from the start of their relationship. And when they'd had Reagan, they'd committed to a minimum of three sit-down family meals a week. Between Reagan's extracurriculars and Liam's teaching schedule, they worked hard to make those happen.

They'd always been a couple who discussed parameters ahead of time and then stuck to them. Accordingly, Liam had assured Payton that their three-meals-a-week commitment with Reagan didn't need to change once they implemented The Plan.

Which felt questionable to her. How could that work? And did she even want it to?

In the last months, Payton had found herself saying no to invitations for dinner or coffee with friends, even if she could fit the outing into her schedule. Eventually people stopped reaching out, which was fine, because she was too exhausted to make it happen anyway.

And yet, Isley was dealing with a son in rehab, plus the traumatic months before that following his arrest—she'd gone into more detail regarding the college party at breakfast this morning—but *she* was still functioning.

Payton would have been jealous if she didn't know better.

Isley's veneer had been cracked and crushed by Aiden's troubles. She'd told them how he was kicked out of school and most of their so-called friends had turned aloof and judgmental, disappearing from their world. How acquaintances had gossiped about them, sharing information that was untrue and hurtful.

It sounded like a grown-up version of what had happened to Reagan.

"How is she?" Isley asked once Payton caught up to her and Clara.

"Fifteen," Payton answered.

Both women laughed.

"Clara, are your children still perfect? Tell me they've turned into normals."

Clara snorted. "They're definitely normal kids. Although,

Ava never went through the ornery stage that most girls go through."

Of course she hadn't.

"Sam, on the other hand, is much moodier. Aaron has his ups and downs depending on the moment. And Talia is still sweet but barreling for the teenage years like a bullet train. That girl might turn out to be our biggest challenge."

"I miss that sweet stage."

"If you can handle nonstop talking, you're welcome to borrow her."

Payton glanced back to see that Hank had also fallen to the rear of the group, and that he and Reagan were discussing something animatedly. Reagan's palms were raised in a defensive gesture, and Hank's expression was concerned. Maybe even frustrated.

Strange.

Clara and Isley continued chatting while Payton strained to overhear what Hank and Reagan were talking about. But they were too far back for her to decipher anything.

Payton was tempted to slow her pace in order to eavesdrop, but the moment she did, Reagan would no doubt shut down the conversation. She was also tempted to catch up to Liam and Trevor and point out the peculiar Hank-Reagan convo to her husband.

But he would just tell her she was overthinking.

Mom radar never quit. Even when it was wrong or missed things, like when the girls in Reagan's class were saying stuff about her online. Payton hadn't known that was happening until the school counselor called.

So, her track record wasn't exactly perfect.

A yelp sounded, and Payton turned to see Reagan bent over gripping her ankle.

Liam and Payton backtracked to her as she released a string of complaints.

They knelt to assess while Hank moved up the trail to join the others and presumably give them space.

"What happened?" Liam prodded.

Tears pooled in Reagan's eyes. "I tripped over a tree root and my ankle twisted."

"How bad is the pain on a level of one to ten?" It was a favorite question of Payton's that she'd used throughout Reagan's childhood. She was a scientist. She needed classifications and concrete answers. And she usually received shrugs.

"It's not that bad."

Or broad answers like that.

Liam manipulated the ankle. He'd played tennis and always struggled with his ankles, so he was the expert in this situation.

"I wonder if we shouldn't just buzz into urgent care and get it checked out."

"Oh, please no. I really don't want to spend an hour or two getting it looked at. If anything, it's a tiny sprain. I'll be fine."

Payton shared a *what do we do?* look with Liam?

He gave a slight shrug. "Do you want to try standing on it?"

"I guess."

Liam assisted Reagan to an upright position. She put slight pressure on her left foot and gave a small squeak, immediately lifting it off the ground.

"We should definitely get it checked out." Liam pulled Reagan's left arm over his shoulder so that he was supporting her on that side.

"Still not interested."

Liam seemed to be wavering over what to do. "If you don't want to get it looked at, then let's head back to the house and ice it."

They'd driven two vehicles today after learning their lesson from only having one at the marina, so the rest of the group could ride back in Isley's SUV.

"I don't want you to miss the hike with your friends. There was a cute little coffee and ice-cream place I saw yesterday that I never went to. So maybe you guys could just leave me there? That way you won't be gone from the group as long and you can catch up with them."

It appeared the ankle was in the zero to two range on the scale Payton had mentioned, while Reagan's desire to be anywhere with her parents was a negative twenty.

The color was easing back into Reagan's cheeks now that her plan was fully hatching. Payton wasn't sure whether to be concerned or impressed by her manipulation skills.

"Trying to rejoin the hike probably doesn't make sense," Liam responded. "But we'll figure that part out once we get you safely down." He sent Payton a grin and slight shake of his head that told her he was aware of what Reagan was up to.

But they couldn't make her hike with the injury, even if it was minute.

"Hang on while I let the others know." Payton strode up the trail. "Rea twisted her ankle but doesn't want to head back to the house yet, so we're going to find a place in town to chill. We'll do that with her while y'all finish the hike." Even though Payton was a transplant to Texas—they'd ended up in Dallas because of Liam's teaching position—occasionally the drawl snuck into her vernacular.

"Poor girl." Isley's brow puckered. "We really can't catch a break on this trip. Should we head back with you guys? It's not like the hike is necessary."

"Definitely finish the hike. It's gorgeous out, and Reagan's fine." Payton lowered her voice to a near whisper. "I'm not even sure she's injured. She just doesn't want to be on this hike."

They watched as Reagan took a few tentative steps with Liam's assistance. No more yelps. No winces. The ankle was healing at a rapid rate.

"She appears to be a normal teenager," Hank offered, earning quiet laughter from the others.

"Exactly." Despite the mishap, it eased Payton's mind to be understood by her friends. And to not be the only one dealing with a contrary kid or a plan that had veered off course. Not that she would wish their struggles on anyone. "We'll check in with you guys in a bit."

"Are you sure you don't want help?" Trevor peered down the trail. "We could call for medical assistance."

"The only kind of assistance she needs is to get away from her parents." Payton's mouth curved. "I don't think emergency responders provide that." Thankfully Reagan's incident had happened in the first ten minutes of the hike, so getting down shouldn't be a huge strain.

She rejoined Liam and Reagan, and the three of them began the descent, which wasn't too steep due to the easy hike Isley had picked.

After about five minutes, Reagan tested her ankle again. "It's a little better. If you guys can get me to the cute place I saw, that would be great. But you definitely don't need to stay with me."

Behind Reagan's back, Liam and Payton shared an amused look.

"Suddenly I'm in the mood for ice cream," Liam announced, earning a groan from Reagan.

If the two of them accompanying Reagan to the coffee shop caused their dear snarky teenager a bit of upset, so be it. They couldn't make her escape from the hike too comfortable, could they?

Chapter Ten

Isley stepped over a root that snaked across the dirt path. Due to the nearby water source, they were commonplace. And one had unfortunately taken down Reagan.

The remaining four of them had kept a slow but steady pace since Payton, Liam, and Reagan had headed down the trail a few minutes ago.

"Do you guys want to keep going?" Isley asked. "Or should we turn around and meet up with the Collins fam? I suggested the hike because it's easy and pretty. But we are on vacation, so we don't need to get in too much of a workout."

Clara laughed. "It *is* vacation. Sort of a working one, but it counts. And I'm guessing that Reagan isn't desperately missing the rest of us."

Isley chuckled. "True."

"How much farther is it to the lake?" Clara asked.

"Maybe ten minutes?" Trevor answered.

"Then I think we should finish, as long as Hank is good with it."

He'd been lagging behind for most of the hike, spiking Isley's concerns that either he hadn't fully recovered from the motion sickness or was still struggling with the altitude.

"I'm good to keep going," Hank answered from behind them.

Isley nodded to the camera looped around Clara's neck. "I may have done the heavy lifting before this weekend, but you're doing it while we're here. You're not getting to relax as much as the rest of us. Last night on the boat, you must have taken a hundred pictures."

"Photography doesn't feel like work. And most of the pictures I've been taking today are for me. I doubt the charity will want the shot of the ladybug on a leaf I just captured."

"They might. Did you donate any of your photographs to the online auction? A piece like the one you gave me with the frame would do really well."

"Goodness no. They're just for fun."

"You're discounting your talent."

"What talent? You're just biased because you're my friend. No one wants my silly stuff."

"How would you know when you never show it to anyone?" Hank rebutted.

"No one invited you to be part of this conversation," Clara called over her shoulder. "Sometimes I give them as gifts," she defended to Isley. "I just can't imagine anyone spending money on them."

"I can," Isley responded.

"There's something different in the air here." Clara inhaled, effectively moving the conversation away from her. "It's—"

"A lack of oxygen?" Hank filled in, earning laughter.

Trevor's phone rang, and he paused and tugged it from the pocket of his athletic pants.

"I need to answer this. Hank, you okay taking a break?"

Hank caught up to them. "If you wusses need to rest, that's fine."

Trevor's mouth quirked as he answered the phone, continuing up the trail a handful of yards to gain privacy.

Hank perched on a fallen tree limb and drank from his water bottle. "Why is it that I'm the only one huffing and puffing? I don't even sit at a desk for work. I'm constantly on the move. I don't get it. I've never felt so out of shape."

"I don't think it's you. I think it's the altitude coupled with your motion sickness last night." Isley felt terrible the hike was affecting Hank like this. "You haven't been here that long in terms of acclimating," she continued. "Not even twenty-four hours." How was that possible? It felt like they'd lived a week in the last day. Especially with the break-in and the note. Isley kept thinking that since it was their home, it *had* to be directed at them. At her.

When she'd woken this morning, she'd feared there would be another one.

Thankfully, all had been quiet on that front.

"I've been drinking a ton of water." Hank capped the bottle and placed it on the ground. "But I still feel sluggish."

"I shouldn't have suggested a hike this early in the trip. I should have given you all more time to adjust."

"This is barely a hike," Hank retorted. "It shouldn't be an issue."

"Isley," Trevor called. "Can you come here for a sec?"

"Be right back." She jogged up the trail to join Trevor, her heart thumping wildly due to adrenaline. Was the phone call about Aiden? Or was it Sergeant Miller with new info?

"I have the phone muted. It's Daria Skor."

Daria was the mom of one of Aiden's high school friends. "Why is Daria calling you?"

"She said she tried you first but you didn't answer."

Isley tugged the phone from the hip pocket of her buttery soft Lululemon leggings. "Oh. I do have a missed call from her." She turned her phone to vibrate versus the low ring volume she'd had it at. "But why is she calling us at all?"

"She says she saw Aiden in downtown Denver and he didn't look well. She was concerned about him."

Dread snaked along her spine, and emotion instantly clogged her throat. *No, no, no.*

This couldn't be happening.

"But that's not possible. Is it? Wouldn't rehab have to tell us if Aiden left?"

"I think they would have at least notified his lawyer or the prosecutor."

Trevor unmuted the phone. "Daria, Isley is here too now. Can you tell us what happened again?"

Trevor held the phone slanted away from his ear so that Isley could listen in, since speakerphone would cause the conversation to resonate through the quiet forest.

"I was downtown meeting a friend for breakfast this morning at Union Station, and I saw Aiden walk through wearing a travel backpack. His hair was long and kind of...unkempt. Sorry." Isley pictured her wince. "I called his name but he didn't turn. I tried a few more times, but either he didn't hear or he didn't want to be stopped. I even got up and tried to follow him but I lost him in the crowd. I wanted to make sure he was okay. That he didn't need assistance or anything. He just didn't look like himself."

If he didn't look like himself, how confident was Daria that she'd seen him and not someone else?

"How certain are you that it was Aiden?" Trevor asked. He must have been thinking along the same lines as Isley. "Because he's...out of town right now."

That was an interesting description for rehab.

But there weren't many people they could trust with Aiden's stuff. It was a bit like Payton had said regarding Reagan. Whatever was going on in her life that had caused them to bring her on this trip was private to her.

"Of course there's a chance I could be wrong. That it wasn't him. But…" Daria's delivery held hints of motherly emotion that caused a contraction of recognition deep in Isley's gut. "I wouldn't have called unless I was certain."

"Thank you for reaching out." Trevor somehow managed to respond calmly while Isley wrestled to quell her rising alarm. "We appreciate you caring about Aiden."

"Of course. Let me know if there's anything else I can do."

They said goodbye and disconnected.

Isley believed that Daria's call had come from a place of concern.

But it still felt like she'd unknowingly unleashed a dam.

"Don't panic," Trevor instructed.

She conjured a wobbly smile. "But I'm so good at it."

Earlier this morning, Trevor had called the rehab center and left a message requesting confirmation that Aiden was still at the facility. They hadn't heard back as of yet.

So, what were they supposed to do now? Worry and wait?

"Think they're okay with a longer break?" Trevor nodded toward Clara and Hank, who were both perched on the tree limb now and appeared to be FaceTiming with someone.

"Seems like it."

"Then I'm going to call Zak Barwick." Trevor searched for Aiden's lawyer in his contacts. "He should be able to get confirmation that Aiden's still where he's supposed to be."

"Smart. We should have done that days ago."

But at that point, Isley had assumed Aiden just wasn't answering her. She'd hoped that was because he was busy healing.

Now it felt as if everything was spinning out of control.

Trevor held the phone to his ear. "The odds that Daria spotted Aiden and not a look-alike have to be less than one percent."

"You can't just make up statistics. That's not how statistics work."

His smile sprouted. "But I'm so good at it."

As the phone rang, Trevor engaged in what Isley labeled his business stance—feet apart, shoulders back, ready to take on the world. He radiated unbridled energy. Always had. A lot of which he directed toward his work. Probably what made him so massively successful.

He was one of those strange creatures who woke early, ran on the treadmill before coffee, and only ate fruit for breakfast.

Although he had set aside his normal routine this weekend. Isley hadn't noticed him working even once. And this morning when he'd woken at his normal time and started sliding out of bed, she'd tugged him back in and he'd acquiesced without complaint.

He'd tucked her against his chest and kissed the crown of her head. "We'll figure it out," he'd whispered. "It's going to be okay."

She wasn't even sure if he'd been referring to the break-in or the note or Aiden. Maybe all of the above.

Isley had been comforted and also swept with guilt over her actions.

She *hated* that she'd explicitly gone against her husband's wishes.

Trevor deserved so much better than her.

He always had.

Isley had fallen back asleep in the confines of her husband's arms, battling the stark fear that she could lose him because of what she'd done.

A receptionist must have answered, because Trevor requested to speak with Zak. A few seconds later, he ended the phone call.

"What happened?"

"They put me through to his voicemail. I'm trying again."

"Could we get in trouble with the police for not telling them about Aiden?"

"Absolutely not. He has nothing to do with the break-in or note." Trevor's mouth pinched. "Right now, our only understanding is that he's at rehab, exactly where he's supposed to be."

"You say that so confidently, when in reality, we don't know anything."

Trev gave a short disgruntled laugh. "We've definitely never done *this* before."

Throughout Aiden's growing-up years, Trevor had always repeated that statement. *We've never done this before. But we'll figure it out.* And they had navigated so much. But the past months had sent Isley careening so off course that she wasn't sure how to even find the highway again let alone relearn how to operate a vehicle.

"I'm starting to feel a little sick of the constant pivoting and adjusting to unexpected circumstances." Frustration weighed down Trevor's statement. "And then last night happened. Can't we just be boring for a bit?"

"Yes. Boring on a beach." Isley's stomach turned to choppy waves at the reminder of the note. They had no idea what thing or person it was referring to. A mystery her mind had been attempting to solve nonstop.

But how could you fix what you didn't understand?

"You name the beach and we'll make it happen. Just the two of us."

Just the two of them made sense. And honestly, Isley had been enjoying empty nesting with Trevor while Aiden was only an hour away at school and they still had the opportunity to see his lacrosse games or him. But that peace had flown out the window after Aiden's possession and distribution charges.

And now that they were uncertain of his whereabouts, she was floundering again.

Isley wanted a beach with Trevor *and* Aiden—her boys,

as she often referred to them. Maybe when Aiden got out of rehab, if he was doing well, they could actually make something like that happen.

"Yes, hello, this is Trevor Stanton. I'm trying to reach Zak Barwick but I just got sent to his voicemail and it's important." He listened, tension lines growing taut across his face. "I see. Is there a way to get a message to him there? Or is there someone else who could handle this for us? We're just trying to get confirmation on the whereabouts of our son, and the rehab center isn't answering." Trevor nodded. "Right. Yes. Okay. That is my number. Thank you." He disconnected with a sigh. "The whole office is at a team building day off-site. She said she'd try to get a message through to him, but she can't promise anything."

"How can they do that? They're a law firm! Aren't they supposed to be available for emergencies?"

"She said it's one day out of the year."

Isley released a disgruntled huff. "We're not going to find out anything until Monday, are we?"

"If that's the case, then we're sticking with the last known scenario—which is that he's at the rehab facility and they're so busy working with him that they don't have time to contact us. Which is stated explicitly on all of their material. It's nearly impossible that he was at the house last night. And then was somehow in Denver this morning."

"If a friend was driving him or he bummed a ride it's not."

"I still think that's a stretch." Trevor frowned. "And the note? What could that have to do with him?"

Good question. Trev was likely right. But Isley couldn't shake the fear that whether from the past or the present, there was a connection in all of it to her.

Chapter Eleven

Payton had assumed Breckenridge was booming in the winter and much quieter in the summer, but the crowds—including everyone's dog—on both sides of Main Street proved her wrong.

Like Trevor had poked fun of, there were people in jackets and jeans and others in shorts and sleeveless shirts. Some appeared to have prepped for their trip with high-end clothing. Others had a mountain vibe—Chacos, hiking boots, faded T-shirts.

They managed to find a parking spot somewhat near the coffee and ice-cream shop, and Reagan walked on her ankle with only an occasional wince, further confirming Payton's theory that the small tweak was simply that. Instead of saying anything, Payton reached for gratefulness that she was fine and they weren't about to spend hours in an urgent care or emergency department getting a broken leg fixed like their friends who, on their first visit to Colorado, did not make it down one ski slope before having that happen to their daughter.

Reagan was right about the coffee and ice-cream shop. It was cute. But also small. The three of them stood inside the door for a few seconds, scanning for a table. Payton wasn't sure they were going to find a seat, and even if the ankle was mostly fine, Reagan should sit down.

"We're leaving if you'd like our spot." An elderly couple stood from a table by the front windows.

"Thank you so much." Payton scooted to the side to let them pass on their way to the exit. "Appreciate it."

The gentleman held open the door for his wife, and she stopped to adjust his wayward collar as she passed him. Once outside, he offered his arm to her, and they carefully made their way down the sidewalk.

"You and Reagan sit and I'll order for us," Liam offered.

Payton cleared the lump from her throat and blinked repeatedly before turning in his direction. "Great, thanks." How had that couple's simple care for each other impacted her so deeply and swiftly? Payton shook off the burst of melancholy their tenderness ignited.

"I could go for some ice cream," Reagan stated as she plopped into a chair with all the grace of a preschooler.

"You know what? Me too."

"Mom! It's before lunchtime. Are you feeling okay?" Reagan tilted her head analytically, a genuine smile climbing her features. Her straight chocolate hair was parted down the middle and pulled into a low ponytail, and her eyes popped with the hint of makeup she'd applied. She was stunning, but she was also that little girl who'd called Payton her bestest friend and wanted to marry her daddy. Fifteen was such a juxtaposition of *I'm an adult!* and yet their gooey middles were all kiddo.

They relayed their orders to Liam, and he joined the line.

"Here. Put your ankle up while we wait for Dad." Payton

scooted the third chair into an accessible spot for Reagan, who surprisingly didn't refuse.

"It doesn't hurt that bad," she stated, vision downcast, as if aware that she'd made a bigger deal out of the ankle than she'd needed to and, in turn, disrupted her parents' morning.

"Just in case, we should baby it for a bit." Payton wasn't going to berate Reagan for being a kid. Not like her parents would have done. But then, nothing about their relationship resembled anything about the one she'd had with her parents. At least she hoped not. That had been her goal all along.

"Thanks, Mom." And with the faintest hint of emotion flickering in her hazel eyes, Reagan actually did appear grateful.

It reminded Payton of when Reagan was sick about seven months ago, and Payton had stayed home from work to be with her despite her protests that she didn't need her *mommy*. They'd watched movies together, and Reagan's poky edges had softened for the day.

"Mom, your face is doing that thing."

"What thing?"

"Where it gets all emo. Like you're gonna cry or something."

Payton laughed. "Just feeling a bit nostalgic. Sorry if that bothers you."

"It does." Reagan delivered the sassy comment with an equally sassy grin.

"When was our last family vacation? Last summer, right?"

"Yep. That trip was *so* much better than this one."

"You mean a vacation focused solely on you and your riding competition is better than one with your parents' friends? How strange."

Reagan snickered. "You forgot the creepy break-in and note."

Payton definitely hadn't forgotten. "We're not winning any awards with this vacation so far."

Their last trip had been pre–Liam announcing The Plan. Looking back, Payton didn't recall anything being off or any fighting or tension between her and Liam.

How had she missed the signs so completely?

"Brunch dessert is served." Liam placed a cup of strawberry cheesecake ice cream in front of Payton and a cup of cookie dough in front of Reagan.

"What flavor did you choose?" Payton peered into his cup.

He scooted it across the table toward her. "Coconut sorbet."

She scooped out a bite and gave a low hum of appreciation before passing it back to him.

It was strange how things like her always needing to taste his ice cream were so familiar to them. Part of their story. How was Payton supposed to know which pieces of *them* would stay acceptable after implementing The Plan and which pieces would end?

"Did you get me a coffee?"

Liam winced. "I forgot. I'll grab one."

"That's okay. I will." Payton popped up from the table and strode to the back of the line, which was now five people deep.

Liam followed her. "Pay, let me. Please. Sorry I forgot."

"It's fine." A rush of tears formed. So frustrating! And so unlike her. "I just need a minute. Hang out with Reagan."

The skin flanking his eyes pinched with concern. "Okay." He returned to the table.

Eventually Payton got her coffee. She added creamer and joined Liam and Reagan at the table, finding them both on their phones.

"Phones, huh?"

She was greeted with a groan from Reagan and a sigh from Liam, who plunked his on the tabletop, screen face down.

After the trouble with the student who'd been somewhat obsessed with Liam, the university had suggested he add a protector to his phone that made it impossible to see the screen from the side. The only person Payton knew who had something like that was their friend who was a lawyer. Protecting his client information made sense.

But she'd felt like it was overkill for Liam to do the same.

The university had said it was to keep students from seeing faculty communication. Everything revolved around privacy and liability these days.

Reagan placed her phone on the table. "What would you like us to do, Mother?"

Payton ignored the sarcastic reply. "Talk? We could play that game we used to." Ironically on a phone app.

Reagan snorted. "I'm not twelve, Mom."

Liam's phone buzzed, and he plucked it from the table. "It's Ashlyn calling," he announced. "She's covering my class this afternoon, so I need to take this."

Ashlyn Browning. Assistant Professor. Kickboxer. A decade younger than Payton with skin that didn't show wrinkles *yet* and hair that didn't sport gray *yet*.

Liam swiped to answer as he walked out of the coffee shop.

The windows perfectly framed his animated conversation. Liam wore chino shorts and a cobalt T-shirt along with an older pair of Vans. Whether outside of the classroom or in, he always looked the part of an English professor. His head fell back, sandy curls bouncing as he laughed heartily at something. The kind of laugh that had been their norm when they first met.

Payton had been focused on building her career when she met Liam, not finding a partner. He'd come out of nowhere, and he'd been so the opposite of her parents.

They were regimented. Liam was easygoing.

They were cold. Liam was warm and kind.

He gave in with Reagan more often than Payton liked, but she also didn't mind because she knew his reasoning—love. He adored Reagan. Always had. Which was amazing, considering they hadn't planned on having children.

Liam hadn't been against having kids, but Payton had. She'd been afraid she would repeat her parents' mistakes, and she hadn't wanted to take that risk.

But their oops baby was the best thing that had ever happened to her.

She and Liam had pivoted together when they'd found out they were pregnant, and Payton would say they'd done a pretty good job.

She'd thought they would always pivot together.

Maybe that's what Liam thought they were doing.

"Mom?"

Payton pulled her gaze away from Liam's conversation. "Yeah?"

"I don't think..." Reagan's lips pressed tight.

"You don't think what?"

"Never mind." She checked her phone screen as Liam re-entered the coffee shop.

"What did Ashlyn have to say?"

Liam picked up his bowl of ice cream that had begun to melt and spooned a bite into his mouth. "Not much. Just had a few questions about the lesson plan for this afternoon." No hint of guilt laced his easygoing tone.

"Everything else good?"

"Yep." His forehead furrowed. "Are *you* okay?"

"Mom's being weirdy." Reagan finished her ice cream and plopped the bowl onto the table.

"I'm not being *weirdy*."

"You most definitely are. Will you two *please* go finish the hike?"

"It's too late now." Payton sipped from her paper coffee cup.

"Then go walk around town. Breckenridge is really cute, and I'm good hanging out here." Reagan lifted her cell from the table and wiggled it in a teasing, taunting gesture. "I've got my phone to keep me occupied." She beamed a mischievous smile at Payton.

"What more could I ask for?" Payton laughed. "What do you think?" She checked with Liam.

He shrugged as he finished the last of his ice cream. "Up to you. I'll do whatever."

Why did a generous response like that ignite Payton's body in an irritable hot flash? She consciously unclenched the muscles that sparked under her skin like live electrical wires.

If they left, at least Reagan wouldn't be a witness to the strain and tension eating at Payton.

"Sure, let's do it." Payton stood and dumped her coffee into the trash receptacle. She...hadn't meant to do that. Evidently her brain was on hiatus.

"Why didn't you take that with you?" Reagan's expression flashed with worry. "Are you *sure* you're okay?"

Confirmation that she wasn't hiding her angst well. "I'm fine. Still a bit tense from the break-in, I guess." *And I'm concerned about you. And Liam. And that stupid, confusing note.*

If only it had been addressed. It would narrow things down so much to know who—or *whom*, as Liam would certainly correct it to—it had been meant for. The note was making Payton second-guess *everything*.

Like that phone call with Ashlyn. Liam had been talking to and about Ashlyn a lot recently. Which probably made sense since she was covering his class.

Payton blew out an aggravated breath. "We'll text you in a bit." She and Liam walked out of the coffee shop and paused before the sidewalk. "Should we call them?" Payton asked.

"See where they're at and find out if we should head back to the hike or meet them somewhere?"

"Sure."

Payton plucked her phone from the pocket of her charcoal capri leggings that she'd paired with a teal tank top. She had a sweatshirt tied around her waist because Isley had mentioned that the morning temp might be cool.

Payton paused before calling Isley. "Did you see Hank talking to Reagan on the hike?"

"I saw they were both at the back of the group if that's what you're referring to." Liam ran a hand through his curls, which had taken on a dryer, less buoyant texture in Colorado. Similar to Payton's skin.

"Yes, but they also appeared to be having a deep conversation."

Liam's mouth pursed with disbelief. "A *deep* conversation? How do you know that? Did you overhear them?"

"Not exactly." Not at all. "I could just tell by their mannerisms."

"Huh. Why does it matter if they were?"

"Doesn't it seem strange? What would the two of them have to talk about? Reagan never has conversations with adults."

"That's not true. She can be terrible about it with us sometimes, but if an adult asks her a question, she always answers. Especially if it's about riding or something she's interested in."

Payton had been right to think that Liam would qualify her concerns as overthinking.

"Are you upset with me?"

"What?" Her response to Liam's question squeaked out like she'd stepped on a dog's chew toy.

"You seem irritated with me. Almost...angry."

How was she supposed to answer that? Payton didn't do

angry. She did calculated. Careful. "I don't—" *think so.* And yet, she wasn't *not* upset with him.

Liam had dropped a bomb when he'd come up with The Plan. And this weekend was the first time Payton had slowed down enough to let it fully sink in. To try to truly understand it and its implications. To not just blindly attempt to get on board so that she didn't lose her tight-knit family completely.

Underneath the tough outer shell she'd constructed, Payton was still that little girl cowering in bed, craving a mother's touch that she'd never received.

Hungry for love and affection.

And ever since her husband had unwanted her, she'd been flailing.

Tension wrapped tentacles around her windpipe. "Honestly, I don't know how to answer that."

"How come?" Liam appeared genuinely curious and concerned. He squeezed her arm, then let his hand fade back to his side. "I thought we were good?"

"I thought we were too."

Chapter Twelve

Cece

My mom has been trying to get my dad to attend tonight even though he's the last person I want here.

I told her as much, but she didn't listen.

She's so intent on fixing me and my dad that she doesn't realize we're not ready to be superglued back together yet.

Plus, it's only homecoming dance my sophomore year. It's not *that* big of a deal.

I can hear her leaving perky *Cecelia would love to see you!* messages for him when she thinks I'm out of earshot.

Our house isn't that big. I'm well aware of what she's up to.

And even though she's campaigning for him to actually show up for his daughter, she keeps warning me that he might not.

Hopefully he can come! But he's been working so much lately! Might be tough with his schedule!

Her list of excuses for him is long. She doesn't want me to

get my hopes up. My hopes were never up. She should listen to her own advice.

I know the justifications she makes for him are her attempt to keep me from getting hurt. She is deathly afraid of me being wounded, and she does everything she can to keep the peace.

We never fight anymore.

And that's not to say we were ever participants in any huge knockout battles. We only ever had typical teenage-parent disagreements.

But after my depression—a word I hate that doesn't convey what I actually *felt*—everything morphed.

Sometimes, when I'm feeling extra *teenagery*, I push back with her to see how far she'll bend. I admit those aren't my best moments. But it's almost a game to see her patience stretch like Gumby's limbs. It's honestly pretty impressive. She could teach a class on how not to react emotionally to a teenager.

When she's reached her limit, her cheeks pop with red and she inhales really deeply and exhales super slowly. I lay off at that point, because I'm aware that she's doing everything she can to make my life easier.

Sometimes it gets old being treated like fragile glass, but I understand why she does it.

In return for her efforts, I attempt to keep my rebellious streak to a minimum. And I picked friends who, even with all of us having our crosses to bear, are similar in that way.

Of course there's always the temptation to numb a particular pain, but during our freshmen year, we made a pact not to go down that path…unless we do it together.

That might sound strange, but it works for us.

It's comforting to think that if one of us is at a majorly low point, we won't be alone.

Despite my mom's poking and prodding, my dad did exactly what I expected him to do tonight.

Nothing.

I'm standing in a room of doting parents—plus Payton's parents, who definitely don't fit that definition—who've gathered to take pictures of us in our homecoming dresses and suits.

We've done photos on the stairs, in front of the fireplace, separately, as just the girls, just the boys, the whole group together.

If we take any more, my brain might explode.

"Cecelia," my mother says, "come here for a second. I want to get a photo of you outside."

I grumble as I cross the room and follow her out the back door of Scout's house. My face hurts. Not from the I-can't-stop-laughing-this-is-so-great kind of smile, but from the forced-for-pictures grinning that always ends up feeling a bit fake.

I hope my face doesn't appear as strained as it felt in the photos, but I won't know for sure until the prints are developed.

Once we're outside and alone, my mom hands me a narrow white box. "I didn't drag you out here for a picture."

I stare at the unexpected gift. "What is it?"

She laughs gently. "Open it and find out."

Inside there's a gold necklace with a dainty thin chain and a small intricate flower pendant.

It looks like something I would see in a jewelry store case and know was way out of my league in terms of price and quality.

I'm not even sure my mom owns jewelry this nice.

I glance up to see her battling tears.

My expression must be asking questions my mouth isn't, because she beams and says, "I wanted you to have something that is a small representation of how much I love you."

She doesn't go on to say what she *could* say: *I'm grateful you're alive.*

Instead she keeps it simple. Light. Or as light as is possible when we've been through such darkness.

I've noticed my mom scrimping and saving and cutting coupons lately, and suddenly I realize this necklace is why she was doing that.

She's been doing those things for *months*. I thought money was tight. But this whole time she knew he wouldn't show, and she was planning for that...and this.

Payton pops her head out the back door. "Cece, time to go!"

"Coming!" I call, and she disappears inside the house. I hand the necklace to my mother and turn. "Can you put it on me?"

"You don't have to wear it tonight. I understand if it doesn't go with your dress."

"Mom." My raspy voice holds humor and tears that I'm fighting desperately, because this definitely isn't the moment for those. "Put it on."

She does. I turn and hug her, and I just sort of...hold on. "Thanks, Mom," I whisper in her ear, and then in a matter of seconds we're back inside and I'm whisked out the front door with my friends.

Which, knowing her, is exactly what she wants for me.

Our crew for tonight is me, Payton, Isley, Scout, Erik, and Clara and Hank.

Clara is the only one of us girls with an official date.

The rest of us are going in a group, as friends. For us to try to couple up would make things weird, and besides, we have an uneven number.

The dance is fine. It's a little awkward when you don't have anyone to dance with on the slow songs. But outside of that, we have fun.

When the dance is over, we head back to Scout's house. His parents are like something out of a movie. They never fight.

They always welcome all of us, even when we're loud and obnoxious. And they always have food.

We're hanging out in their basement, which has a basketball game and a Ping-Pong table along with some older couches and an entertainment system. But none of us are playing anything. I'm lounging on one end of the flowered couch, my now jeans-clad legs spread across Isley's lap, as we listen to U2 because the boys have control of the CDs.

My eyes are starting to close when someone suggests we play two truths and a lie.

Have I mentioned there's not much going on in this town?

"Who's going to start?" Payton drops into a beanbag chair across from us with a red Solo cup full of popcorn in hand.

"Scout's house," Hank says from his perch next to Clara on the other couch.

"Scout starts," Erik fills in. He's got his back against the unlit fireplace, his legs spread across the floor. Erik is one of those people who floats in and out of various friend groups. But he and Scout are close, so that often brings him circling back to us.

Scout is on the far end of the couch I'm on. He gives a good-natured groan and starts right in. "My grandfather calls me Skeeter. I write in a journal almost every day. And I have a *huge* crush on someone in this room." His last pronouncement earns laughter, and his eyes flash to mine, a challenge and humor written there. My mouth curves. I can't believe he just did that!

"Way too easy, dude." Erik rolls his eyes. Everyone assumes Scout's last one is the lie. Only I know it's one of his truths. "But seriously, you keep a journal? Lame."

I'm curious as to which of the others he mentioned is the lie. Probably the Skeeter one. I wouldn't put it past him to process his thoughts in a journal every day. He's weirdly mature like that. Then again, sometimes he operates at third-grade levels.

I've told him as much on more than one occasion. He usually just laughs and agrees with me.

"Cece's next," Payton calls out.

I resist echoing Scout's groan because mine would hold far more annoyance and less humor than his. I don't mind truth or dare because I can always choose dare. But this game is all about the truth. I mean, we get one lie, but we know each other so well it's a little pointless.

I should have been thinking ahead about what I was going to say. Now I'm on the spot, so I start tossing things out.

"I'm so different from my dad and his side of the family that sometimes I wonder if we're actually biologically related. I would do anything for my friends. I almost died in the eighth grade."

"That one's *so* obvious, Cece." Clara's eyes sparkle. She looks beautiful tonight. She always does. But there's also something about her being with Hank. They just make sense together, and it's almost as if she's even brighter and more *Clara* when she's around him. If the two of them don't end up married, I'll be shocked. "There's no way you almost died in eighth grade and didn't tell us the story. If that had happened, we'd all know about it. Who's next?"

I don't correct her, conceding she's right, when in truth, I only told truths.

When I get home, I wash off my makeup and take more bobby pins out of my hair than I can count. I'm about to remove the necklace my mom gave me when my fingers freeze.

I don't want to take it off. So, I just…don't. At first it feels strange to sleep with it on, but I get to the point where it feels odd when I'm *not* wearing it. Eventually the necklace becomes a part of me, and I'm careful not to delve too deeply into why.

Chapter Thirteen

The hiking group made it to the reservoir. Clara had taken more photos than necessary of the small scenic body of water, and then they'd turned around and met up with Payton and Liam in the town square.

"We're so doing that." Clara pointed to the large boulder in the center of the area, which had two holes in it that people—mostly kids—kept sticking their heads into to pose for pictures.

If she was in charge of photography this weekend, she could demand a fun picture too. There were only two holes in the rock, but they could get creative. They had so many silly pictures of the four of them from high school that Clara had filled four heavy albums—one for each year.

"I've made Aiden do that since he was little. Now that he's older, he gets so annoyed when I demand a pic, but he also knows not to fight me."

"I'm sure he loves that as much as Reagan would." Payton sprouted a mischievous smile. "I'm totally going to force her to do that before we leave town."

"What's our plan when The Husbands get back?" Clara asked.

The men were in an outdoor sports store located a few steps away.

"Trevor and I can go to the jewelry store to grab the donated necklace. And then we need to pick up gift certificates from three local stores." Isley ticked off items on her fingers. "Cheese, soap, clothing. Do the four of you want to handle those three? Or is that too much?"

"We're good with that." Isley had done so much for this weekend. It amazed Clara that she wasn't afraid to ask for contributions wherever she went and that so many places donated. Clara needed to borrow some of her friend's bravery. "What's the necklace like?"

"It is *so* beautiful." Isley's eyes sparked with embers of emotion. "And it totally reminds me of Cece's. It has that same type of superthin gold chain, but the pendant is different. More of an abstract shape. Trev's bought me quite a few pieces from this jeweler over the years because I really love his stuff. I sent the email asking for a donation not really expecting anything. But he was so generous. Belinda is going to list the necklace as a separate auction item from the vacation weekend because it's worth a fair amount on its own. That's why I want to swing by with Trevor—so we can thank the owner in person."

Clara edged fingertips under her lower lashes. "How does just the thought of Cece's necklace make me teary?"

"Because it wasn't just something she wore," Payton supplied quietly. "It was literally part of her. I never saw her take it off. Ever."

"Same." Isley's hair flipped around her face from the breeze, and she secured it with a clip she produced from her small crossbody bag. "I brought it up once when we were in Scout's hot tub because I was afraid the chlorine would discolor it.

But she thought that necklace could survive anything. And it did. At least until..."

"Did Belinda ever find the necklace?" Cece hadn't been wearing it when she'd been found. Removing the necklace before her death might have made sense if she had left a note or given a reason for it. But nothing about that time or her passing fit that definition.

Her last words to Clara had been, *It's gonna be okay. Love ya!* accompanied by a smacking, silly kiss on Clara's cheek.

But it had never been fully okay again after that.

"Nope. I mentioned the necklace to her since it has some similarities to Cece's. I didn't want her caught off guard. She said she searched for that necklace for years. She thought it would show up somewhere in Cece's things, but it never did."

"I wonder what Cece did with it." Had she stuck it in a box somewhere? Lost it? "Was she wearing it that night when we were at her house?"

On their last friendcation, Clara had brought up the idea of leveling with Belinda about the night Cece died. About admitting they'd been at her house that evening...and what they'd been up to. She'd wanted to be done with the responsibility and remorse they'd all shouldered over the years.

Clara was the one who saw Belinda the most. They lived in the same small town. They met for lunch a handful of times per year.

Payton and Isley didn't understand the weight that created for Clara.

Her friends had agreed that unloading the truth would be a relief in so many ways, but they felt it was too late and unearthing those skeletons would only cause turmoil and pain for Belinda, who they all adored.

And Clara agreed with them on that.

Plus, like they'd feared as teens, their involvement in the events of the night Cece died could be looked upon as accessories to her demise. Not that they wouldn't have done everything in their power to save Cece if they'd known what she was considering.

"She was," Isley supplied. "Because when I hugged her that night as I was leaving, my earring caught on her necklace. Which makes the fact that Belinda never found it so strange."

Clara shook off the melancholy of the conversation before it could grow talons and latch into her. It made sense that nothing would ever feel like *enough*, but they were doing all they could to honor Cece's memory and assist the charity in saving lives.

The Husbands rejoined them, and Isley texted the location of the three stores to Clara and Payton.

Trevor and Isley headed in one direction while the four of them took off in the other. They were at the end of the street before Clara realized she'd forgotten to orchestrate the rock picture of their group.

They would have to capture it later.

At the stoplight, waiting for the crosswalk sign, she tugged her camera from her tote bag, which she'd grabbed from the car after the hike, and began snapping pictures of Main Street.

Most stores appeared to be local and not chains, including the restaurants. And with the dotting of older 1800s buildings joining the newer developments, the town was quaint and historic and would photograph really well for Finch's Hope and the auction vacation package.

The crowd began to cross the street, Liam and Hank included. Payton waited for Clara to finish taking pictures and then joined her as they walked a few yards behind The Husbands.

"How's Reagan's ankle?"

Payton dodged the leash of a smiling golden retriever. "It's fine. She's parked at a cute little coffee and ice-cream shop with her phone and her foot up on a chair. Once Liam and I got her to where she wanted to be, she basically told us to leave."

"I shouldn't laugh at that, but—"

"I know." Payton's mouth curved begrudgingly. "We were the same way. Or at least I was." Payton *had* pushed back at her parents, but even as a teen, Clara had known it was an attempt to gain their attention and affection. An attempt that had sadly failed. Clara didn't understand people who had children but then didn't love them fiercely. It seemed counterintuitive.

Clara's mother had been her staunchest supporter. She'd expected a lot from Clara, but her love had somehow been gentle and fierce at the same time.

It was easy to put her mom on a pedestal since she'd passed away when Clara was so young. She tried not to do that. She tried to emulate her mother's strong, compassionate spirit instead.

"Did Ava ever go through girl stuff?"

"What kind of girl stuff?"

"Rea had some classmates making up things and lying about her online and we didn't know it."

"Oh, Pay." That broke Clara's heart. "How would you have known?"

"No clue, but that doesn't stem my guilt. I don't understand that world since we, *thank God*, grew up without social media. But not realizing what was going on felt a bit like Cece's situation all over again."

"We probably all have a bit of PTSD because we lost Cece. I keep a Finch's Hope magnet on our fridge with the number for their text and phone line. And I use an app on the kids' phones that sends me notifications if they search for or use certain terms. Like *unalived*. Did you know that's how they refer to suicide now?"

"That's what Reagan calls it too. How are we supposed to

know what's going on with them when we can't even understand what they're saying? Cap, sus, bus, bet."

"Right? What's happened to the English language?"

Payton's smile grew. "Oh, man. It's official. We're old."

"I'd rather be old than illiterate."

"And there you go sounding ancient again."

Clara laughed at the teasing and then grew serious. "There's no denying that Cece's death changed our DNA. I'm sure that's why things feel so giant when they happen with our kids. I mean, they might *be* big, but we're also on high alert."

"True. Maybe that's why I tend to overreact with Reagan."

"But overreacting is better than underreacting." Wasn't it? Clara fully understood Payton's desire not to miss the signs of something happening with their kids.

Payton snorted. "Not according to Reagan."

"She'll understand some day when she has kids of her own."

Payton's eyes squinted against the sun, carrying a smile. "I cannot wait to see her deal with a little version of herself." She laughed. "Probably what my parents once thought about me."

"You are *nothing* like your parents." Who'd been the definition of selfish and self-focused. "Your love for Reagan is *so* obvious. Despite whatever she might be telling herself at this moment."

"Thank you." Payton squeezed Clara in a quick side hug, leaning her head against her shoulder.

"Anytime you need a reminder that you've created a completely different story for your kid compared to what was handed down to you, I'm your girl. Makes me think I did a good job choosing you as a friend in the sixth grade."

"You definitely don't get credit for that!" Payton protested. "*I'm* the one who came up to you at church."

Technically true. Clara had attended Veil Community Church from the time she'd been born. Payton, on the other hand, had asked to be dropped off for Sunday school in the sixth grade because she'd wanted out of her house.

They'd become friends with Isley during that school year too, and then Cece had shown up their freshman year of high school, and they'd instantly bonded with her.

Clara and Payton caught up to The Husbands outside the cheese store, and they entered together, the door jingling overhead.

After receiving the gift certificate and thanking the owners for it, Clara snapped a couple photos of them behind the counter and a few of the store itself for the blog.

Then they crossed the street and did the same thing in the soap store. Clara tucked the gift card into her tote as they exited.

"Hang on." Hank paused outside the building full of shops. "I'd like to check this place out." He pointed to the oxygen bar, which, according to the lettering in the window, also boasted everything from printing services to internet to oxygen in a can. "Would it be okay if we grab the other gift certificate in a little bit?"

Was Hank serious? He must be feeling worse than Clara realized, because visiting an oxygen place sounded like something he would make fun of versus participate in.

"Works for me," Liam responded. "There's a used bookstore up ahead that's been calling my name."

Payton groaned. "There goes two hours."

"I won't be that long," Liam protested. "I can be done whenever you need me to be. And this will give me more to write about Breckenridge. So technically, me visiting the bookstore is for Finch's Hope."

Clara laughed. "How can anyone argue with that logic? Besides, this weekend *is* supposed to be a vacation in the midst of supporting Finch's Hope." Though last night's events had certainly put a damper on that.

"I wouldn't mind picking up the gift certificate from the clothing store. It looked like it had some cute stuff, so I'm sure I could be convinced to do a little shopping. Want to come with me and do some damage?" Payton asked Clara.

"I would but I don't really need anything." Nor did they have the budget for shopping right now. "I'll stick with Hank and check this place out." *And figure out what's going on with my husband.* "We'll catch up in a bit."

Payton and Liam continued down the sidewalk while Clara and Hank entered the oxygen store. Inside they got the lowdown on how it worked from a scrawny kid behind the bar, whose "yeah, man" responses and relaxed body language gave major snowboarder vibes.

After the employee finished his spiel, Hank pulled his wallet from the back pocket of his shorts. "I'll do a forty-five-minute session."

"How about you, ma'am? Are you interested?"

Clara shook her head since her stunned voice refused to function. "No, thank you," she managed to croak out.

She followed Hank to a couch in the corner where the snowboarder—aptly named Pine—got him set up with oxygen.

Clara picked up a magazine and thumbed through it, her chaotic, concerned thoughts ricocheting off the front glass windows and burrowing inside her.

Pine returned to the bar, and Hank closed his eyes and leaned his head back against the sofa. "You don't have to stay. You can walk around town if you want."

"I'm fine." If that was true, why did she feel so agitated? She scratched the inside of her arm. The back of her neck. "Hank, are you okay? Like really okay? Should we be going to urgent care or the ER?"

His eyes popped open. "Why would we do that?"

"Because you're hooked up to oxygen."

"They have an oxygen bar. That must mean I'm not the only one rocked by the altitude."

"But we live in Colorado."

"We live on the edge of Colorado. It's basically Nebraska."

True. "I'm still concerned about you."

"You don't need to make this bigger than it is." Hank's eyes sparked with mirth. "Not that you would ever do that. I didn't have some master plan to come here. I just saw the place and thought, why not? We're technically on vacation. It would be nice not to feel so winded and tired. That's all it is. I haven't been secretly diagnosed with a rare illness that I'm not telling you about."

Clara tossed the magazine at him. It bounced off his chest and landed on the sofa.

'How are you doing with the news from Brent?"

While they'd been catching their breath and waiting for Isley and Trevor to finish their phone call on the trail, Hank's brother had FaceTimed to discuss an issue he was having with one of the tractors.

Clara was attempting to be grateful to Brent for covering the farm while they were out of town versus irritated that he'd brought the failures to them through the phone and laid them at their feet. As if they'd forgotten the albatross back home and he'd rushed to deliver it.

Hank had relayed to his brother all he'd done so far to correct the overheating problem on their John Deere 4450. Before they'd left, Hank thought that he'd gotten it fixed. But according to his brother, it still wasn't working.

Brent enjoyed troubleshooting machinery issues. He'd mentioned asking about the problem in an online machinery talk forum. Maybe that would yield some answers. Clara appreciated that Brent wanted to help, and she also couldn't blame him for calling to discuss things with Hank because he didn't know the farm was in dire straits or the stress the conversation might cause.

Despite Clara repeatedly encouraging Hank to talk to his family about the farm issues, he'd so far refused to do so.

Obviously he wanted to turn things around on his own. But he'd been trying for so long.

The lowest point had been two months ago—on the exact day Isley had texted about using friendcation to assist in raising money for Finch's Hope.

Hank had visited the bank to renegotiate the terms of their loan, but they'd refused.

There was a reason the nicest buildings in Veil and every other small town were the post office, firehouse, and the bank. Because two were government-funded, and the other didn't make risky decisions. And right now, they—and the farm—were a gamble.

"Not much I can do from here. I'm hoping Brent figures it out for me while we're gone." Hank flashed a grin that reached for teasing and landed somewhere closer to dejected.

"Me too." If they had to hire a mechanic, the price would skyrocket.

Hank's eyes closed again, and Clara popped up from her seat so she didn't disturb his rest. She walked around the small place, checking out some of the artwork, the television showing a soccer game in the back.

"You sure you don't want to try it?" Pine asked from behind the bar.

"Thanks, but I'm not having the altitude issues that my husband seems to be. But I do have a question for you." Hadn't Clara just thought about borrowing some of her friend's bravery? Why not ask for a donation? The worst they could do was refuse.

"I was wondering if your business might consider donating

a gift certificate to a charity auction." Clara gave Pine a thirty-second spiel about Finch's Hope and the Breckenridge vacation package being auctioned off. "If you do end up donating a session, the store will be mentioned on the blog."

"Right on. Let me check with Dewey and I'll let you know." Pine pulled out his phone and began texting.

"I'm just going to take some photos if that's okay." That way if they ended up donating, they'd already have the content.

"'Course."

Clara snapped pictures inside and then strode outside to capture the storefront. She could see Hank through the window, eyelids shuttered, head resting on the couch cushions.

She missed her husband.

The one who was present in their marriage. Who wasn't so swamped by stress that he actually heard what she was saying. The one who slept through the night and could therefore engage with her during the day.

They'd gotten married when they were only one year older than Ava. A wild, outrageous concept now that their daughter felt so young. And from the beginning, their relationship had been like two forks of a river that swept into the same waterway without so much as a ripple. Now, because of the farm stress, they were opposing currents twisting, turning, struggling to redirect each other until the water was so jumbled they couldn't tell which way was up.

Clara was ready to throw the farm out and start over. She didn't care where they lived or what they did for work.

She cared about Hank and the kids.

Nothing mattered beyond that.

But lately it felt as if the waters were slipping over Hank's head.. and he'd stopped trying to stay afloat.

Chapter Fourteen

"Why did that make me emotional?" Isley stepped outside through the jewelry store door that Trevor held open for her and donned her sunglasses to combat the sunlight and hide the remnants of tears.

"I can think of a couple reasons. For starters, you wear the bracelet Aiden helped pick out from there all the time."

She did.

Isley had even worn it the day they'd dropped Aiden off at rehab as a reminder to all of them that he was still the same kid who'd asked Trevor to drive him to Breckenridge to pick out a piece of jewelry for her for Mother's Day because he'd known she loved this store.

He'd been ten at the time.

Isley had tried so hard to infuse Aiden with hope that day, but he'd been forlorn and pensive.

Understandably so.

Trev, on the other hand, had given Aiden his version of a pep talk on the drive there.

We could be dealing with felony charges, A. This alternative is a godsend. Take it. Be thankful for it. Use it.

Aiden didn't need a reminder of how much worse it could have been from Trevor. They'd lived it, and the stark, debilitating fear and stress of that time was part of them. Like a tweak to their DNA or a tattoo they could never remove.

Isley had stated as much to Trevor.

They'd fought on the car ride.

And they'd dropped Aiden off in the midst of that argument.

It was one of Isley's biggest regrets—not that she didn't have a list.

She searched in her crossbody bag for a tissue as Trevor led her over to a bench. They sat, and he put an arm around her shoulders.

"This weekend has been stressful. It makes sense to feel frustrated by what happened last night. Especially when you're trying to help Belinda and the charity. And not hearing back about Aiden isn't helping anything."

Trev was right. The lack of communication was, in a word, terrible.

After their phone call from Daria on the trail, he'd sent a follow-up email to the rehab facility—in addition to the voicemail he'd left earlier this morning—explaining their situation in more detail and asking them to *please* confirm Aiden was still on-site.

Isley understood that the rehabilitation center believed the patient needed separation from their former life to heal. And the place had come highly recommended.

But now she wished they would have searched further. Asked more questions.

But how could they ever have known that they would encounter an issue like this in the middle of Aiden's rehab stay?

Either Aiden's counselor would eventually get back to them

to confirm or deny that he was present at the facility. Or Aiden's lawyer would provide an answer. But now that they'd learned Zak's whole staff was out of the office for the day and it was Friday, Isley didn't hold out hope that they'd hear from him before Monday.

The unknowns yawned wide in front of them.

Especially after that phone call from Daria.

If Daria had actually seen Aiden, they were about to deal with a host of problems. But Isley's main concern—and she imagined it always would be—was: *Is our son okay?* Was he safe?

"Do you want to check where the others are?"

"Sure." Isley pulled out her phone and sent a text to Clara and Payton just as a toddler veered in their direction.

The mother called for her, chasing the little girl with gorgeous black curls while also pushing a baby in a stroller.

"Hi." Isley waved at the toddler, effectively stopping her in her tracks. She studied Isley and then broke into a smile.

"Thanks for the assist!" The mother snagged her daughter's hand, and they continued down the sidewalk. The little girl grinned over her shoulder at Isley twice before they turned the corner.

She missed those younger years with Aiden, though she'd done her best to relish every moment. Isley and Trevor had experienced secondary infertility after Aiden, and even with medical intervention, she'd never been able to carry another pregnancy to term. After the third miscarriage when Aiden was seven, they'd closed the door on trying for more children and Trevor had gotten a vasectomy as a precaution.

Because continuing to hope had been...excruciating.

That turmoil had only made Isley more grateful they had Aiden. She'd doted on him, of course. Had probably given in too much with him. No doubt some would claim that's how they'd ended up in their current predicament.

That or the family traits she'd passed down to him.

Isley's mother certainly hadn't done Aiden any genetic favors. Iris Tordoff was a cynical serial dater, likely an undiagnosed alcoholic, and a chain-smoker.

No matter how much Isley had tried to distance herself from her childhood, she was still a Tordoff. And she certainly wasn't blameless when it came to making terrible decisions that affected those around her.

Her phone buzzed with texts from her friends.

"Sounds like Payton's in a dressing room filled with a stack of clothes," Isley relayed, a genuine smile forming. She wasn't a stranger to a little shopping therapy herself. "Good for her. Maybe we'll all get out of this funk yet. And Clara says Hank's at the oxygen bar."

"Is he really? That doesn't sound like Hank. He must be feeling worse than he's been letting on."

"It would be like him not to complain. It *is* just an altitude issue, right?"

"I would imagine. He's not the first person to need a boost of oxygen up here. They sell it all over the place. I'm glad he thought to try it."

Another text popped up on Isley's screen. "Payton says that Reagan just checked in with her and she's still at the coffee shop. And that Liam's at the used bookstore."

"We might not see him for the rest of the weekend."

Isley laughed. The store was organized chaos, with vintage and used books filling every nook and cranny. But if you asked the staff where something was, they always knew the precise location.

Trevor's phone rang, and Isley's heart climbed into her throat. "Is it the rehab facility?"

He held up the screen for her to see. *Garrett Turner Cell.*

Garrett was the contractor they'd used to replace tile in one of the basement bathrooms at The Haven when they'd first purchased the house. Trevor had left him a message last night asking if anyone from his company could repair the front door. Or if he could refer them to someone else better suited to the task.

The Husbands had secured the door last night with a fix that held it permanently closed, so they would all be using the garage entrance to go in and out until it was repaired.

"Hey, Garrett." Trevor listened for a few beats. "You did not need to call me back while you're on your honeymoon." Trevor laughed at something Garrett said. "That's true. Yeah, anyone you can send would be great. Appreciate it. Congratulations and have a good trip." He disconnected. "Did you know Garrett was getting married?"

"I didn't, but I'm happy for him. He's such a good guy." In his early sixties, Garrett was the embodiment of calm and helpful and seemingly at peace with his life. The romantic in Isley was delighted to think that he'd be sharing the rest of his with someone.

"He said his son Cyrus is going to head over to the house shortly to check out the door and see what he can do."

"Nice. We should head back, then. We have two vehicles, so you and I could do that and get lunch ready while the rest of the group finishes in town."

At Trevor's agreement, Isley sent another text letting the others know about their updated plan. Their responses came back quickly.

"They said they'll grab Reagan when they're done and meet us back at the house."

"Then let's head out."

Isley was quiet on the drive, her mind a hundred miles away at the rehabilitation center.

Trevor stopped at a red light on Main Street, and a surge of people flooded the crosswalk. A young teenage couple held hands, their backs to Isley and Trevor. Something about the girl's demeanor reminded Isley of Reagan. Her hair was parted down the middle, her dark locks similar in length and style to Reagan's, and she had on an oversized green hoodie along with the same type of fitted bike shorts that Reagan had been wearing this morning on the hike.

"Is that—?" No. It couldn't be. But... "Trev, does that girl look like Reagan to you?" Isley pointed her out just as the light changed and Trevor accelerated.

"Sorry, I didn't see who you were talking about."

The couple faded into the throng of pedestrians. "That girl looked so much like Reagan. But she was with a boy. It couldn't have been her, right? Payton just confirmed she was at the coffee shop."

Certainly Payton and Liam knew the whereabouts of their daughter.

Except...last night on the sailboat they'd mentioned the location app wasn't working on Reagan's phone. Isley had found that suspicious since they never had issues in the mountains. But she hadn't voiced skepticism because the Collins family was obviously already dealing with plenty.

"Does Reagan know anyone here?" Trevor asked.

"I don't think so. It must have been someone who looked like her because they were dressed in a similar fashion." An extremely common look for any teenage girl.

"Are you going to say anything to Payton?" Trevor turned into their neighborhood.

"No. We have literally no evidence it was her. Mentioning it when we're uncertain feels like repeating what Daria just did to us. She created all this—" Isley made a frazzled motion with her hands "—anxiety and fear over what could be nothing. I'm not going to do that to Payton."

"Smart. I agree."

They parked the SUV in the garage, and Isley entered the house first.

She hesitated immediately after crossing the threshold, her athletic shoes superglued to the floor.

"Did we leave that package of pastries there?" She scanned the island. "And does something smell weird?" Her pulse surged to a gallop.

No note filled the island, and the front door still appeared secure, yet Isley was transported right back to last night's scenario.

Trevor slipped by her, squeezing her arm reassuringly. "I think this one is all us. Someone must have grabbed another pastry after we cleaned up breakfast." He stowed the box in the pantry cupboard. "Which is exactly what we want, right? For everyone to feel comfortable and at home and help themselves."

"Right." Isley exhaled shakily. "Of course." The thought of shutting the door behind her made her feel trapped, so she left it open.

She was being so dramatic. What was wrong with her?

Trevor flipped on the kitchen and living room lights. "Want me to check the house?"

"No, that's okay." Everything was silent. There were no signs of an intruder. The lights helped. As did the sunshine flowing through the wall of glass doors.

Trevor turned on music, and familiar jazz played through the built-in speakers, morphing the house from crime scene back to home.

Isley closed the door leading to the garage. "Sorry I froze there for a minute."

"It's going to take time to get over an intruder being in our house. I'd say you're normal."

"You're always too easy on me." Though Isley didn't believe she'd receive the same calm, understanding response if Trevor were to learn that she'd reached out to Freya's mother, Bianca, after her daughter's overdose...and near death.

Isley had mentioned her desire to speak with Bianca Edwards one time after Aiden had broached the same topic and been shot down. Outside of their stress-filled drive to rehab, it was the only occasion during Aiden's ordeal when Trevor had gotten upset.

His anger hadn't been directed *at* her, but his opinion on the issue had been clear—reaching out to Bianca would put their family at risk.

He'd been right. And Isley had been wrong. The idea of confessing to her husband that she'd met with Bianca when he'd been her and Aiden's rock during the legal issues was, in a word, demoralizing.

Trevor had saved their son and family. And Isley had taken a step that could destroy both.

She put Trev to work slicing onions, tomatoes, and lettuce for the sandwiches while she plated the sliced cheeses and meats. She'd known that their schedule would be somewhat fluid over the weekend, so she'd stuck to easy meals that didn't require much prep. Like for tonight's dinner, she'd purchased premade enchiladas and Spanish rice from a store by their home in Cherry Creek, which she would pair with chips, queso, guac, sour cream, and salsa.

Cooking caused Isley to break out in hives. She could host with the best of them. She just didn't want to be the one creating meals from scratch.

Growing up, the kitchen in her home had carried the scent of cigarettes more often than food, and Iris had never taught her how to make even the most basic of meals.

When they'd lived with Gary—the best of her mom's many boyfriends—he'd taught Isley how to make Hamburger Helper and had her assist with grilling.

He'd been the closest thing to a father figure Isley had ever experienced. After Iris broke things off with Gary, he continued to stay in touch with Isley. They still communicated to this day.

It would be easy for Isley to blame her issues on her upbringing, but she refused to use that cop-out. So many people endured so much. Her mistakes were unfortunately all her own.

The sound of a vehicle pulling into the driveway through one of the windows Trev had opened when they got back made Isley pause in the middle of slicing a fresh sourdough roll.

"Friends or Garrett's son?" she asked, tossing the roll into the basket with the others.

"I'll check." Trevor stepped into the garage, and the overhead door rumbled open. In the past, they would have thought nothing of leaving the garage door open until their friends returned. But last night had increased their caution.

It had to be Garrett's guy. Surely Hank's oxygen and the shopping would take a bit longer.

If it was friends, Isley would put out one of the dips she'd bought as an appetizer to tide everyone over until lunch was ready.

Trevor reentered the house with Sergeant Miller following, and Isley's chest hiccupped with surprise and a sliver of dread.

Did he have information for them? Would they have to watch surveillance footage? Her stomach churned.

"Sergeant Miller," she greeted him. "Excuse the mess. We're just getting lunch put together. Can I get you anything? Glass of water? Soda?"

"Actually, water would be great. It's a warm one out there today." The sun hit differently in the mountains. Seventies in Denver was about perfect. Seventies at high altitude sometimes felt like it could sear skin.

Isley filled a glass with ice and water.

"Sorry to drop by without warning. I was nearby and thought I'd see if you were home since I had an update."

The glass slipped in Isley's hand, but she managed to catch it before it slid through her fingers completely and crashed to the floor.

"Glad you checked." Trevor motioned to the dining table. "Should we sit?"

"Sure. Though I won't take much of your time."

Isley handed the glass to Sergeant Miller. She wiped her hands on a towel and then followed the men to the dining room, her steps shaky.

What had Sergeant Miller found out? And who did it involve?

If the note had to do with Cece's death or with Isley contacting Bianca without Trevor's knowledge, either scenario ended in a dumpster fire.

The first would devastate Belinda and could easily cast blame for Cece's passing on the three women. The second could cause her family to be sued civilly or their reputations once again tried in the court of public opinion. Trevor's business could be affected. Aiden's future impacted.

Aiden's arrest had demolished their world. Like she'd told the group this morning at breakfast, they'd been abandoned by their so-called friends. Gossiped about. Ostracized. Isley was amazed that Trevor's work had survived as well as it had.

If someone were to out either scenario—past or present—she imagined people would be just as venomous...if not more so.

Chapter Fifteen

When they pulled up to the house and spotted Sergeant Miller's vehicle outside, palpable tension filled Payton's small SUV.

Was it only radiating from her? Or did the rest of them feel the same?

Reagan's breath hissed out when she looked up from her phone in the back seat, where she was sandwiched between Payton and Clara.

"Can't we go two seconds without drama?"

The irony of Reagan delivering a line like that had Payton tamping down amusement. And she was almost certain she heard Clara stifle a similar response, though she attempted to cover it with a cough.

"We don't have to go in," Payton offered. "We could just sit in the car until he leaves." Like they'd done last night.

Liam parked behind the garage stall housing Hank and Clara's minivan.

"Why would we do that?" He glanced in the rearview mirror as he turned off the engine. "Maybe he has good news. Maybe they found a match for the prints."

Would that be classified as good news? Perhaps. Depending on the information.

"Maybe they even caught someone." He hit the button for the back hatch to open.

Payton's stomach gurgled as a stress response. She would love to leave the mess of last night in Isley and Trevor's hands, but despite it being their house, until they knew the source of the note, they were all equally involved.

"I'm definitely going in because I have to use the restroom." Hank glanced back from the passenger seat, eyebrows lifted with a hint of humor. He exited the vehicle and then leaned the top half of his body inside, confusion evident. "You're not actually going to stay out here, are you?"

"Of course not!" Clara chirped. "We're just moving slowly, that's all." She and Payton exchanged a glance behind Reagan, whose head was once again bent over her phone.

They got out, and Liam retrieved two bags of books from the back while Payton grabbed the brown paper bag filled with her shopping therapy session.

She followed the group inside through the open garage door.

Clara called out a greeting as they stepped into the kitchen, which Isley and Trevor answered.

"Sergeant Miller just got here with an update if you guys want to join us," Trevor said.

Want was a strong word for what Payton felt.

With a typical break-in, information from the investigating sergeant would be a good thing. In this strange case, Payton was experiencing mostly dread.

If only the threatening note would have come with more information—like being addressed to a specific person. And signed by someone who graciously included their phone number in case the group had further questions as to *what* truth it was referencing. And a deadline would be helpful too. Who knew how long they had until this truth would be revealed? And once it was, which one of them would be forced to deal with the fallout?

Payton and Liam placed their bags on the island stools since the island itself was covered in lunch prep.

"Be there in thirty seconds." Hank retreated to the half bath while Clara, Payton, and Liam took seats at the table.

Reagan remained in the kitchen, her gaze downcast, her countenance drawn.

Even though she'd agreed to stay for the rest of the weekend, perhaps Payton and Liam should have still made the decision to go.

At least then they wouldn't be walking into another unknown right now.

Hank came out of the bathroom and joined them at the table while Reagan rummaged in the drinks refrigerator and pulled out a soda. Then she turned to the pantry cupboard and began searching for something in there.

Isley had told her repeatedly to make herself at home. She appeared to be taking that command literally.

Payton was tempted to remind Reagan she'd just had ice cream, but that would officially turn her into her own mother, who'd loathed junk food and never let her have it. Which had only made Payton seek it out wherever she could find it.

Eventually she'd grown up and found some balance. And Reagan would do the same one day. Right?

"As I was just telling Mr. and Mrs. Stanton, I stopped by since I have an update."

"Do you want to listen, Rea?" Liam pulled out the chair next to him. "Otherwise you can head downstairs and we'll fill you in later."

Payton would opt for giving their fifteen-year-old the Cliffs-Notes version after the fact so they could protect her in case the information Sergeant Miller delivered was disturbing or upsetting. But she'd been working incredibly hard to make the *right* decisions lately for herself and Reagan and Liam. And she felt as if she kept failing over and over again.

So she would let Liam head to bat on this one and see how he fared.

"Um, I think I'll..." Reagan pointed downstairs. "Actually—' her posture straightened, reminding Payton of her stance and attitude while horseback riding "—I'll stay."

She dropped into the chair Liam had scooted back from the table, her hair covering her face like a curtain, her soda in front of her.

"Unfortunately, the Elrods' surveillance system wasn't working last night, so he doesn't have any footage for us to view. He wasn't aware of the outage until he tried to send it to us."

That was weird. Wasn't it?

Surprise echoed around the table, and Payton was almost certain a barely visible shudder reverberated through Reagan.

Exactly why Payton would rather have filled her in after Sergeant Miller left.

"Isn't that kind of strange?" Trevor questioned.

"There was a power outage in this area about a week ago so it could have something to do with that. Kyle's trying to figure out what's going on with the system now. But that doesn't change the fact that we don't have anything from last night and the fingerprints aren't back yet. If those pan out, then we have something to go on. If not, I'm afraid we're in a bit of a bind without surveillance footage or an eyewitness. This is an unusual case. The note wasn't threatening bodily harm. The person who broke in didn't steal anything. Could be some teens messing around for all we know. I'm sorry not to have better news."

Payton wasn't sorry. Now they could focus on Finch's Hope again.

At least until the fingerprint information came back.

Unlike Trevor, the only thing Isley felt about the missing surveillance footage was relief.

Logically she knew Aiden wouldn't have anything to do with the note, but after Daria's phone call, the fear that he'd left rehab was growing. She was incredibly thankful not to be identifying him on video right now.

She and Trevor were still sitting at the dining room table, processing the sergeant's news—or lack thereof—while the rest of their guests were in their rooms getting ready for lunch... and likely doing the same.

Isley's brain felt as if it had been filled with cotton stuffing. She couldn't think clearly. Everything felt undone.

Including lunch, which still occupied the island. "We should finish prepping the sandwiches."

Trevor stood and offered her a hand, pulling her up from the chair. Instead of moving into the kitchen immediately, he wrapped arms around her. "I know this is all stressful, and I'm sorry." His chin rested lightly against the top of her head. "Try not to jump to conclusions or overthink. All we can really do at this point is let the police do their job."

Like Trevor advised, Isley kept directing herself to set aside any theories about the break-in and note until they knew more. Because until they had at least one concrete detail regarding the intruder, guessing was as productive as spitting into the wind.

But she was also having a hard time following that decree.

"And I'm certain Aiden's okay and still at rehab. Which means he's safe and in the best place he can be."

Isley glanced up to find her husband's mouth pursed. She framed his smoothly shaved cheeks with her palms. "You're right. I'm sure he is okay." She wasn't, but it was high time she gave back to him an ounce of the support and encouragement he gave her.

At her statement, his eyes softened with relief. On top of his concern for Aiden, he was worried about her. She needed to pull herself together and not cause any more harm than she already had.

Trevor pressed a chaste kiss to her lips. And then, as if reconsidering, he returned for a slower, more intentional connection. Warm, gentle, a little demanding.

He'd always been able to melt her like chocolate on a car dash in the summer.

And it wasn't because he looked even better at forty-four than he had at twenty. How did men *do* that? Isley was constantly masking, hydrating, even the occasional Botox. And Trev did nothing of the sort and aged backward.

It was and always had been Trevor's caring, generous nature that drew her in.

Because she'd *never* deserved him. Jeremy was right about that.

Trevor eased back. "Why does it feel like we haven't done that in forever?" Because they hadn't. Once Isley had reached out to Bianca, she'd pulled away because the guilt had been destroying her.

"I know how hard you worked planning this weekend." Trevor hugged her again. "We're going to keep heading toward the goal of helping Finch's Hope. We're not going to let any of this derail us." She tightened her arms around his waist and leaned against his chest as he continued. "You make it all look easy. Raising Aiden. Planning a fundraising gala or a school event. This weekend. I might not always say it, but

I notice everything you do. Not in the creepy, stalkerish way that just came out."

She laughed.

"Just because I don't always comment on everything, doesn't mean I don't see you."

"Thank you," she whispered as moisture flooded her eyes and throat. "Trev, I—"

Footsteps sounded on the stairs, so they moved apart. At the same time, a vehicle pulling up to the house carried through the open front windows.

Isley tensed. They kept getting surprised by people and incidents, and she was *over it*.

"That's probably Garrett's son here to fix the door. I'll meet him outside and let him in through the garage."

Right. Her shoulders unhinged as Reagan came up the stairs, appearing a bit lost.

Isley strode for the kitchen. "Lunch should be ready soon, Reagan." She flipped on the faucet to wash her hands. "Sorry if you're starving. We got waylaid with Sergeant Miller."

"I'm not starving. Is there anything I can do to help?"

Isley was about to say no when she realized that Reagan might need something to keep her occupied. And if she was willing to assist, why not include her?

"Do you want to pick one of the dips from the middle shelf in the fridge? There's salmon, artichoke, and gouda cheese. Crackers are in the pantry cupboard. Platter is in the corner cupboard."

"'Kay. Sure. My friend does that." Reagan motioned toward the running water.

Isley flipped off the faucet. "I had that going for a while, didn't I?"

"There's something calming about water. I get it."

"You're right. There is. How's your ankle, hon? Should you be icing it for a bit instead of standing on it?"

Reagan's head shook, her long hair swinging with the movement. "It's fine now. I guess I overreacted."

"In high school, I once thought I was coming down with something terrible. I didn't leave the couch for eight hours and moaned and complained until suddenly, I got my period. After the fact, it was kind of hilarious." Reagan wasn't the only one who had a monopoly on teen drama.

Reagan laughed and pulled a white platter from the cupboard. "Periods are the worst though."

"Amen, sister."

"How come you're so chill?" Her vision bounced from Isley to the stairs, as if she could see or sense her parents from her spot in the kitchen.

"If Aiden heard you ask that, he would howl with laughter."

Reagan's mouth curved as she grabbed the cheese dip from the fridge. "Does Aiden like where he goes to college? I've been thinking that maybe I should come to Colorado for school. I know it's a ways off, but..." She shrugged. "The weather is amazing here. So cool even though it's summer. Dallas is a stinky armpit."

Isley laughed at that description. She assumed Payton hadn't gone into the details of Aiden's arrest with Reagan. Or mentioned that he'd been kicked out of his school after "the incident." The university had acted as if they were completely unaware of the culture on their campus. So frustrating.

"Aiden did like college, but he's planning to switch schools in the fall." *Providing he's not in jail.* Isley quickly skipped over that traitorous thought. "We're still figuring that out."

"Wish I could live here and just...start over," Reagan said quietly.

Isley wasn't sure if she was supposed to hear the comment or not, but she answered anyway.

"I've had that thought on occasion in my life too." Especially in recent months. If only there was an actual slate Isley could wipe clean. She and Reagan could both zoom backward in time and have redos. "And I do think there's something special about the mountains. That's why Trevor and I have loved coming up here so much over the years. You're always welcome to visit. Bring a friend. We'd love to have you here or in Cherry Creek. The area where we live in Denver has shops and restaurants close by. It would be fun to have some girls in my house for once. But no pressure," Isley added quickly. Staying with one of her mom's old friends probably wasn't high on Reagan's wish list.

"That would be fun, but I don't see Payton letting that happen."

"She might if I ask."

Reagan laughed. "True."

"And if she doesn't want to send you alone, your mom could come too. And Clara and her daughter Ava." Clara could decide whether to also include Talia or if she was too young. "We could make a girls' weekend out of it."

It could be a new tradition, and they wouldn't have to wait two years to see each other.

Without realizing it, Isley had been on pause.

Waiting for Aiden to graduate from high school.

Waiting for Aiden to go to college.

Waiting for him to finish college.

And once that plan had veered off course, waiting for him to avoid a jail sentence and finish rehab.

Now, she was waiting to find out who'd broken in and left a note demanding the truth from one of them.

When did it ever end? It was time to stop waiting for life to happen.

Reagan went up on her tiptoes to reach the crackers in the cupboard, and her gray long-sleeved shirt shifted with her movement.

Gray long-sleeved shirt.

The girl on Main Street had been wearing an oversized army green hoodie.

"Reagan, did you change clothes when you got back to the house?"

"Nope. Why?"

"Just curious. I like that shirt."

"Thanks. I just got it last week."

Isley's whole system heaved a massive sigh of relief. At least that was one concern she could set aside.

Who would have thought she'd find a shirt such a win.

Chapter Sixteen

"'Stroll through quaint small-town streets and experience the ambience of a late 1800s gold mining town with upscale dining and local wares. Shop the day away with the included gift certificates or spend it outdoors hiking, relaxing, and enjoying the beautiful scenery,'" Liam read from the laptop perched in front of him at the dining table, remnants of his sandwich filling the plate next to him.

He'd opted to work on the wording for the auction package while they ate lunch so it was fresh in his mind. Clara would need to edit the digital photos when they returned home, but she enjoyed that part of photography and could do it at the kitchen table while their kids flitted in and out. When she was in the midst of her crew in some way, she felt content.

"How do you *do* that?" Half of Isley's sandwich remained on her plate.

Clara added some of the cheese dip to hers even though *she'd* already finished her whole sandwich. Outside of rare instances like the night of the break-in, Clara's response to stress—and to good times, if she were being honest—was to eat.

The information Sergeant Miller had delivered a short while ago was like a storm cloud hanging over them, darkening what was supposed to be a good weekend. They didn't know anything more about the break-in or note *and* the three of them were still carrying the burden of the night Cece died.

But Clara was relieved that no one had been forced to relay the truth about something.

Yet.

Interesting how one little word could create such a massive sense of foreboding.

"If I tried to come up with that it would take me a month and sound like a kindergartner wrote it." Clara scooped dip onto a cracker and popped it into her mouth.

"Same!" Payton tossed her napkin onto her plate. "If it doesn't involve a scientific theory, I'm out."

"And when it comes to a scientific theory, *I'm* out," Liam quipped. "I need to make some notes about the hike. Get my creative juices flowing. Tell me what you liked about it."

"Not dying," Hank delivered dryly.

"To poor Hank," they said in unison.

This time, Hank joined them in raising his water glass in a toast.

"Liam, maybe you could talk about it being kid friendly or on the easy end of the spectrum—at least when it comes to hikes here." Isley winced. "Outside of us breaking Reagan."

Their teen guest had promptly filled a plate with food and retreated to some alone time in the basement versus joining the adults for lunch.

Clara didn't blame her.

Especially since Cyrus had been making a bit of noise fixing the front door. He'd left just a few minutes ago, refusing their offer of lunch because he'd needed to get to another job.

Isley's attention swung to Hank. "Speaking of breaking people, Hank, how are you feeling after oxygen?"

"Better. Hopefully it will help me get out of the funk I've been in since we got here."

Maybe they needed to install an oxygen bar at their house too. Clara's eyelids shuttered at her vicious thought.

"Did Clara tell you she got a gift certificate from the oxygen place while we were there?"

And of course Hank was building her up, celebrating her.

Maybe Clara was the one who needed the emotional overhaul instead of her husband.

"That's amazing, Clara!" Isley beamed. "I'm so glad you asked them. Oh, I meant to make a note." She pulled her phone from the pocket of her leggings. "There's a local social media account that shares Breckenridge news and reels. I wanted to ask if they'd be willing to post about the vacation package when bidding starts. It would be nice to get some traction outside of the consistent Finch's Hope supporters."

Smart. "Good idea, Is."

Isley's phone began buzzing in her hand. "It's Belinda." She swiped to answer. "Hey, Belinda, you're on speakerphone with everyone. We're just eating lunch and working on the vacation package blog content."

A chorus of hellos rang out.

"Hi, my favorite children!" Belinda was a mother hen to all of them. Even The Husbands got a card in the mail on their birthdays. "I know you all are busy with this weekend, so I'm sorry to interrupt, but I just *had* to say thank you for the photos! They have been so fun to look through, and I do think we can use some for the blog. People will love seeing flashback pictures of Cece and the rest of you."

Confusion reverberated around the table.

"I...don't think any of us sent you photos." Isley's vision bounced from Clara to Payton, confirming her statement.

"Not me," Payton supplied.

"Me either," Clara echoed.

Isley turned up the volume of the call. "What did you say the photos were of?"

They heard shuffling in the background. "There's one with just the four of you girls. And a stack with other kids from high school, but you're in those too."

"Were they mailed to you or how did you receive them?" Clara asked.

"The package was on my front step. It has Mrs. Finch written on it along with my address. But there's no return address and no postage on it."

"Was there anything else in the package?" Payton frowned.

"There's a Post-it note that says, *For the Finch Hope fundraiser.* But it isn't signed."

The food Clara had just enjoyed turned sour in her stomach.

"Finch Hope?" Isley confirmed. "Not *Finch's*?"

"Correct."

"Belinda, it's Trevor. They didn't put initials or anything like that on the note? No signature at all?"

"No." Her voice dipped with worry. "That's why I assumed it was from one of the girls."

"Of course." Trevor's tone held reassurance. "I'm sure it has a simple explanation. I wouldn't be concerned."

He was obviously trying to alleviate Belinda's apprehension, because his countenance didn't support that statement.

"Can you send us a picture of the note?" Isley questioned. "Maybe one of us will recognize the handwriting."

And then we can see if it matches the note left during the break-in.

They all had to be thinking the same thing, though no one burdened Belinda with the details of last night.

Veil was a little over three hours away. It wasn't impossible that the notes could be connected.

"Can you send us some pictures of the photos too?" Payton added. "Maybe we can figure out who they might be from or where they were taken."

"Yes, of course. I'm not sure I know how to do that while I'm on the phone with you all. Let me hang up and send them."

Belinda disconnected, and the group sat in stunned silence.

Hank snaked an arm over the back of Clara's chair and laid a comforting hand on her shoulder. "Could be as simple as someone wanting to help. Everyone back home knows about this weekend and the fundraiser for Finch's Hope."

Could be. But coupled with last night, the unsigned package felt almost sinister.

Clara's nerves fired off like tiny continuous firecrackers.

The women's phones began to ding and buzz simultaneously.

They scanned the texts as they came in. Hank looked over Clara's shoulder while Liam and Trevor did the same with their wives.

The Post-it note came through first. "I don't recognize the handwriting." Payton glanced up. "Do you girls?"

They shook their heads.

Clara pulled up the photo of the Breckenridge note, thankful she'd thought to snap a picture before the police had confiscated it.

"The handwriting is nothing like the note left at the house." She texted it to Payton and Isley so they could compare it too. "Not even close."

Clara scrolled to the first photo from Belinda, which was of a large group of kids at a lake.

"Hank and Clara," Isley studied her phone screen, "why aren't you in this picture?"

"Maybe that was the scorching day everyone went to Red Lake but Hank and I had to work." Clara had been green with envy to miss out on the fun.

"That seems right," Payton agreed. "And it would explain why you weren't with us. I still remember how hot that day was."

"Here's the four of us in Cece's backyard." Isley's lips compressed.

"Looks like maybe fall of our senior year. I think." Clara had a faulty memory when it came to high school. She could recall some events like they happened yesterday and others were blank spaces in her mind.

"Here are other group shots from Cece's," Payton said. "Same clothing so it must have been the same day."

Another picture rolled in along with Belinda's notification that it was the last of the batch.

"This was *right* before Cece died." Isley expanded the final photo. "It was Erik's birthday."

"Who's the guy looking at you like you're a piece of dessert, Pay?" Liam's mouth quirked with humor. "Old boyfriend?"

"What?" Payton squinted at the screen.

"There. That guy." Liam pointed.

"Oh, Scout?" Payton gave a short laugh. "He's not looking at me. He's looking at Cece next to me. She always said he wasn't her type and that they were just friends, but we were all sure that he was in love with her or at least harbored a pretty major crush."

And Payton had harbored a pretty major crush on Scout. Not that Clara would ever say that. She'd only figured it out during their senior year because she'd been observant and picked up on a few small clues. When she'd asked Payton about it back then, she'd begged Clara not to say anything because she hadn't wanted to cause strain in the girls' relationship.

Plus, like Payton said, Scout had formed an obvious attachment to Cece. It had appeared as though he was into her even though she wasn't into him like that, and he'd settled for friendship with her.

Payton thought throwing her feelings into the mix would only complicate things.

It had been as close to a love triangle as the four of them had experienced with each other.

"What are we supposed to do now? What do we do about these?" Isley dropped her phone to the table with a clatter.

"I suppose we could ask Sergeant Miller," Liam intoned. "Though I'm not sure what advice he would have."

"And I doubt he would get involved since it's not here in Breckenridge." Trevor raised his palms. "Plus, the note with the photos was helpful, not threatening. I would guess law enforcement would view the package as a goodwill gesture. It just doesn't feel like it to us because of what happened here."

"I agree," Hank added quietly. "If we hadn't experienced the break-in and note, we wouldn't think anything of the photos. Someone probably just thought Belinda would know who they were from and didn't even think to sign the message."

It was possible. But that explanation felt like the equivalent to wrapping a cloth bandage around a leaking water pipe.

"Could one of our families have sent the photos?" Isley asked. "I can't imagine Iris doing that."

"I have all my old albums. They're not at my dad's house. But I'll check with him just in case." Clara sent her father a quick text.

Payton was estranged from her parents, and they would never have sent the pictures, so she stayed silent.

The unsigned photo package made as much sense as the break-in and *tell the truth* note.

Were the situations connected? Or were the photos truly an attempt to help Finch's Hope?

The only thing they knew for sure was that now they had a second note without a signature.

Everyone was readying for the mine tour scheduled for this afternoon, but Payton couldn't seem to make herself change out of her casual leggings and tank top from this morning into something...else.

She wasn't sure what outfit she'd packed that would be a fit for a mine tour.

Maybe exactly what she had on?

Learning about the package of photos Belinda received with the unsigned Post-it note had exhausted her. Instead of changing clothes as planned, she'd crawled under the covers and pulled her phone back out.

Looking through the pictures a second time sent Payton spiraling back to those tumultuous teenage years.

They'd had a *lot* of fun.

But she'd also felt so lost at times.

The group shots resurrected her years of feeling like leftovers in the fridge that someone forgot to toss out.

Liam had gotten the photo wrong. *She'd* crushed on Scout in high school, not vice versa. And she'd struggled to navigate that crush while observing Scout liking Cece...and Cece not liking Scout in that way. And yet the two of them had been *very* close.

And the whole time, Payton had been standing in the wings, attempting to appear as though all was well when her heart had been breaking.

Teenage love was so theatrical and dramatic. But her angst during that phase had been very real.

Payton had refused to do anything that would wreck her

relationship with Cece, Isley, and Clara, so she'd attempted to move on.

She'd dated other guys for a minute.

Despite moments of rebellion outside of school, she'd focused on her grades, because they'd been her ticket out of Veil.

And she'd put her friendship with her girls first, because they'd been her family.

Then and now.

Outside of Clara, who'd discovered her crush during their senior year, Payton had kept her feelings for Scout—and plenty of other things—under wraps.

Even as an adult, it was hard for her to open up to people.

She wasn't sure she would have ever fallen for Liam if Isley, Clara, and Cece hadn't loved her unconditionally and taught her the definition of the word.

Payton stalled on the photos from when they'd driven to the lake to get relief from the heat. That day, instead of getting in the water with her and the rest of the kids there, Scout had stayed on the towels talking to Cece.

Like always.

One of the other guys from their class had flirted nonstop with Payton that day. Now she couldn't even remember his name. But she'd used his attention as a balm to the wound that Scout's lack of interest in her created.

Payton had spent over two years of high school shoving down and hiding her crush on Scout. And she'd managed to do a good job of it. Until the end. Payton felt ill when she thought about that last night with Cece.

Once the shower kicked on behind the closed bathroom door, meaning Liam wouldn't be popping back into the room, Payton exchanged her phone for his.

He'd left it on the nightstand, and that awful hidden screen had been taunting her ever since.

Payton knew Liam's pattern, so she logged in and scanned his texts. She didn't know what she was looking for. But she just couldn't shake the feeling that something was off. That she was missing something.

No doubt the photos delivered to Belinda coupled with last night's events were compounding her conspiracy theories.

Liam's most recent texts in order were to her, his friend Parker, his mother, and then Ashlyn.

Payton clicked on the Ashlyn messages and scrolled backward. Everything was school- and class-related. She went back about a month before giving up on that string and returning to the main screen. The man had nearly a thousand unread emails in his personal account. Seeing that number every day would drive her nuts.

"Mom." Reagan stood in the door frame.

"What's up?" She returned Liam's phone to the nightstand.

Reagan closed the door behind her and dropped onto the bed. "Was that Dad's phone?"

"Yeah. I was just...looking something up." Payton decided less was more. If she tried to explain, red flags would start going off for Reagan. They probably already were.

Reagan propped a pillow between her back and the headboard, legs stretched across the comforter. "I really don't want to go on this mine tour. I trust Isley and all, but it sounds terrible."

Payton tamped down a smile. "Why does it sound terrible?"

"It seems like something either an adult or a five-year-old would want to do."

Payton laughed. "It's not my first choice either, but it won some huge award. So, it'll probably be better than we think. And it will show well for the auction vacation package. Especially if adults or someone with a five-year-old buys it."

Reagan gave an amused snort.

"I can't imagine letting you stay at the house right now by yourself because of the break-in."

"I know. And it's not like I'm ready for that, anyway. Don't you think it's strange that the person who broke in didn't steal anything?"

"I do."

"What do you think that note was about?"

"I honestly don't know." Certainly they feared it could be about Cece's death, but Payton wasn't opening up that can of worms with her daughter unless she knew for certain. "The whole thing is just really odd."

Reagan's head tipped to rest on Payton's shoulder—something she hadn't done in months if not years. Payton was afraid to breathe lest she ruin the moment.

"Is...everything okay?" Again, Payton didn't want to disrupt the tender touch, but how could she *not* ask?

"Yes, Mom." Reagan responded with a hint of both annoyance and humor. "Everything is fine."

"There hasn't been any more online stuff?"

"Nope."

Payton desperately wanted to believe her daughter. But all she could think about was the many months before the discovery of that box under her bed when Reagan hadn't told her *anything*.

"Rea, you know you can talk to me, right?" She leaned her head lightly against her daughter's.

"Yep. You know you can talk to me too, right?"

Hmm. What was that about?

When Payton looked at herself in those old photos, all she saw was a broken girl with a wild look in her eyes. So basically, all of Payton's angst over Reagan had one purpose: to prevent her daughter from turning into her.

Chapter Seventeen

Cece

Today Veil will break a heat record set over sixty years ago, so it's not a huge surprise to find twenty-plus kids from our soon-to-be junior class along with a smattering of seniors and sophomores are all at Red Lake.

Clara and Hank are both working, so neither of them are here. Payton and Isley are in the lake floating on tubes. I'm lying on my towel next to Scout beneath the shade of a tree, eyes closed. Every couple minutes, I recognize Isley's laugh-screech that ends with a splash when one of the guys flirting with her tosses her from the tube into the water. Payton's experiencing the same level of male attention, but her response is less vocal.

Cold water sprinkles over me and I sit up with a gasp.

Konnor grins. "Are you getting in?" His hands land on his hips. He doesn't have a shirt on because he just got out of the lake, and his muscles are... It takes a few seconds for my eyes to finally reach his face.

"No. I'm not getting in." My reply comes out clipped. "I was sleeping before you so rudely interrupted me." I wasn't. But Konnor is not on my list of favorite people right now. I'm not sure how he has the audacity to approach me so nonchalantly after what I told him two weeks ago and his subsequent vanishing act.

"Fine. You're missing out." He saunters away and is quickly occupied by a game of football on the sand.

"What is going on with you two?" Scout asks from the towel next to me. His arms are propped behind him so that he's semi-reclined, and his vision is on the lake and the group of kids occupying it.

"Nothing."

He shoots me a look that screams, *Really?*

"I may have admitted that I was a little bit into him," I whisper, as if that will somehow erase my mistake. I don't know what I was thinking. But Konnor had been flirting with me *so* much, and I'd thought for certain he was interested in me. Plus, I've liked him since partway through sophomore year. In teenage years, that's like a decade of unrequited like.

Scout knows the feeling. His eyes widen. "When was *this?*"

"Almost two weeks ago."

"What did he do when you admitted you were into him?"

"Nothing. He didn't say anything back. And that's the first time he's talked to me since."

"What a player." Scout's upper lip curls with disgust. "He doesn't deserve you, Cece."

If anyone overheard us right now, they'd think Scout was into me. Isley, Payton, and Clara all believe as much.

Payton gets tossed off her tube, and one of the senior guys steals it. She tries to take it back, and a wrestling match erupts with water flying everywhere.

"Dude, your crush is showing."

Scout winces and turns toward me, likely in an attempt to block out the scene in front of him.

"Are you ever going to tell her?" I ask for the thousandth time.

Payton's laugh floats across the water.

Scout smiles as if this whole scenario isn't excruciating for him. "I don't know what you're talking about."

"Ten years from now, you're going to wake up and realize you missed out on her. You do understand that the more you hang out with me, the more all my friends think you like me, right? They don't know you're talking to me about her. *She* thinks you like me. That's not exactly working in your favor."

I can't reveal Scout's crush to Payton because I'm loyal to a fault. When my friends ask me about my life before Veil, I skirt over most of it. But when your so-called friends tell everyone a secret you shouldn't have told them in the first place, things get dicey.

Especially when the secret is beyond juicy. And *so* painful.

My loyalty is the only thing that keeps me from spilling all to Payton. I am a vault, and Scout knows it. It's the reason I'm privy to what's really going on in his mind.

I will not do to him what some girls did to me in the eighth grade.

Despite his short-lived attempt not to focus on the water, Scout's attention is glued to Payton again.

"Why don't you get in the lake? Who knows what could happen if you do."

"I don't fit in with those jocks."

"I'll say it again. You are going to miss your opportunity with her. Ten of those *jocks* would go out with her in a heartbeat."

"You're not helping anything!" Scout lays down on his towel and covers his face with his arms. "What am I supposed to do? Tell her I like her and then she doesn't like me and now we're all stuck with awkwardness for our last two years of high school? This is our friend group we're talking about. It would make things so weird."

"Only if she doesn't like you. May I please, *please* fish around to figure out if she does?" Payton is a closed book. She keeps her feelings tucked close to her chest, and even though she's one of my best friends, I honestly have no idea how she feels about Scout.

It could be platonic. She could be in love with him.

"At least then you would know."

"That's so second grade. I might as well just give her a note that asks if she likes me and include *yes, no,* and maybe checkboxes."

"That's not a bad idea."

Scout quickly sits up and shoves me off my towel. I laugh, scramble back onto it, and then push him back.

We're in the middle of something that closely resembles that wrestling match in the lake from a few minutes ago when I notice that Payton is returning to her towel and is only a couple steps from us.

I cringe and shoot Scout a panicked look. I'm sure Payton thinks we're flirting. We definitely weren't helping Scout's predicament just now.

"Pay, I put your towel in the shade since the sun moved." Scout nods toward the brightly striped towel next to him.

"Oh, nice. Thanks." Payton's mouth softens. She drops onto the towel, lies on her stomach and closes her eyes, then adjusts her position...until she's facing away from both me and Scout.

I could practically kick him right now.

No matter how many times I tell my friends that I'm not into Scout like that—that we are *just friends*—no one believes me.

And why would they? Because I'm only allowed to share *my* feelings with them.

I resist the urge to punch Scout in the arm to release my aggression. I feel irritated with him, and I really shouldn't. It's not his fault he's not ready to say anything to Payton. If I had to guess, he never will be.

He's told me about the stutter he had when he was younger. Sometimes I still catch it or the way he adjusts to an alternate word. He's told me how painfully shy he was as a kid and how he's never fully grown out of that. He says his brain literally stops working sometimes when he's trying to talk to someone, like there's a wall between it and his mouth.

I wish he would tell Payton this stuff. I see her reacting so kindly even if she's not romantically interested in him.

But I also understand where he's coming from. After all, look what happened between me and Konnor two weeks ago and how awkward I feel around him now.

If anyone should understand Scout's predicament, it's me.

A water balloon lands at my feet and shatters all over me. Even though they were also sprayed, neither Scout or Payton react.

I scan the lake to locate the source of the airborne strike and find Konnor beaming in my direction as if he just won the Nobel Prize.

What is his *deal*? Why does he act into me one second and then, when I actually admit I like him, totally disappear?

Still...he *is* paying attention to me.

Do I want to be like Scout and Payton and miss out on what's in front of me? Or do I want to be the kind of person who grabs onto life and takes risks?

"I'm getting in," I announce to no one in particular, since Scout also appears to have conked out on his towel.

And then I push up from the ground and join Konnor in the lake.

Chapter Eighteen

The group returned from the mine outing late that afternoon. They'd eaten enchiladas with rice and all the fixings for dinner, and now, sated and exhausted, planned to do a chill movie on the deck.

After they'd cleaned up dinner and while everyone changed into comfortable clothing or pajamas for the movie, Payton power-napped for ten minutes.

She didn't understand why she was so tired. They were literally vacationing for charity.

Maybe it was Reagan's stuff, which was always heavy on her mind.

Or the break-in slash note.

Or the photos Belinda received.

Or maybe it was altitude and she should have done the oxygen thing with Hank.

He'd seemed to perk up after that. But then, Hank wasn't the type to complain. For all Payton knew, he was still experiencing altitude sickness symptoms and downplaying them.

In high school, he'd been easygoing and unassuming. And *so* in love with Clara.

So basically the exact same person he was now.

Payton strode upstairs. Only Liam occupied the living room, his nose in one of the suspense novels he'd picked up at the used bookstore today.

The doors to the deck were open, and Payton spotted Reagan on the outdoor L-shaped sofa. There'd been a short rain shower this afternoon while they were at the mine, but the weather cleared quickly after. Now, the sun filtered through the pine trees behind the house and cast a pretty glow on Reagan.

If Payton wouldn't get into trouble for it, she'd snap a picture.

For not wanting to go on the mine tour, Reagan had actually rocked a pretty good attitude. Granted, the tour was really well done and interesting. Payton should never doubt Isley's planning skills. They were always impeccable.

Reagan hadn't brought up her ankle on the outing, so Payton assumed it wasn't bothering her. After touring the mine, they'd all taken part in the option to pan for gold. Reagan had competed with Liam to see who could discover the most, and Payton had glimpsed the little kid in her daughter again.

This afternoon Reagan had barely checked her phone, and for a couple hours, things had felt peaceful. Void of girl drama or even the need for Reagan to keep up the pretenses of being a snarky teen.

Honestly Payton understood that turmoil and the way the adolescent years caused emotional highs and lows.

She remembered those days clearly. She'd pushed. Her parents had reacted strongly, often with anger and judgment. But after, they'd burrowed back into their distant emotionless state. And she'd been left drained. Payton sometimes thought maybe she'd missed the mark with her parents. That she'd been expecting too much. After all, they'd provided for her physical needs. She'd never been without clothing or new shoes, or a haircut, or a meal. Things that had at times been hard to come by in Isley's world.

But she also knew there'd been abuse in both of their childhoods, and Payton wondered if that abuse had turned something off in them. Almost as if the connection she'd craved had been impossible. To this day she'd never confronted them, because she was certain they wouldn't see anything wrong with her upbringing.

Clara, Isley, and Cece had stuck with her through her rebellious periods without participating in the same reckless decisions. Except for the one time she would never forgive herself for when she'd taken them all down. Payton was certain they'd lost Cece because of it.

Because of her.

Payton stepped onto the deck. Reagan must not have heard her approach, because her head was tipped forward, her hair covering most of her expression as she focused on something in her lap.

Flick-flick-flick. A flame leaped from the lighter in her hand. She studied it and then lowered it to her wrist.

"Stop." Payton wasn't even aware that she'd moved, but suddenly she was next to Reagan on the sofa, the lighter in her hand instead of her daughter's. "Whatever's going on, we'll figure it out." Payton kept her volume low and soft. The last thing she wanted to do was cause Reagan shame.

Payton had been searching for wayward laundry under the edge of Reagan's bed when she'd discovered the doodled-on box filled with matches and lighters and candles.

She'd been so confused. At first she'd thought maybe Reagan was just into lighting candles. But why hide that?

Even Liam hadn't known what the box contents might be for when she'd asked him. And he worked with college students.

An internet search had clued Payton in to the fact that some people used a flame to self-harm. She'd only ever heard of cutting before.

It had all made sense then—the long-sleeved shirts even on warm days, disappearing into her room for hours on end, the way Reagan snipped at Payton whenever she inquired about her mental health.

Payton had believed herself to be hyperaware of any changes in Reagan's demeanor.

But she'd missed this *and* the online girl drama.

Just like with Cece.

The week before her death, Cece had been upset about something, but they hadn't known she was suffering at such a deep level. They'd been so unaware.

Payton would give anything to take on even a small piece of the pain that would cause Reagan to hurt herself in any way. Just the idea of it tortured Payton, often keeping her awake at night.

She wrapped her arm around Reagan. "Rea—"

"Mom, *stop*," Reagan hissed and jumped across the cushions, landing out of Payton's reach. "I wasn't *doing* anything."

"But—" Payton motioned to her wrist "—you were going to—"

"*No*, I wasn't. You just jumped to conclusions. I offered to help Isley even though I don't even want to be part of this movie on the deck, and she asked me to light the candles."

Reagan pointed to the coffee table, where two lit candles flickered...and a third stood flameless.

Wounding flashed like visible thunder in her dark eyes.

"But..." Reagan had been about to hold the flame against

her skin, hadn't she? Payton covered her mouth with her hand. *Had* she overreacted? "Oh, Rea. I'm so sorry. I just saw the—"

"You saw me with a lighter and you literally lost your mind."

It was true.

"I haven't touched any of that stuff since I started seeing Ms. Tilda." She tugged her thin long-sleeved shirt away from her wrists and yanked her bracelets up her forearm. Bracelets that Payton had learned after the fact were part of Reagan's cover for her scarred skin.

She held out her healed arms defiantly.

"I didn't know. I was trying to give you space. You've still been wearing long sleeves, so I just thought..." It was such good news, but it was tainted by Payton's misplaced reaction to seeing the lighter in Reagan's hand.

Since they'd found out about the self-harm, Payton had tried *so* hard to respond to Reagan with patience and grace and love. And never judgment. But the emotional thrashing she'd just released on her precious kid was the opposite of everything she'd strived for.

And eerily reminiscent of a reaction Payton might have experienced herself from the two people who'd raised her.

When they'd first purchased The Haven, Isley had entertained the idea of movie nights on the deck with Aiden and maybe even his friends. It had been a silly dream, perhaps, because they didn't watch the same movies as Aiden and he was already in his freshman year of college. But Isley would put up with pretty much any genre for quality time with her son.

She'd bought the screen and projector on a whim, and this was the first time they'd used it.

She was still glad she'd made the purchase though. The night was lovely—the stars bold and bright, the temperature cool and requiring a blanket, the company as comfortable as a favorite soft sweatshirt. The movie had also provided a welcome distraction from the fact that, despite Trevor's additional phone calls this afternoon to both the rehab facility and the lawyer's office, Aiden's whereabouts were still unconfirmed.

Once again he'd been forced to leave voicemails at both.

From his reclined position in the corner of the outdoor sofa next to Clara, Hank let out a quiet snore.

The group exchanged amused glances, raising their drinks in a toast.

"To poor Hank," they chorused quietly.

According to Clara, it was normal for Hank not to make it five minutes into a movie or television show without falling asleep, so that at least alleviated the worry that something was still going on with him physically.

When the credits rolled, Clara nudged Hank. "Let's get you to bed, old man."

He rubbed a hand over his shaved head. "Is it over?"

"Yep." Clara stood and pulled him up from the couch. "We watched three movies and you slept through them all."

"Seriously?" Hank's eyes widened.

"No." Clara laughed. "Is, I'll be back to help with the dishes once I get this guy safely in bed for the night. I'm not sure I trust him not to fall down the stairs in his current state."

Hank's nose scrunched in offense. "I'm not *that* out of it. I can get myself to bed. But I feel like I should be on dishes duty since I probably snored through most of the movie."

"You did," Clara confirmed with amusement. "But I'll handle our portion of cleanup tonight."

"Fine. Sign me up for something helpful tomorrow."

"I'm with Clara." Payton stacked popcorn bowls. "The two of us can get this."

"The three of us," Isley amended. "Husbands, go to bed. All of you were either asleep during the movie or close to it."

Liam raised his palms. "I know better than to argue. I'll assist with Hank tomorrow."

Trevor scanned the deck and the trees behind the house. "You feel safe out here? Sure you don't want me to stay?"

Isley followed his line of vision. The deck didn't have stairs. It was suspended high enough off the ground that no one would be able to scale it without effort. Things she'd never analyzed before.

"I'm good." She glanced at Payton and Clara, earning nods of agreement from them.

"Okay. Get me if you need me." Trevor kissed her forehead. "Night."

The Husbands carried the projector and screen inside and then broke off toward their respective bedrooms.

"Oh, no!" Clara paused in the middle of folding a blanket. "I didn't take any photos tonight."

"This isn't part of the auction weekend, so we're fine. I don't think the resort is going to offer whoever wins a personal outdoor movie under the stars. Although it would be a nice touch."

"Okay, phew. I feel better now. I panicked thinking I missed such a good photo op. Tonight was beautiful, Is. This was the perfect relaxing end to our day."

"Right?" Payton stacked drink glasses. "It was ninety-eight in Dallas today."

"Wait." Clara dropped the blanket onto the couch and pulled out her phone. "We should take a picture just for us. Especially after we missed the one in the town square."

The three of them scooched together and Clara snapped selfies from a few different angles and settings due to the low lighting.

After, Payton grabbed the bowls she'd set down for the pictures. "Have you both been thinking about the photos Belinda received too? Or is that just me?"

"I have." Isley carried glasses as she followed Payton into the kitchen.

"Me too." Clara placed the blankets in a basket in the living room.

"Iris answered me during the movie. She didn't send them." Isley had assumed as much, because the note with the photos appeared to be helpful. And Iris was a one-woman show.

Clara's dad had already confirmed it had nothing to do with him earlier this afternoon.

"Who could they be from?" Payton rinsed bowls and handed them to Isley to be loaded into the dishwasher.

"So many kids were in the photos." Isley placed them on the bottom shelf. "The pool of who could have sent them is wide."

"The whole thing wouldn't feel so disturbing if the note with the photos had been signed." Clara's lips pursed as she wiped the countertops.

"Exactly." Isley fit the glassware into the nearly full dishwasher. "That feels a bit creepy. But maybe we're overthinking it because of what happened here." She added soap to the dishwasher and started it, then turned to find the kitchen sparkling. Just how she liked it. "Thank you for helping."

"Thank you for letting us." Payton's brows rose with humor.

Isley's friends knew her idiosyncrasies regarding cleanliness well and where those traits had stemmed from. "I'm exhausted but..."

"I'm not sure I can sleep," Payton filled in.

"Same. Does anyone want Sleepytime tea?"

Both Payton and Clara raised their hands in answer.

Isley laughed. "How are we this old?" She retrieved mugs from the cupboard and heated water.

"Should I close the doors to the deck?" Clara motioned to the open wall. "Between the note here and the photos at Belinda's, it's hard not to feel like there's something sinister out there." She shuddered. "Just waiting to out *something*, and we don't have any real direction as to what. The past? The present?"

Both options were debilitating to Isley. It was as if her world was teetering on the edge of a cliff and about to roll down the steep incline.

"I'll shut them." She added tea bags to the mugs and handed them out, and Clara held hers while she closed and secured the deck doors.

Once they sat in the living room, Clara continued. "I'm at the point where if someone is trying to out us, so be it. At least," she grew pensive, "that's what I would think if it didn't have the potential to hurt Belinda."

"I can't imagine that Belinda wouldn't be blindsided." Payton blew on her tea and took a tiny sip. "And if anyone tells her or takes the blame, it should be me. We all know that."

Clara's head shook vehemently. "We did it together."

Even though Clara had been the only logical one that night. Isley had thought when they'd made that pact freshman year that they were being smart. Like they were watching out for each other. A musketeer's vibe. As a mom, she saw it differently. In her rearview mirror, it looked a lot like peer pressure.

Isley wished she could follow Clara's lead, but she couldn't handle another piece of her life imploding.

If it all fell apart—if Trevor couldn't forgive her for the conversation she'd had with Bianca, if Aiden had left rehab early and ended up serving time, if their reckless decision the night of Cece's death was brought to light, if the perfect facade she'd been crafting and honing all this time imploded—who *was* she?

Isley didn't know the answer to that question. And that scared her as much as everything else combined.

Payton wrapped hands around her mug. "Do you think the photos are connected to the note here at the house?"

"It would seem odd because the handwriting is so different," Clara responded. "But I guess we really don't know."

Isley sipped her tea, but it did nothing to alleviate the Sahara Desert filling her mouth. "There's no way *to* know if they're connected or not. Or what the note here was referencing. Maybe it was just kids messing around like Sergeant Miller said."

Though if any of them thought that last option was the case, they wouldn't be so troubled by it.

"What *is* the plan if someone knows about that night and follows through with sharing the details?" Clara asked. "I do dread the thought of my kids finding out."

Isley understood the desire not to have her foolish decisions made public. If Aiden's arrest had caused upheaval in their world, then her presence and participation the night Cece died would certainly do the same.

"You didn't even do anything, Clara." Payton spoke quietly. "You're not guilty by association."

"Did I try to stop it from happening?" she responded, her free hand jutting into the air. "I was just as much a part of it as you both were."

Payton finished the last of her tea and then stared into the bottom of the mug as if the answers they were searching for were written there. "I suppose since we can't solve any of it, we should go to bed. Tomorrow will be a busy day."

In the morning, they were riding electric bikes on the Breck bike path—another donated activity for the auction weekend—and then Isley had a non-charity related surprise planned for the women in the afternoon while Trev had one scheduled for The Husbands.

After that, the caterers would arrive to prep for the Finch's Hope dinner party.

Isley hoped the survivor interviews they planned to capture

at the dinner would be a huge boon for the charity...and that nothing strange happened tomorrow night when Belinda and the guests were here.

They hadn't told Belinda about the note or the break-in, nor did they plan to.

Not when they were still clueless as to what it was about.

"It's like we're in limbo." Payton placed her mug in the kitchen sink. "Like we're waiting for another shoe to drop."

"Right?" Isley barely resisted the temptation to handwash their mugs. She would unload and load the dishwasher in the morning. "What was the point of the cryptic note? Why not just state whatever truth they wanted unearthed?"

"Maybe they're trying to make us suffer," Clara offered.

Payton gave a derisive snort. "If so, it's working."

Chapter Nineteen

Payton descended the stairs quietly in case Liam was already attempting to sleep on the sofa bed, but she found Reagan there instead of him.

She rounded the couch to speak to her. "Are you planning to sleep out here tonight?"

Reagan pulled out an earbud. "What?" Her voice snapped with an edge that Payton ignored.

She repeated her question.

"Yeah. No offense but sleeping with you isn't my favorite."

Ditto, kid. Reagan had flipped and flopped for an hour before falling asleep last night.

"The house alarm is set, right?" she asked.

"Isley was doing it when I walked down."

"Then I'll be fine here."

Payton wanted to argue. It felt so much safer to have Reagan next to her. Even if it meant her own sleep being disturbed. But she didn't want to create fear in her daughter. Life was full of unexpected circumstances. Learning to pivot and adjust was important.

Payton perched on the edge of the pull-out sofa bed. "Rea, about earlier—"

"I don't want to talk about it."

"I'm just trying to apologize." Payton wouldn't be able to sleep unless she expressed her remorse. "I was wrong. I'm sorry for jumping to conclusions. And for being overprotective. I always want to know how you're doing, but I don't want to bug you by asking all the time."

"You should stick with that plan and not ask."

Payton swallowed a sigh, willing herself not to be hurt or engage with Reagan, who was the definition of that word herself. "I'm trying to give you space to heal on your own. But I'm always here. I'll help with anything that I can—"

"Mom, please, *please* stop talking."

Ouch.

"I just need a little space from *you* right now."

Ouch times two.

"Can you at least acknowledge my apology? I'm not saying you have to accept it. You can be mad at me. I just... I need you to hear me say I messed up." It certainly wasn't something Payton had ever heard from her mother.

"I agree that you messed up. There."

Payton nearly laughed. Sometimes Reagan was so *her* as a teen. Walls up. Cannons locked and loaded. Assuming everyone was out to get her when in fact, so many people—teachers, friends, church families—had fought for her.

"Just what I asked for. Thank you." She stood, leaning over to press a kiss to Reagan's head, managing to complete the action before Reagan realized what was happening and squirmed away. "Love you, Rea. Sleep well. And we're right here if you need us or it feels weird out here. I can always kick Dad out of bed. You know he doesn't care."

Reagan snorted. "Too true."

What was that about? "What do you mean?"

"Nothing. I'm just tired, okay?" A notification popped up on Reagan's phone screen, and her face erupted in a smile as her thumbs power-texted back. She didn't look fatigued at the moment.

I'm tired too. Not that you were asking.

It was a toss-up as to which issue was exhausting Payton more—Reagan, Liam, everything they'd just discussed on the deck.

If Payton had a number two pencil, she'd fill in all of the above.

"Wait, Mom."

"Yeah?" Payton paused just outside the bedroom door.

"Can you turn off the light?"

Had she really expected some sort of understanding from Reagan just now?

"Sure." Payton flipped the switch, leaving Reagan's curved mouth illuminated by her phone screen.

At least that meant the communication was a good thing, right? And not problematic like the online stuff she'd dealt with.

Payton entered the bedroom to find Liam filling the side of the bed that had been *his* throughout their marriage.

Most nights at home, Liam fell asleep on the couch and stayed there. Since he woke earlier than Reagan, Payton assumed their daughter was unaware of the new sleeping arrangements they'd developed since their discussion about The Plan.

She thought he might say something about the awkwardness of them sharing a bed tonight, but he was reading. Another consistency throughout their marriage.

"You two doing okay?" He glanced at her over the top of his book.

He'd overheard the lighter situation on the deck earlier and had attempted to smooth things over with Reagan. Which, based on her snark just now, hadn't worked.

"She's still in hating-me mode."

"I promise I tried. I know you didn't mean anything by what happened. It was just a weird situation."

Payton blinked back tears. "Thank you." It was so nice to have Liam recognize her heart. "I—"

He'd already returned his attention to the pages in front of him.

Payton grabbed her pajamas from the dresser drawer, entered the bathroom, and engaged in her normal nighttime routine. She washed her face, used her electric toothbrush for two minutes, flossed, applied a generous helping of expensive night cream that had, so far, not reduced her appearance of aging like it claimed to. Then she donned her short-sleeved button-down pajamas with matching shorts in the bathroom like a teen hiding out in a shower stall versus the locker room, because the idea of changing in front of her husband made her feel way too vulnerable.

Not that Liam would even look up from his book.

Payton was clothed in something that she could easily wear walking down a street, but she still felt exposed. Which had everything to do with the scenario she was about to walk into and nothing to do with her pj's.

She closed the bathroom door behind her so that Reagan could use it as needed from the living room entrance and slid into bed quickly, tugging the luxurious, fresh-scented sheets up to her chin. The temptation to build a pillow barrier between her and Liam like two characters in a forced proximity rom-com rose up, but Payton dismissed it.

Liam turned a page, unaware of her awkward turmoil a mere foot away.

He'd bought so many books at the used bookstore today, which Payton had known would happen. Throughout their marriage, she often accused him of collecting more books than he could ever read. He had numerous overflowing bookshelves at their house, and whenever Payton suggested he consider purging some, he responded with fearful hesitation that caused her to laugh.

How strange that he planned to remove the books—and himself—from their home.

As she listened to the sound of his breathing, her irritation from after the hike this morning rose up again. It was mere embers at the moment. A smoldering cigarette butt tossed into a ditch. But Payton feared the ashes could start an angry, raging forest fire if given even a hint of oxygen.

She didn't know what to do with all the feelings rumbling around inside her like rocks in a metal dryer drum. Payton had finally realized what she'd been upset about this morning. Unbeknownst to even herself, she'd been harboring hope going into friendcation.

Hope that her husband would wake up, see what he was orchestrating with The Plan, and change his mind. Hope that being with her and Reagan on the road trip and for the weekend would help him grasp what he was throwing away.

Except...if he still had Payton and Reagan in his life, still had family dinners and holidays and school events together like he'd talked about, was he really losing anything at all?

"I have a question." Or ten.

Liam's focus swung to her, and the walls of the room pulled an Indiana Jones stunt, closing in around them.

"How may I be of assistance?" he quipped, teasing crinkling

the corners of his mouth as he inserted a bookmark and set the hardcover nonfiction book on his nightstand.

His demeanor was so reminiscent of the many times throughout their marriage they'd hashed out a plan or dreamed about something together that Payton had to inhale shakily before she could continue.

"When you first talked to me about us separating, you mentioned that we operate better as friends. What prompted that? Were we fighting? Because I don't remember us fighting."

Her heart. It couldn't be good for it to thump and pound like this, could it?

"I don't know that we were fighting so much as..." His palms lifted and landed back on the bedspread. "We were just different. Remember when we were friends before we were dating?"

That was like questioning if she remembered Reagan's birthday. "Of course." She would like to ask him the same. Along with, do you recall how we've always been friends while married?

"Everything just kind of fit and made sense. We didn't have to try overly hard. Which was consistent during the first part of our marriage."

"When did that stop?" And how had Payton missed that too?

"About a year and a half before I talked to you." A *year and a half*? Payton would have said that the last couple years of their marriage—pre–The Plan announcement—were the best. She'd felt like they'd meshed better than ever.

Apparently her instincts were completely untrustworthy.

"I kept trying to make adjustments," Liam continued. "Thinking maybe something had fractured that we could piece back together. But in a way, we were doing all the same things we'd always done and it just stopped working."

"Stopped working?" That was a broad statement.

"Stopped being easy."

"I don't know a lot of marriages that qualify as easy. I think they take work."

"I'm not doing a good job of explaining."

Payton agreed with that part.

"Something just changed without us realizing it. And I started thinking about how we operate so well together. Almost like business partners. We're great at making decisions together. We're great at doing life together, but we weren't really doing anything else together anymore."

Business partners? Tack on yet another *ouch* to her night.

"Are you referencing spending time with each other?" Payton wasn't sure what his last comment meant, because quality time was another thing they'd mapped out. They still did date nights—or at least they had before he'd announced The Plan.

"Sort of."

Sort of?

"More like we stopped…connecting."

Maybe he'd stopped connecting while she'd been plugging along, thinking everything was good between them.

"It's more of an instinct versus something I can describe."

And Liam was the one who was good with words.

What was Payton supposed to do with this information? Or lack thereof.

It sounded like he'd stopped loving her and was unwilling to just state that.

Liam yawned, turned off his bedside lamp, and settled onto his pillow facing away from her.

Evidently their conversation was over.

Chapter Twenty

When Clara woke to Hank's nudge and found him sitting on her side of the bed, the room still clothed in darkness, she panicked.

"What is it? Did you hear something? Are the kids okay?"

"Nothing's wrong. Everyone is fine." Clara's galloping pulse resumed a semi-normal rhythm. "I just have a question for you."

"You have a question for me in the middle of the night?"

He emitted a low quiet laugh. "It's six thirty in the morning."

"I repeat, you have a question for me in the middle of the night?"

She earned another chuckle from Hank as she closed her eyes, planning to go back to sleep. If nothing was wrong, surely he could wait another hour to ask her something. Maybe two.

"I am aware of the risk in waking you this early. I'd planned to mention it last night, but then I slept through the movie and transferred straight to bed." Clara opened her eyes to see him wince. "I sound so old."

Her lips curved as she fought the gravity of her weighted eyelids again.

"I heard about a photo spot just outside of town, and I wondered if you'd like to go. There's a small lake and the views are supposed to be amazing."

Ooh. Interesting. Yes, Clara was taking photos for the charity this weekend, but this option sounded like it was for *her*.

"How did you hear about this spot?"

"I found it online."

Her eyes popped open. "You used The Internets for me?" Hank wasn't exactly tech savvy.

"I did."

"You have my attention." She propped a pillow between her back and the headboard and moved to a semi-sitting position.

Now that she was conscious, Clara recognized the early morning light slipping around the blinds.

"I would have woken you for the sunrise but that seemed like pushing it."

"Oh, goodness. I'm thankful you didn't do that." Clara wasn't picky when it came to photography. She didn't need the perfect lighting or setting. She found beauty in simplicity—a cornfield, hay bales, an old barn, a rusted tractor.

Maybe because their life was simple, and she found beauty in that too.

That's what she was waiting for Hank to rediscover. The joy in the mundane. The pockets of good in the midst of troubles.

"If you're interested, I'll grab you coffee and a pastry for the car." Hank knew her love language well. Quality time and food. Usually in the same setting. "If you're not interested, I won't be offended. You can go back to sleep and we'll pretend this conversation never happened. Just please don't be mad at me for waking you up."

Clara laughed. "You're a little scared of me, aren't you?"

"Only when it comes to disrupting your sleep." His cheeks creased and then swiftly switched to broadcasting regret. "I know I haven't been very present lately. At home or on this trip." Hank was rarely serious, often choosing humor to mask a deep-seated emotion or to lighten a mood. "This is my peace offering."

How could she say no now?

Especially with him making an effort to find a great photography spot.

About five years ago, Hank had built her a darkroom as an anniversary gift, and for his gift that year, she'd made his favorite rib recipe for dinner. Sometimes marriage was lopsided like that. Sometimes one person was in a funk and couldn't climb out, like Hank presently.

There was always an ebb and flow. Expecting both partners to be equal in all phases of life made absolutely no sense.

Yet that's exactly what Clara had been doing lately. She'd been so impatient and irritable with Hank. Even if she'd only allowed those emotions to bubble up internally, they were still unlike her.

Maybe she was the one who needed to rediscover herself.

Clara rested her forehead against Hank's. "I'd love to go." She framed his stubbled cheeks and kissed the lips that were as familiar to her as her own. "Thank you for planning it. I'll get ready."

"I'll get the van packed." He grabbed her camera bag and exited the room quietly since Reagan was sleeping on the sofa bed.

Clara dressed quickly in leggings and a T-shirt, then brushed her teeth and tossed her hair into a ponytail. She donned tennis shoes and a sweatshirt, assuming the morning would have a chill.

In the kitchen, she found a notepad in the drawer. She didn't want to text in case someone had their phone volume up, so she left a note on the island regarding their whereabouts, making sure to sign it. Surprised she could find humor in the break-in note situation, she underlined her and Hank's names at the bottom for good measure and added a smiley face.

They disarmed and reset the alarm on their way out of the house—Trevor and Isley had given everyone a rundown on how to use it yesterday after Cyrus had gotten the front door functioning again—and then loaded themselves into the van.

Clara didn't ask where they were going. She just rode shotgun with her to-go coffee and a caramel roll placed on a paper towel. Hank had located a travel mug with a lid in one of the kitchen drawers, but said he'd done a short-lived search for a paper plate and come up empty. Clara wasn't surprised by that. Adult Isley wasn't a paper plate kind of girl.

"I'm impressed you figured out how to use the coffee maker." Clara sipped, finding the dark brew that filled the van with its rich, nutty scent doctored with just the right amount of cream. Alas, it wasn't a latte since Isley was the mastermind behind those, but it tasted almost better because of Hank's efforts.

"Trevor showed me yesterday in case I was up before him today. It wasn't quite as complicated as it appears."

She tugged a fragment from the warm roll and popped the buttery, caramel pastry into her mouth. "I'm also impressed you heated this up for me. You're doing excellent husbanding this morning."

"Thank you." Hank laughed, his vision remaining on the road as they exited town and the scenery switched from condos and townhomes to evergreen forest dotted with an occasional cabin, house, or quiet neighborhood.

Even the drive was pretty. Clara itched to ask Hank to stop and let her get her camera out now, but she opted for patience since her husband had masterminded this thoughtful plan.

"When was the last time we did this?"

Hank turned off the main road. "Got up early to take pictures in Breckenridge? I'd go with never."

"Not exactly what I meant," she said wryly. "Outside of the drive to Breckenridge, I don't know the last time we did anything with just the two of us that didn't revolve around the kids or the farm." Or money issues.

"I agree." Hank kept a slow careful pace as the dirt road they were on increased in elevation. "We need to be better about that."

And yet, this outing wasn't about them as much as *her*—another sighting of the original version of Hank.

He parked in the nearly empty dirt lot that lined the side of the road and overlooked a small gorgeous lake hemmed in by mountains still boasting patches of snow.

"Stunning."

"There's another lake at the top." Hank motioned to where the dirt road continued but vehicles weren't allowed. "Doubt we have time to hike up there for pictures though."

"And I'm not sure I'd survive that ascent." The path rose at a steep incline.

"I certainly wouldn't be able to this weekend." Hank got out and slid open the back door. "Which camera do you want first?"

"Film, please."

He looped the digital around his neck and handed her the Minolta.

"Thank you." She kissed his cheek.

A couple stood near the bumper of their car in the lot. "Do you see the mountain goats?" they called out to Clara and Hank.

After a bit of guidance, they located the nearly camouflaged animals lying on boulders about halfway up the ravine.

Clara snapped photos, they thanked the couple for pointing out the wildlife, and then she and Hank worked their way down the dirt path toward the lower lake.

The water was like glass, creating a mirror of the mountains that rose up on each side. She captured the scenery while Hank found a rock to perch on and, with permission, sipped the remainder of her coffee. After ten minutes, she exchanged cameras with Hank. Perhaps the charity would use a few shots for blog content. This was another easy outing that could be included as a free option with the auction vacation package. But even if the photos were just for her, they still filled her soul. She couldn't wait to get home and pull the digitals up on her laptop and lose herself in the darkroom with the film.

She glanced over to see Hank relaxed on his perch, studying the view, and she covertly snapped a few pictures of him.

Photography wasn't his thing, but he was good at creating space for it to be her thing. Clara was starting to understand that seeing the world through a lens was a part of her in a way she hadn't recognized before. She'd always downplayed her photography because she didn't consider herself to have talent. She just enjoyed it and deemed it a creative outlet. But she was also starting to understand that while she'd been so focused on taking care of Hank and the kids and even her community back home, she'd forgotten herself along the way.

Self-care was a foreign language to Clara. But maybe she could try to notice herself a little more. To acknowledge that she existed outside of her family and the farm they'd worked so hard to build that was now floundering.

Maybe she, much like Hank, needed to see her value and worth outside of those things.

She joined Hank on the rock, leaning her head against his

shoulder. "Thank you." She inhaled the aroma of pine mixed with wet earth and melting snow. "I didn't know how much I needed this."

In answer, he pressed a kiss to the crown of her head.

"I miss you. And us. Lately it's just been..." Stress and fear and worry and more stress.

"Me too."

Clara straightened, and Hank reached for her hand. "I'm not sure if you realize this, but—" he focused on their entwined fingers, his mouth arching with his trademark hint of sarcasm "—I'm not handling the farm issues very well."

Clara gave a small pained laugh. "What? No way!"

"What do you think my grandparents would say if they were still alive?" he asked quietly, emotion adding a gravelly pitch to his tone.

"That they love you and they're *so* proud of you." She squeezed the hand laced with hers.

"Everything they built and sacrificed for and I'm just—"

"Doing everything in your power to save it," she finished for him.

A chipmunk scurried in front of them and then darted over the rocks and into the trees.

"This might sound strange, but I'm glad to hear you say you're not handling things well."

Hank snorted. "Why's that?"

"Because you admitting as much means we can face it together. Whatever happens, I choose you. Always have, always will. Now and when the next hardship comes."

Hank remained silent, processing, seemingly unaware that Clara would like to have those same sentiments repeated back to her.

She *knew* it, but it would be nice to hear it. And asking for that assurance felt needy.

"It's supposed to be my job to take care of you," Hank said tenderly.

"No, we're supposed to take care of each other." Yet Clara had been attempting to fix this for Hank. Even to fix Hank.

"I hate that I can't provide for you and the kids. I'm doing my best to enjoy this weekend and focus on Finch's Hope—outside of the strange events, at least—but all I can think about is that even this simple road trip is a strain. And it shouldn't be."

"In terms of not taking care of us, our family is okay, so that's not true. No one is starving. We *are* surviving. And we *are* here for Finch's Hope. We made it happen."

"This might be the last vacation we ever have, so you should enjoy it."

Clara's head shook, her mouth curving. "Stop. You know that's not true. This is just a phase."

"I hope you're right. I can't believe we might lose what's been in my family for generations. I'll say it again since you enjoyed it so much the first time—I don't know how to handle that."

Clara slid her arm through his and leaned her head against his shoulder again. "I didn't say I enjoyed it. I said I appreciated you being honest."

There was definitely a difference.

Chapter Twenty-One

They'd heard nothing from Sergeant Miller since his visit to the house before lunch yesterday.

Nothing from the rehab center in answer to their calls or emails.

And nothing from the lawyer's office.

They were zero for three, and Isley didn't know what to make of any of it. She was trying to follow Trevor's advice and assume all was well until proven otherwise.

Add that in, and she was zero for four.

But she was looking forward to the early afternoon surprise activity she'd planned for herself, Payton, and Clara.

The group had returned from riding electric bikes on the Breck recreational path shortly after eleven this morning. The outing had been easy and relaxing because of the assistance—10/10 recommend versus having to do all the work oneself. Even Hank had managed without issue, giving Isley hope that he was past the motion and altitude sickness. The rental place had been booked solid, but Isley had called and basically begged them to find a bike for Reagan. It had taken a cancellation on someone else's part to make it happen, but thankfully it all worked out.

Isley hadn't relayed her efforts to the group, but she got the impression Reagan had overheard part of her phone call to the bike shop, because she'd been purposeful about thanking Isley for including her.

Sweet girl. She might be going through some struggles, but she was honestly a delight. Even with the side of occasional sass. Which she usually reserved for her parents. Payton had been prone to the same edgy fierceness as a kid. It was one of the things that drew Isley to her that first year of middle school.

While she waited for Payton and Clara to get ready for their afternoon activity—The Husbands had already left for their fly-fishing outing—Isley bustled around upstairs, making sure everything was pristine for tonight's dinner party.

The catering company was providing linens, tables, and chairs along with the food and dishware for tonight, so all Isley and Trevor had to do was provide the space.

It would be a tight fit for the twenty-plus guests, but the hope was that without rain, two tables could be placed on the deck.

The other option for gathering Finch's Hope supporters, survivors, and staff had been renting a space, and that would have cost far more than hiring caterers for The Haven.

It might take money to make money, as the old saying went, but the less expense Finch's Hope incurred in their fundraising attempts, the better.

Isley hoped and prayed that the interviews from tonight's dinner party would create testimonials for Finch's Hope that would assist in propelling the charity back into the black.

She still got red-hot angry when she thought about the charity's bookkeeper pilfering funds.

"I don't like not knowing where we're going," Clara said as she walked upstairs. "How am I supposed to know what to wear?"

Isley had told Clara and Payton to dress casually for the afternoon activity and not to overthink their wardrobe options, because they would likely want to shower after.

Clara wore a pink sleeveless shirt that complemented her olive skin tone and ankle-length cuffed jeans. "You look perfect. Did you pack your swimsuit?"

"Yes, ma'am. You look like you're heading out on a yacht. I'm going back down to change."

Isley had on a matching linen navy tank top and trousers. "No, you're not!" She scooted around the island and grabbed Clara's hand, pulling her back into the kitchen.

"Sit," she directed, and Clara dropped dejectedly onto one of the stools lining the island. "Are you pouting, Clara Weber?"

"Maybe a little. But I'll stop if you tell me where we're going."

"Have you always been this terrible about surprises?"

"Yes, she has," Payton called out as she jogged up the stairs. "Remember when her dad threw her that surprise birthday party our senior year and she ended up crying at it?"

Clara groaned and covered her face with her hands. "I forgot about that. But Hank surprised me this morning and I handled it fine!"

"Didn't he tell you he found a photo spot?"

"Yes."

"How is that a surprise?"

"He didn't say exactly where it was."

Payton snort-laughed. "Nice try. That doesn't count. Sorry for making you guys wait. I was just going over the house rules with Reagan."

"Pay, are you *sure* she shouldn't come with us?" Isley kept her volume low. "I can tell her what we're doing and she can—"

"It doesn't matter what we're doing. She told me she's *done* with adult hangout time." Payton winced. "No offense to you guys. You've been great. She's just super annoyed with me right now. Plus, in Reagan logic, she paid her dues by going on the bike ride with us this morning, and now she deserves downtime by herself before tonight's dinner party."

Isley grinned. "Smart girl."

"Bossy girl," Payton countered. "She also says she's not worried about the break-in or note anymore."

"Good for her. Wish I could say the same."

"Me too," Clara seconded. "Questioning who left it and why they left it and what they want from one or all of us is constantly on my mind."

"Same," Isley and Payton responded simultaneously.

"Do you think you'll be able to enjoy this afternoon?" Isley certainly understood if Payton didn't feel comfortable leaving Reagan at the house. "We can always cancel and stay here."

"No. I mean, yes." Payton's head shook, a smile forming, though her eyes shimmered with a hint of moisture. "Yes, I can and will enjoy whatever you have planned for us. We can't live in fear, can we? I mean, I can because I'm good at it. But I'm really trying not to. Reagan will be fine," Payton reiterated, giving Isley the impression she was convincing herself.

"Rea," Payton called downstairs. "We're leaving."

"Coming." Reagan bounded upstairs. "Isley, can you show me how the alarm works again for while y'all are gone?"

"Of course." So maybe she wasn't quite as relaxed as she'd claimed. Isley explained how she would set it to *stay* so that it wouldn't trigger with Reagan being inside the house, she outlined how to turn it off if she needed to go in the garage or outside, and she showed her the panic button. "But I'm sure you won't need that. And we won't be far away if you need us. Are you certain you don't want to come? I can—"

"No, thank you." Reagan grinned and made a shooing motion that caused Clara and Isley to laugh and her mother to groan.

They loaded into Isley's vehicle. "Now, we relax," she announced as she drove out of the neighborhood. She'd been looking forward to this for weeks and getting to surprise Clara and Payton made it even better.

After the stressful events this weekend, they needed it more than ever.

When they pulled up to the resort valet, Clara leaned between the two front seats. "Is, what are we doing here?"

"You'll see." She handed the key to the valet. "This is the place that donated the stay for the auction vacation package. Isn't it gorgeous? Trev and I used to stay here with Aiden and sometimes one of his friends when we came up to ski."

"It's definitely gorgeous," Clara said, sounding a bit stressed. That would melt away shortly.

Isley led them to the spa area and then checked them in at the desk. Since she'd preregistered and filled out the paperwork ahead of time, they were whisked into the dressing room within seconds of their arrival.

"It smells amazing in here." Payton inhaled. "Like cucumber and mint and lack of teenager. Massages are a great idea, Is. Thank you for planning this."

"I'm so excited about it. And when I scheduled them, I didn't even know how much we would *need* it. Our massages aren't for a little while, but we can take advantage of the amenities. There's a cold plunge, sauna, steam room, hot tub."

"I'm game to start in the hot tub." Payton rotated her shoulders. "I can feel the Reagan stress slipping away already."

"Exactly what I was hoping for." Now Isley just needed

to have the same happen with her list of stresses... Was her son okay? Did Trevor's brother know about her conversation with Bianca and how she'd put their family at risk, specifically going against her husband's wishes? Isley loathed herself for being so weak. For reaching out to Bianca and then burying the debacle as if it never happened. When she contemplated admitting her mistake to Trevor, she felt feverish and shaky and tormented. Especially since Bianca had left the conversation upset. And then followed up with a text asking Isley not to contact her again.

Or maybe the note was addressing the night of Cece's death. Or something else entirely not on their radar! How were they supposed to know for certain what it was about? And when did the threat of someone else revealing the truth come to fruition? Was the deadline this weekend?

If so, they were running out of time.

Clara was frozen. Numb. And unsure how to navigate this bump in the road.

Massages did sound wonderful. And expensive. Especially at a resort like this. She understood why Isley wanted to patronize the place that had donated the stay for the vacation package, but what was Clara supposed to *do*?

Payton rifled through her bag and pulled out her swimsuit while Clara floundered.

She should leave.

But she didn't want to ruin this for her friends.

And if Clara backed out right now, they would protest or try to leave with her.

Dutifully, she changed into her swimsuit and followed Isley and Payton into the grotto with its soothing gray stone walls and dim lights and eucalyptus scent.

Everything in the gorgeous welcoming space encouraged

Clara to release the tentacles slithering from her shoulder blades to her neck.

But she couldn't give in.

All she could think about was the cost.

The three of them entered the fiery water of the hot tub.

"There's also a rejuvenation room." Isley and Payton sat on the ledge seat that lined a majority of the rectangular stone spa, and Clara perched on the same across from them. "It has a waterfall and lounge chairs and tea. If we don't have time before massages to use everything, maybe we can stay after. Caterers will be at the house at four to prep for guests at six. But since we're not setting up ourselves—" Isley waved her hands in celebration "—we don't *have* to be back until we need to let them in."

Clara closed her eyes, listening faintly as Payton and Isley discussed the spa and the resort and the last time they'd had massages.

It had been over a decade for Clara, not that she planned to admit it.

Had Isley paid when they walked in? Or would they do that on the way out?

Or...could this be one of the covered auction items and Clara just hadn't heard about it?

Her eyes popped open. "Is, are massages part of the auction package too?"

"No, just the resort stay."

Clara swallowed hard. "Gotcha."

"Make sure you tell us what we owe you for all the activities before we leave this weekend." Payton lifted her hair from her neck and dipped farther into the water. "It would be just like you to accidentally not relay that information."

Wait. What? Clara's mouth dried out instantly.

"I don't know what you're talking about." Isley studied her ombre manicured fingernails, feigning innocence.

Me either! Clara barely resisted shrieking.

Isley looked up, read Payton's menacing eyebrow lift, and laughed. "I'm kidding! I know we said we'd split the cost. I promise to honor that."

Clara's stomach rolled and pitched. Split the cost of what exactly?

Her breathing shallowed and her chest ached as realization struck. Hank had been right. Their group activities for this weekend *weren't* donated. They must be covering the cost of those themselves.

But *why, why, why* had Clara thought otherwise?

Had she misread a conversation? Had she just assumed?

"When did we talk about that again?" Clara kept the emotion from her voice with sheer determination. "We communicated so much about this weekend I can hardly remember."

"I think it was the first day we were texting about the trip. Right, Is?"

"Sounds right," Isley said, eyes closed, head tipped back against the edge of the hot tub.

That had been the day Hank met with the bank and they'd refused to refinance the terms of their loan.

There'd been so many texts flying back and forth...and so much stress and panic within the walls of their home. Clara must have missed that extremely important detail somehow.

And she'd wanted to assume the auction activities were covered because if they weren't...that meant she and Hank shouldn't be here.

And she'd been *so* desperate not to miss out.

"Clara?" Isley maneuvered across the hot tub and perched on the ledge seat next to her. "Are you okay?"

Payton's eyes crinkled with concern, and she moved to Clara's other side.

"I'm fine. Why are you both looking at me like that?"

"Because you're crying," Payton supplied gently.

"No, I'm not. I was probably just sweating." Clara had never been the type of girl who glistened. When she overheated, her body had something to say about it.

She swiped her cheeks to prove her point and came away with more moisture than expected. She blinked and felt a new rush cascade.

She *was* crying. She just hadn't been paying attention to herself. Which appeared to be a theme with her.

"Sorry." She scrubbed her cheeks again, begging her brain to shut down the waterworks.

"What is it? What's going on?" Isley's empathetic tone appeared to be Clara's undoing, because the dam holding back the truth broke into a million little pieces.

"I can't afford this, Is. I'm going to get out and see if they can cancel my massage. I'll sit outside and read a book on my phone while I wait for you girls. I don't mind. I promise," she rushed to assure them. "I would have said something right away but I didn't want to disrupt your chance to get massages."

"Oh, Clara, I don't want anything for this. I was excited to gift this afternoon to you and Payton. But I am so sorry for not being more considerate and saying something earlier. You mentioned that money was tight because of Ava's college. I should have—"

"We're not having money issues because of Ava's college. I mean, yes, we are trying to help her, but the real issue is that we might lose the farm."

Isley's eyes widened. *"What?"*

"There was a drought and then after, our attempts to improve things backfired. We haven't been able to recover from the tailspin. I think that's part of why Hank is acting and feeling like he is. Altitude yes, but also so much stress."

Clara sniffled and continued, "I'm sorry for not saying something sooner. You both know I'm an open book. But then we got here and Hank didn't say *anything* when Liam asked him about the farm." Her husband might not be one to disclose their problems, but she was. She appreciated and craved her friends' support. "That was the perfect opportunity to be open and share the burden with people we trust. And then, I missed the fact that we're splitting the activities cost for the weekend! Somehow, I thought those were also donated. I feel so foolish. That was the day Hank met with the bank, and I was distracted. Is, I *will* pay our part. I just might need a little time to do it."

"I couldn't care less about that." Isley slid fingertips under her lashes where sympathy tears had surfaced. "You're not paying for anything. Payton will cover your end."

It took a moment for the well-timed sarcastic comment to register, and then Clara gave a burst of laughter.

"Sure, why not?" Payton grinned. "I'm getting divorced anyway, so I'll be making financial decisions myself."

"What?" The smile fell from Clara's face.

Isley's jaw slacked. "Pay? Tell me you're just continuing this humor shtick we have going."

"I wish." Payton swallowed, her appearance stricken as the bomb she'd just dropped registered with all of them. "About six months ago, Liam announced that he thinks we should divorce and operate as friends and co-parents. He says that things changed between us, even though he's terrible at explaining *what* changed. I'm so confused by him right now."

"He doesn't have a reason?"

"He does, but it's like listening to someone talk in circles. Something is different but he can't explain what." Her breath rushed out. "But the gist is... I'm afraid he's done when I'm not."

Isley scooted so that she was floating in the water directly in front of Payton. "How could he? Doesn't he realize there isn't anything worse he could do to you?"

Precisely what Clara had been thinking.

Payton had grown up with so many wounds. And she'd craved affection from her parents when what she'd received instead was an obligatory upbringing.

For Liam to disregard that, for him not to give her the full love and acceptance and place in his world that he'd once vowed... Clara couldn't fathom the way that was destroying her friend. For the second time in her life.

"And you're here with him!" Isley recoiled. "No wonder you said he'd sleep on the couch."

"I know!" Payton lamented. "I thought maybe this weekend would wake him up. Make him realize what he was losing. But if anything, he seems more content with his decision than ever. Like us being able to travel together with Reagan proves his point that we can operate as a team even if we're divorced."

"This is a lot." Isley stood. "I think I should cancel our massages so we can head back to the house and process some of this before tonight. Are you good with that?" She directed her question to Payton since Clara had already attempted as much.

Payton nodded. "Now that I've spilled all, a massage would be a waste on me. I'm too upset."

"But if you cancel, they'll charge you." Clara couldn't help but focus on the money.

"They're not going to charge me." Isley flashed a confident look in their direction as she waded out of the hot tub. "I'll work it out. After you two change, meet me in the lobby."

Despite the seriousness of the conversation they'd just started,

Clara and Payton exchanged matching grins and headshakes after Isley's exit.

"She's the only person on earth who can figure out how to cancel a massage minutes before it's supposed to happen and not get charged."

"Right?" Payton laughed. "It's a skill."

A skill Clara wished she had.

Maybe if Clara had some of Isley's moxie and fierce determination, then she could have helped dig her family out of their current predicament.

Clara and Payton changed back into their clothes and waited for Isley in the lobby. After about ten minutes, she appeared looking fresh and perfectly put together.

"All set!" She breezed by with a winning smile that told them her endeavors had been successful.

"But how—?" Clara expected as much but was still shocked.

Payton's laughter was *so* good to hear. Whatever was happening in her friend's world and marriage, they would trudge through it with her *and* come out on the other side.

It was what they did. And it was what they would have done for Cece if they'd understood the depths of what she was going through.

Chapter Twenty-Two

While the tension pulsating through Payton's body told her she could have used a massage, she was grateful they'd ditched the spa and were on their way back to the house.

Ever since she'd admitted Liam's plan to her friends, she'd been shaking. Not enough for them to notice—she hoped—but enough that *she* was aware that her body wasn't listening to her pleas for it to calm down.

Payton could finally acknowledge that The Plan and everything that would snowball after it was monumental. She'd tried to tell herself it wasn't. She'd tried to take the scientific, logical approach. She'd even tried to convince herself to get behind it.

None of that had worked.

And her friends' responses in that grotto had confirmed everything that Payton had been thinking and feeling. In just a few moments, they'd confirmed *her*.

Payton was equal parts terrified to have admitted what was happening in her life and relieved to share the heavy burden of it with two friends who loved her like Isley and Clara.

Who knew how deep her wounds stretched.

Why hadn't she or Clara spilled their issues before now?

For Payton, that answer probably had something to do with pride—she and Liam had always been so purposeful in their marriage. She'd thought they were above divorce. That the decisions they made and the safeguards they'd put into place would protect them. But they'd shattered like New Orleans' seawalls during Katrina, and Payton hadn't even seen the waters coming.

And then of course there'd been that pesky little thing called denial.

After all, she'd come on this trip with the hidden hope that it would change Liam's mind.

As for Clara, she'd obviously kept the farm issues quiet because Hank didn't want to discuss them. Which Payton wholeheartedly understood. She knew how much Hank loved his family's land and how tirelessly he worked to ensure the farm's success. Certainly this hardship would be debilitating to him.

Isley pulled into the garage, and the three of them exited the vehicle. The door from the garage into the house was still locked, so Isley used her key to gain access. Once inside, she disarmed the alarm.

Payton was about to call out to Reagan when she heard her daughter's voice travel up the stairs.

Who was she talking to? Maybe a friend over FaceTime.

A male voice sounded, and every muscle in Payton froze. Usually Reagan used her AirPods on FaceTime, but maybe she'd decided not to since she was the only one home.

Laughter trickled up the stairs, and Payton followed the sound, leaving Clara and Isley in the kitchen.

When she reached the bottom step, it took her a few seconds to assess the scene in front of her.

Reagan was on the couch, and a teenage boy filled the spot

next to her. Fear roared through Payton's body. Despite the alarm causing her heart to stampede in her chest, Payton registered that the two of them were playing a video game together—and laughing—so the kid wasn't an intruder who'd broken into the house.

But then who was he? And why was he here?

"Reagan?" All Payton managed to do was squeak out her daughter's name while her brain jumbled any chance of relaying her other questions.

Reagan leaped off the sofa and swiveled to face Payton in one combined movement, pupils wide, ligaments strained. "Mom, you freaked me out!"

"Same," Payton replied, her voice deadly calm.

The teenage boy twisted in Payton's direction, though his expression carried more concern than outright panic.

It was the kid from the movie theater parking lot.

Had Reagan met him there or something? Payton was so, *so* confused.

"Everything okay down there?" Isley called from the top of the stairs, checking in while still giving them privacy.

Everyone is alive at the moment. "Yes, we're okay," Payton called up. "Thank you!"

Normally Payton didn't find herself prone to anger.

Logic? Yes.

Willing to discuss things in a calm manner? Always.

But right now she'd morphed into an unrecognizable version of herself.

The shaking that had begun after she'd confessed the status of her marriage to her friends intensified until she was forced to brace her hands on the table flanking the sofa. Her neck careened forward as she fought for a solid breath.

"*Mom?* Are you okay?"

"No, I'm not."

The fright she'd experienced upon entering the basement was morphing into white-hot anger.

Payton felt so foolish. She'd been duped by her teenage daughter, and she should have known better, because she'd *been* Reagan as a teenager.

But things were supposed to be different with them. Reagan was supposed to trust her because Payton had raised her daughter in a manner one hundred and eighty degrees different than the way she'd been raised.

Was Payton more upset that she'd been conned by her daughter or that she'd initially feared for Reagan's safety?

Yes.

"I'm sorry." Reagan raised her palms in a defensive gesture. "I can explain."

"Sit." Payton barked out the command. "Just sit down. I can't think right now."

Reagan's teeth pressed into her lip, but she plopped onto the couch. "Just don't freak out, okay?"

"Too late." Payton heard the mania in her tone and inhaled unsteadily in an attempt to corral it.

She wavered between kicking the boy from the theater out or interrogating him, quickly settling on door number two.

"Who are you," she asked, "and why are you here?"

To his credit, he hadn't moved from his spot on the couch or tried to speak yet. *Smart kid.* Payton would let him live another minute for that.

"*Mom!* Don't be rude!"

Payton lifted a finger toward Reagan in a silencing motion, waiting for their mystery guest to answer.

"I'm Zion. Sorry that I'm here." The end of his statement ramped up an octave as if it was a question. As if he was trying to figure out what to say to placate Payton.

Too bad she didn't know the answer to that herself.

Where had Payton heard that name before? She filtered backward, landing at the moment she'd dropped Reagan at the grocery store to pick up period supplies and a text from Zion had popped up on her phone screen.

Supplies that Payton had seen no sign of in the bathroom, she now realized.

Why would Reagan make up getting her period? What else was her daughter hiding? And why?

"How do you two know each other? Do you live here?" Before anyone could answer those questions, Payton refocused on Reagan. "And *what* in the world were you thinking letting a boy into the house?" Because it definitely appeared he hadn't forced his way inside. "It was just broken into the other night!"

"Mom, chill. Calm down and I will answer all of your questions."

"I am not planning to employ either of those options right now."

Reagan had the audacity to risk her very life with an eye roll, and Payton morphed into a cartoon character with fire shooting out the top of her skull.

"I need you to leave," she said to Zion. "I need to speak with my daughter right now."

"Yes, ma'am." He popped up from the couch. "Sorry." He winced in Reagan's direction. "Let me know if I can help."

He strode past Payton, expression apologetic and a little fearful—rightfully so—then up the stairs. Payton listened for the sound of the front door opening and closing. Once it did, the rigid tendons in her neck released a smidgeon.

"Mom, that was dramatic. You didn't have to kick him out." Reagan sounded like an exasperated parent dealing with a miscreant teenager.

"You're right. I didn't have to. But I did. Because I don't

know who he is or what he's doing here." Payton crossed her arms. "Now start explaining."

"Okay, give me a sec."

"Nope. No seconds. You're the one claiming to have a perfectly good explanation for all this. So, let's hear it."

"Can you at least come sit down? You're kind of scaring me right now."

"Good." Payton was delighted to cause fear in her daughter, because her daughter had certainly invoked plenty of the same in her.

Even so, Payton acquiesced, aware that calming down enough to have a conversation with Reagan was more important than the righteous anger coursing through her.

Payton sat on the other end of the sofa, legs at a ninety-degree angle, back straight and not touching the cushions.

Reagan popped up from the couch and began to pace in front of it. "Zion is cousins with Killian."

"Killian from Dallas? From our neighborhood?"

"Yes."

"Why do these children have such unique names?"

"Really? That's such a mom thing to say."

They *did* have unusual names. "So, you've met him in Dallas? At Killian's house? Why wouldn't you tell me that? What am I missing here?"

"I didn't meet him in Dallas. When you started talking about making me go on this trip, I was upset." Shocking. Really, though, Payton didn't blame her. It probably hadn't been her best decision. "I told Killian and she mentioned her cousin lives in Breck. She FaceTimed with both of us and then we started snapchatting and texting and stuff after that."

"So you've been communicating with him for weeks?"

"Yeah. He's actually so nice, Mom."

Payton really didn't want to hear it. Because if that was the case, why wouldn't Reagan have mentioned him? Why did everything have to be secretive?

"Wait." Payton felt as if a wall was slowly crashing down on her, each brick delivering a new blow. "This is what's been going on with the GPS tracking on your phone, isn't it? You turned it off because you've been, what, meeting up with him?" Reagan gave a succinct nod. "The sailing night too? You were with him at the theater even though you made me feel irrational for thinking that?"

Reagan swallowed. "Yes."

"So, you going on the bike ride this morning in order to get to stay home this afternoon was a ploy to see him?"

"It wasn't a ploy."

To Payton, it appeared to be the definition of that.

She'd thought Reagan joining them on the mine tour and bike ride hadn't just been about not being at the house alone after the break-in. That maybe she'd been letting them in the tiniest bit. Now, that theory had been disproven.

And honestly? That betrayal stung.

"I just don't get why you wouldn't tell me."

"I didn't think you would understand or let me see him."

Probably correct on the second part. "When else *have* you seen him?"

"After the hike."

The ankle drama made sense now. Reagan had been trying to get back to town to meet up with Zion. "I'll take more details for a thousand."

"He met me at the ice-cream shop and then we walked around town."

That's why Reagan had attempted to convince them to return to the hike! "On your injured ankle," Payton filled in dryly.

"I didn't fake that," Reagan protested. "It really did hurt at first."

Payton felt so deceived by the rest of it. She'd had no idea what her daughter was up to. Absolutely none.

"Weren't you afraid that we would run into you?"

Reagan cringed. "I could see where you and Dad were from the tracking app."

Of course. Because they hadn't turned theirs off. "And you just took the risk with the rest of the group."

She nodded.

"What else? When else? This is the time to tell me. Wait, is this why you asked me to stop at the grocery store after the movie? Did you really get your period or were you meeting up with him at the store or something?"

"That wasn't about Zion, but I *was* trying to buy time."

"Why?"

"Because..." She exhaled long and slow. "Because Zion and I were at the house that night for a couple minutes. It was barely any time," she rushed to explain. "I was just grabbing a sweatshirt, but when Dad mentioned the surveillance video, I panicked because I thought Sergeant Miller would know I was here. So, I asked you to stop at the store, hoping the police would leave before we got back."

"You were at the house the night someone broke in and left the note? When? What time?" Payton slapped a hand against her chest as terror consumed her. What if Reagan had come across the intruder? What if he'd caused her harm? Payton suddenly found herself standing even though she had no recollection of the movement.

"Right when Hank got back. We didn't notice him, but he saw us driving away from the house." Reagan dropped dejectedly to the couch. "He wasn't sure it was me until he talked to me on the hike the next morning. I begged him not to tell you guys. I said I would tell you myself."

"I *knew* that was a strange conversation between you two on the hike. It's not like you and Hank have so much in common that you'd be chatting it up on the trail. I told your dad that and he thought I was overreacting."

"Shocking."

"What does that mean?"

"I don't get how you can just ignore stuff."

"What am I ignoring?" What was Reagan referring to? What was Payton missing yet again?

"Nothing." Reagan's head shook.

"So, after you promised Hank you would tell us, why didn't you? How could you keep that from us *and* the police?"

She bit her lip. "I knew how mad you'd be. Especially with the break-in."

Correct.

"And once we learned the break-in had been *after* Hank returned, I knew we weren't here at the time."

"Thank God for that mercy."

"And then the video surveillance became a nonissue. So I didn't think the police necessarily needed to know."

"Or your parents."

Her shoulders lifted in a "what can I say" gesture. "I definitely wasn't *excited* to tell you."

"I can't believe Hank didn't say anything. Especially with the break-in."

But then, it was easy for Payton to judge. What would she have done in the same situation if it had been her and Ava? Not that Ava would sneak around the way Reagan had been.

After all, she was Clara's daughter. And similarly, Reagan appeared to be following in Payton's footsteps.

"It's not his fault. I literally pleaded with him not to say anything. And this morning on the bike ride, he told me that if I didn't tell you before the dinner party tonight, he would."

Compassion for Hank surfaced. No doubt he'd tried his best to navigate a no-win scenario.

"You're right. It is your fault, not his."

"This is why I can't talk to you! You're so judgmental."

Reagan's accusation was a punch to Payton's jugular. She'd done everything possible to be the antonym of that word with Reagan.

"I want to understand what happened every minute of Thursday night. Talk me through it."

"I met up with Zion in town after you guys dropped me off. We hung out for a bit but then I was cold so we swung back here to grab my sweatshirt. He stayed in the car. He didn't come inside the house. I just ran in, grabbed it, and left."

"Then what happened?"

"Then we went to the movie."

"So this kid who we don't even know was driving you around." Payton hated the idea of Reagan being in a vehicle with a teenage boy in general, let alone one they didn't know anything about. Was he a safe driver? Was he even allowed to have passengers in his car? "Exactly how old is he? And was that his car parked across the street when we got back this afternoon?" Payton had assumed someone was visiting the neighbors.

"Yes, that was his car." Reagan pulled a pillow onto her lap. "Sixteen. He's not even a full year older than me."

That difference felt vast to Payton. Especially when she was in "overprotective mama bear" mode.

"So, after you left the house you went straight to the theater? Any pit stops?"

"No pit stops. Just the theater and then you picked me up after. I was exactly where I told you I was."

Payton snorted. "Well, good job getting that one portion of your weekend correct!"

"Sarcasm doesn't look good on you, Mother."

"Lying doesn't look good on *you*, Reagan." Payton felt the fight slipping from her, leaving her weary down to the marrow of her bones. All she wanted to do at this point was cry. "I don't even know what to say to you right now so..." Her arms rose and then dropped to her sides. "I'm going to walk away so that I can calm down."

"What? I need to know what you're going to do to me."

Do to her. Like Payton was such a vicious dictator. Like she hadn't told Reagan *so many times* that she could come to her with *anything*. Anything! And instead she'd chosen to hide so much.

"I need time to process. That's why we're going to discuss this later. But I want to know where you are at all times. Don't step foot outside the house without notifying me."

Reagan huffed. "So I'm basically in prison?"

"You were almost at the house when someone broke in, Rea. That is *all* I can think about right now. What if you'd been injured?" Or worse?

"If I hadn't convinced you to let me walk around town, I *would* have been at the house that night during the break-in. That's where *you* wanted me to be."

It was true. Apparently there was no protecting her. And no right decisions.

"I'm extremely grateful you weren't here." Payton's voice wobbled with emotion. "But I'm also not going to celebrate that you were meeting up with a boy who we don't know in a town that we don't know. So, like I said, I'm going to walk away right now. We'll talk later when Dad gets back."

"But that could be hours!"

"Did you have some fantastic plans for this afternoon?"

Reagan's vision cast to the floor. "No."

"That's right. I ruined your plans, didn't I?" Payton paused at the bottom of the stairs. "Oh, and turn your phone tracking back on. Enough pretending it's not working when you're the one who flipped a switch."

And then Payton strode up the stairs as if she was confident and poised to take on her teenage daughter fearlessly when in truth, she was anything but.

Chapter Twenty-Three

Payton joined Isley and Clara on the deck, her body hunched over as if the last ten minutes had added twenty years to her frame. She shuffled to the corner of the outdoor L sofa and nearly fell onto it, grabbing a pillow and clutching it against her chest.

"Tell me I wasn't like that as a teenager."

They answered in unison. "You weren't like that as a teenager."

Payton threw the pillow at them, and it bounced off Isley's leg and crashed to the deck.

She picked it up with a laugh and tossed it back to Payton.

Isley and Clara had booked it onto the deck in an attempt to give Payton space once they'd pieced together that Reagan had someone in the basement with her and that everyone was safe. But of course Isley was curious as to what happened. And pathetically, it made her feel better that she wasn't the only parent flabbergasted by their child's choices.

"We were out here when he left," Clara said. "He looked like a pup with his tail between his legs. I do think he felt bad."

"Good." Payton produced a millisecond smile.

"Do you want to talk about it?" Isley tucked her legs underneath her on the couch.

"Nope. I think I need a minute."

"You can have all the minutes." Clara patted Payton's leg.

"Tell us what's happening with the farm, Clara." Isley had waited for Payton to join them before broaching the conversation.

"There's not much to it. Obviously Hank's unwilling to discuss it. But as you know, I'm a verbal processor."

"Which is why you're going first." Payton nudged her, a small grin sprouting. It appeared as if she was slowly blooming back to life after whatever had just transpired in the basement.

"If people don't talk about stuff—" Clara propped her feet on the outdoor coffee table "—how do they deal with anything?"

"We don't," Payton quipped.

Isley laughed. "Or I make Trev listen to whatever I'm sorting out, and about halfway through he gets a glazed look and it's obvious he's no longer hearing me."

"Hank does the same thing."

"And The Husband gunning for a break-up is typically a perfect conversationalist. Go figure." Payton made a shooing motion when she realized the attention had landed on her. "Keep going."

"After the drought, the additional income streams we added stretched us too thin. Failing at something is hard enough. But the pressure of the farm being in Hank's family for generations complicates everything." Her expression pinched. "I'm worried about him."

"I would be too," Isley agreed. "He definitely hasn't been himself this weekend."

"I'm sorry, Clara." Payton's brow furrowed. "That's a lot to carry."

"But it's smaller than so many other people's problems. We'll be okay no matter what happens. I just need Hank to believe the same." Clara's vision swung to Isley. "I'm sorry I was an idiot about the money for this weekend. I promise I'll figure it out."

"Please don't. I expect nothing. Which probably doesn't help, but it's the truth. And like I said, in so many ways, I planned this weekend selfishly. All we did this spring was deal with Aiden's arrest. I was desperate for a distraction from worrying about him and from the judgment we received. Not that Aiden didn't do anything wrong. He did. Absolutely." Isley was thankful every single day that Freya had lived. And not just because it would have majorly changed Aiden's punishment. But because she was a mother, and the loss of that young girl would have shattered all of them.

"It's not like Aiden and his friend had intended to hurt that poor girl. He made a stupid decision, and the results were really awful." Clara cringed. "Sorry for using the S word."

Isley laughed. Clara's household had been big on word choice, and there'd been many off-limits. "He did make a stupid decision. And that's what I keep coming back to. He made an awful mistake that could have had catastrophic consequences but thankfully, gratefully, did not. Sadly, substance abuse is an issue that so many kids are struggling with these days. It's heartbreaking."

"It is," Payton affirmed. "Reagan's school is constantly talking about this stuff."

"That's the worst part. We did too. And he always assured us that he would never."

"I can't believe you were dealing with this all spring," Clara said sorrowfully.

"Sometimes you just...hunker down," Payton supplied. "Fight the fight in front of you. I get it."

"Yes. Exactly." There hadn't been time to analyze or reach out to her friends. Isley had been in survival mode.

"True. I suppose Hank and I have been doing the same with the farm."

They'd all been battling their individual troubles...and now, a new one had been laid on their kitchen island. A threat that could refer to past or present, one or all of them *and* didn't give a definite deadline as to when someone would reveal the truth.

And a second had been delivered to Belinda's doorstep in the form of unmarked photos that were possibly helpful, possibly creepy.

And a third had arrived in the form of her possibly missing, possibly at rehab son.

"Remember how I told you girls that we hadn't heard from Aiden at rehab recently?"

They nodded.

"After the break-in, I kept wondering, could it have something to do with him? What if he left rehab and was trying to get into the house to stay here or something? So Trev and I reached out to the rehab facility and Aiden's lawyer just to confirm he's still there. But no one has gotten back to us. I'm panicking a bit."

"Wouldn't they have to tell you if he'd left?" Clara questioned.

"I think so, but because he's nineteen, I'm not entirely sure." Isley didn't mention the phone call from Daria, because it felt so convoluted.

"I'm sure he's still there," Payton said with confidence. "The events of this weekend are probably making everything feel worse. Bigger. Besides, what would the note have to do with him?"

"Nothing that I can think of." That was Isley's saving grace in all of this.

"Payton's right. I'm sure he's still there."

Isley wished she could say the same.

This weekend was supposed to be a break *for* them. Instead Isley worried it could break them.

"Pay, are you ready to talk? Or do you still need more time?"

Payton winced at Clara's question. "About which thing? My rebellious teenage daughter or my mess of a marriage?"

"Um...either?"

Payton would start with the subject currently at the forefront of her mind thanks to Reagan's antics today. "Isley, I'm sorry that Reagan invited someone into your home without permission. That was incredibly disrespectful of her."

Isley waved a dismissive hand. "I'm just glad she's okay. But how does she know the boy who was here?"

Payton outlined the connection to Killian. "I just found that out from Reagan. Along with the fact that she and Zion were at the house the night of the break-in. She said Hank saw them driving away."

"What?" Clara sat up ramrod straight. "Hank saw Reagan that night and didn't say anything?"

"He wasn't confident it was her until he talked to her on the hike the next day. And then Reagan begged him not to say anything, claiming she'd tell us. Sounds like Hank gave her an ultimatum on the bike ride this morning that if she didn't do it by tonight, he would."

"My husband knew all of that?" Clara's back collided with the couch. "I'm in shock. I had no idea."

"Of course you didn't. You would have spilled right away."

The current situation mirrored the past in so many ways. After Cece passed, the girls had been messes and desperate to absolve their guilt. They should have gone to an adult with their problems—just like Payton wished Reagan would have done this weekend and in the last year. But their options had been slim. Payton's parents weren't trustworthy allies. Isley's mother either. And Clara's dad, although approachable, had been focused on raising her younger brothers. Ironically, the person they would have gone to about it all had been Belinda Finch.

But they'd been too petrified to do that.

"I am so sorry. I can't even believe that Hank—"

"Did his best. It's easy to judge when you're not the one forced to make a fraught in-the-moment decision. Which we all know from firsthand experience. Evidently, Reagan and Zion have been hanging out all weekend."

Isley flinched, her head bowing.

"Did you know, Is?"

"No. But I saw a girl in Breckenridge after the hike who looked like Reagan. She was with a boy and wearing a different sweatshirt, so I thought it couldn't be her."

"Maybe she was wearing his sweatshirt. She did say she walked around town with him yesterday." How had Payton missed so much? "I can't even talk about her stuff right now because I haven't processed." She flashed a sad grin at Clara. "And I have to do some of that on my own. And on the other subject... Liam thinks we make a 'great team.'" Payton used air quotes. "And that we should separate but keep raising Reagan and doing life together. Family dinners. Holidays. School and equestrian events."

Clara snorted. "What does that even mean? Does he have any idea what he's doing? Is he *stupid*?"

The Clara rampage and another use of the S word eked a laugh out of Payton despite the awful conversation. "I should never have married him." Her gut dropped to her toes. "I should have known—"

"Stop," Isley said with conviction. "You've been together almost seventeen years. This doesn't negate that."

"I'm so angry." Clara's eyes sparked with unshed tears.

Same. Though Payton hadn't allowed herself to engage with that emotion until this weekend. "Listening to your responses makes me realize how far down the rabbit hole I've gone with this. Of trying to assume the best about him and this situation. Trying to get on board even when I didn't want to. Reagan doesn't know what's going on." Though her comment downstairs did raise suspicions.

"I'm starting to think Liam just wants out and this is his way of doing it. The illusion of friendship. The illusion that we can dissolve our marriage amicably. But maybe he's right. Because I'm so logical that what did I do when he brought it up? Did I question him? Did I yell at him? Did I ask him if he was cheating on me? No. I just went along with it because I thought he must be seeing something that I wasn't. But this weekend..." Payton swallowed, fighting to speak over the lump in her throat. "It's like you girls have given me back myself. That intuition I taught Reagan to trust—I stopped using mine. Maybe because when I did, it caused pain. But I can't stay in denial. It's not working to live that way. Thanks for making me feel like I'm not being irrational."

"You're definitely not." Isley frowned. "Every question you have deserves an answer."

Payton wasn't sure she was going to get any of those. At least, not ones that made sense.

"We're home!" Trevor's voice rang out from inside the house.

The Husbands were back already? And also, how much longer would that title fit?

"Terrible timing." Clara winced. "We're not done yet."

And now they had to pivot from revelations to a dinner party to support Finch's Hope. How were they supposed to do that? This weekend had raised so many questions for Payton and left her utterly confused. This whole time she'd been shoving down and burying the idea that the break-in and note could have anything to do with her and Liam.

But the more their marriage dissolved, the more her wariness grew.

"Nothing leaves this deck, right?" Clara spoke softly and quickly. "Just because I need to talk about it doesn't mean Hank does."

"Of course," Payton assured her. "Same for me."

"Agreed," Isley added. "Nothing we discuss ever leaves *us*."

Again, the past and present collided. They were certainly good at keeping each other's secrets. They'd been doing it a long time.

Liam poked his head outside. "How's it going?"

A pain started under Payton's ribs and radiated through her chest. The idea of her world imploding was debilitating. She was more distant from Reagan than ever. The end of her marriage appeared to be nipping at her heels. She'd never felt more undone. More lost.

And now she had to figure out how to co-parent her teenage daughter with the man who wanted out of the vows they'd made nearly seventeen years ago.

"I need to talk to you about Rea. Walk?"

"Is it urgent? We were all gunning for lazy naps before the dinner party tonight."

"Unfortunately, yes." And even if it wasn't to him—even if he would consider Reagan's antics of the last few days typical teenage stuff—the situation felt enormous and overwhelming to Payton. Because she couldn't lose Liam *and* Reagan. And her daughter not talking to her about *anything* felt like the definition of that.

Chapter Twenty-Four

Clara had been waiting impatiently to speak to Hank ever since The Husbands had returned from fishing.

But the minute she'd gotten him alone in their room, he'd raised a palm and rubbed his other hand over his eyes.

"I need to rest for a few, okay?" He'd dropped on top of the bedspread—shoes off, fishing clothes on, palm centered over his heart—and had been snoring ever since.

The dinner party started in an hour and a half. From her perch on the bed next to him, Clara listened to the scrapes and thumps of the caterers setting up one floor above them.

She'd attempted to nap herself, but after today's revelations, she'd been unable to quiet her mind. Especially since all she wanted to do was confront Hank about the night he'd returned to the house early from sailing and spotted Reagan with Zion.

Clara had switched from attempting to nap to reading, which had also failed. And then she'd texted with Ava a bit. When she'd reached out to her younger children, Talia was the one who'd responded from her grandmother's phone. The boys had phones of their own but couldn't answer her simple text.

Which was actually a good sign because it meant they were okay. When they needed something, they blew up Clara's phone with their requests.

Apparently the boys, much like their father, were not in a conversational mood.

Clara slid quietly from the bed so as not to wake Hank and moved into the attached bathroom. Since she couldn't seem to concentrate on anything else, she would get ready.

She showered and then peeked in on Hank.

Still sleeping.

She shut the bathroom door a little louder than necessary, then dried and styled her hair, certain that noise, at least, would rouse Hank.

Not that she did it for that reason.

Another peek into the room.

No change. She sighed loudly and plugged in her curling iron, then added eyeliner, eyeshadow, lip color, and a layer of foundation and blush, because Ava had told her blush was back in. If Clara wasn't so desperate to talk to Hank, she would have asked Isley to do her makeup. She did that whole contouring thing like a pro.

Once the iron was hot, she added loose waves to her hair, spritzing with hair spray to hold everything in place.

Clara wouldn't be surprised if the curls relaxed back to her usual straight locks within the hour. But still, pampering herself felt nice. As did having the bathroom to herself.

She finished and reentered the bedroom to find Hank in the exact same position. And discovered that her patience had run out.

"Don't you want to shower before dinner tonight?"

His eyes popped open. "What?" He raked his hands over his face.

"You need to get ready at some point, right?"

Granted, he was the epitome of those Instagram reels about husbands who hopped in the shower as their wife was ready to walk out the door and still was somehow always ready on time.

"Yeah. Sure."

Yeah, sure? That didn't exactly sound like a raving endorsement. Hank didn't move from his prone position on the bedspread.

"How are you feeling? Did the rest help?"

He sat up, propping a pillow between his back and the headboard. "Still waking up but pretty good. Although, it was a little hard to fall asleep with you seething at me."

Really? He'd been out in less than ten seconds according to her calculations. "I wasn't seething." Except that description wasn't far off.

"What's the deal? I thought you girls had a relaxing afternoon?"

"We did. Sort of." Basically they'd tried to support Payton after the Reagan incident. And each other. "Hank, how did you not tell any of us about Reagan being at the house when you got back from sailing? You lied to the police!"

He groaned and swung his legs over the side of the bed. "I didn't *lie* to the police. The car she was in was pulling away as I got here. I wasn't sure it was her until I talked to her on the hike the next morning. And I wasn't about to announce something like that unless I was confident. Besides, Reagan being at the house didn't have anything to do with the note. Bringing it up to the police felt unnecessary. But I have been trying to get her to tell her parents what happened since then. Especially since she promised she would."

"But you didn't even tell *me*." Clara recognized the hurt in her voice.

"Because it would have put you in a weird position. I knew you wouldn't be able to keep something like that from Payton. And I was trying to give Reagan a chance to do what she said she would. I kept thinking if it was Ava—"

"You would want someone to tell you!"

"I'd want Ava to step up and do the right thing on her own. It was a mess, Clara. I did my best."

Clara exhaled with agitation and hints of exasperation. "Are you going to apologize to Payton and Liam?"

Hank's sigh mimicked hers. "Of course. I've been waiting to do that until Reagan did what *she* was supposed to do. How did you guys find out? Did she actually talk to her mom?"

"No. We got back to the house today and she was here with the same kid."

"She didn't."

"She did. And Payton was blindsided."

Hank grimaced, head shaking. "I guess I should have said something. Not sure why I thought Reagan would actually follow through on her promise."

"Maybe because Ava would have." Clara's tone softened. Their daughter wasn't perfect by any means. But she also hadn't rebelled in the way many kids did. They were thankful. And aware of how unusual that was.

"I'll go talk to them now."

"I can come with you."

"No need. I'll handle it." He exited the room, shutting the door behind him.

To occupy herself, Clara plugged in the handheld steamer she'd borrowed from Isley to get the wrinkles out of her dress for tonight. It was burgundy, sleeveless, and landed above the knee. It had also been in her closet for at least five years, but no one here knew that. And it made her feel good. Clara was curvy, and this dress hugged and hung loose in all the right places.

A few minutes later, Hank returned to the bedroom and dropped back to a sprawled position on the bed.

"How'd it go?"

"Fine. They understood my predicament. They're not upset with me."

"Good. I'm glad to hear it."

Hank's eyes closed.

"Are you okay?"

"Yeah. Just tired."

"Was fishing that hard?"

"No. It was fun." His smile sprouted and then crashed. "Clara Rose, I'm not sure I can do the dinner party thing tonight. I'm just exhausted."

"What?" Clara set the steamer on the dresser and turned to study Hank, whose eyelids remained shuttered. And felt anger bubble up. "Are you serious?"

She was tired too. Someone was still demanding a truth from one or all of them, and that was eating at Clara. When would whoever left the note follow through on their threat to reveal all if one of them didn't? What if the photos left at Belinda's had something to do with the note at Isley and Trevor's house? It was a lot to handle, and certainly, there were moments Clara wanted to run and escape.

But supporting Finch's Hope was the main reason they were here. How could Hank not attend the dinner?

What was going *on* with her husband?

"Hank, something has to change." Clara's voice broke as she attempted to keep her tone gentle but firm. She couldn't *do* this anymore. She couldn't carry this weight on her own. "I keep trying to lift you up, but you're not making any effort to assist and help yourself. If you're going through depression, which would be *completely* understandable, then let's get some help." She fought tears. "Please."

A few beats of silence filled the room. "I'll rally for tonight." He pushed off the bed. "I'm going to shower and then I'll be up in a few to help with whatever." He passed her on the way to the bathroom without so much as a touch or a glance.

When they'd found that note after the break-in on Thursday night, Clara had thought she didn't have anything to hide in her personal life. That her only connection to *telling the truth* would be linked to the past.

But she'd been lying to herself.

Because she was angry with her husband for disappearing on her.

Angry that he couldn't admit he was in such a dire spot.

Angry that he'd just ignored her mention of getting help.

Angry that he'd rewritten their life without her permission.

She'd had *no idea* how much angst she'd packed with her in her luggage. Or what to do with it now that it had all tumbled out.

Isley had thought that because the dinner party was being catered she would be able to stay out of it.

She should have known better.

She'd hosted so many events like this that it was second nature to roll up her sleeves. And it had been nice to focus her mind on mundane tasks for tonight instead of the stresses of the weekend.

Now, guests were supposed to arrive in thirty minutes and she'd just finished showering and styling her hair.

She slipped on her dinner-party dress—it was fitted, with black lace and cap sleeves—and then her Jimmy Choos. She returned to the en suite bathroom to put on her face, as her mother had always referred to it.

She was mid-application of bronzer when Trev called out from the bedroom. "Is, videographer's here." His voice carried through the slightly cracked bathroom door.

Belinda had opted for professional video and photography tonight, despite Clara's offer to take pictures. Which made sense since she needed to be in the photos, not behind the lens.

"Okay! I'm almost done." She quickly added her cream contour and moved on to her nose, jaw, and hairline. "Give me a few and then we can show him the interview spot and make sure it works." As requested, they'd set up a chair and side table in the corner of their bedroom as a backdrop for the videos. "Can you check my texts to see what time Belinda said she was planning to arrive? My phone is charging on my nightstand."

"On it."

She added lip color and mascara.

"I don't see anything on your group text string with Payton and Clara," Trevor responded.

"I think maybe she texted me separately." Isley wanted to be at the door to greet Belinda. No matter how amazing this night was supposed to be in terms of supporting Finch's Hope, there was always an emotional thread at play. Especially since Belinda's loss was the catalyst for someone else's survival.

The bathroom door opened, and her husband stood inside the frame, leaning against it like it was holding him up.

Isley's heart climbed up her throat so swiftly that she thought she might be sick. "What's wrong? Is it Aiden? Is he—"

"While I understand why you reached out," Trevor began reading from her phone, "I am asking you not to again. Please allow Freya and our family time to heal and move forward."

Isley's eyeliner clattered to the countertop. "Trev."

"I couldn't find Belinda's texts." He held up the phone screen toward her. "And when I searched for hers, this popped up. You have Bianca Edwards entered in your contacts as BE?"

What was there to say? Isley gave a painful, guilty nod.

"When did you communicate with her?"

She could barely hear him over the whooshing in her ears. "A week after Aiden left for rehab. She agreed to meet me."

His pupils darkened. "That long ago? And you didn't say anything?" He scrubbed a hand over his face. "What happened during the conversation?"

"I just had to apologize to her, Trev. I *had* to. My heart was so broken over Freya. So traumatized that she almost died. And mom-to-mom... I was desperate to express our remorse for what happened." And in doing so, she'd inadvertently heaped blame on her son. Exactly why Trevor had asked her not to talk to Bianca. "I'm sorry. I understand why you didn't want me to. I get that I was wrong and that I could have caused issues for Aiden or you or any of us. I was just in the throes of grief and I...made a stupid decision." It felt like exactly the right timing for Clara's *S* word.

His grip tightened around her phone, which he still palmed. "What was her response?"

Isley pressed a shaky hand against the bathroom countertop. "Not good. Bianca was so upset that she left the coffee shop after only a few minutes. Which made me even more afraid to admit what I'd done. Because I was certain I'd made things worse."

"Her kid almost died, Is. I'm not shocked that she was upset."

Isley hadn't been either but she'd *had* to try.

A knock sounded. "Belinda's here," Payton called through the bedroom door. "Just wanted to let you guys know."

Isley raised her voice. "Be right out!" So much for being at the door when she arrived.

"When you first brought up talking to Bianca, I understood

why you wanted to reach out to her. But I was trying to protect Aiden. And our family." Trevor's shoulders sagged, voice gravelly. "Even though the possibility of Freya dying was just as awful for me as it was for you. And not just because our son could have been punished for it."

Isley's heart thumped wildly. "I know. I understood why you asked me not to. And I hated myself for doing it anyway."

Voices grew louder outside the bedroom door. More people must be arriving.

"We have guests."

A crease formed on the bridge of his nose. "They can wait."

"But—"

"It will look like we don't have it all together? I hate to be the bearer of bad news, but no one is under the illusion that we do. Our kid is basically serving time in rehab." Trevor set her phone down on the bathroom counter as if it were tainted and he wanted to distance himself from it. "The thing I'm most upset about isn't that you endangered our son's future or even that you basically implied we were liable for Freya's near-death." His delivery was deadly calm, which only made the situation worse. Isley would prefer that he yell and rail at her. She deserved it.

"And I can't even imagine the legal ramifications of that," he continued. "It's that you don't trust me. I'm not sure you've ever fully trusted me. Or believed that I love you without stipulations. Without you needing to act or be a certain way. You still view yourself as Iris Tordoff's daughter instead of Isley Stanton. Or Aiden's mother. Or the woman I've loved since I was the TA in your class and you did everything you could to avoid going out with me. You think that one day I'm going to wake up and see you how you see yourself and be gone, yet I've been proving the opposite to you for over twenty years."

Isley's cheeks were wet. She would have to fix her makeup.

"I know you love me, Trev." Though in this moment, she certainly didn't feel deserving of that love.

"You might know it but you don't *believe* it. Because if you did, you would have come to me with this. Before you did it or after. I might not have agreed with your decision, but I know your heart. Apparently, you don't know mine."

Chapter Twenty-Five

Payton had assumed that she and Liam would bring the awkward to tonight's dinner party. Especially after their fruitless, frustrating conversation with Reagan this afternoon.

But based on their friends' behavior so far this evening, they might come in third instead of first in that regard.

Isley and Trevor had been holed up in their bedroom when guests started arriving. And since then, it appeared as if they hadn't spoken to each other.

Clara was her usual cheerful self, greeting everyone she knew from Veil and the charity and engaging with the survivors and guests who were attending tonight. Yet, every time her vision landed on her husband—who was sitting at one of the tables even though they hadn't been directed to take their seats—she appeared to be near tears.

Payton would like to pull her aside and check on her, but she didn't want to be the reason the dam broke for her tender friend. So she was biding her time.

And in what was perhaps the worst twist of the evening so

far, after she'd readied for tonight and donned her sleeveless deep blue cocktail dress, Liam had kissed her on the cheek and told her she looked beautiful.

The only reason Payton hadn't batted him away was because she'd been stunned by his sudden attention. They definitely had to figure out their new normal, because this no-man's-land wasn't working for her.

Originally, Reagan had planned to attend the dinner party tonight. But after the events of this afternoon, she was currently holed up in their bedroom downstairs, wearing pajamas, rejecting food, and refusing to speak to Payton or Liam.

Like she'd put herself in solitary confinement.

Their attempt to talk to her calmly about Zion and her lying to them over the course of the weekend had quickly derailed this afternoon.

Payton's only solace was that Liam was the one who'd lost his temper with Reagan when, instead of showing remorse, she'd reacted to their concern with anger.

No doubt he was as rattled as Payton that Reagan had been in the house shortly before the break-in, and that fear had demolished his typically composed demeanor.

"Trevor, have you seen Isley?" Payton wanted to ask her if they were supposed to be doing interviews tonight too. And since Belinda was in conversation with two of the guests who'd used Finch's Hope's services over the years, Payton didn't want to interrupt her.

"I haven't. Sorry." Trevor raised his palms and continued toward the kitchen.

Strange. Everything and everyone definitely seemed off tonight.

A utensil clinking against glass sounded, and the group quieted. Venette, who was second-in-command at Finch's Hope, beamed at the group. "Thank you all for making this night happen! We're so grateful you've gathered to support Finch's Hope and assist in keeping our doors open."

Cheers and whistles followed.

"If we didn't grab you for an interview before dinner, please flag down me or our videographer, Chet. We want to capture as much footage as we can tonight."

That answered Payton's question. She would let Venette know she was willing to be interviewed if they wanted the footage and happy to sit out if they didn't have time for her.

"If everyone could find a seat, dinner is ready." The scent of stuffed wild-rice chicken and vegetables caused Payton's mouth to water as she joined her friends, The Husbands, and Belinda near the end of the indoor table the caterers had provided that filled the center of the living room.

People also seated themselves at the Stantons' indoor dining table and the two additional long tables that had been set up on the deck, which were easily accessible through the open wall of glass doors.

Cece's high school boyfriend, Konnor, sat diagonally across from Payton, flanking the end of their group and leaving room for his fourteen-year-old daughter, Remmy, to be tucked between himself and Clara.

Payton kept up with Remmy news through Facebook when Konnor or his ex-wife posted about their tenderhearted girl, who'd been born with Down syndrome. According to plenty of Veil sources, Konnor's short marriage in his twenties had ended badly, though Payton didn't know specifics. In the past, she might have had a chip on her shoulder about that because her marriage to Liam had always been so easy. Now? She felt sympathy.

But Remmy was definitely the good that had come out of that scenario.

Over the years, Konnor had fluctuated in his involvement

with the charity, sometimes going off-grid and other times—like this evening—showing up to support Finch's Hope.

But then, he was in an awkward position. It wasn't as if he and Cece had been engaged or married. They'd been dating—on-again, off-again—like normal high school kids.

It had to be hard to navigate a world where your high school girlfriend was gone, but her legacy lived on through the charity started in her honor. Certainly he'd done his best to navigate the aftermath of her death just like the rest of them had.

"Remmy, I'm Payton and this is Clara. We were friends with your dad in high school."

Remmy speared a bite of dinner salad with her fork. "And Cece?"

"And Cece."

"I'm glad you came tonight," Clara said. "And I love your dress."

It was cornflower blue with small white flowers and flared just below the knee. Her necklace was tucked under the high neckline. If Payton were sitting next to her, she wouldn't be able to resist sliding it out.

"Thank you." She preened at the compliment, as she should. "A girl in my online Downs group was sad and I told her about Finch's Hope. But now she seems better."

Sweet girl. "I'm so glad she's doing better. That was very kind of you to help her."

"I like helping people. It makes me feel good."

Same.

The girls hadn't understood all that Cece had gone through before moving to Veil until after her death. But once Belinda had shared those details with them, her passing had made more sense. Payton, Isley, and Clara had been heartbroken regarding Cece's past and that she hadn't felt she could share that burden with them.

But then, would Payton have disclosed such a terrible season if that had been her story? She'd been the queen of keeping her feelings tucked close.

She still was.

Conversation flowed well during dinner. Payton enjoyed small talk as much as she did having a stick poked into her eye, but she found that with tonight's guests, conversation came easier than it normally did in these situations. Maybe because Cece was their tie. Or maybe because there were people alive in this room tonight because of Belinda's brainchild and passion for Finch's Hope.

At the end of dinner, while chocolate soufflés were being served, Belinda asked Trevor to pause the background music, then stood to address the group.

"I'm terrible at public speaking." Belinda spoke loudly so her voice would carry to the tables outside. She was a petite woman with paper-white skin, silver-streaked hair, and a fiercely determined personality. "Though, this group feels like family, so that makes it a little easier."

"Hear, hear!" sounded from one of the outside tables.

"I just wanted to say thank you to everyone for being here to support Finch's Hope. When the money issues were first discovered at the charity, I thought maybe it was a sign that it was time to close our doors. But then people began to rally and support us in amazing ways. Venette reached out to the families in our database. And my bonus girls began planning this weekend and helped us get started with the online auction." Which of course Isley deserved full credit for. "Cece's friends were everything to her." Belinda sniffled and beamed at each of them. "They changed her life when we moved to Veil, and for that I will forever be grateful."

Again—*same*. Payton truly didn't know who or what she would have become without her friends.

"And now here we are celebrating so many years of Finch's Hope and fighting for more to come," Belinda continued. "Thank you to those of you who traveled here to share your survivor stories. They're going to be an amazing help to so many. I *love* thinking about all the lives that have been affected for the better because of Cece. There have been so many nights I laid awake wondering what went through my daughter's mind in the minutes and hours leading up to her death."

Payton's nervous system screeched to a halt.

"Of course, anyone in my shoes is desperate to understand what would prompt their child to make a decision like that. You wish that they hadn't been alone."

Isley and Clara appeared stricken at Belinda's subject matter—just like Payton.

Hank passed each of them a tissue. So evidently, they also seemed to be teetering on an emotional ledge.

"It's hard not to think that maybe if someone had been there, they would have sensed something. To stop the worst from happening." Payton felt like an elephant had plunked down on her chest. She couldn't catch her breath. She inhaled in little bursts and pressed her fingernails into her thigh as a distraction from what felt eerily close to a panic attack. "But eventually, you realize there are some answers you'll never get. It was that torment that led me to Finch's Hope. I became obsessed with stopping suicide and that pain for others. I was desperate to create something good from the loss of my precious daughter."

Payton risked a glance around the end of the table.

Clara was silently weeping.

Isley stared vacantly forward, appearing to be in a battle for control of her body that Payton felt in her core.

The Husbands had their attention—and nonverbal support—focused on Belinda.

Sweet Remmy had tears in her eyes.

And Konnor's vision was homed in on the untouched dessert in front of him, the tendons in his neck tense. Immobile.

Belinda gave a watery laugh. "I told myself to keep this short! Sorry I went on and on. What I really want to say is thank you, thank you for loving Finch's Hope and in turn, loving my baby girl even though some of you didn't get the chance to know her. It means the world."

A round of applause ignited, and a newly married couple—the husband a survivor because of Finch's Hope—popped up to talk with Belinda.

Payton literally never spoke about the night Cece died. It was a vault inside her. A murky abyss of regret. She knew it was the same for Isley and Clara.

And now that hidden truth had become a monster.

How were they supposed to admit to Belinda decades later that they'd been with Cece before her death?

But after that speech, how could they not?

People began to rise from the tables and mingle.

In nonverbal agreement, the women stood. Isley walked toward the front of the house, and Payton and Clara silently followed.

Once on the front step, door closed behind them, all three of them physically sagged under the same weight.

"What are we going to do?" Clara asked softly.

Payton crossed arms over her thundering heart. "We have to tell her."

"We do." Isley pressed shaky fingertips against her lips. "If we're held responsible, so be it. Maybe we deserve to be."

"Maybe we do." If Payton could rewind time, she would have told Belinda right away that they'd been drinking with Cece the night she died. She would have told her that *she* was the one who'd purchased the alcohol with a fake ID. And even if they'd been blamed for Cece's death in some way, she would shoulder that responsibility. It was the right thing to do.

But they'd been frightened teenagers. They'd panicked. No one had questioned if they'd been at Cece's house that night. There'd been no proof that they were there. And so they'd kept their mouths shut.

Payton hated the thought of Reagan witnessing that side of her. The person she'd once been. The person she'd worked so hard to distance herself from.

"How can Belinda ever forgive us for this? For all the things we didn't say and the years we left them unsaid?" Clara voiced the question on all of their minds.

But just like with so many other scenarios this weekend, no one had an answer.

Chapter Twenty-Six

The women agreed that they would speak to Belinda tonight after the guests left.

She was their mother hen. Their bonus mom. She'd filled a void for each of them. And now they had to confess something that would wound her deeply.

But if Isley had learned any lesson in the last couple hours, it was to lay everything on the line—just like she wished she had done with Trevor—and then deal with the ramifications.

They would get through this.

Somehow.

"Could everyone gather out on the deck?" Suri called out. The photographer for the evening was a young woman with gorgeous dark skin and braids that skimmed her shoulders as she flitted about the party. "I'd like to get a group shot before people start heading home."

They moved en masse to the deck, and Suri directed them where to stand to fit the whole group into the shot.

"Could a few of you slide that table to the side to make more room? I'm going to grab my ladder. Be back in a sec."

Trevor assisted with moving the table and chairs and then snaked his way through the guests to stand next to Isley. Anytime they'd spoken to each other since that awful conversation in the bathroom, it had revolved around the logistics of the evening.

"Did we get the interviews needed for Finch's Hope?"

Case in point. "Yes. I think they have more to do, but Venette told me they've gotten great footage already."

"Good."

Tension crackled between them. Isley needed to talk to him too. And it should also wait until a more opportune time. But her spirit was crumbling. "Trev, I'm so sorry."

He gave a succinct nod. "I know." His mouth opened as if he planned to say more, but Suri returned to the deck with a ladder, effectively silencing him.

She climbed up a few rungs and began snapping photos, then checked the screen on the back of the camera. "The couple on the right, can you scooch in a bit? Perfect." Her camera clicked as she continued to capture them, then examined her screen again. "Okay, these look great. Thanks, everyone!" She climbed down the ladder and tugged a paper list from her pocket. "Whoever is part of the friend group staying at the house this weekend, can I get a couple group shots of you with Belinda?"

"Just the women?" Trevor asked with a hint of hopefulness.

"That's up to the boss." Suri motioned to Belinda.

Belinda laughed and patted a palm to Trevor's cheek. "That's fine. You boys can sit this one out."

The Husbands cleared from the deck before Belinda could change her mind.

Suri arranged Payton, Clara, Isley, and Belinda in the corner of the deck, with evergreens as their backdrop. They smiled and posed as directed, but Isley's heart was cracking down the middle at the pain she'd caused Trevor...and the pain they would soon cause Belinda.

"Thank you!" Suri dismissed them and turned, her attention and her camera focusing on a group of guests who stood in a circle, laughing and talking together.

"This night was a great idea. Thank you for all of your help, girls." Belinda opened her arms, gathering the three of them in a hug.

When they stepped back from the embrace, Clara's cheeks were wet with tears.

"What's wrong, dear?"

"Belinda, your speech—"

"Was very touching," Isley interrupted Clara. This wasn't the time or place for their conversation with Belinda. They needed the guests to be gone first. They needed to sit Belinda down and prep her as best they could.

"We have to talk to you about the night Cece died," Clara continued in a rush, tumbling down a slippery slope with no signs of stopping her descent. "There are things we never told you."

Belinda frowned. "What are you talking about?"

"But..." Recognition that people were still milling about the deck finally registered in Clara's panicked expression. "We can discuss it later."

"You girls can tell me anything. You know that."

"We were at your house drinking with Cece the night she died," Payton filled in rapidly, leaving Isley stunned.

So...they were doing this *now*?

People were a handful of yards away.

"Cece was upset about something that week, though we don't know what it was. She never told us or we would have told you." Payton spoke quietly. "I'm sorry we can't give you better answers to your questions. And I'm sorry we were drinking with her that night and never told you. I bought the alcohol. It was my fault that her cognitive skills were diminished."

"We're *all* sorry," Clara said with hushed emotion. "Not just Payton. We were all there. We were all part of it."

"We were." Isley nodded her agreement. "And we should have told you right away. At first we didn't say anything because we were young and afraid of getting blamed or held accountable for Cece's death. We thought we could go to jail. We were petrified. And then eventually, when we got older and realized that likely wouldn't have happened and maybe we were overthinking, we were so desperate not to hurt you. You were—*are*—our bonus mom. If we admitted what we'd hidden back then, we thought you'd be crushed beyond comprehension that we hadn't told you right away. We couldn't fathom the thought of causing you additional pain."

If someone had asked them directly if they'd been there, they would have admitted it. It wasn't a lie they told. It was a truth they kept hidden.

Belinda's eyebrows joined together, and her mouth opened.

"We are *so* sorry," Payton said with anguish, effectively cutting off Belinda's response. "We should never have concealed it."

"We don't want to lose you." Clara's delivery caught like a snag in a favorite sweater. "If we could go back—"

"Remmy, dear." Belinda interrupted Clara, her sight line skimming over their shoulders.

Was she warning them Remmy was there and to stop talking? Or was she done with them?

Belinda stepped around their group and approached Remmy, leaving a stunned Payton, Isley, and Clara in her wake. "That's such a pretty dress, dear. Let me adjust that for you." A few beats of silence echoed. "Have you been wearing that all night? It's lovely." Belinda's voice shook as it trailed away and she led Remmy inside the house. "Suri," they heard her call out. "Could you get a picture of the two of us?"

"I can't believe I just did that," Clara lamented. "That I just brought it up like that. I'm so sorry, girls. What was I thinking?"

"You weren't." Payton raised her palms. "I didn't mean that how it sounded. I'm just saying that you were stressed by her speech and our plan to tell her. I get it. That's why I went along with it. I thought maybe once we started, it was best to just get it out there."

"We should go after her, right?" At least that's what Isley desperately wanted to do.

"I'm not sure we should," Payton responded. "Maybe she needs a minute."

"Clara." Trevor stepped onto the deck, his voice taut with stress. "Something's going on with Hank."

Trevor led Clara to the front step, where they'd been a short while ago making decisions that had seemed like the right thing to do.

Payton was shocked that Belinda had just walked away from them mid-conversation.

It was so unlike her.

And yet, the information they'd relayed was twenty-plus years too late.

They deserved all of her angst and ire.

And she'd deserved to know those details long ago.

Payton couldn't imagine that Belinda would cast blame on them for Cece's death, but in truth, they didn't know what she would do with the information they'd just handed over to her.

Hank was sitting on the front step. He opened shuttered

eyelids to find the five of them gathered around him, staring with stark concern.

"Stop it." He attempted a laugh that morphed into a cough. "I know what you're all thinking. Poor Hank. Go ahead and say it."

Payton certainly hadn't been thinking that, but Hank's comment caused a small laugh to erupt from everyone except Clara.

She knelt next to her husband and pressed fingers against his wrist, her other hand checking his forehead.

"You feel clammy. And your pulse is *racing*. How does your left arm feel?"

"Like an arm," Hank supplied, eyes crinkling.

She groaned in annoyance.

"But we should probably go in," he acquiesced, "because my heart is acting strange."

The moment he said *heart*, everyone took a collective inhale. That was one important organ.

Clara stood. "Are we taking an ambulance or am I driving?" She was visibly trembling, much like Payton after this afternoon's confession and departure from massages.

How had that only been today? It felt like a week had passed since then.

"I'll drive," Trevor stated. "Your van has vehicles behind it. We can take Isley's SUV since it's parked on the street."

They'd moved it out of the garage earlier to make room for the caterers to park there. And they'd left the driveway open for guest parking. Isley and Trevor had also gotten special permission from their HOA to allow the influx of vehicles lining their street tonight.

"I'll get the key." Trevor hurried into the house, shutting the door behind him, likely in an attempt to keep the dinner party from being disrupted by what was happening outside, since Hank would abhor the attention.

"Purse," Clara said. "I should—"

"Where is it?" Liam asked.

"Top of the dresser."

"I'm on it." He disappeared into the house after Trevor.

"Make sure they get all the interviews," Hank dictated to Isley and Payton.

"Hank." Isley's pupils darkened like storm clouds. "Stop it. You're more important than tonight. Maybe we should call an ambulance." Her vision swung to Payton and Clara. "It's not worth the risk."

"One hundred percent agree." They definitely didn't need to lose another one of them because Hank was being stubborn.

As if in answer, a faint siren wailed in the distance.

"*Did* someone call an ambulance?" Accusatory lines erupted across Hank's forehead.

"Hank, we've been right next to you since we found out. Of course we didn't." Somehow, Clara's chiding registered as caring. And despite the situation, a bit humorous. Because this conversation was so *them*.

Trevor exited the house, Liam on his heels. "Is that for us?" He nodded toward the sound of the siren as he closed the door behind them.

"Not that we know of." Isley raised her eyebrows. "Unless you called for one."

"I'm too afraid of Hank to do that."

His quip earned a nod and laughter from Hank. "Good. Because if it is for me, I'm not taking it." Hank pushed off the step and started walking toward the street and Isley's vehicle.

"Pretty sure that's a police siren. Not an ambulance." Liam handed Clara her purse—a large black tote that was at odds with her dressy outfit—and both she and Trevor hurried to catch up to Hank.

They loaded into Isley's car, and Trevor backed into the

driveway to turn around just as a police cruiser raced up the street, sirens now off but lights still flashing.

Liam had been correct.

The police vehicle screeched to a halt in front of the other house at the end of the street, and two officers popped out and strode toward their front door.

Trevor took off with Clara and Hank.

"Why are the police at Kyle Elrod's house?" Isley asked as a blonde woman—Kyle's wife or girlfriend?—answered the Elrods' door.

"Maybe they had a break-in and note delivery too," Liam offered.

The blonde woman engaged in conversation with the officers for a few seconds before granting them access to the house.

What a strange turn of events. But then, how many times had Payton thought *that* this weekend?

"So weird." Isley frowned. "Also, how odd is it that now whenever I hear sirens, I assume it has something to do with us?"

Payton was about to follow her over the threshold of the front door when Liam's phone buzzed and he slid it from his pocket to check that stupid—*thank you for the fitting word, Clara*—screen she couldn't see.

"Is, we'll be there in a minute."

Isley turned, read Payton in a millisecond, and jutted her chin in nonverbal support. As if to say, *Go get 'em girl*, and, *You've got this*, all with one quick movement.

Payton shut the door and faced her husband. It was just the two of them on the front step now. The neighborhood had turned quiet again. And it took a full four seconds for Liam to stop texting, wipe the goofy grin from his face, and realize any of that.

His mouth pinched with confusion. "What's up?"

"Liam." Payton swallowed hard, her throat filled with the jagged edges of the many years of trust and love between them. "Are you cheating on me?"

Seeing Clara and Hank interact with each other just now had shattered something in Payton. They might fight or lose it in a moment of stress. But they were solid. Just like Payton and Liam had once been.

It wasn't that Liam didn't care about her. At least he'd claimed he always would. But in so many ways, her husband had already left her. She was already on her own.

"*What?* Of course not. We have too good of a relationship for me to ever treat you like that."

They had too good of a relationship, but he wanted a divorce. So confusing. "Tell me the reason again."

"The reason for what?"

"Getting divorced." Payton refused to refer to it as The Plan anymore. She would call it what it was—being abandoned, dumped, left behind, discarded.

"You want to talk about this here. Now?"

Payton nodded.

"We function better as a team than in a romantic partnership. I don't know how else to say it." A sliver of irritation crept into his response.

The phone remained in his grip. Payton's mind bounced back to that note on Thursday night and how it had instantly made her think of the student from earlier this year.

And his teaching partner.

Even though both of those scenarios felt like *such* a stretch.

She thought of how, after Liam had suggested The Plan, she'd gone from being confident and content to doubting everything and everyone.

She would never wish a relationship like this on Reagan.

"I'm not *leaving* you. We're just...changing the parameters of how we operate."

Liam had always had a way with words. And Payton only understood numbers and science and proof. And the end result in this scenario didn't match up with what Liam was offering.

Did you try to convince a person to keep loving you when they'd stopped?

It went against every protective instinct in Payton to do what she was about to do. But if she didn't try, she would always wonder if she'd done enough. If she could have said more. And the biggest lesson she'd taken from Cece's death was to never leave things unsaid.

"I don't want a divorce, Liam. I meant our vows. If you want out, you're going to have to leave me. Because I'm still in this and I'm not going anywhere."

Payton's heart pounded like bongos inside her rib cage. She hadn't known it could ache so much and keep on beating.

Liam's jaw slacked. His mouth opened. Closed. And then, "I'm sorry, Pay. I'm just not there anymore."

What else was there to say? He didn't deserve to know the depths of the wound he'd just carved inside her. Right on top of the scars of her childhood.

"It doesn't change any—"

"It changes everything." Payton had spent her childhood waiting and hoping to be genuinely loved. She wouldn't spend her adulthood doing the same.

She would figure out how to love herself and her daughter.

And that would be more than enough.

Chapter Twenty-Seven

Cece

This week has been *the worst*. And not just for me. Payton's gaze has been glued to the ugly, stained, low-pile carpet at school. She keeps snapping at everyone over the smallest stuff, then realizing it and apologizing.

She's made me feel better, because Godzilla is trapped inside my chest. The turmoil going on in my world is so convoluted that I don't know how to process any of it.

All I can think about is how to *stop* thinking about it. How do I turn it off?

Apparently whatever is going on with Pay and me is pretty obvious, though neither of us have gone into details as to what's making us so irritable, because Thursday at lunch, Clara started gently asking questions in the hopes of digging our issues from us.

Like using a planting trowel.

Isley was much more direct. "You two are absolute messes. What in the world is going on? Spill already!"

Like using a pickax.

I love both of them for their patented approaches, but I wasn't ready to dish.

Neither was Payton, because her lips stayed tightly sealed and she gave a headshake that said *nope*.

And then suddenly, we were making plans to drown our sorrows at my house on Saturday night while my mom is visiting a friend in Denver.

Some kids in our class party every weekend. Our friend group doesn't. But one night of escape from this painful processing is exactly what I need. In a terrible friend move, I let Payton believe that tonight was her idea even though I planted the seed. All Payton did was give it a little water. Isley jumped on board without issue, and Clara claimed to do the same, though we all know she has no interest in drinking.

But she also must sense that whatever we have going on is bigger than typical teenage problems, because she didn't protest.

Or more likely it's because of that pact we made freshman year.

The one where we vowed that if anyone felt like they were standing at the edge of a deep dark pit and needed to escape the pressure of that place, we'd all do it together.

It's a relief to think that when you're on the precipice of something menacing, there will be people on both sides to keep you from falling.

I hear the moment Clara's old car turns down my street because it sounds like a ninety-year-old with emphysema. But somehow, it continues to get all of us where we need to go. I run out to the attached garage and open the overhead door, motioning for her to park inside.

I suppose I'm being overly dramatic. No one would think

anything of Clara's car being here since my friends are constantly at my house. But considering our agenda for the evening, a little privacy isn't a bad idea.

I close the garage door behind them, and Payton, Isley, and Clara follow me into the house. Payton is gripping a brown paper bag, which she sets on the kitchen counter.

She opens it and takes out a bottle of strawberry daiquiri mix and what I assume is a really cheap bottle of rum.

Do we like rum?

We're about to find out.

My mom has one bottle of alcohol in the house, which she offers to guests since she rarely drinks. We discussed borrowing from her stash but decided it would be too obvious.

One, the bottle has dust on it, which would get disturbed or displaced. And two, with the four of us girls partaking, the volume level would diminish enough to get noticed.

I don't know how closely my mom watches that sort of thing, but ever since my eighth-grade issues, she's a literal hawk when it comes to observing my life and habits. I wouldn't put it past her to have the amounts marked somehow.

It's been so many years since the incident it almost feels like something that happened to someone else. Except this week, the devastation I felt at that time has all come tumbling back like bright orange construction signs placed throughout my day, reminding me of how *bad* it got.

"Do you have a blender?" Payton asks.

I climb onto the countertop and retrieve the blender from the top shelf in the cupboard.

"Ice too."

Payton morphing into a bartender would give me the giggles if I were in a better mood.

I take out two trays from the freezer and place them next to the blender for her. I'm not sure how much ice she needs.

She's probably not sure how much ice she needs because she's never gone down this particular road of rebellion before.

Payton pushes with her parents more than the rest of us do—dating boys she doesn't even like just to ignite their anger, staying out way past her curfew, occasionally pilfering cigarettes or other small items from the store, surfing on top of some of the guys' cars—a small-town activity I'm not a fan of. But to those close to her, it's easy to see her rebellion is an act—a way to get back at her parents for being stone-cold robots.

"I brought snacks." Clara carries a grocery bag into the living room and pulls out two bags of chips and a sleeve of cookies.

She's probably trying to make sure we're not drinking on an empty stomach.

"Are we doing music or movie?" Isley asks.

"Music," Payton responds.

"I'm on it." Isley goes into the living room and puts on a Dave Matthews CD as Payton measures and blends like the scientist she plans to be.

No one else has their future all laid out like Pay. She's going to attend School of Mines—just as soon as she's off the waitlist—and has had her major picked out since sophomore year.

She's so ready to get out of her house and Veil that I'm sometimes a little surprised she hasn't already bolted.

But her phenomenal grades and that salutatorian tag are her tickets out of here, and she's too smart to mess any of that up. Which only proves my earlier point about her so-called defiant tendencies.

When the obnoxiously loud blender stops, I locate glasses and bendy straws for our drinks. The bendy straws give off elementary vibes, but they're all we have.

Daiquiris in hand, we migrate into the living room and lounge on the floor versus the furniture.

"How many times did we spend the night here freshman year?" Clara places her drink on a coaster on the coffee table.

"More than we can count." Isley takes a small sip, wrinkles her nose at the taste, and then inclines her head as if it wasn't *that* bad. "Cece, truth or dare like the old days. Actually, just truth."

Ah, man. That was the option I always avoided.

"Does your mom ever get sick of us being over here?"

That's a question I have no problem answering. "No. She loves you girls like you're her daughters too. And some days, she likes you better than me." I'm teasing, because of course I know my mom loves me. She uprooted our life for me. At the time, I didn't realize the move to Veil was to provide a place for me to start over. I thought she was being *so* self-centered.

But she got me out of Denver.

She got me away from those girls, the constant reminders, my guilt. Though of course that last thing moved with us in some capacity.

"Your mother definitely likes me better than mine does." Payton takes a long slurp through her straw that appears to have nothing to do with the taste and everything to do with the alcohol content.

Normally we would protest a comment like Payton's, but in this situation we don't because Payton's family is so unusual.

The older I get, the more convinced I am that Payton's mom has an undiagnosed mental disorder and that her dad has his hands full focusing on her.

"Are the two of you ready to tell us what's going on?" Clara asks in her tender way, and tears spring to my throat.

Instead of answering, I take another sip. The daiquiri would be good outside of the rum part. But at the same time, the small tastes start to warm me. And something inside of me unknots. I both dislike and like the feeling at the same time.

I tip my head toward Payton in a *you first* motion.

"I got into Mines."

We all shriek at once. "Pay, that's amazing!" I'm *so* happy for her, I could—

"It would be amazing if I could afford to go." She draws a pattern in her drink with the straw. "The money that my great uncle left for me..." Payton's head swivels, and she swallows hard. "They lost it. My parents lost my college fund on an investment. Supposedly. But I don't even know if I believe them."

"They wouldn't." Isley leans forward, fire sparking in her eyes.

"Maybe they would." Payton shrugs. "My mom got that new car about six months ago. And when my great uncle Damien left me the money, she complained numerous times that it should have gone to her and not me."

We all sit in stunned silence. This feels bigger than us. Like Payton should get a lawyer.

"Do you want to ask my mom?" It's a flimsy offer, but I do trust that she'd try to help Payton if she could. But how would she do that? It's not like she can march over to Payton's house and confront her parents.

"Thanks, but that's okay. I'm sure they've tossed enough dirt on top of whatever they did that it's well covered up at this point. Plus, what really matters will still be true. Without a doubt, the money is gone."

There are likely options for loans and financial aid, but I quickly realize that we're not here to solve this even if we could. We're attending a wake of Payton's dreams.

We're here to stand on this ledge with her and hold on so she doesn't fall.

Clara scoots over and wraps Payton in a hug. "I'm sorry, Pay. You can always stay here and go to community college. I'll be here."

Payton's expression turns venomous. "I am not staying in this town!" At Clara's wince, Payton rushes on. "I'm sorry for being such a witch, Clara. It's not about you."

"I know," Clara responds graciously as she returns to her spot. "It's okay."

Payton pops up from the floor and starts pacing the living room. "All I want to do is get out of this town and it's like there's a vortex sucking me down, keeping me here." She still has her drink in her hand, and it's sloshing around the rim. I hope it doesn't spill and stain the carpet, because I'm certainly not planning to tell my mom any of this happened. She'll put up with a lot from me, but she would freak if she knew what we were doing right now.

The thought stresses me out so much that I inhale a bunch of my daiquiri really fast. Now I'm not sure if the room is spinning or if Payton is walking in circles.

"Cece." Payton raises her drink toward me, though it's emptier from her recent slurp, so the threat of spilling has diminished. "You're up." She drops to the floor as if the fight has gone out of her.

There is no reason for me not to tell the girls. I can trust them, obviously. They are completely different than the friends I had that year. Now, in hindsight, I can see the red flags those girls had been obnoxiously waving.

But what happened in eighth grade coupled with my backstory coupled with this new development is too much.

I feel physically sick.

"Is it about prom?" Isley suggests. "Did Konnor not ask you or something?"

I'm so relieved at the out that I take it, even though this subject has its own issues.

"He hasn't asked me yet." I keep my answer simple, because there are some things the girls don't know about me and Konnor. Some things I've been trying to work through on top of the stuff with my dad.

"Do you want to go with him?" Payton asks.

Konnor and I have been on and off a couple of times since we got together the fall of junior year, so Payton's question has merit. But it feels like there's an undercurrent to her inquiry.

Payton doesn't wait for an answer. "If you're not going to go to prom with Konnor, are you going to go with Scout?"

What? "No, I'm not going with Scout." The CD switches songs, filling the room with silence. I'm not sure if it's the alcohol or Scout putting me in this position for so long that has me internally seething.

When Payton dated a couple of guys our junior year, I thought Scout moved on from her. But once we ramped into senior year, I could see that his feelings had grown versus fading.

But he still wouldn't give me permission to do anything about it. Or do anything himself.

"There is nothing between me and Scout." If I've said it once, I've said it a million times. But I also understand why the girls think there is something between us. Especially lately, since Scout's the only one who knows about certain recent events in my life. He's been…helping me with some stuff, so it looks like we're talking more than ever.

I set my drink on the coffee table. It's making me feel icky. Or this conversation is.

Payton stares at me. "You should stop leading Scout on," she says with an underlying hint of resentment. "He's a nice guy."

Suddenly that mask Payton keeps in place drops away, and I can see that she cares about him. She *likes* Scout. It's written in her sad eyes and her pained expression.

How has she been so good at keeping it from us all this time?

It's the alcohol, I realize. That's why I'm able to glimpse

what I usually can't. Her ability to keep up a protective shield is diminished.

Thinking about all the time Scout's wasted being in love with Payton makes me want to scream at him. Why didn't he just *talk* to her?

But a surge of hope follows my upset—about this issue, at least. My dad's stuff and Payton's lost college fund might not be fixable, but *this* is.

Payton starts to cry softly, which is *so* unlike her that we're all a bit shocked. Clara hugs her, and they sit on the living room floor together while Isley and I clean up.

We meticulously load any evidence that they were here or that we drank into the dishwasher, including the blender. Then I start it on a short cycle so that I can clean it out before my mom gets home.

Clara stands and pulls Payton up with her. "I'm going to get you home and into bed. I'll tell your parents you're not feeling well if they're around."

"They won't care or notice." Payton slumps against Clara.

"Should you be driving, Clara? Maybe you girls should stay here for a bit." Although, I am excited for them to leave so that I can call Scout. This has been a long time coming, and I feel like I'm about to hand him one of those extra-large checks for a hundred thousand dollars.

"I wasn't drinking mine," Clara responds. "I just pretended to sip from it. I hate the taste of alcohol."

We all laugh, because this is *so* Clara. And because we were too caught up in ourselves to notice.

"I want to go home," Payton says quietly. "I don't like this version of myself."

I understand what she's saying. And that she's probably frustrated we ended up doing what we did tonight. But we're allowed to make a couple stupid teenage mistakes, aren't we?

We've done a pretty good job navigating high school even with each of us having our own trials.

I don't want Payton to beat herself up. And I want to instill some hope in her even though I can't tell her anything. Yet.

I walk over and hold her face in my hands. "Pay, I need you to listen to me. You will figure out a way out of here, even if it's not Mines." I so badly want to tell her about Scout being madly in love with her, but even now, in my compromised state, I somehow manage to keep his secret for him. "Call me tomorrow, okay? I promise something good is going to happen."

Clara shoots me a concerned look, as if to say, *Don't promise her something you can't follow through on.* But they don't know what I know!

"Don't worry. It's going to be okay." I smack a kiss to Clara's cheek.

Her eyes spark with mirth. "Whatever you say, Cecelia Finch." She packs the rum and daiquiri mix back into the paper bag. "I'm putting this in the car so we can dump it in a public trash can on the way home."

That feels like overkill and yet...it's not like I can stick it in the garbage can at our house. "You're a mastermind." For how well-behaved we've been throughout high school, I'm a little surprised at our ability to hide what we've been up to.

Clara reloads the food we didn't touch into the plastic bag she brought it in.

"I'll carry." Isley takes it from her, and Clara loops an arm around Payton and assists her into the garage.

Isley pauses next to me on her way out. "Haven't forgotten about you, sis." People often comment on how the two of us look like sisters, and the nickname was born from that. "Is prom really what's bothering you?"

Of course not! I want to yell. I'm tempted to tell her everything. To let it all spill out. How I did the unthinkable in eighth grade because I'd believed there was no other way out of my pain. In hindsight I can see there were other options and answers, but at the time, I'd been desperate to escape the visual of my dad cheating on my mother *in our house* with our neighbor's daughter—a girl who was barely twenty years old and used to be my babysitter. That, in and of itself, felt sick enough on its own. But then he asked me to hide it for him.

I was freaking out. I didn't know how to handle something that big. How to keep it from my mom...or how to reveal it to her. Either road was a dead end. Either road was torture. In my desperation, I relayed a portion of the details to my so-called friends, hoping for support or insight from them.

But instead of being true friends, those girls told everyone at school. My mom found out about my dad's dalliance with the neighbor girl from another parent.

This week my dad relayed to me that he's in a new relationship with a twenty-two-year-old and he wants me to meet her, because he's going to *marry her*. What for? It's not like it will last. But he's still willing to destroy what's left of our family in the process. Because while he apparently loves to be in relationships with women only a few years older than me, my mom once loved him wholeheartedly. Despite their divorce, sometimes I'm afraid she still does. Though she's too wise to allow that emotion to surface after the choices he's made.

"Is, you coming?"

"Yeah!" she calls back. "Love you. Call me tomorrow, okay? Maybe you'll be ready to talk then."

"Love you too." I hug her tightly. It was nice, for a couple minutes, to think about Payton and Scout and prom and other normal teenage things instead of the deep dark *blech* of my dad being a complete jerk yet again.

We step back, but Isley yelps. "My earring is caught on your necklace."

"That's what you get for being so short." We laugh as we untangle, and then she's out the door.

After my friends leave, I shut the garage door behind them and double-check that the living room and kitchen don't show evidence of them being here. I even open the dishwasher early, dry the blender, and put it away before restarting the cycle. Satisfied, I call Scout at the diner where he works.

I'm shocked when he answers but I quickly recover. "It's Cece. I *have* to talk to you."

"What's going on? Are you okay?"

Of course his mind would go *there*. Oops. "I'm fine. It's good news."

I hear his exhale of relief. "I'm almost done with my break so you've got two minutes."

In the same way that Clara is the most gracious person I've ever met, Scout is the most stand-up, responsible, do-the-right-thing kind of guy. Of course he would think nothing of answering the diner phone while on his break.

"Tonight, you either need to stop by Payton's after work or call her when you get home. *Tell her*," I emphasize.

"What? Why?"

"I need you to trust me. I've kept your secret all these years. Would I steer you wrong now?"

A few beats of silence fill the line. "Are you sure?" His question is quiet, and the hubbub of the diner can be heard in the background.

"One hundred percent. Plus, she could use some good news right now. Her parents—never mind." It's not my story to tell. If Payton wants to share that update with Scout, she can.

"What did they do now?" he growls.

Payton has no idea how protective Scout is of her or how

many times I've had to talk him down from confronting her parents about something they said or did to her.

I'm so excited for her to see this side of him that if I could, I would buy a front row ticket to one of their future dates.

"Just talk to her."

A puff of annoyance slips over the line. "Fine." There's a smile in his response, and I raise my fist in silent victory. "I work the late shift, so I'll have to do it tomorrow." The diner is open until eleven.

"No dice. It *has* to be tonight."

"What am I going to do? Call her house after work? Knock on the front door?"

He's right. Neither of those will work. "Go throw some pebbles at her window."

"You're being dramatic."

I *am* being a bit dramatic. But I just need some hope right now. "I need something good to happen, and if it's not for me, then even better that it's for a friend. *Two* of my friends."

"What are you not telling me?"

"Nothing like that. Just some family stuff that I gotta figure out."

"Do you need me to come by after work?"

"Are you looking for an excuse not to go over to Payton's and confess your undying love?"

He laughs. "That's exactly what I'm doing."

"Just tell her you like her and ask her to a movie. That's all you need to do. You don't even have to say you *like* her. Just ask her to a movie. She'll figure it out."

"All right, I've got to get back to work."

"Promise me!"

"Fine. I promise."

"Good boy."

He laughs and the phone disconnects.

I hang up my end and do a little dance around the living room, then decide to use this good momentum to tackle another conversation. I'm about to dial the phone when a knock sounds at the front door, interrupting me.

I check the peephole to find it's the exact person I was just about to call.

Chapter Twenty-Eight

Clara sat in a chair next to the hospital bed Hank occupied in the emergency department, her pulse thrumming so wildly she was afraid if her body didn't calm down soon, they would need to find a bed for her too.

Thankfully, in the hour-plus they'd been at the hospital, the staff ruled out a heart attack and pinpointed Hank's issue: atrial fibrillation.

Things moved quickly when the organ keeping you alive was involved.

Currently, the doctor was answering their questions about the diagnosis.

Correction—the doctor was answering Hank's questions because Clara couldn't seem to form a coherent thought. She'd lost it after learning that A-fib could cause a stroke or heart failure.

Logically she knew it was good they were here so they could address the problem.

Emotionally she was sixteen and reliving the moment she'd

answered the phone and heard the words, *Hank's been in a farm accident.*

She'd dropped the cordless phone to the kitchen floor in shock. Her brother Niles—closest in age to her—had picked it up, confirmed that Hank had a broken arm but would be fine, calmed her down, then proceeded to make fun of her over-the-top reaction for the next couple years.

That moment had cemented how she'd felt about Hank. Because the idea that he'd been injured or worse had taken her out at the knees. And she'd instantly known she didn't want to do life without him.

She felt the exact same way now, decades later.

"The good news is you don't have blocked arteries or blood flow," their young doctor relayed. Dr. Caddel looked to be twenty, though she was obviously older than that. "A-fib is an electrical problem versus a plumbing problem."

"What do we do for it?" Hank was handling the discussion regarding his diagnosis with ease while Clara's body continued to react to every bit of information as if the hospital ceiling was caving in on top of them.

And to think, her concern levels regarding her husband going into this weekend had been high. And that had only been because of his emotional health.

"First option, which I'd like to start with, is antiarrhythmic medication, and if that doesn't work, then we'd need to look at doing a catheter ablation."

That sounded dangerous. Didn't it?

"Is this something that can go away on its own?" Hank asked. "Do we have to treat it?"

"It's possible it could go away on its own." Dr. Caddel made a note on the tablet she held. "But with the symptoms you named, it's also possible you've been dealing with this for days. If it were me, I wouldn't take the risk of it forming a clot."

"He'll do the medicine," Clara piped up. Both sets of eyes swung to her. Did she sound as manic as she felt? "Sorry. I mean, we'll start with that, right?" she asked Hank.

"Yep. Let's do it." Hank sounded like he was agreeing to a game of catch with one of their boys.

Their children. How was Clara going to relay this information to them?

Treat it first, then let them know. Why upset the kids when they hadn't even tried the medicine yet?

"Great, let me get this ordered." Dr. Caddel sent them a reassuring smile before leaving the small room where they were stationed.

Hank's brow creased. "You doing okay?"

"I'm fine." Clara gripped the arms of her chair in an attempt to quell her nerves. "How are you feeling?"

"Like there's a wild bird trapped inside my chest. I'm glad it's not a heart attack, but I hope whatever they do helps."

"It will! Right? Gotta trust the experts! They know what they're doing. I'm going to text our friends so they know you're okay."

Although, *okay* was a relative term. But there were worse scenarios than the one Hank was experiencing.

When Clara glanced up from her phone screen, Hank was studying her with a quizzical expression.

"What?"

"I'm trying to figure out why you're talking like a record player that shouldn't be set to seventy-eight rpm."

"I'm not talking fast. I was just relaying a bunch of information so it probably sounded like I was." Even her denial came out at hyper speed.

Clara's phone buzzed with a notification. She checked it. "Everyone says they're glad we got a diagnosis and they're praying for you." Trevor had dropped them at the hospital, stayed until Hank had been brought back to the emergency department, and then returned to the house.

Again, Clara looked up to find her husband staring at her like she'd just landed on planet Earth and descended from a spaceship.

"What?" This time her question came out a bit churlish.

Hank leaned forward and motioned for her to do the same. Then he careened as if trying to see the back of her neck.

"Hank Weber. What are you *doing*?"

"Looking for the switch so I can adjust your rpm."

Clara burst into tears, and Hank sat back in shock. "I'm teasing." His palms rose in a placating manner. "Care to tell me what's going on?"

"You could have died, that's what's going on! And it's all my fault. I should have made you go to the doctor earlier this weekend, or even back home. I shouldn't have—"

"You tried, remember? You brought it up. I'm the one who shut down the idea. It matched so many symptoms of altitude sickness that I thought it had to be that. And I didn't almost die."

"You could have! The A-fib could have caused a stroke or worse!"

"But it didn't."

"But it could have!" Was that wailing coming from her? Clara clamped her mouth shut and slumped against the back of her chair. "I was *terrible* to you today. If you'd died tonight, I would have had to live with that guilt forever!"

Hank laughed. "I'm sorry for almost causing you to live with the burden of guilt over my non-death and our last conversation." His head shook, mouth curved with amusement. "You weren't terrible. You were trying to get me out of the funk I've been in. Just like you've been doing for the last year plus. If anyone should be apologizing, it's me. And I am sorry.

I was so caught up in the farm it became my identity. I thought if it failed, I failed. But now, after tonight, I'm seeing things more clearly."

That made a new batch of tears form. Who would have thought a health problem would be the catalyst for Hank to finally crawl out of the dark hole he'd been cowering in?

"Would you stop with the tears?" Hank's smile was tender. "Come here." He tugged her hand until she was sitting on the bed with him. And then he gave another tug that sent her crashing against his chest.

"Hank! You have so many wires and things attached to you. What if—"

"If something starts beeping, we'll adjust." He kissed her temple as she acquiesced and tucked into the crook of his arm. "I've been wallowing for so long I'm not sure how to un-wallow."

Clara smiled.

"But I'm going to work on it."

That was really good news. "I was *so* impatient with you today."

He leaned his head against hers, his eyes closed. "You were pretty patient with me for a lot of days, weeks, months. You're allowed."

"No, I'm not!"

He laughed at her petulant response. "Yes, you are."

"I was really angry with you," she whispered, a breath shuddering out of her. "I didn't know what to do with that level of emotion. I couldn't even admit it to myself."

"This afternoon was the last straw in a cupful of straws. You should have been angry with me a long time ago. You're allowed to be upset when your life is derailing and you don't have any control over your husband's response to that."

Clara had spent so much of her childhood being the peacekeeper. Especially after her mother's death. Smile. Choose gratefulness and happiness. Encourage and lift others up. Rinse and repeat. Sometimes she didn't even realize she was taking on that role. But if she could trust anyone with her whole truth—even her anger—it was Hank.

"I'm actually proud of you for letting yourself be upset with me and for admitting it."

"That's strange."

"Not when it's you we're talking about." Funny that he knew her better than she knew herself. "I've been a brat for over a *year*. I would have gotten tired of me too if I'd been in your shoes."

Clara toyed with Hank's hand, her vision cast there instead of at him. "The thing is, I'm not tired of you. I just miss you. I know people change during marriage. I get that it's normal and to be expected that with time, pieces of who we are adjust and shift. I want to and will love you through that and I hope you can do the same with me. But..." She exhaled. "Maybe you're right that I need a little more than you've been giving me."

Hank's mouth bowed. "You need a lot more than I've been giving you."

"This whole time, all I've really wanted to hear from you is that if the farm fails and we have to start over, that me and you and the kids...we're enough. That whatever we do, we'll figure it out together."

"Of course that's true. Always."

"I might have needed to hear you say it."

"I'm saying it. Why didn't you tell me you needed to hear it?"

"I thought I did. I asked you so many times...but I may have been asking in roundabout ways."

"You talking in circles? Never."

"Argh." She slapped a hand against his chest and laughed. And then panicked. "Did that hurt? I just slapped your heart!"

"With the strength of a mosquito. Pretty sure all's still well in there. Or at least not any worse." His face contorted in mock distress. "Wait! I think that slap caused a stroke."

"Hank, that's not funny!"

"It's a little funny." He grinned. And then his eyes closed as if a wave of something—maybe exhaustion—came over him. "Is Dr. Caddel coming back at some point? I'm ready to stop feeling like there's a helicopter inside my chest."

Clara slipped from the bed. "I'll go check to see how long it will be before they start the medication." She paused before leaving the room. "Love you."

His mouth creased, his eyelids still shuttered. "Love you more."

For the first time in a while, she believed him.

Chapter Twenty-Nine

Isley was sitting at the island nursing a cup of tea when the door from the garage into the house opened. The caterers had left with their supplies about twenty minutes ago. Trevor had returned to the hospital to pick up Hank and Clara and she knew they were on their way back to the house. Still, she jumped, because due to the events of this weekend, that was her new mode of operation.

"It's just us." Trevor stepped inside.

Clara carried her heels, and Hank's typically ruddy skin had a whitish hue.

When Isley rose to hug him, he pasted on a smile. "I'm fine, Is."

"Your definition of *fine* might be skewed," she teased, because humor was Hank's love language. She stepped back. "Thank you for not dying."

"Happy to oblige."

Isley hugged Clara next, and her friend sagged against her.

"You're back!" Payton joined them from the basement, doling out embraces. "Are you guys exhausted?"

"Like I just ran a marathon." Hank shuffled into the living room and dropped onto the sofa.

Clara joined him there, and Isley and Trevor took the love seat while Payton poured herself into the chair.

Isley was tempted to ask if Liam would be joining them, but she stemmed the curiosity. Payton appeared almost as exhausted as Hank. Maybe there'd been a new development in their relationship tonight. Or maybe, between her marriage issues, her teenage daughter, and the women's confession to Belinda, her friend was just overwhelmed.

"Did we get everything we needed for Finch's Hope?" Hank questioned.

"Venette said the interviews went great. Of course the videographer will need to edit everything before the charity can use it, but the Finch's Hope staff considered the night a success."

"So glad to hear it." Clara's breath puffed out in relief. "And Belinda? How was she?"

"Belinda..." Isley wasn't sure how to relay this information without causing Clara more stress.

"Belinda spoke to Remmy for a long time after you guys left for the hospital," Payton filled in quietly. "And then, when the crowd started thinning out, she just...took off. We haven't seen or heard from her since. Isley and I both texted and called a couple times."

"What?" Clara covered her mouth with her hand. "What are we going to do? Is she *okay*?"

"We've been wondering the same." It was concerning that Belinda wouldn't at least answer one of their texts. "I might run over to the hotel to check on her. I won't be able to sleep if I'm not sure she's all right."

Trevor unbuttoned the cuffs of his dress shirt. "I could have checked on the way back from the hospital."

"I assumed Hank and Clara were drained, so I thought I'd save them the trip and just pop over."

"Good point. I'll go with you."

Relief flooded Isley's system. At least her husband wasn't so upset with her that he refused to be in her presence.

Or maybe he wanted to discuss the Bianca-slash-Freya situation.

"Keep us updated and let us know if we need to come," Payton said with concern, and Hank and Clara nodded their agreement.

"Will do. Do you want to change first?" Isley asked Trevor.

He'd ditched his tie and suit jacket from earlier and now wore the blue shirt with his dress pants. Once the caterers left, Isley had changed into a white sleeveless shirt and brown wide-leg pants that could pass for casual or pajamas.

"That's okay. Let's just go." They loaded into her vehicle, and Trev backed out of the driveway. "What happened when the police showed up tonight as I was driving Hank and Clara to the hospital?"

Trevor had returned to the house between trips, but with guests still present, they hadn't delved into the neighbors' dynamics.

"They knocked on the Elrods' door, and a woman answered and let them in. I assume it was Kyle's wife. Clara told Pay and I that the night of the break-in she overheard Officer Sanchez making a comment about how the Elrods are frequent customers of the police. Or something like that."

"Interesting. I wonder what that means." Trevor turned toward Belinda's hotel, which was located on the edge of town. "Are you going to tell me why we're checking on Belinda right now? What happened? Did she leave because she was upset about something?"

"Are you sure you're ready for two revelations from me in one night?"

His gaze transferred to her and then back to the road. Trevor didn't answer, and Isley didn't blame him.

What he'd uncovered about her earlier this evening was hard enough. But the idea of unveiling her part in Cece's passing produced so much shame her skin heated and broke out in goose bumps simultaneously.

Isley stared through the windshield, unable to look at her husband as she relayed the details of that night.

She told him about Cece and Payton both being upset that week. The pact. The alcohol. How the fear over admitting they'd been with Cece had turned into decades of keeping quiet. And that after Belinda's speech, they'd decided to confess their presence and involvement.

"How did she take it?"

"Based on her early exit, I'd say not well." She studied her hands in her lap. "Can you believe that we would do that?" Disgrace closed off her throat, causing the question to slip out barely above a whisper.

"Do I believe that you were a bunch of frightened teenage girls? Absolutely."

"But we should have never waited so long to tell Belinda." Tears slipped down Isley's cheeks. She was a perpetual fountain this weekend. "Personally, I didn't want to hurt her or lose her, because—"

"She's been more of a mother to you than Iris."

"Exactly. And to Clara. And to Payton. It was like by the time we realized what we'd done in not speaking up sooner, it felt too huge to unravel."

The signal in the vehicle clicked quietly as Trevor waited to turn into the hotel lot. "In a way, what you girls were afraid of is what happened to Aiden. Only he was held accountable for Freya's near-death."

"I've thought the same so many times. It's been hard not to blame myself or even my mother for what happened with him. Like his DNA dictated his choices."

Trevor turned into the lot and headed for an open parking spot. "Lots of people come from hard things and don't continue down the same path. Like you." He inclined his head.

"Because of you."

"That's not true. You were well on your way to not being Iris when I met you." He parked and turned off the engine. "You'd already made far different choices than she had. You were working to pay for college. You studied constantly. You basically lived in the library. And you avoided me like the plague when we first met. Iris wouldn't have done any of those things. She *didn't* do any of those things. And in the same vein, Aiden made his own choices. We gave him all the tools, and he still decided to decompress with oxy versus the other options available. He's just a kid who made a mistake. More than one, I'm sure. Just like you. Just like me."

Her, yes. But Trevor's version of a mistake was forgetting the number of years they'd been married or falling asleep while she was in the middle of talking to him.

"What you girls did is understandable, Is."

A sob released at the absolution. She'd always wondered what Trevor would say or do if he knew the truth. If he would look at her differently.

But like he'd told her earlier...she was the one who saw Iris Tordoff's clone when she looked in the mirror. He saw *her*. And he loved her as is.

"Were you three concerned the note was about Cece's death?" he asked gently.

"We wondered. But we also don't know who would want to out something like that. I'm sorry I didn't tell you. Times two." Isley blotted under her eyelashes with a tissue. "We vowed to never talk about the night Cece died. It was... We hated ourselves for it. Talking about that night made it real, and it was like we had to put it in a vault in order to keep functioning. To keep living...when she didn't."

Trevor reached across the console and squeezed her hand.

"Trev, I am so sorry about Bianca."

"I know. I also know that you care about her. That you were putting yourself in her shoes."

"Yes. I just wanted to make amends for Freya's near-death. But I went about it wrong, and I've come to realize that I can't fix it for her or us. It's just...there. I can't earn her forgiveness. We may never get that. And we and Aiden have to live with that."

"We do."

"Bianca was so upset when we talked that I was afraid she might consider a civil suit. I worried I'd made things worse."

Trevor didn't comment, because what was there to say? That was a possibility. All they could do now was wait and pray that she didn't.

"The night of the break-in, we were worried the note could be about us, but I also..." Isley closed her eyes, her words releasing in a rush. "I questioned if maybe Jeremy had discovered that I'd contacted Bianca and was trying to out me."

"You thought my brother broke into our house to leave a note?"

"I didn't think he would do it himself. But what if he'd hired someone?" She groaned. "I'm hearing myself now though."

"I know you two aren't on the best of terms, but I don't think he'd do something like that. If Jeremy was privy to any information, he would call to tell me in a heartbeat." *Unlike you.* Isley filled in the unsaid jab she deserved.

"You're right. I was just so caught up in my own guilt that I couldn't think clearly. I was a little surprised that you didn't notice me acting strangely after I talked to Bianca, because I've been a mess."

"*I* was so caught up in dealing with the fallout of missing work while we handled Aiden's case that I didn't even notice."

"Wait, what? You never said anything."

His shoulders rose. "I was trying not to create more stress for you on top of what we were already dealing with."

Her husband had been carrying this burden, and Isley had been so focused on herself that she hadn't even realized it.

That, and so many other things, had to change.

"I'm sorry work's been tough. Do we need to make adjustments? Sell The Haven?"

"We don't need to sell the house. I've just been putting out fires and trying to get ahead versus scrambling to catch up."

"Trev, our life is amazing, and I'm grateful for it, but I don't *need* it."

His mouth twisted wryly. "Iris would disagree with you on that."

She laughed. "Yes, she would tell me to stick it out during the good times and move on when things took a turn for the worse."

"I would say we've trudged through plenty of *worse* this spring with Aiden's arrest."

"And yet here we are."

"Exactly." The skin around his eyes softened as he studied her, and then he leaned across the console and wrapped her in a hug.

"I don't deserve your forgiveness," she whispered against his neck, because she knew that's what he was offering.

"I've made plenty of mistakes myself over the years."

"Have you though?" At the moment, Isley could only see her own in the rearview mirror of their relationship.

His chest reverberated with a silent laugh. "If you think I'm going to remind you of any of the things I've done that have upset you, you are sorely mistaken."

Trevor started to ease back, and Isley tightened her arms around him. "Not finished." It felt like ages since they'd connected without the albatross of her choice between them. "What do we do now?"

Despite this healing, so much still felt undone. Aiden's whereabouts, the note at the house, the photos that had arrived on Belinda's step. They hadn't even gotten a chance to discuss the box of pictures with Belinda because she'd left so quickly.

"We do the next thing," Trevor stated in that calm, consistent way of his. Which was what drew her to him the most back when they'd first met. Isley's world had been so chaotic growing up. And her mother's constantly revolving door of boyfriends hadn't helped.

There'd been one in particular who had given her the creeps. Scout had helped Isley install a lock on her bedroom door while Iris had been dating Kent.

A girl had to trust her instincts.

Even still, Kent had taken every opportunity to torment Isley. And one night, in a drunken stupor, he'd gotten angry about something having nothing to do with her and put out a cigarette on her back.

He'd branded her permanently as trash. And she'd never been able to fully rid her body—or her soul—of that scar.

To Iris's credit, when she'd learned what had happened, she'd kicked Kent out. She'd made a dramatic fuss, yelling at him, throwing his possessions onto the lawn.

Nobody touches my daughter! she'd screeched loud enough for the neighbors to hear—not exactly helping the situation.

To this day, Isley's desperate need for organization and cleanliness in her home stemmed from her hatred of the disorder and chaos that had marked her childhood.

"We check on Belinda," Trevor continued, his arms still wrapped around her. "And then on Monday when Zak's back in the office, we get him to confirm Aiden is still at rehab. Which I expect him to be."

"Full transparency—if no one confirms he's safe at rehab by Monday, I'm driving there and demanding to see him."

"If no one responds by then, I'll drive." She smiled at Trev's answer. "And if something comes from the note or the Bianca conversation, we'll deal with that too." He pressed a kiss to her neck, and Isley squeezed her eyes shut to prevent a new rush of emotion.

Like he'd accused her of, she wasn't sure she'd ever let herself trust him completely.

Too many Iris warnings lived in her head.

Men only want one thing, and once they get it, they move on. Never give away your heart fully. Always hold back a piece of yourself so when they leave, you don't break.

Practically poetic of Iris.

Isley hadn't realized the lies her mother had spouted off during her childhood and adolescent years had been operating in her psyche like silent but deadly parasites.

But now that she was aware, it was long past time to surgically remove those.

A knock sounded on Trevor's window, causing them to jump apart as if they were teenagers out past curfew.

Belinda waved, and Trevor popped open the door.

"Are you two done making out? And if yes, are you here for me?"

"Yes, we are." Trevor laughed. "And yes, we're here for you."

Chapter Thirty

When Clara read the text stating that Trevor and Isley were returning to the house with Belinda because she wanted to talk to them, she began pacing the living room.

Would Belinda be able to forgive them? The thought of losing her was nearly as painful as the idea of grieving her own mother all over again.

Sure, Clara had mentioned on their last friendcation that they should consider revealing all to Belinda, but she hadn't accounted for actually *doing* that.

Or what this moment of reckoning would feel like.

"Hank." Clara gripped Hank's arm and gave it a gentle shake. He'd fallen asleep on the couch after Isley and Trevor left. "Belinda's coming over to talk to us. Let's get you downstairs to bed." Unless he wanted to snore through the conversation up here, which, according to the powers of sleep he seemed to possess this weekend, wasn't impossible.

Hank blinked. "Why is Belinda coming back? Is she okay?"

The question of the night.

"I'm sure it's about what we told her earlier. Belinda could hate us or—"

"Want to talk to you about something completely different."

Clara doubted that. She resumed pacing.

At the hospital, Clara had relayed the conversation that they'd had with Belinda to Hank. She hadn't expected anger because that wasn't really Hank's way, but maybe some hurt that she'd withheld information from him. Clara had never spoken about the night Cece died to anyone outside of Payton and Isley. As girls, they'd vowed not to bring it up *under any circumstances*. And as women, they'd been trapped inside the confines of that original promise.

"Huh. So that's why you always shut down when anyone mentions the night Cece died," Hank had said. And then he'd moved on to another topic! As if she'd relayed the contents of a grocery list to him instead of something demoralizing.

"How do you not see how awful it is that we kept that from Belinda? And that I didn't even tell you about it!"

"You were just girls, Clara. You needed advice and wisdom. And you didn't have anyone to talk to. Your dad did his best, but he had his hands full raising the boys after your mom died."

He was right. But that didn't make what they'd done right.

"Is Belinda here?" Payton asked as she came upstairs.

"Not yet," Clara responded. "Is Liam joining us?"

"No, he's hanging out with Reagan." Payton dropped onto the love seat, an air of exhaustion wafting from her. "Would it be out of the way for you guys to drop Liam at the airport on your drive home tomorrow?"

"Of course not," Clara quickly supplied. Logistically, it might take them slightly off course, but she would never admit as much.

Hank's vision toggled between the two of them. "What am I missing? Does Liam need to be back for work or something?"

"He does actually. But I—" For a second it appeared as though Payton might cry. But then she wrangled all of that Payton fierceness together and her mouth formed a sad smile instead. "It appears that I'm going to have to find a divorce support group or a new hobby. Maybe bowling. Something to occupy me since Liam and I are splitting up and Reagan will kill me if I focus all of my attention on her." Payton's voice dropped. "We actually just finished talking to her about it."

"Oh, Pay." Clara marched over and hugged her friend long and hard. When she stood, Hank was waiting behind her.

He bent to hug Payton. "If anyone can rock this, it's you."

She sniffled. "Thank you."

"Do I need to beat him up or anything?"

Payton gave a watery laugh. "Not today but I'll let you know if I need to take you up on that offer."

The door from the garage into the house opened. "We're back," Isley called out.

Belinda scanned the kitchen. "When did the caterers leave?"

"About twenty minutes before Trevor and I headed over to check on you. Why, did you need to talk to them?"

"No, I was just hoping there was food left. I was so busy tonight I barely ate anything."

"We can fix that." Isley scooted around the island and washed her hands. "We have enough food in this house to feed an army."

She appeared relieved to have a task, which Clara understood.

"Belinda, where would you like to sit?" Trevor asked. "Living room, dining table, deck?"

"Outside, please. I feel like I didn't get to enjoy that tonight either."

"You three head out." Clara motioned to Trevor, Belinda,

and Hank—who evidently planned to stay awake for this conversation. "We'll grab the fixings and be right behind you."

They exited onto the deck through the partially open wall of glass doors.

Isley peered into the fridge. "I've got a bunch of leftover appetizers in here. Does that sound good? Or should I do something else?" She sounded as frazzled as Clara felt.

"Apps are perfect," Clara assured her. "And quick. The faster we know what Belinda wants to talk to us about, the better."

"Agreed." Payton gave a determined nod. "Whatever happens, we'll navigate it together, because you two along with Belinda are my family. I wouldn't have survived this long without you, and I'm going to need you on the next leg."

Isley paused from arranging appetizer options on a large tray on the island, her vision bouncing to Payton.

"It's official. We told Rea tonight not because the timing was good, but she brought it up and it just sort of…came out."

"I'm sorry, Pay." Isley hugged her. "A break-in, a weird note, strange photos and a divorce is definitely not what I had on the agenda for this weekend."

"Same." Payton added silverware to the small stack of plates she'd procured from the cupboard as Clara filled glasses with ice water.

"Whatever happens, we'll navigate it together." Clara reiterated Payton's statement. And they would continue to fight for and celebrate Cece's legacy in the future too. As long as Belinda didn't prevent that from happening.

They delivered the items to the coffee table on the deck. Trevor and Hank had pulled over two chairs to face the L sofa.

Isley, Payton, and Clara sat with Belinda on the outdoor couch.

"Thank you, girls." Belinda filled a small plate with an assortment of dips and crackers and vegetables.

"Belinda, we're so sorry that we didn't come to you earlier to confess that we'd been drinking with Cece that night," Payton said quietly. "We all regret letting our fear keep us from giving you information that could have provided even an iota of relief."

"I appreciate that." Belinda popped a cracker with dip into her mouth, chewed, then swallowed before continuing. "I remember at the time how much I craved details leading up to Cece's death. Especially since she didn't leave a note. Once I learned from the coroner there was alcohol in Cece's system, it crossed my mind to inquire if you girls were with her. Alcohol didn't seem like something she would partake of herself. But then, suicide felt off too."

Belinda ate another cracker, shoulders drooping. "Although, I've learned that's what every parent thinks after losing a child in such a manner. I'd planned to ask you girls, but then at the funeral, I saw the way people avoided you. Like you were damaged or tainted because of your friendship with Cece. I decided whether you girls were drinking with her or not didn't change the fact that she was gone. Instead, I asked the three of you if you had any insight into why Cece made the choice she did. And I believed you when you said you didn't. I could tell by the way you grieved and responded to her passing that you were just as shocked as I was. That she hadn't relayed anything to you that would make it all make sense."

Isley shifted forward on the couch. "We would never have kept that from you. She was upset about something that week, but she never told us what it was. I knew there was more going on, but I thought we had time. I gave her space, and I shouldn't have."

"Don't shoulder that blame. Cece wouldn't have responded well to pressure or pushing." Belinda set her plate on the coffee table. "I suppose, maybe part of me also knew that if you girls had been drinking with Cece and it became public knowledge, that people would have judged you and tried you in the court of public opinion."

"So...you were protecting us?" Payton asked, her brow furrowed.

"In a way, yes. Because you three saved Cece. I know you didn't learn about her suicide attempt in eighth grade until after her death. But that was because Veil was her chance to start over. And you provided that opportunity for her. She changed *so* much once she became friends with you girls. It was as if she blossomed back to life. You brought *both* of us back to life. No matter what caused Cece's decision that night, you three were the solution, not the problem. I'm sure it gets old that I'm constantly inserting myself into you and your spouses' lives, but you became my substitute daughters."

"We feel the same about you being our bonus mom. None of us consider your love and support intrusive." Clara sniffled as Payton and Isley nodded in agreement. "We're so grateful for you."

"I like being doted on," Hank supplied. "It's nice to have someone recognize all my amazing qualities."

Laughter and groans followed.

Payton shook her head, lips curving. "We needed you then. And we all need you now. Especially humble Hank."

Belinda's cheeks creased. "And after Cece passed away, *I* needed you girls. And your *phenomenal* spouses, of course. Speaking of... Where is Liam?"

Payton froze with a water glass to her lips. "Um." She placed it on the coffee table with a loud *clink*. "Liam's downstairs with Reagan right now. I don't know how to say this so I guess I'll just... We're going to be separating when we get back to Dallas. He wants a divorce. It's not what I want, but..." Her hands jutted into the air and then dropped to her lap.

"Oh, my dear girl." Belinda opened her arms, and Payton scooted toward her to accept the embrace she offered. "If anyone understands that exact pain, it's me." Belinda leaned back and held Payton's gaze. "I'm sure right now you're wondering how you're going to survive." Payton's eyes shimmered with tears as Belinda continued, "But you're not only going to do that, you're also going to flourish. I promise. And I'll be here for you every step of the way. You call or text me anytime, day or night."

This was why they couldn't survive without Belinda. She loved them fiercely. The fact that she'd been protecting them after Cece's death was astounding...but also less surprising than it should be.

"I'm sorry for leaving early tonight." Belinda's vision encompassed each of them. "I think when you hear why I did, you'll understand. Did you girls know that Scout came to me after Cece's passing?"

All three shook their heads in answer.

"He told me that Konnor had been abusive toward Cece before her death."

"What?" Isley's fists clenched. "How would he know that? Why didn't *we* know that?"

"That's why she was acting so weird about Konnor during senior year," Payton filled in. "I thought it had something to do with her liking Scout or him liking her." She scowled. "I *never* liked Konnor. I tried to include him for Cece's sake. But to me, there was always something off about him."

"Same," Isley said.

"Same," Clara added.

"Yep." Hank's expression was thunderous. It was a subject Clara and Hank had discussed back in high school and after. But they'd never had a concrete reason for their distaste.

Obviously they'd all been trying to get along with Konnor

for Cece's sake. Maybe if they'd been more vocal, she would have opened up to them about what was going on.

Or maybe they would have alienated her by giving their opinions of her boyfriend when she wasn't ready to hear them.

"I didn't see the appeal with him either," Belinda said. "According to Scout, she was one hundred percent done with Konnor. Which made me wonder if that aggravated him. I went to the police with Scout, and he relayed to them what he'd told me about Konnor being abusive. I begged them to fully investigate Cece's death. I told them she would *never* have hung herself. After her attempted suicide by intentional overdose in eighth grade, she told me that she knew she would have been incapable of taking her life in any other way. But once the police learned about her suicide attempt in eighth grade and that she'd struggled with depression, it was case closed. They just slapped on a label." She released a growl. "They were *so* condescending to me. Like my mother's intuition didn't count for anything. I kept telling them that Cece wasn't in that frame of mind her senior year, but they didn't listen.

"It wasn't like I could hire a private investigator," Belinda continued. "I didn't have the money for that. So eventually, I moved on. Sometimes Konnor was willing to be involved with Finch's Hope and other times he disappeared from having anything to do with the charity for years on end. I only invited him tonight because I thought it would look strange if I didn't. I certainly didn't expect him to accept. But apparently, he RSVP'd yes because of Remmy. She's taken a big interest in the charity because she almost lost a friend in an online group to suicide."

"She told me about her friend," Payton spoke up. "Remmy is absolutely precious. It's hard to believe that Konnor was part of creating someone as amazing as her."

Belinda inclined her chin in agreement and took a sip of

ice water. "Tonight, after you girls talked to me on the deck, Remmy asked me if I got the photos she dropped off at my house."

Wait. What? "But how would Remmy have access to those photos? I don't think I ever saw Konnor with a camera in high school." Even then, Clara had been their resident photographer.

"Maybe Cece gave him some doubles of hers," Isley supplied.

"Could be. She always had stacks of pictures in her room," Belinda said. "But here's where it gets really convoluted. Of course you all know that I've been on the hunt for Cece's necklace since she died. And I am one thousand percent sure that Remmy was wearing it tonight."

A bomb of confusion exploded, causing Clara's hearing to warble as if an actual explosive had detonated.

"What?" Isley hissed. "How is that even *possible*?"

Belinda unlocked her phone. "Here it is." She opened her photos app and passed it to Clara.

It was, without a doubt, Cece's necklace. Clara trembled as she gave the phone to Payton. This was *so* strange. *How* did Remmy have Cece's necklace?

"That's definitely it." Payton handed the phone to Isley, who nodded her agreement before passing it to Trevor and Hank.

Belinda stood and retrieved the phone from Hank and then paced from the chair to the outdoor couch and back.

"I walked away from you girls on the deck because Remmy was just behind you and could easily overhear. But then I noticed the necklace she was wearing was tucked under the high neckline of her dress, and in a typical mom move, I pulled it out for her. I about fell over when I saw it was identical to Cece's. And I was immediately reminded of Scout's accusations back when Cece died. I had Suri take photos of me with Remmy so that I could get proof of the necklace, and then I had her take some on my cell phone too. Remmy told me she'd found the necklace in a box of old things in her dad's closet. She didn't want me to tell him that she'd borrowed it, because she hadn't asked permission. Of course I assured her that I wouldn't say anything. She was under the impression it was her mom's necklace because there were some things in the box that pertained to her mother."

Payton ran agitated fingers through her hair. "So, Konnor took it? Or he was there when Cece died? Or he upset her enough to hurt herself? Or *what happened*?"

"My questions exactly. I left as soon as I could to contact the Veil Police Department. I relayed everything to the new young investigator, sent him photos of the necklace, and gave him the details of where Remmy said she found the box. I told him that if he didn't immediately look into why Konnor has had Cece's necklace all these years or if he was somehow involved in her death, then I would go to every online crime syndicate and scream about the inadequate investigation when Cece died…and decry that the new regime is refusing to re-examine her death now despite new evidence." Belinda smiled victoriously. "I get the impression he's going to do his job."

Chapter Thirty-One

On Sunday morning, Payton woke next to Reagan on the sofa bed and did her best not to move in the hopes of not waking her daughter.

Payton had been incapable of sleeping in the same bed as Liam last night, and now that Reagan knew everything, there was no reason to pretend or continue what was, evidently, their terribly enacted charade.

Last night, between the end of the dinner party and Belinda's return to the house, she and Liam had checked on Reagan. But instead of ironing things out after their contentious afternoon conversation, tensions had imploded further when Reagan had plucked out her earbuds and said, "Is this the conversation where you two finally admit that you're splitting up?"

Payton had dropped to a seat on the bed in complete shock. She'd thought they'd done a better job of keeping their issues under wraps.

Even Liam had appeared stunned, though he'd adjusted to the question-slash-accusation faster than Payton. He'd started on a spiel about how much they both loved Reagan—that part was true. And how things in her life wouldn't change—a complete sack of lies in Payton's opinion.

"But yes, we are planning to separate when we get back home," Liam had quietly admitted. "You are correct."

Reagan had rolled her eyes. "Separate in order to try to fix something? Or separate in order to get divorced?"

It was just like Reagan to demand the truth. To not let them sugarcoat the details.

Liam's shoulders had drooped dejectedly when answering his daughter. "Divorce. I'm sorry, Rea."

They'd ended up talking openly with her after that. Reagan had cried. Payton had cried. Liam had been emotional. Payton had thought that if anything could change her husband's mind, it would be their daughter, but he'd stayed strong in his decision. And he'd repeated all the same platitudes to Reagan that he'd uttered to Payton.

Reagan's reaction to those had been a wrinkled nose and a disbelieving squint.

Their daughter wasn't naive as to how this would affect her future. But in some ways, she'd appeared relieved to have it out in the open.

In the midst of the conversation, Payton had asked Reagan if her self-harm had been because of their marriage problems. Reagan had denied that was the catalyst.

"It wasn't one thing," she'd told them. "It was everything. All this pressure kept building with school and riding competitions, and my friends were already acting weird at that point, and everything just felt massive. I was trying so hard to hold it together, and it was just too much, I guess. I know that probably doesn't make sense."

Payton had assured her it made perfect sense.

She had a similar tendency to stifle pain. Hadn't she been

doing the same by telling herself she was okay with Liam's plan? She'd been trying to minimize the agony of being left—un-loved, un-chosen, unimportant.

Ultimately, even if the self-harm was a response in part to their disintegrating marriage, Payton couldn't rewind and fix that.

She couldn't even fix them now.

Some things required building a bridge over instead of forging a road through.

Now, Payton attempted to scoot to the side of the sofa bed in a stealthlike manner, but Reagan's dry, amused tone stopped her.

"It's okay, Mom. I'm awake."

Payton winced. "Sorry."

"It wasn't you. I just…didn't sleep great."

"Me either. I'm sorry that Dad and I are the source of that lack of sleep."

Reagan rolled to face her. "Mom, are we going to be okay?"

Interesting that Reagan was asking her even though Liam was the one orchestrating the divorce. Of course it took two people to create issues in a relationship, but when one wanted to repair it and the other didn't…

They ended up here.

How was Payton supposed to answer a question like that?

"If there's one thing I know, it's that your father adores you. He always has. And since I do too… Yeah, we're going to figure out how to be okay."

"I feel like part of him loving me should include him loving you. He shouldn't get to separate the two."

Last night Payton and Liam had both been careful not to cast blame on each other regarding the divorce. But Reagan had obviously deciphered that splitting wasn't Payton's idea. Or maybe she'd figured that out a while ago too.

Payton swallowed a sob, determined not to break when Reagan needed her strength. "I'm with you on that. Unfortunately, it doesn't seem to be how things are turning out this time."

She ran her fingertips across Reagan's temple. "You don't have to solve any of this, honey. Your job is just to be our daughter. And let us love you and take care of you and support you. Your job isn't to fix us or worry about what our relationship looks like. We will get along because we love you. Just like we told you last night."

Reagan sniffled.

"Rea, how would you feel about taking a road trip?"

"We're on a road trip."

"I know. But suddenly I'm not in a huge rush to get back to Dallas. I have some vacation time available and it's summer break for you. What if we take a couple days and see some other places?"

A hint of interest flickered. "Dad has to teach this week, doesn't he?"

"I was thinking we might do it without Dad."

"Mom." Reagan's voice dipped with humor and admonishment. "I thought you guys were going to get along perfectly and all that other sus stuff you told me last night."

Payton laughed. Sus = suspicious. That was one bit of teen slang she actually understood. "We never said *perfectly*. Since Dad has to get back, Hank and Clara can drop him at the Denver airport on their way home. They already said they're willing." And knowing her friends, they would drive ten hours out of the way if she asked. "We could see more of Colorado or we could drive up to see Yellowstone or Grand Teton National Park. Or anything you want."

"Actually, Zion mentioned a few places that we should see while we're here. I didn't think that was an option, but your idea is...interesting."

Of course she couldn't say *good* or *great*. But Payton would take *interesting*. Interesting was a win.

"Plus, if we don't have to rush out of Breckenridge today to get on the road, then I could meet Zion before we leave town."

Reagan had been toying with the sheet, and her fingers froze. "What?" She sat up straight. "Are you serious? I thought you were *so* mad at me about him."

"I was upset that you didn't talk to me or Dad and that you hid things from us. And I'm still not over that. But, I think you're incredibly smart and have great instincts when it comes to making friends. So, if you see good in Zion, then I need to trust you on that. But you're still definitely getting some sort of punishment for lying to us."

Reagan's chin slanted with acceptance. "That's fair."

"What do you think? Want to text Zion and see if he's available to have a late lunch with us today after we pack up and leave Isley and Trevor's?"

Reagan's teeth pressed into her lip and then she shrugged. "'Kay. Sure. Will Dad be able to get a last-minute ticket?"

"Yeah. We'll definitely figure that part out. Don't worry about Dad."

Payton hated to sound like a scorned woman, but Liam owed her this. He was getting his demand—dissolving their marriage. Her request was small in comparison.

Plus, it was the perfect opportunity for him to prove all those platitudes he'd been spouting were true.

"After I get ready, I'm going to head upstairs and eat breakfast. See if you can go back to sleep for a bit." Payton slid out of bed and walked to the bathroom. Inside, she shut the exterior door and knocked lightly on the interior one that led to the bedroom so that if Liam was sleeping, she wouldn't disturb him. "Are you awake? I need to talk to you about something."

At his affirmative answer, Payton opened the door and stepped through it.

★ ★ ★

"I feel like I have a revelation hangover from last night." Isley sipped her latte, inhaling the comforting dark roast aroma from her perch at the dining table. A plate of untouched fruit sat in front of her. Her stomach had soured after last night's conversation about Konnor and Cece's necklace. About what the implications of him having it could mean.

What are we missing, sis? If only Cece could actually answer.

"I have one from this whole weird weekend." Clara cut an almond pastry in half and slid it onto her plate. "And I don't know why, but I'm still in shock that Belinda was protecting us back then."

"It's so her, isn't it?" A sheen of moisture surfaced in Payton's hazel eyes. "Belinda is the definition of selfless love. For years, I've considered myself not to have parents. But in truth, I had a replacement mother before I was even estranged from mine. So many people never get to have that kind of influence and support in their lives. I'm grateful that I do."

"Well said." Isley cupped hands around her coffee mug. "And it's so freeing that she knows everything now. I don't think I understood what a relief that would be. Clara, when you brought it up on our last trip, you were right."

"Easier said than done. I'm glad it worked out, but the process itself was awful. Speaking of, Is, have you guys heard back about Aiden yet?"

"Nope. If we don't get an answer from someone tomorrow, Trev says we can drive to the rehab center and storm the gates looking for him."

Trevor's quiet laugh sounded. "That wasn't our exact conversation by any means. But Aiden's lawyer will be back in the office tomorrow, and I'm confident he'll get us confirmation."

"Good." Clara gave an encouraging nod. "So, you just have to survive until then."

Isley couldn't think of a more apt description.

Liam crested the stairs. "I got a ticket for early evening. Think that works for driving me to the airport?" he asked Hank and Clara.

"Sure," Hank nodded. "No problem."

Liam filled a mug with coffee and joined them at the table. "Thanks." A sad smile claimed his mouth. "Sorry I brought the awkward this weekend."

Isley appreciated that he said *I* versus *we*, because she knew where Payton stood on their separation. And it appeased a bit of her anger at Liam that he did too. It was tempting to rail at him, to force him to explain his reasoning. But Payton had tried that already, and it hadn't procured any understandable answers. Isley wanted Payton and Liam to salvage their relationship for her friend's sake and for Reagan's sake.

But it didn't appear they were going to get a fairy-tale ending this time.

Though the women did have each other. And was there a better fairy-tale ending than friends who'd loved each other for decades, supporting each other through life's hardships?

Cece might be gone, but she was still part of them—and always would be.

"What's one more unexpected development in this weekend full of surprises?" Clara said, adding a melancholy smile of her own. "I'm not going to lie... I'm brokenhearted over this chasm in your relationship."

"I can understand that." Liam's Adam's apple bobbed. "I... changed the script." His apologetic gaze swung to Payton. "I get that it messes with everything."

It was good to hear him say that too.

"I guess we'll just have to be adults about it all and get along like we always have," Clara said in an attempt to smooth what felt wrinkled. But she was right. They were big kids. They would navigate their friend's split.

"Personally, I'm never speaking to Liam again." Hank's mouth twitched with humor. "He didn't even say good morning to me today. And earlier, I sneezed while upstairs and he didn't say bless you from his bedroom down in the basement. Lot of red flags there."

Laughter and shaking heads followed. And then suddenly, thanks to Hank and Clara, the world righted again and things felt normal. Or as normal as they could feel when a friend's life was imploding and you were sitting on the sidelines, helplessly watching it happen.

Trevor squeezed Isley's arm in a show of nonverbal support, likely sensing her surge of sorrow. "Liam, did you get filled in on what Belinda told us last night?" he asked.

"I did." Liam's features relaxed at the switch in topics. "Wild stuff. Any other updates this morning?"

"Nope. Which might be a good thing." Trevor stood and strode into the kitchen, where he refilled his coffee. "We could use a day off from drama."

The doorbell sounded.

"Seriously?" His eyebrows rose, and a collective groan came from the group.

"Maybe it's Belinda. She mentioned stopping over this morning if she had time before her drive back." But Isley hadn't heard from her today.

"Whoever we guess it is, we'll be wrong." Trevor opened the front door. "Sergeant Miller," he greeted the man with an almost comical come-in hand motion. "Join us. We're just having breakfast. Can I get you some coffee?"

"No, but thank you." Sergeant Miller followed Trevor to the dining table. "Sorry to drop by again, but I thought it would make sense to deliver this news in person since it's..." his head shook "...convoluted."

That description sounded on par for this weekend.

"Please, have a seat." Trevor motioned to the chair at the head of the table and then returned to his spot next to Isley.

"We uncovered who broke in and left the note at your house. It was a man named Darren Loyd."

Stark relief that the break-in didn't have to do with Aiden resonated through Isley, causing a shudder. She wanted to throw her hands into the air and screech in victory! She wanted to cry from the release of her fears. That had to mean Aiden was safe at rehab, didn't it?

"*Who* is Darren Loyd? We don't know anyone by that name. Do we?" She checked with Trevor and then the rest of their friends, receiving *no's* from everyone present.

"That's because the note wasn't meant for you all. Apparently, Mrs. Elrod was having an affair with this Darren. She broke things off, but he didn't want their relationship to end. He continued to contact her and eventually took some drastic steps in the hopes of breaking apart her marriage. He thought if her husband learned about their affair, he would leave Renee—Mrs. Elrod—and that she might come back to him. And the note was his attempt to orchestrate that. He was also aware that Renee had turned off the surveillance system because of the affair. She hadn't wanted Kyle to be able to track her coming and going from the house."

"But..." Trevor's forehead furrowed. "How did he end up here instead of the Elrods'?"

"He said he knew the name of their street but not their house address. But Renee had mentioned they were located at the end of the street. Which left two options—your house or theirs. He also knew that Kyle and Renee were full-time residents while many of their neighbors were not. When he got here, the lights were on at your house and it appeared occupied while Kyle and Renee's was dark with no signs of occupancy. He was aware they were attending an event Thursday evening and assumed they'd left a couple lights on to make it appear as if they were home. So, he broke into the wrong house to leave the note."

"That *is* convoluted." Clara sat back against the seat of her chair. "I thought Kyle was a little off when he came over here Thursday night. Guess my radar was off too."

"It was more on than the rest of ours." Even with the police activity there last night, Isley had barely given the Elrods a second thought.

Payton's mouth hitched with a sardonic curve. "I like how Mrs. Elrod's tryst thought that forcing her to out her affair would give him another chance with her. On what planet would that approach work?"

Sergeant Miller released a fatigued sigh. "None of his choices make sense. But then, most criminals aren't known for their logic. After questioning, Darren also admitted he was under the influence of alcohol the night he broke in, so I'm sure that played into him getting the wrong house. At this point, he's been arrested and charged. And Mrs. Elrod is filing a restraining order."

"So..." Liam drummed his fingertips against the table. "That's why the police were at the Elrods' house last night?"

"Not exactly. The Elrods tend to have a...tumultuous relationship. We went to the property because we received a call from Mrs. Elrod seeking assistance in diffusing a domestic disturbance between herself and Kyle. Renee told the officers her husband had found out about an affair she'd been having and that she felt threatened by both him and Darren. She said Darren had been harassing her the last couple days, claiming he'd broken into the house and that she needed to *follow through on what he'd told her to do.* But she was of course confused as to what that meant. That's how we pieced together that your home invasion was meant to be theirs."

Trevor's mouth pursed. "This is all a lot to process."

"It is. That's why I stopped by instead of calling."

As strange as it all was, Isley felt utter relief.

Aiden hadn't been at the house, which hopefully meant he was still at rehab.

The note hadn't been directed at them, which meant they could stop fearing that another shoe was going to drop or someone was out to destroy their lives.

Instead someone had been out to destroy their neighbor's life. And somehow they'd gotten caught in the crosshairs.

After Sergeant Miller left, the group had discussed the strange details he'd relayed along with the rest of the events of the weekend before dispersing to pack for their return trips home.

Clara and Liam had loaded the van, despite Hank's protests. But Clara wasn't taking any risks with her husband, especially when Dr. Caddel had dictated that he needed to take it easy and eliminate stress in his life.

Once they were ready to depart, the group met in the kitchen for goodbyes.

Payton sipped from a water glass as she leaned against the kitchen counter. "Did anyone ever hear from Belinda this morning?"

"Oh, she did text." Isley winced. "Sorry, totally forgot to mention it. She said she had to get back to Veil and would update us when she knows more."

Clara filled her water bottle for the drive with ice and water from the fridge. "Waiting is torture. I'm so angry that Konnor has Cece's necklace that when we get back to town, I'm going to—"

"Let the police do their job?" Hank's eyebrows rose. "And not say a word so that Konnor doesn't disappear before the investigators can question him?"

Clara huffed. "That is not what I had in mind."

Payton placed her now-empty glass in the top rack of the dishwasher. "It's weird that you live in the same town as him." Her forehead puckered with the anger they all felt. "I'd for sure be tempted to head over to his place and interrogate him."

"At least it won't be decades without answers this time," Isley added.

"It had better not be. Sorry we're talking about this dire stuff." Payton squeezed Reagan's arm as she leaned against the counter next to her. She'd obviously filled her daughter in on the latest happenings.

"It's okay. I want justice for Cece too. All you guys need is a few TikTokers to get a hold of this and—"

"Rea. Don't you dare." Payton's pupils spread wide with panic. "Like Hank said, we have to give the police time to do their job."

"Even though they didn't do it the first time?" Reagan crossed her arms.

Trevor chuckled. "Next time I need something done right, I'm calling Reagan."

Liam's eyes crinkled with his smile. "She's smarter than me, that's for sure." His adoration of Reagan was evident, and it gave Clara hope that he and Payton would be able to navigate this next step with grace and dignity for their daughter's sake.

Of course the split would force them all to choose sides in various situations, and of course Clara was always going to be one thousand percent Team Payton.

But she also hoped to be able to get along with Liam when the occasion called for it.

Because in truth, they were all Team Reagan.

Protecting her mattered most of all.

"What a strange weekend. I'm still shocked that note was for the wrong house." It had caused so much worry and stress... and yet, Clara was grateful for the end result. Coming clean to Belinda was a huge relief. As was finally admitting to Hank how frustrated she'd been feeling.

"Right? We need a friendcation redo," Isley stated. "Next summer. Just the girls." She sent an apologetic glance to the men. "Come to our house in Cherry Creek. Or here. Bring Ava," she said to Clara. "And of course Reagan wouldn't miss another trip with us for the whole wide world."

Reagan snorted. "Of course not. Who would have thought that hanging with teenagers would be less drama than hanging with a bunch of ol—" She cut herself off and then grinned. "Adults," she clarified, to a round of laughter.

"So, this is goodbye?" Clara felt the tears form before she gave them permission. But then, what else was new?

"It's 'see you soon,'" Payton countered.

With the changes between Liam and Payton, this felt different than leaving any other friendcation. Like the end of an era. Though they *would* figure out how to muddle through this next hurdle together. And having a girls' trip to look forward to next summer sounded like a perfect plan.

But next time, Clara would save her pennies beforehand to cover the cost of any activities. Right after she figured out how to repay her friend for the ones they'd done on this trip.

Hugs commenced, and within a few minutes, she and Hank were loaded into the van with Liam while Payton and Reagan waved from their small SUV as they backed out of the driveway.

Trevor and Isley stood outside as they pulled away, Isley leaning against Trevor. Even with all the mayhem this weekend had brought and not having confirmation yet that Aiden was still at rehab, they appeared to be at peace—or as close to that emotion as they could be without answers. Like they would weather whatever came next together.

Clara's vision bounced to Hank in the passenger seat.

She knew the feeling well.

Hank intercepted her glance and reached over to hold her hand. "Love you, Clara Rose." He raised his chin. "Love you too, Liam," he called to the back seat.

Liam's low laugh sounded in answer.

Chapter Thirty-Two

Cece

When I first see Konnor through the peephole, there's a catch in my gut that tells me maybe I shouldn't open the door. But I need to talk to him and doing it in person makes sense.

After all, we've been dating off and on for almost two years of high school.

Plus, I want to trust that he's a good person.

I unlock the door and swing it open. "I was just about to call you."

"Me being here in person is better than a phone call, right?" His smile is bright but registers like a Photoshopped toothpaste ad.

Just like that, my attempt to be civil dissipates, and I want to slap the smarmy grin off his face like he would probably do to me if I let our relationship continue.

At first, Konnor was a doting boyfriend. Flowers. Notes.

Swinging by the parking lot of my work when I got off just to steal a kiss. During junior year, there was the occasional degrading comment or flirting with other girls and then gaslighting me as if I was to blame.

Senior year, the passive aggressive comments ramped up until I found myself avoiding him without realizing it...while we were supposedly still a couple. We ended up breaking up a couple of times over the course of our relationship, and I wish I had let one of those instances be the end. But one of us always caved and reached out to the other.

I can't let that happen this time.

Once Konnor's anger ramped up to involve the physical, I knew I *had* to get out.

The first incident happened two months ago. Konnor and I got into a fight about something in his kitchen, and he threw a glass against the wall. Not *at* me, but some of the shards bounced off and hit me. It was frightening, but he convinced me it was a one-off situation. He was also completely well-behaved and repentant for weeks afterward.

Then about a month ago, he prevented me from leaving a room by gripping my arms so hard that I had to hide the bruises for the next week.

More apologies and excuses followed.

And then last week, I saw his anger ignite, and I basically ran from his house. I've been avoiding him ever since by telling him I was busy with work and family stuff. He makes me nervous, and not in the good butterflies-in-my-stomach kind of way. I've been biding my time trying to figure out how to get out of the relationship without causing issues. But tonight, something has loosened in me and I feel strong. Maybe it's the alcohol giving me courage, but I would like to think that I'm just stepping into who I really am. Into the person my mom raised me to be.

I *know* I'm capable of handling Konnor and the new developments with my dad because of her and the friends I gained in Veil.

In the aftermath of my suicide attempt, my mom never cast shame on me for what happened. Her anger was only directed at my dad for putting me in that position.

And despite how badly I didn't want to move to this Podunk town, being welcomed into a friendship with Isley, Payton, and Clara my freshmen year, and Scout and Hank too, was like being given not just a second chance at life, but an actual second life. A do-over.

Thanks to all of them, even with my dad's latest decision, I've come so far from that place I once existed that I have no desire to end my life.

At least when my mom learns about my dad's wedding plans, I'll be able to alleviate her fears over my well-being. She deserves that peace and more.

"I was driving home from work and realized that we never talked about prom," Konnor says. "Do you know what color your dress is? I should probably get a tux rented soon."

I love how he assumes we're going together. But we are technically a couple, so I guess he's not off base.

I also cannot believe that he's ignoring what happened last week. We were playing a game at his house, which he was losing and I had the audacity to tease him about. When I got up to grab a soda from the fridge, suddenly he was standing too and he just...slammed into me. I went flying and my head bounced off the arm of the couch so hard that my neck was sore for days.

"Sorry, we got up at the same time." He'd laughed—*laughed!*—as if the whole thing was a silly mix-up. "You okay?" And then he'd turned all tender, trying to hug me, to check on me.

I'd wanted to scream that I wasn't, but deep down I knew he'd done it on purpose...and I had to get out of there.

"I forgot that I told my mom I'd be home in five minutes," I'd declared, grabbing my keys and heading for the door. "Even if I leave now, I'm going to be late!" After getting into my car, I'd immediately locked the doors and tore out of there.

Honestly, I shouldn't be surprised by Konnor's actions. I've seen the bruises on his mother that she attempts to hide. I've witnessed the way his father talks to her...and to him.

Being in that household is glimpsing a future I want to avoid at all costs.

"I don't think we should go to prom together."

"Why not?" His eyes narrow, and I realize they're bloodshot. Lately Konnor seems different. Like maybe he's on something, though I'm not sure what.

"I'm done with us, Konnor. Last week at your house, you hurt me." I know I need to be careful, but I'm also so *mad* that it's seeping out my pores.

"It was just an accident. You're being dramatic." He catches himself casting blame on me and changes his tune. "I'm sorry that I bumped into you, but I promise it was just a fluke."

The organs inside my chest give a lengthy exhale. It would be *so* easy to believe him. And maybe he's telling the truth. But does it matter? How do you keep going out with someone who you're afraid of?

"I'm glad it wasn't on purpose." The alcohol may have loosened my tongue, but I'm not stupid. "But I do think it's still time for me to move on. I'll be leaving for college in the fall, and you'll be here. We can be one of those cool couples who stays friends after they break up."

"I'm not going to be friends with you," he states, pupils darkening.

A sliver of trepidation threads its way up my spine.

"Well, maybe we'll get there at some point. We had a lot of fun together, and I'm grateful for that." We did. In the beginning. Before Konnor's true colors started coming out.

"Whatever. We'll just get back together in a week or two. It's what we do."

It's what we used to do before his dark side came out. "This time is different," I say as kindly as possible. "We're not getting back together. I just... My feelings have changed."

Konnor's typically pale face reddens and his hands form fists. "It's Scout, isn't it? I knew there was something between you two."

My nervous system screeches like a warning alarm at a nuclear power plant. Konnor has always had jealousy issues during our relationship. He's accused me of flirting with other guys or even cheating on him more times than I can count. I'm certain he hates the idea of us breaking up for good not because he loves me, but because he loves to control me.

"There's nothing between me and Scout." *Except that he knows about you.* I was too embarrassed to tell my mom and friends that Konnor has gotten physical with me. But Scout somehow figured it out...and almost lost his mind when he did. I had to make him promise to let me handle it—to let me break things off with Konnor *without* him getting involved. But he's definitely holding me accountable. If I don't end this relationship, Scout will. And that's enough to make me follow through, because I'm not putting my friend in that position.

My appreciation for Scout's support must have registered on my face, because suddenly Konnor's contorts and he's screaming obscenities and accusations at me. I don't recognize this person. It's like he's *gone* and something evil has taken over.

"Why don't you go and we'll talk tomorrow when we're not upset." And I won't be naive enough to think I can do this alone. I'll have someone with me. I'm practically yelling to be heard over his screeching. "I'm sure you're right. We'll just get back together." I'll tell him anything he wants to hear right now to get him out of my house. But it's obvious that nothing is getting through to him.

He's blocking my path to the front door. But the door to the garage is behind me. I take a small step back, then another. But I trip on one of the pillows still on the floor from earlier and crash to the carpet, narrowly avoiding hitting my head on the coffee table. I'm so grateful I didn't, because I need to be conscious to talk Konnor down and get him out of here.

I start to scramble up, but suddenly his weight is on top of me and then—*dear God*—I can't breathe. I fight back with every ounce of my strength, but everything is just fading to black.

And then, there's a bright, stunning light that's more beautiful than anything I've ever encountered before.

And I reach for it.

Epilogue

One Year Later

Instead of being on a beach with her boys like she'd originally wished for, Isley was attending a Finch's Hope fundraising gala with them at an event venue in Denver. But she considered this option just as good, if not better.

Over the last year, the reopened investigation into Cece's death and Konnor's subsequent arrest had skyrocketed the charity to fame, causing an influx of attention and support.

Every online news persona and TikToker and even the larger mainstream news channels had something to say about the case, and #JusticeForCece had been trending ever since.

When Cece's autopsy had been reexamined, the updated pathology report labeled the cause of death as manual strangulation, with the staged scene happening after the fact.

The coroner's first findings had incorrectly deduced that Cece's injuries were from suicide, which had propelled so many other facets of the investigation—or lack thereof.

Isley, Payton, and Clara hadn't understood all Belinda had been going through back then or how she'd begged the police to look beyond Cece's depression and suicide attempt in the eighth grade.

Investigators had also confirmed that the necklace in Konnor's possession was Cece's. And that the photos Remmy found *were* doubles of Cece's pictures, which Konnor had pilfered from her room. The picture from their friend Erik's birthday had been taken a little over a week before Cece's passing... and, according to the receipt shoved inside the old envelope, wasn't developed until one forty-three p.m. on the Saturday she died. Konnor had worked from noon until 8:00 p.m. that day, so he couldn't have gone to Cece's until after the friends left her house.

Which placed him there within the window of her death.

After Cece's passing, Belinda had boxed the stacks of photos in her room in their original developing envelopes—often with the receipt still inside—planning to organize them at some point in the future. She'd had no idea at the time how fortuitous that would turn out to be.

No one knew why Konnor had taken Cece's necklace and the photos, but as Sergeant Miller said, criminals didn't make logical choices. Thankfully, Konnor's irrational actions back then had spurred the renewed investigation now.

An eyewitness had also come forward. A neighbor who'd returned home after getting off work at 9:00 p.m. on the night of Cece's death stated that Konnor had nearly rammed into her vehicle with his truck while leaving the Finches' driveway.

Since his arrest, Konnor had been claiming innocence. But last month, he'd accepted a plea deal for one count of second-degree murder with a set term of twenty-four years, and in exchange, the prosecution had dropped the additional charge of tampering with a deceased human body.

Isley hated the clinical nature of viewing Cece as a case versus a person, and the equalization of her life to a number. From an emotional standpoint, no time Konnor served would ever be enough.

But Belinda was grateful that Konnor was being held accountable for taking Cece's life and that she and Cece's friends and family wouldn't have to endure a drawn-out trial. Especially since there was always a risk with a trial that he could be found innocent.

Recently the women had been chatting with Belinda over FaceTime when Payton had asked her about the future of the charity.

"Belinda, are you going to continue running Finch's Hope? It's okay to take a step back and give yourself time to adjust to all of the recent developments."

Belinda had squared her shoulders. "I absolutely plan to continue running the charity. What man intends for evil, God intends for good. So many lives have been saved because we thought Cece had taken her own. Do you know how many Ceces and Cecelias have come from survivors the charity has assisted? Six little girls have been named after her. How could I step away from continuing that kind of legacy for my daughter?"

It was so Belinda.

And it made Isley wonder how they could have ever doubted what her response would be to their stupid, fearful teenage decision not to disclose that they'd been drinking with Cece the night she died.

Isley had a bit of PTSD from all that had happened and been discovered during friendcation last summer.

But ultimately, she, Clara, and Payton were grateful for the end results of the note mistakenly delivered to The Haven.

Even though it hadn't been meant for them and at the time

had been painful and frightening, they'd all needed to unburden their truths. And their guilt.

And that awful note had helped make that happen.

The Monday following that weekend, she and Trevor had finally been able to confirm that Aiden was at rehab and had never left.

All of the worry and fear had been for naught.

After he was released from rehab, Isley had asked Aiden why he'd stopped communicating with them during those last weeks.

He'd said it was because he and his counselor had decided to use the time to hash out any issues that could deter him from lasting change. He'd wanted to take full responsibility for his actions, and they'd decided to forgo distractions and any outside communication.

In retrospect he'd made an impressive, mature decision. But during... Well, Isley was sometimes surprised they'd survived.

The women were following through with their girls' trip in the next few days. They'd decided to head to The Haven again. Reagan was hanging out with Zion tonight but would be joining them for the weekend. They'd added in Ava, who would be arriving tomorrow, and Belinda, who was more than ready to relax after all the effort that had gone into making this fundraising gala happen.

Venette had wisely capitalized on the public interest from Cece's story and Konnor's arrest to drive donations to the charity—thus the reason for the large sold-out gala this summer. Though thankfully last year's online auction had done very well, raising slightly over the goal they'd set. Venette had also roped Isley into assisting in planning tonight's gala. But she was glad to give her time to Finch's Hope now that Aiden was settled at a new school and doing really well. He'd even started dating a sweet girl about three months ago.

Makayla was with him tonight, and she looked stunning in a deep burgundy dress that complemented her brown skin and striking green eyes.

Seeing Aiden happy and healthy and making good decisions brought Isley so much joy. She and Trevor were proud of him and so grateful for where they were versus where they could have been if things had taken a more dire turn. They all understood how quickly the trajectory of life could change.

Trevor leaned in her direction from his seat to her right. "I'm going to confirm with the DJ that he's ready and get the dance going."

"Great, thank you. I know you didn't want to emcee tonight, but you're exceptional at it."

His eyes narrowed. "Don't be getting any ideas for next year. You and Belinda promised me this would be a one-off situation."

They had. But he was such a fantastic emcee that they might have to renege on that.

A discussion for another time.

"And then I'm done for the night. Right?"

Isley laughed. "Yes, that's the last item on the agenda." They'd finished the program portion of the evening and the caterers were delivering the cheesecake desserts to the tables now.

Isley slid her arms around Trevor's shoulders and pressed a kiss to his cheek. "You've done an *amazing* job tonight. Thank you."

His eyebrows rose suggestively. "How good of a job? Is there some sort of reward for my performance?"

"I'm sure we can come up with something."

"*Ew.* I'm sitting right *here*," Aiden announced from his seat to Isley's left.

She'd thought they'd been quieter just now. But also, how

was she supposed to know that he'd actually torn his attention away from Makayla to focus on them? The two twenty-year-olds had been enthralled with each other all night. It was endearing and almost comical to see their typically indifferent son so gaga over a girl.

"Dad, leave Mom alone. That's gross. Aren't you two too old for that stuff, anyway?"

Isley laughed. Trevor opened his mouth to respond and then shook his head, amusement creasing his cheeks.

Over the last year, Isley and Trevor had made a conscious effort to focus on each other—and Aiden when he would allow it. They spent weekends at The Haven whenever possible. They'd begun playing pickleball together. Apparently they were in the right age bracket for that. And they had a planned date night every week. She felt the shift in their relationship, and Trevor said he did too.

Isley was still working through her trust issues in counseling. Maybe she always would be. But striving toward something was just as important as reaching the finish line. It was a constant battle for her to believe she was worthy of love as is, without conditions or having to prove herself. But she was doing her best to change the script she'd unknowingly been following all her life...and Trevor was her greatest ally in that regard.

"Makayla and I are going to check out the silent auction items to see if there's anything you and Dad should be buying me." Aiden sprouted a teasing grin, grabbed Makayla's hand, and off they went.

Isley and Trevor laughed.

Trevor stood. "Meet me on the dance floor when I'm done with this announcement, because someone has to start this party, and according to you and Belinda, that person is me."

Isley watched her husband take the stage and command the room with his strong, appealing presence. In a matter of seconds, people were laughing at something he said. No wonder they'd forced him to be the emcee.

He had that *something* about him.

The thing that had captivated her decades ago and never released its hold.

And she was eternally grateful that despite her mother's many cryptic warnings, he'd never let go of her.

After Trevor introduced the dancing portion of the evening, Isley met him on the dance floor.

"We'd better get out there." Hank sighed good-naturedly. "Is told me we had to dance to at least the first song to get people to join in."

Clara glanced at Payton, who filled the seat next to her and was attending the evening alone. "I really don't think they need us."

"They do." Payton nodded toward the dance floor. "They're still the only ones out there. Don't worry about me. I'm going to check out the silent auction items, anyway. Reagan has a whole list of things she wants me to look for."

"I'm excited to see her tomorrow."

Payton beamed. "I feel the same about Ava. I think this girls' weekend is going to go way better than last year's friendcation."

Hank laughed. "It had better."

At Payton's continued prompting, Clara and Hank joined Isley and Trevor on the dance floor, and two other couples subsequently followed.

Clara moved into Hank's familiar arms, once again overcome with gratefulness that the A-fib scare last year hadn't been a worse diagnosis and that they still had each other.

When they'd returned home from Breckenridge last summer, Hank had leveled with his parents and family about the farm troubles. With their help, they'd been able to adjust the loan payments to something manageable.

Clara hadn't known what she'd wanted to happen when it came to the farm. But once everything fell into place, she'd been so thankful that they could continue doing what they loved.

Hank had been keeping his A-fib in check with medication and stress reduction.

And even Ava had come home this summer. Clara felt as if her family had been pieced back together. She knew changes were coming and that this might be the last summer Ava lived at home. She knew to expect the unexpected. And she was learning to adjust to that.

In many ways, surviving this last year with all the developments surrounding Cece's death and Konnor's arrest had been a study in that very thing.

"By the way, both of your photographs have numerous bids."

"Really?" Clara was shocked. She'd only donated them because Isley and Belinda had pleaded with her to.

Hank's mouth arched. "Clara Rose, *when* are you going to start seeing your hobby as talent?"

"Oh, I'd say probably...never."

Clara had also let herself get talked into consigning a few photographs at a local gift shop in Fort Collins. So far, she'd sold two pieces. It was nice to bring in a little income outside of the farm, but it still felt like such a wild, unfathomable concept that someone would buy something she'd created.

She'd used the money to pay Isley back for the friendcation weekend activities.

Hank spun her out and then back toward him. They were terrible dancers. Terrible! Like two toddlers shuffling around together. But Clara didn't care what anyone thought of their antics. She fit with Hank perfectly.

"Remember how awful we were at dancing during the homecoming dance our freshman year?" she asked.

"I remember how nervous I was."

"You didn't show it. And you've never told me that."

"I have my secrets too."

"Oh, really," she said with amusement.

"On top of being nervous, I remember being so relieved you said yes. Asking you was the scariest thing I'd done up until that point in my life."

More information he'd never mentioned. "I feel like I gave you all the signs that I would say yes."

"You did. But back then there was no texting. I had to talk to you in person!"

She chuckled.

"I also recall feeling like I'd been waiting for you for years at that point."

"We were fifteen."

"Exactly."

Clara's heart gave a sweet tug. She paused their movement, palms framing Hank's face, and pressed her mouth to his for a long second. "Sorry, I know you hate PDA, but—"

He cut her off with a kiss that lasted longer and was accompanied by hands pressed into her lower back.

His smile sprouted when he pulled away. "Maybe it's growing on me."

Clara fanned her face. "Who *are* you?"

"Quit making out!" Trevor called as he and Isley floated by, their movements mimicking professional dancers. Or at least people who did this more than once a decade like Clara and Hank.

"Quit showing off," Hank quipped back, earning laughter from them.

Clara wrapped arms around Hank's neck and held on, their

feet barely moving as the crowd who now filled the dance floor swept by.

They definitely weren't the best dancers here tonight, but the other couples had nothing on them.

This was the portion of the evening Payton had been dreading.

She'd told herself that if she needed to escape at any point tonight, she could, and that just attending an event like this alone was a win.

Technically Payton had her friends and their husbands. And of course she knew the Finch's Hope staff and people from Veil who were attending.

But still...going solo after being married for so long was quite an adjustment.

The last year had been filled with those.

True to his word, after they'd returned to Dallas last summer, Liam had moved out of the house, leaving her and Reagan in their familiar territory.

Sometimes Payton wished she'd been the one to start over in a new place void of all the memories of their marriage.

But she'd known that consistency was key for Reagan, so instead she'd redecorated the bedroom she'd once shared with Liam.

She'd painted it a dark plum and then filled it with gorgeous whites and beiges. It felt a little like a spa to her and a lot less like *theirs*.

She and Liam had gotten along well during the divorce. Mostly because he hadn't fought her on anything. Sometimes she was thankful for that and other times she wanted to engage in the biggest brawl with him. But of course, for Reagan's sake, she'd chosen that first option on repeat.

About three months after they'd separated, Liam had started dating Assistant Professor Ashlyn Browning.

Whether he'd cheated on Payton or not, she really didn't know. Ultimately it didn't matter anymore. Because he'd moved on and someday she would too. But right now, she'd moved on to focusing on Reagan—much to Reagan's chagrin.

Payton was about to slip from the table into the adjacent room that held the silent auction items when a man pulled out Clara's empty chair next to her and slid into it.

She released a squeak of surprise and excitement. "Scout?!" She lurched forward to hug him. "It's so good to see you!" His shoulders were broader than they'd been in high school, and he smelled like a combination of subtle mouthwatering cologne and *him*.

Amazing how a scent could instantly transport her back to fall nights and football games, hanging in Scout's basement, and studying at the same table in the school library.

"I can't believe you came from Germany for this." Isley had mentioned that Scout had purchased a ticket to tonight's gala. Payton had been on the lookout for him earlier this evening but had eventually assumed something waylaid his plans.

"I was going to be in the States for some interviews and the timing lined up, so I decided to make it work."

"You're thinking of moving back?"

"Maybe. Two places are trying to convince me to. Depends on what they offer me."

Of course Scout would be well sought after. "I don't even know what you do."

"Just IT stuff."

Just. And yet he was being wooed back to the states for work.

"Have you been here the whole night? Why didn't you say hi earlier?"

His mouth curved, his peach skin crinkling around sky blue eyes.

"My flight was delayed today, so I didn't get here until about fifteen minutes ago."

But he'd still come. Payton's smile felt cheesy and overdone, but she couldn't seem to stem it. And then the reason for tonight and all that had happened in the last year regarding Cece and Konnor hit her like an SUV barreling through a pedestrian-filled crosswalk.

"I'm sorry that you went to the police about Konnor and they didn't listen. And you've had to live with that all this time."

A divot divided his forehead. "There's only one person to blame in that situation. And hopefully every year of his prison sentence will feel like a decade."

Payton raised her water glass. "Cheers to that." She took a sip because her mouth was suddenly so dry.

Instead of sporting a tux like many of the men tonight, Scout wore a black suit that appeared as if it had been tailored just for him. His tie was charcoal, his shoes high-quality leather. When had the lanky kid she'd hung out with in high school turned into this dapper 007 character? Fortunately he still had the smattering of freckles that she'd always found endearing.

"Still, though...thank you for fighting for Cece. I know how close the two of you were."

His face softened with empathy. "No different than you girls and her."

Not exactly true. "I used to wonder, if she'd lived, if the two of you would have gotten together at some point."

Scout winced. "I can see how you might have thought that. We *were* close. But we were just friends. I..." His lips pressed together. "Honestly? I was always talking to Cece about you. I had such a massive crush on you in high school. Sorry if that makes you uncomfortable," he rushed on, his light laugh coupled with a *what can I say?* gesture.

Payton set her glass down so hard it created a *clink* through the tablecloth.

"But...you liked Cece. The two of you were always—"

"Talking about you or Konnor."

Payton's equilibrium betrayed her, and for an instant she thought she might fall right out of her chair. How was this possible? "Why didn't you ever say anything?" All those years she'd suffered watching her friend and the guy she'd liked together.

"I was shy and insecure and certain you were out of my league. Plus, I thought if I said something and you weren't interested in me like that, it would make everything awkward with us and our friend group."

"That's understandable." Navigating high school was incredibly tough. And it wasn't like Payton had given him any indication of her feelings for him, because she'd been so determined not to wreck her relationship with Cece, and in turn Clara and Isley.

She'd chosen the girls who'd been her family, because she'd known she wouldn't survive life without them. And even all these years later, she'd been right on that account.

"That last night..." Payton pressed fingertips against her mouth. "I snapped at Cece. I accused her of leading you on. I thought you liked her and..."

"Huh." Scout's smile formed. "So that's why she called me that night. She told me I *had* to go straight to your house after work and ask you out. I promised her I would. But I got off late, and I totally chickened out that night. There was no way I was going to throw a rock against your window like she suggested."

Payton laughed.

"And then the next morning we found out she'd died and everything just..."

"The world stopped."

"Exactly."

Payton's nose wrinkled. "We just had the most serious conversation within five minutes of seeing each other. After *not* seeing each other for decades."

"True. Maybe we should backtrack to something more normal." He motioned to the dance floor. "Would you like to dance?"

Social media made details so accessible. Like that Payton had divorced in the last year. And that Scout—at least according to Clara's snooping—didn't appear to be in a relationship.

But still... Payton certainly didn't need to read into a little dance.

"Is there any chance you'd be interested in going for a walk instead? I wouldn't mind getting out of here."

Scout didn't answer immediately, and Payton panicked. Why had she made it awkward? Why hadn't she just said yes?

"But you just got here," she hastily filled in. "I'm sure you have people to see, so leaving doesn't make sense. Never mind what I said. A dance would be great."

If that offer was still on the table after her rambling commentary.

Scout stood and offered her a hand. "The only person I needed to see—Belinda—I talked to already. And a walk sounds way better than dancing."

She accepted his assistance as he tugged her up from her chair.

With her in heels, she was only about three inches shorter than him. Payton forgot what they were discussing as Scout's presence registered like an icy poolside drink on a hot summer day.

"With how stunning you look, you absolutely deserve someone who can make dancing worthwhile," he said quietly with a grin. "But I'm the same awkward nonathletic kid I was in high school, so by walking, we'll be saving your toes from certain doom."

Did Scout just call her stunning? Payton followed him through the maze of tables as they made their way out of the ballroom.

She'd found her dress for tonight on clearance, which made the fact that she felt amazing in it even better. It was long and black with a gorgeous slit that showed off the thigh muscles she'd been toning since she'd needed to throw herself into something during the divorce, and exercise had fit the bill.

She'd added bright fuchsia earrings for a pop of color.

Payton had been discovering things about herself this year. Like that she preferred a simple wardrobe of white, black, gray, and blue and then enjoyed accessorizing with artistic jewelry pieces.

Occasionally she liked popcorn for dinner versus a meal. Reagan was game on. Her teen had even started cooking one night a week without any prompting.

Payton did not appreciate bookshelves in the house. Which was likely a result of Liam's overflowing ones that had once filled their space.

But she wasn't going to overanalyze why she preferred an e-reader or an audiobook these days. Because she was also learning to take things at face value.

Scout held open the door for her to exit into the evening that registered at a lovely mid-seventies temperature. As Reagan liked to say, Dallas was already a stinky armpit at this point in the summer.

"Which way?" he asked.

"Any way."

"Feels like a left kind of night. But if I'm making this weighted decision now, you are in charge of the next one."

She laughed. "Deal."

In unison, they turned, keeping a slow casual pace along the sidewalk.

Payton plucked her phone out of her small black clutch. "I need to text Isley and Clara to let them know where I am so they don't panic when they can't find me." The girl code they'd adhered to in their teens was still going strong in their forties.

"Good idea." Scout offered her his arm. "If you're going to text while walking in those heels at least hang onto me."

"Are you calling me clumsy?" Payton tucked her arm through his and sent a quick text, covertly inhaling the heady mixture of Scout along with the remnants of an earlier rain that had begun to dry on the ground.

"I definitely am *not* saying that."

Clara's reply came back quickly. It was a GIF of a girl yelling, *It's Actually Happening*.

Payton laughed out loud.

"What did they say?"

She held up the phone for him to see.

"What's that about?"

"Clara's the only one of the girls who figured out in high school that I had a crush on you."

Scout's footsteps faltered, and he faced her, effectively disengaging their arms. "So when Cece demanded that I ask you out that night... You *were* actually interested in me?"

"I was. And I suppose me snapping at her about you clued her in. Didn't you believe her?"

"She had no proof for her claims." Scout's grin sprouted as he lifted one shoulder. "She just told me to trust her. I thought maybe she was just being Cece and overly optimistic. Why didn't you say anything?" He tenderly repeated the question she'd asked him earlier. "I mean before she died, obviously. After, none of us were functioning."

"I couldn't risk messing up my friendship with the girls. They were—are—my family. And I thought you and Cece liked each other despite her claiming otherwise."

The half-mast curve of his lips held hints of understanding and acceptance. "It appears we both had our logical reasons."

"We did."

Scout started walking again, and Payton fell in step beside him, considering claiming that she needed to send another text just so she could resume their lost physical connection.

"You know I have a teenage daughter?"

He nodded. "What is she like?"

"A thousand times better than I was as a teen."

"Impossible. I liked that girl." They approached an intersection. "Left, right, or straight?"

"Straight," she answered. Scout's attention focused on her as they waited for the crosswalk sign, and Payton's face warmed. "What?"

"I was just thinking about how Cece once told me that I was going to wake up in ten years and realize I'd missed out on you."

Cece! Why didn't you say anything? Why didn't you tell me?

"But she was right *and* wrong," Scout continued. "Because it's been over twenty."

The light turned and Scout resumed their pace like he hadn't just delivered the most tender blow to her heart.

When he realized that Payton was still glued to the sidewalk corner, he stopped and turned back.

"You coming?" He held out a hand.

Payton took it, the feel of his skin against hers sending electrical currents zipping along her nerves. "I am."

Reagan's Epilogue

It's about time that my opinion is taken into consideration.

My mom has been dating Scout since the end of June, and she's finally introducing me to him three months later.

That could have something to do with the fact that he's only lived in Texas for about two months.

Or it could be Payton being overprotective.

She acts like I can't handle meeting her boyfriend. I can handle more than she realizes. Just look at the last year and a half. I survived high school girl drama, my parents' divorce, my mom turning all schmoopy over Scout, *and* my dad dating an assistant professor at his college before he'd even signed the divorce papers.

That one shook both Mom and me. I know Payton wonders if he started seeing Ashlyn while they were married or if he had feelings for her during that time.

I asked my dad once because I was curious about the same thing.

I mean, the timing was definitely sus.

Dad said no... I think. But his answer was so wordy I'm not even sure what he said.

He does that sometimes.

At this point, my parents have both moved on. Which helps, because now when they discuss me or our annoying whose-house-is-Reagan-going-to-be-at schedule, things are less strained.

Scout gets to the restaurant and makes his way through the tables to ours.

"Hi." He greets my mom with a kiss, and she turns as red as a tomato.

She introduces us. We order. We eat. Everything goes pretty well if not a little beige.

I'm definitely not a fan of surfacey conversations.

Where do you go to school?
What activities do you like?
Blah-blah-blah.

At the end of the meal, my mom gets up to use the restroom. Finally!

I've been waiting for this moment.

"So, Scout," I say when she's far enough away not to overhear. "Did you move to Austin because of my mom?" It's about a three-hour drive from Dallas, and the two of them are constantly going to see each other or meeting in the middle. "Because if so, why didn't you just move to Dallas? It would have made things easier."

He inclines his chin like he's acknowledging that I'm right. "When I was offered the job in Austin, your mom and I had just reconnected. I wasn't sure where it was going to go. And the last thing I wanted to do was scare her off or put pressure on her. Especially since the divorce was recent."

Good answer.

"You know how you feel about Zion?"

I nod. We've been together ever since that awful but somehow still good trip to Breckenridge. The best part about dating someone long distance—outside of how hard it is to never see them—is that Zion and I have become *really* good friends.

We talk about literally everything.

"Well, how you feel about him is how I feel about your mom. Only I had to wait over two decades to be with her because I didn't get up the courage to ask her out in high school."

"But if you had, I wouldn't exist."

"Exactly. So it all worked out like it was supposed to."

My eyes narrow. "Did you practice these answers?"

Scout's head swings back and forth, a slight curve to his mouth. "No, ma'am. I would never panic over meeting my girlfriend's daughter or spend any time prepping for meeting my girlfriend's daughter by watching advice videos on YouTube or TikTok."

I laugh. If he put that kind of effort into today, he might be as great as my mom seems to think he is. "So, listen, I have a dad."

"I'm aware."

"Which means we don't have to do that whole *thing*."

"Got it."

"And my mom is like the best person in the world." After last year's Breckenridge trip, Mom leveled with me about the stuff that happened the night Cece died and how much guilt she had over her friend's death. She acted like she'd been this terrible kid in high school. I told her that she's too hard on herself. I don't know why she thought she couldn't share that with me earlier. In some ways, those mistakes she thinks she made make her edges softer.

"I'm aware of that too."

"So don't hurt her." My voice dips. "Please." It took Payton months to return to normal after Dad moved out. We're not doing that again.

"Not planning to."

"And I'm not moving to Austin before I graduate from high

school. So don't do anything stupid like asking her to marry you for at least a couple years."

Scout nods, that small smile forming again. "Noted."

I spot my mom leaving the restroom. "I'm glad we had this little talk."

Scout laughs. "Me too."

"Oh, and listen," I continue as my mom slides into her seat. "I'm going to need you two not to be like constantly hugging or kissing or anything like that. Just...please don't."

My mom releases a squeak of surprise as Scout gives a regretful sigh. "No can do on that one. I've read way too many studies on how physical touch decreases a host of medical problems. And since your mom and I got started late, I'm filing for an extension on our lives with that."

I laugh. "Oh, my word. You are such a sap!"

"Reagan!" Mom's eyes go massively wide like I've done or said something terrible.

"It's fine, Mom. Scout and I are buds now. We talked through some things while you were in the bathroom."

Her vision toggles between us. "What did you—?"

"Sorry," Scout interrupts. "It was a private convo."

"I was gone two minutes," Mom mumbles.

"Reagan, tell me about this Zion. Is he a good kid? Kind? Hard worker? How does he feel about drugs and drinking?" Humor sparks in Scout's eyes with each additional question.

"I *just* told you not to pull the dad card."

"I know, but I'm still allowed to care about you, right?"

I laugh and roll my eyes. Great! Another adult butting into my life. Perfect.

Except... I don't mind nearly as much as I pretend to.

And if Scout being in our lives accounts for bonus birthday and Christmas gifts, I *suppose* I can figure out how to adjust.

★ ★ ★ ★ ★

Acknowledgments

To those who have lost loved ones to suicide, my heart and deepest condolences go out to you. And to those who've contemplated suicide and are reading these words, I'm exceptionally glad you're here.

A huge thank you goes out to the Harlequin publishing team who made this book happen. I would not be here without my editor, Shana Asaro, and the team at Love Inspired. Thank you for partnering with me for ten years. I'm so grateful!

Breckenridge is one of my family's favorite places to visit in Colorado. I fictionalized the town of Veil and picked the name because of its meaning. Any mistakes in the setting or story are all mine.

Once again, thank you to Jessica Patch for talking me through changes to this book and for brainstorming a creative plot twist. I couldn't do this writer thing without you.

To the readers who took the leap with me to a different type of story than my first ten fiction books, thank you. I'm so glad you're here! To the Bookstagrammers, Facebookers, and BookTokers who take the time to read, write reviews, and share your love of books, thank you! Special thanks to Becky's Bookshelves, Kim at Inspirational Fiction Reader, Beth at Faithfully Bookish, and Tina Radcliffe—rock-star author and organizer—for all you do.

So many people have helped me get to this point in my career: my agent, Rachelle Gardner, my über-supportive parents, who, along with my sister-in-law Debbie, are the best free marketers a girl could ask for, my in-laws, who are the quickest to help with anything we need, my extended family, who hunt down my books in stores across the country, and our friends, who are the greatest support system in the world.

I am so grateful to my kids and husband for the ways you adjust to deadlines and all the other writing nuances that affect our lives. Love you all so much. All glory goes to God for making this dream of writing books come true.

Harlequin Reader Service
Enjoyed your book?

Get more novels that reflect traditional Christian values with a mix of contemporary, Amish, historical, and suspenseful romantic stories with the Essential Inspirational subscription!

Start with a Free Welcome Collection with 2 free books and a gift—valued over $30.

See website for details and order today:

TryReaderService.com/Inspirational-Fiction